BLOOD
OF
WOLVES

BOOKS BY G.N. GUDGION

THE RUNE SONG TRILOGY

Hammer of Fate

Runes of Battle

Blood of Wolves

BLOOD
OF
WOLVES

G.N. GUDGION

SECOND SKY

Published by Second Sky in 2023

An imprint of Storyfire Ltd.
Carmelite House
50 Victoria Embankment
London EC4Y 0DZ
United Kingdom

www.secondskybooks.com

ISBN: 978-1-83790-480-8
eBook ISBN: 978-1-83790-479-2

For Sophie

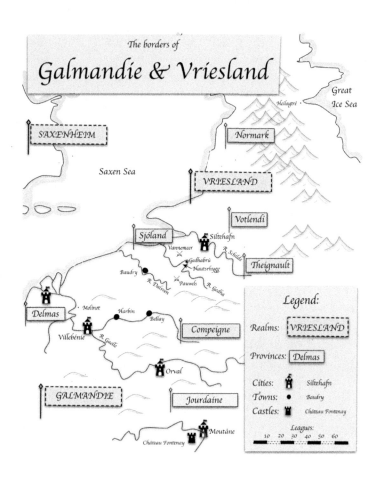

The borders of
Galmandie & Vriesland

Great
Ice Sea

SAXENHEIM

Normark

Saxen Sea

Heilagtré

VRIESLAND

Votlendi

Sjóland

Siltvhafn

Vannemeer

Godhabrú

Nautsrhvegg

Baudry

R. Thálven

Pauwels

R. Scâlde

R. Geálva

Theignault

Delmas

Molinot

Harbin

Bellay

Villebénie

R. Geádle

Compeigne

Orval

GALMANDIE

Jourdaine

Moutâine

Château Fontenay

Legend:

Realms: VRIESLAND

Provinces: Delmas

Cities: Siltvhafn

Towns: Baudry

Castles: Château Fontenay

Leagues:

10 20 30 40 50 60

PART ONE

THE FASTING MOON (GALMAN) | THE WORM
MOON (VRIESIAN)

CHAPTER ONE

1.1 FYLGJA

She does not know why she has woken thus, surrounded by the soft susurration of the flock. Though she is not so much waking as becoming aware, amidst the ruffling of a thousand unseen wings, huddled in the waiting that is not quite sleep. Their movement is a constant, comforting whisper beneath the rise and fall of the wind. There is snow; the wet almost-sleet of early spring that chills more than the crisp cold of winter. In the pre-dawn half-light it eddies in the lee of the dune where they shelter, settling on their backs, and turning to water between their feathered warmth and the damp sand. It smells clean against the salt of the flood tide. There is a soft, rhythmic thunder as unseen waves churn sand and bladderwrack on the shoreline.

The flock waits. The storm will pass. Light will come. The tide will bring food. It is the way of things in this hungry, bickering, beak-clacking world.

Yet she spreads her wings and lifts into the storm's rush, above the flock's soundless *why?* Flapping from nearby tells her she has panicked others into flight, though they settle back at the absence of threat. And as the storm takes her, there is joy in her mastery, in the strength of those energy-sapping downbeats that keep her alive even when the storm threatens to sweep her out over the estuary, tumble her over and slap her into a wave. Joy too in her conquering the urge to return to the safety of the flock, for she has remembered her purpose.

She angles into the wind, beating upstream with the tide until the clouds lift and the eastern sky shows a line of light, grey-brown like a plover's wing and cold as ice. The river below her reflects that light, but all else is dark; she smells the fires of man-kind before she sees the city. Within the smoke and stink are hints of offal and rot, and she must dominate the urge to swoop and feed, for in the city is a castle and in the castle is the girl. With that knowledge, understanding takes shape, the way a day assembles itself after a deep and dream-troubled sleep.

For she has slept. How long, she does not know. In that former time there was a wolf, whose body she knew as she now knows the gull. Knew better, for the wolf accepted her, knowing her lineage. Once, she was a woman of the people of the wolf, but now she is spirit. She is guide. She is *fylgja*. That wolf she released when the danger to the girl had passed. And she has woken once more.

This gull feels too wild, too instinctive, too *basic* to be of use. As the sun lances under clouds, rolling back the storm, the gull's need for its flock and feeding ground is a headwind to her flight.

Yet the girl calls, without knowing. Or perhaps it is the gods that call her on the girl's behalf. Such understanding is hidden from her. There is a bond between her and the girl, as strong as any Norn-woven thread of fate; this girl who is stronger than she knows, and who is weak for her innocence. And the smell of menace around her is as strong as fish guts on the wind.

The sun's rim gilds the horizon, and with that glare understanding dawns.

A *fylgja* cannot be summoned, and yet she has woken.

A wolf would not be tolerated among the dwellings of men. This body is all she has.

It may not be enough.

1.2 ADELAIS

Adelais fought her way out of the nightmare, pulling the bed coverings away from her neck as she struggled to breathe. *This is not real.* But fingers were high on her shoulder, almost at her throat, and she swatted them away. Her hand connected with flesh. Real flesh.

'Mistress?'

A known voice. Ulfhild. *Thank the gods!*

Adelais lay gasping, staring upwards. Shadowy roof beams loomed above her, half-seen in the tiny light of an all-night candle burning in the hearth.

She turned her head, reached for Ulfhild's forearm and squeezed an apology for the blow.

'Sorry, Ulfie. Bad dreams.' *Again.* Adelais struggled to remember. There had been a hand, reaching for her, coming ever closer. A great, putrid-yellow, disembodied hand that walked on its fingertips like a spider. She'd tried to keep it away by throwing fire at it, or was it firebirds? They'd flown, anyway, but the hand kept coming closer and Adelais had a precipice at her back so she couldn't run, not even when the hand reached her neck and started to choke her. Her firebirds had scattered, making the mewling cry of seagulls.

The window shutters rattled in the wind. Traces of light around their frames told Adelais it was dawn outside.

And cold.

'I will light the fire.' Ulfhild busied herself at the hearth. Adelais sat up, pulling her cloak around her shoulders, and watched. She didn't want a servant. Didn't need one. But she welcomed Ulfhild's company; her laughter lifted the spirits, and she wasn't part of the politicking cesspit of Duke Ragener's court.

Shadows danced as kindling caught, and Ulfhild twisted to face her, still kneeling. Long hair, unbraided for the night, hung in a golden curtain in front of the flames. 'My aunty, her what learned rune lore, said some dreams foretell the future.' Ulfhild was wide-eyed, as if Adelais's dreams had to be significant, like a prophecy.

'And some simply relive the past.' Adelais paused, remembering. 'There was certainly some of that last night.'

'Tell me, mistress?' Again that breathy thrill; Ulfhild lapped up stories of Adelais's adventures as keenly as a cat with fish, though Adelais rarely spoke of them. Duke Ragener was already feeding the court's rumour-mill avidly enough with his own version of the truth.

But this dream had been disturbing enough to share, at least with Ulfhild.

'Galman soldiers came to seize me at an inn near Bellay,' Adelais began, and realised she couldn't tell the whole story. She'd been alone with a man who might have become her lover, yet, when the soldiers arrived, it was not with passion that he instructed her to take off her shirt. *Distract them,* he'd said, as he backed into the corner. She'd felt so vulnerable, so exposed, facing the troopers bare-chested as they burst into the room. Their eyes had locked on her breasts, not on the man-at-arms behind the door. And they'd missed the sword hidden behind her trailing shirt.

'There was a fight. I cut a man's wrist.' That was the place to start the story. Adelais swung her arm, flexing her wrist as if repeating the strike. She'd already taken down that soldier, but he'd flailed at her from the ground and she'd made an instinctive, sideways, defensive swipe with her sword. The scything tip had almost severed his hand. That was another memory that wouldn't go away: an arc of hot, red blood splashed across one breast, across skin that had been caressed just moments before. From woman to warrior in one flick of her blade, and she'd seen the lust die in her erstwhile lover's eyes.

'And?' Ulfhild prompted. Her eyebrows seemed always to be arched in wonder.

'I almost chopped his hand off. Last night I dreamt that hand was attacking me. It was able to move.' Adelais reached from under her cloak and walked her fingers along the bed covers. 'It was a horrible colour. Dead but shiny.' She didn't want to say more. Somehow, talking about it made it seem real.

'*Skit!*' Ulfhild was open-mouthed. In the firelight her buck teeth looked like a circle of standing stones. She was shivering, holding her threadbare cloak tight under her chin.

'Come back to bed, Ulfie, until the chamber warms up.' Ulfhild had a straw-filled mattress in the corner but Adelais insisted they share the feather bed, for warmth. Ulfhild was happy; the former scullery maid also had unlimited logs for their fire, candles to burn, and her duties were light. Adelais was a very cosseted captive.

For your own safety, she was told. *There are those who wish you dead, even in Vriesland.* A whole tower of the castle had been assigned to her. She could walk the battlements above and look down upon the River Schilde flowing beneath the walls, but the way into adjacent towers was blocked. The chamber below was a guard room, where there were never less than four soldiers 'protecting' her. She could ride her warhorse, Allier, in the exercise arena just outside the walls, but only when an escort could be arranged. And she was not allowed to leave Duke Ragener's castle. The bustling life of Siltehafn, beyond the gates, might as well have been another country. Ulfhild, whom many saw as a mere drudge, had more freedom.

How alike, and how unlike they were. Both tall, both blonde. Adelais lean and slender from hard exercise, Ulfhild thin from malnourishment. Ulfhild thought she was residing in luxury. Adelais was bored. They were like the two cloaks over the bed: one rich and warm, a gift to Adelais from her great friend Lady Agnès de Fontenay; the other a shirt-thin cast-off that no one else wanted.

'Ulfie,' Adelais began. She had the beginnings of an idea. 'Will you lend me your cloak?'

It was two full turns of the spiral staircase down to the guard room. Time enough for Adelais to whisper the rune song of *bjarkan*, the birch-rune, for this was the rune of the earth mother, and the earth mother protects and hides her children from danger. *Bjarkan er laufgat lim, ok lítit tré, ok ungsamligr vidhr.* She tugged the hood over her face and stooped a little in the way that Ulfhild did to conceal her height. She cradled a basket between hip and arm, full of crumpled, dirty linen, and the four soldiers in the room scarcely looked up. The laundry girl was invisible to them. She did not even merit a ribald comment.

Adelais hunched over the basket across the outer courtyard, a servant at her chores. She dumped it outside the laundry and kept going through the gates, still bent, with one hand holding the cloak's hood closed against the cold. It was only on the cobbled streets of Siltehafn that she began to feel guilty. If she was caught, would Ulfhild be punished? But she'd only be gone a little while. She had two gold crowns in her scrip and she was going to buy Ulfhild a cloak.

As she walked, she straightened her shoulders. This was what she had yearned for – to walk tall as a Vriesian woman, free and unremarked upon in a world of bustling people and screaming gulls. With her pauper's cloak held tight at throat and waist, no one noticed the gown flashing beneath. The duchess herself had given her this; they were a similar height and build, and the man's clothing in which Adelais had escaped from Galmandie was too scandalous for a woman to wear at court. The gown's blue velvet was worn and faded, and no longer fit for a great noblewoman, but it was still the finest dress that Adelais had ever owned. She even welcomed the mud and *skit* that oozed over the cobbles, for within a hundred paces her magnificent boots, Agnès de Fontenay's gift last Yul-tide, were hidden beneath a coating of muck. As she turned into Drapers Lane she laughed aloud for the joy of being outside, and free, and unknown.

At first, her chosen draper would not take any notice of her; no one wearing Ulfhild's cloak could ever afford his wares. But his eyes widened at the sight of gold in her palm and Adelais was ushered into his shop. A fold-down shutter to the street served as a counter for sales to ordinary folk, but so great a lady must be offered a seat, and, perhaps, a little mead?

Adelais declined, and described her needs. The man's wife came to help, leaving two small children standing wide-eyed in an archway to the rear. The older one held a toy bear made from scraps of fur and leather in one hand, and his thumb-sucking sibling in the other. They looked well fed, and Adelais decided she would buy from this man. She made faces at the boys and they giggled. Life. Uncomplicated. Real. Wonderful.

She forgot herself. The draper sold leather belts as well as cloth and ready-made cloaks, and Adelais was trying a belt around her own waist, with her head bent to admire the way it dipped over her stomach, when she heard the man gasp.

'It's you, isn't it?' His eyes were fixed on her hair, no longer masked by the cloak's hood. 'Adelais Leifsdottir?'

There could be no other woman with short, blonde hair, uncovered by any matron's cap. All women wore their hair long and braided when they were maidens, and covered after marriage with a linen cap, folded in styles that were unique to each region. Except Adelais, whose hair had been cropped in a sisterhouse and was still too short to braid. She tugged the hood forwards, pleading for silence, but the man's wife was already at the door, calling to her neighbours.

'It is the she-wolf! The *örlaga vefari*! She buys from us!'

For several heartbeats the noises outside were the everyday life of the commercial quarter: cartwheels and iron-shod horses on cobbles, tapping hammers, snatches of passing conversations, the occasional shout. But faces appeared at the hatchway, peering in, disbelieving. Adelais lifted her fingers to her lips, begging for secrecy, but the merchant beamed with pride and opened his hand as if displaying his richest possession. The men and women outside turned and called to others, and the street sounds swelled in a tide that lapped against the counter. Faces blocked the light, jostling for position, peering inwards. Men held out their Mjölnir hammer pendants to her as if to prove that they had never renounced their beliefs in the old gods. Some thrust them over the counter, inviting her to bless them. One dropped his pendant and touched her wrist, the way an Ischyrian would touch a relic. Another grabbed her hand; he seemed to want to pull her into the street. The craftsman's wife retreated backwards through the door, pushing at bodies who tried to follow her, and the merchant ran to help her, forcing it shut with his shoulder while his wife slammed home the bolt. She ran to the back of the house and there was the sound of more bolts shooting home. The infants began to cry.

Adelais realised her head was shaking, slowly, as if to deny the crowd's adulation. *It's just me*, she wanted to say. *The daughter of Leif the weaver. I'm one of you.* But there was such hunger in their eyes, such need. Across their shoulders she saw a passing Ischyrian priest knocked to the ground as men vented the raw anger of people denied their gods.

A chant began, a chorus of two, then five, then fifty, echoing between the houses of Drapers Lane. '*A-de-lais! A-de-lais! A-de-lais!*' Those nearest the counter began to beat it with their palms. Further back in the crowd, a fight began as a craftsman wearing a pendant of the Hand of Salazar had it ripped from his neck to be trampled underfoot.

A young man with the light of a zealot in his eyes began to climb into the shop, and the draper crouched underneath the counter, heaving it upright with his back and tipping the youth into the street. A retaining beam dropped down to hold it vertical, protecting and trapping them. The chanting turned to '*She-wolf! She-wolf! She-wolf!*' and hands thumped the shutter in time with the shouts. Behind her the infants' sobs turned to screams.

Adelais stared at the merchant. His body was jolting where his shoulder leaned against the shutter, and his eyes were now wide with worry. Adelais peered through a crack in the wood at a scene of riot; at least two fights were happening within sight, and a workshop opposite was being looted.

It was a long, anxious wait before the chanting faltered and another sound echoed down the street, a sound Adelais knew; weapons beating on shields in a rhythmic challenge. She shut her eyes and swallowed. 'Thank the gods. They've sent soldiers.'

Through the chink in the counter Adelais saw a mounted squire arrive at the head of a troop of foot soldiers. He held Adelais's warhorse, Allier, ready saddled with her sword hanging from the pommel, and watched as his soldiers cleared the street with brutal efficiency. By the time they had formed a cordon outside the draper's door, two men lay senseless in the street and another sat against a wall, holding his head. At least one more had staggered away with blood pouring from his nose.

Adelais picked up a cloak from the range that had been offered and fastened it around her shoulders. It was a warm, quality cloth, but modest enough for Ulfhild to wear without embarrassment. She'd tie Ulfhild's to her saddle. 'I will take this one.' She'd had to clear her throat before she could speak.

The draper waved away her gold. 'Please, mistress. You honour us. Now many will come because of you.'

She left a gold crown anyway, and kept the belt as well. It was still too much, but she could not rob them. Outside, the glowering squire held out Allier's reins.

'Wear your sword, mistress.' His thunderous face was vaguely familiar, as if she should know him.

'Even with your men around me?'

'They want the she-wolf. We'll give them the she-wolf.'

There was a cheer as she mounted, a great roar of noise that she acknowledged with a raised hand. It felt good. Here were no courtiers with their honeyed flattery; these were real people, and their faces were shining. Allier was restive, curvetting and dancing amidst the tumult, and she had to work to master him until he dropped his head, arched, proud, skittish. She realised how she must seem through the people's eyes: the weaver's daughter on a great destrier, with a knight's sword hanging so easily from her hip, and her still-short hair falling barely to her shoulders. A glimmer of understanding pushed another thought at her; the loose hair sent a bridal signal, almost as if they could claim her. Bed her. In their eyes she belonged to them. She was one of them. They *needed* her.

It was a fine wine to drink.

More people came running as they pushed through the narrow streets. Windows opened on the upper floors, arms reaching out, waving, some so close in the overhanging houses that she could stretch up and touch fingertips, laugh with them. Their shouts reverberated between the houses, making mere speech impossible. Hands reached through her encircling escort towards the skirts of her gown, or her scabbard, as if she were some holy icon. Others, further back in the alleys, called down the blessings of the gods.

There were those who did not smile. One was seized by the ring of soldiers and hit out of the way with a shield to the belly, but not before he had spat into her path and shouted '*witch*'. Yet even that could not dampen her joy, nor the need to follow the squire's rigid back towards the castle. She was outside. On Allier. And the day was brightening, loud with the cries of seagulls and the shouts of people. She rode a wave of adulation and she could believe herself capable of anything, because they believed it of her.

There are times when things happen so fast they must be assembled, afterwards, at a pace where the mind can make sense of what the eyes see and the ears hear.

Adelais knew only that a seagull flew screaming into her face, red beak gaping, but disintegrated before it could strike. She'd rocked backwards in the saddle, and saw the bird burst into a hundred white fragments, the way a storm-driven wave breaks against a rock. There was a spatter of something wet and warm against her face, and feathers flew like spume around her; as she recovered her balance they were drifting downwards past Allier's neck, snow-pure against black.

And there had been a noise; a left-right *snap-thunk* that she ought to have recognised. But Allier understood, and reared, throwing her backwards again. Then Allier's fore hooves came down and he spun, dancing, so the clatter of his hooves was the dominant sound in the quietening crowd. The faces that had been shining a moment before, or scowling, were now all blank with shock. And on the cobbles, within the ring of soldiers, lay the mangled remains of a seagull. Half a seagull, for its head and one wing had been sliced clean away; the wing lay upside-down an arm's length from the body.

'Crossbow!' The squire's shout broke the moment. Allier spun again, contained within Adelais's hands but oh-so-alert. The turn was enough to show her an open, empty, upstairs window, so close she could have tossed a coin into it; and on the opposite side of the street, more feathers – a little tuft on a stick that her mind slowly recognised as the fletching on a crossbow bolt, embedded into the end of a beam.

'Move!' The squire's sword was out. He looked slightly ridiculous with nothing to wave it at.

Adelais moved, in an icy daze, but at a walk. Quite deliberately. She would *not* lame Allier by cantering him on icy cobbles. Besides, this is what all those faces would want of her – to see her ride calmly away from danger, straight-backed, regal, on a destrier that was arched and proud and beautiful beneath her. They would not know that her back was braced against the fear of another shot. What if there was a second crossbow? The noise of the crowd began again, a different note now, one of shock not triumph, and she strained through it for the *tick-tick-tick* of a windlass. Or what if it was a hunting weapon? Faster to re-span. Less sound.

From behind them came the sounds of soldiers splintering the door into the house with an axe. She kept her eyes forwards, still tense across her shoulders as she waited for another impact.

'You are hurt, my lady?' The squire fell in beside her where the road broadened on the approach to the castle.

Adelais had not expected that respect. She looked at him, perhaps too jerkily. Soon she might start to shake. She was holding herself together so tightly that her whole being might crumble at a touch.

'Your face,' he added, gesturing with his sword, still upright in his hand.

Adelais lifted a hand and wiped a finger to the wetness. It came away smeared with blood. A tiny, white, downy feather waved at her from her fingertip and blew away on the wind.

'Not mine,' she said. She had an inexplicable need to weep. A numbness was creeping over her; some reaction to the nearness of death. One thing was sure – that crossbow bolt might have missed her, but it had killed her dreams of walking free in Vriesland.

1.3 GAUTHIER

Gauthier Ferreau moved calmly, taking steady, methodical steps out of the back of the house into an empty alley. He had no need to rush; everyone would be on the street side of the buildings, watching the girl. The front door was bolted and would hold for long enough, and the downstairs windows were shuttered. As added security he wore the robes of an Ischyrian priest. No one would suspect a priest. He'd left the crossbow in the room, where it had been waiting for him. A nice weapon, that, but replaceable. Hit or miss, the escape plan was the same.

It had taken Gauthier's charm and a little gold to persuade a devout Ischyrian widow to leave her home and make a long visit to her family in the provinces. And Gauthier could be very charming, especially when he was dressed as a priest. The gold had come from Gauthier's paymaster who would not be pleased at the day's results; it would be hard to find another empty house in such a strategic position.

He was a hundred paces from the house before he saw anyone else; he almost collided with a man hurrying down a cross-alley. The man shoved him, hard, and Gauthier had to master the urge to strike back, remembering he was supposed to be a man of the God. As his assailant turned, almost snarling at him, Gauthier smiled as disarmingly as he could. 'Easy, friend!' The charm didn't work. The man pulled a Mjölnir hammer pendant from around his neck, pushed it into Gauthier's face, and shouted *'one shall come!'* before running off towards the rabble around the witch.

Gauthier knew the prophecy. *One shall come, born of wolf-kind and of mud, who shall unite the peoples of the north against the march of Ischyrendom.* It had been screamed from the flames by *seidhkonur* as they were burned as witches, and now it was told again in taverns by all who followed the old gods. And Duke Ragener was feeding the flames, saying this girl Adelais was the promised *örlaga vefari*, the fate-weaver. Two moons before, no one would have dared whisper it. Now they felt free to shout it into a priest's face.

Gauthier flexed his fingers, releasing tension, and followed the man onto the market square. He turned left, towards the castle, rather than right towards the noise, forcing himself to look benign; a man of peace.

Behind his calm exterior, Gauthier was seething. He took professional pride in completing such assignments cleanly. No mistakes. No trails that might lead to his employer. Well *executed.* Half a moon they'd been planning this, and all in case the girl was allowed out of the castle. He'd expected more warning; word had only just reached him in time, and he'd still been breathing heavily from running, but it didn't spoil his aim. At that range the crossbow bolt should have split her skull like an egg.

One house. One shot. One chance. *And it had all been wrecked by a fucking seagull!*

Gauthier made the Ischyrian sign of benediction as he passed through the gates. The guards ignored him; priests prayed regularly in the castle's temple, converted from a small hall. A larger, grander structure was being built in the town, but for now this served the castle's faithful. Behind him, the noise was swelling; no longer joyous shouts but the heavy murmuring of an angry crowd, swamping the clatter of hooves on cobbles.

He knelt at the sanctuary rail, made the ritual sign of the God, and waited. The courtyard outside soon echoed with hoofbeats and shouts. Troops were being assembled, searches organised.

Gauthier did not turn when a side door opened, but stayed on his knees, facing forwards in an attitude of prayer, like a prisoner awaiting execution.

'What happened?' The voice was quiet, as menacing as the click of a crossbow being spanned.

'Fucking seagull. Flew into her face as I fired. Her horse reared.' If his master spoke freely, then Gauthier could too. The temple would be empty.

His words were met by a long, deep breath behind him. 'You were supposed to be good with a crossbow.'

'I am.' That made Gauthier angry. 'I'm the best.' He was, too. Though he preferred to get in close, with sword or knife. He could see their faces that way. That moment when his target knew that their life was about to end was worth more than the gold.

'This was unfortunate.' The man he'd been told to call 'Roche' spoke with heavy understatement. He crossed to the priest's chair beside the sanctuary and sat. Gauthier risked a sidelong glance. A fresh, open face, framed by a well-trimmed beard, looked back towards the door. Roche's clothes were respectable but not over-rich; the dress of a steward or functionary rather than a noble, though he wore no retainer's badge. A man could mistake him for an innocent until you looked at his eyes. Those were cold. Calculating. If anyone darkened the entrance, 'Roche' would be on his knees in an instant so

Gauthier could slip into the Ischyrian rite of unburdening. For now, they could talk safely.

'I know all about you, *Pateras* Gauthier.'

Gauthier waited. This man had power. One day Gauthier would like to follow him and find out who he was really working for.

'You were a priest once, weren't you? A *real* priest.'

'Yes, Roche.'

'You were known for giving quite severe penances.'

'They were sinners.' Gauthier had liked being a priest. He'd had respect. And young women would unburden their sins to him. He'd liked that a lot.

'Which you sometimes delighted in administering yourself.'

'They wanted it, messire.' Usually they'd been pathetically grateful. Maybe he had taken it a bit too far, once in a while.

'If your superiors had believed that, you'd still be a priest. But that's none of my concern. It is simply useful to me that you can pass as a man of the God.'

Gauthier began to relax. He sensed he was not going to be punished for the morning's failures.

'So let me tell you what's at stake here, *Pateras*. There will be war with Galmandie.'

'Last I heard, Roche, Galmandie is divided,' Gauthier objected. 'Both the Duke of Delmas and Prince Lancelin claim the throne. Neither will invade Vriesland until the succession is resolved.'

Sometimes it was worth reminding people like Roche that he could think as well as wield a blade.

The long pause told him a lot. *So, Vriesland is not as safe as it thinks.*

'When war comes, my master would like Vriesland to be divided as well.'

Gauthier's smile froze. This was treason. The game of lords and *episkopes*, not of men like him.

'To field an army of sufficient size, Duke Ragener needs the support of the heathen jarls of Normark. The chief among them, Jarl Magnus, is travelling to inspect this Adelais. If he decides she is the fate-weaver, the northern jarls will follow his lead, and an army of berserkers will assemble south of the Schilde. Therefore the girl must die.'

'Magnus may decide this Adelais is not the fate-weaver.' Gauthier risked showing a little wisdom.

'Let us not take that risk.' The way Roche spoke reminded Gauthier how alike they were, despite the gap between their stations in life. They were both capable of putting a knife into a man's back, or a crossbow bolt into a woman's head. The difference was that Roche could pay someone to do it for him. Gauthier was expendable. Deniable.

'There are no more houses. No chances of a prepared ambush.'

'There will be a feast to welcome Jarl Magnus. Undoubtedly the witch will be paraded. I offer you the chance to redeem yourself.'

Gauthier breathed deeply. His professional pride demanded that he kill the girl, but after today the guard around her would be tighter than a duck's arse. Getting close enough to kill, even at a feast, would be hard enough. Getting clear afterwards would be nigh impossible.

'An escape route will be important.' Gauthier spoke out of mutual interest, not fear. They both knew that a captured assassin would be tortured until the identity of his employer was known.

Though Roche probably had the power to have him killed even inside a dungeon, before any questions were asked.

'Meet me here tomorrow, after second office. You may have a chance to show me just how good you are with a crossbow.'

1.4 ADELAIS

Adelais expected to face anger when she was returned to the castle. The squire's meticulously polite 'my lady', spoken for the crowds, had changed into a rant as soon as they were within the castle's gates; she had abused Duke Ragener's protection, she was wilfully irresponsible. Adelais held herself together, more hurt by the knowledge that he was right than by his words. But his rant did not last long; the squire needed to send word to the duke, return to his troop, and coordinate searches.

Word had already reached her guards, and they glowered their resentment as she climbed the stairs. Adelais muttered an inadequate apology.

She let Ulfhild pull her into a hug. She really needed a hug. Perhaps Ulfhild needed one too; she'd be punished, unless Adelais could shield her from blame. The excursion to Drapers Lane had seemed so reasonable, at the time. The consequences of discovery simply had not occurred to her. Ulfhild's wide-eyed wonder at her new cloak made Adelais feel a little calmer; enough to answer Ulfhild's questions about her adventure.

'You was saved by the gods, mistress!' Ulfhild exclaimed.

'Well, if that seagull was an instrument of the gods, it won't be helping me any more.' Adelais couldn't settle, and she paced as she spoke. The snap of the crossbow, the *thunk* of its impact, and the slashed-pillow burst of feathers had all happened in the same instant, as if the bird had been ripped apart from within. *So close.* Close enough for the bird's blood to splash her face.

Seagulls were everywhere in Siltehafn; irritating scavengers who'd snatch a pie from a vendor's cart, but they didn't attack people. Yet that one had flown right at her.

'I'm going to groom Allier,' Adelais said, restless and in need of distraction. She and Allier could calm each other.

In the gloom of the stables she stroked a brush down Allier's neck, making long, gentle sweeps from the warhorse's ear to his shoulder. A soothing hum came from deep in her throat as she worked, almost a purr, animal to animal. Soon, as she knew he would, Allier rested his muzzle into the angle of her neck and held it there. Warm breath caressed her skin. A few more strokes of the brush and whiskery lips began to play against her; teeth that could tear out a man's throat now nibbled at her ear with eye-filling tenderness.

She needed that. She needed the honest stink of the stables, that fug of piss-damp straw and horse *skit.* It was warm among the horses' bodies even though a biting draught cut at her ankles, hoof-high, blowing from a gap beneath the stable doors. Out there her guards stamped blood into their toes and muttered about the extra duties they now faced. The rhythm of the castle had changed; more movement, more shouting. Servants passing in the courtyard would pause to gossip. *Have you heard?*

In the shadowed light of the stable, Adelais could not see the effect of her brushing, nor where it was needed, but that did not matter. The bonding mattered. After a while she let the brush fall to the straw, rested her cheek against Allier's neck, and scratched gently with her fingernails at his shoulders, where he liked it. In response, the stallion's great head arched over her shoulder to groom her back with his teeth, pulling her into his chest. It was as good as a hug with a human. Nobles' mounts snorted and moved around them, their hooves rustling the straw as the time for their morning feed drew close, but Allier was calm beneath her hands and warm against her face; a warhorse with the gift of peace.

Did warhorses imagine what might have been, but for the random flight of a bird? Did they remember killing, or have nightmares after doing what they'd been trained to do? She thought not. Allier was the same horse now as he'd been when she first knew him. Back then he'd been the destrier of Humbert Blanc, a knight of the Order of Guardians, and she'd been a fugitive from a sisterhouse. Now he was the closest thing to a friend she had. Humbert was dead. Her lover Arnaud was dead. Her great friend Agnès de Fontenay was far away in Galmandie. Ulfhild was still too much in awe of her to be a friend. Adelais hoped that would change.

The court of Duke Ragener was not a place where she could make friends; here she was either feared or patronised, and sometimes both. She saw it in the nobles' eyes, especially in those who worshipped the new god Ischyros. Even those who'd clung to the old gods saw her as a curiosity; a weaver's daughter who'd set aside her womanhood to dress as a man and wield a sword. Quite effectively, it seemed. If she'd been a knight, she'd have been honoured for her prowess, but she was a woman and they recoiled from her perversion. Only Allier, nuzzling at her back and neck, accepted her. Wanted her company.

The stable door swung open and Allier lifted his head, alert, the bonding moment broken. Adelais turned to face the light, angry at the intrusion, but bit back a snarl when she saw that the figure silhouetted at the entrance was no stable boy. He was tall, clean shaven, and carried a sword on his hip with the easy familiarity of a veteran. Duke Ragener must trust him to allow him to wear that inside her guards. Beyond him, the castle's outer courtyard dazzled in the morning sun; the light was sharp and clean after the storm and the man with the sword was all greys against the glare. It took her a moment to recognise the squire who'd led the rescue party.

'My lady.' He spoke respectfully, now his anger was spent, in the clear Galman of a courtier. He even extended a leg and made a slight bow, though with as little warmth as a herald. At least he wasn't sneering at her; some courtiers pronounced 'my lady' as if she were a harlot and they shared a secret. Noble-women would say it with exaggerated, scornful tones to remind her of her birth.

'*Mynherra*. I did not thank you for rescuing me.' Adelais responded in the Vriesian of the people. Her Galman was fluent, only lightly accented, but she wanted to make a point. Those whose mother tongue was Vriesian called aristocrats like this '*gykes*'. The word was often spoken with a limp-wristed, back-handed wave in imitation of courtly manners. The hostility was mutual; she'd seen courtiers lift their noses and say 'peasants' with similar contempt. And for this *gyke* Adelais made a token dip of a curtsey, just enough not to be rude.

'You don't remember me, do you?' He still spoke Galman. His cloak moved as a gust tumbled into the stables, pushing the wet-cold smell of spring into the musty air.

'We have met before today, *mynherra*?' Adelais frowned. He did seem slightly familiar.

'One night in the strawberry moon when you kicked an anakritis into a sewer.'

That could only be the night Arnaud and a group of ruffians tried to rescue a tortured Guardian from her sisterhouse. They were all dead now, or far away, except...

'*Mynherra* de Warelt? Forgive me, it was dark that night...' And nine moons before. A lot had happened.

'And I wore mail across my face for much of it.' De Warelt moved towards her, out of the glare.

Adelais remembered him now; a tall, well-favoured man, old enough for crinkles to form around his eyes when he smiled. Ischyrian. *Gyke.* She touched Allier's neck one more time – *later, my friend* – and dipped her head to acknowledge de Warelt. 'I envied you your horse.' She'd been thrown out of the sisterhouse for her part in that raid. 'I had a long walk, after that.' Several hundred leagues, in fact, with the king's men and anakritim on her heels.

'An eventful walk, I hear. You killed the king.' He sounded more amused than upset.

Adelais waited. Every courtier wanted to hear the story, first-hand. She was bored with telling it.

'And now you have a fine destrier of your own.' He nodded past her towards Allier. 'And I have seen that you ride him well.'

'He was a gift from a Guardian knight.' Adelais ran her hand along Allier's side. After nearly a moon of enforced inactivity the horse's belly was slightly fuller. 'And he's getting fat.' Was that too subtle a protest at her being confined to the castle *for her safety?*

'Duke Ragener will be even less inclined to let you ride out after today's adventure.'

'Don't let them punish Ulfhild. It was my idea.'

'I will tell the steward.'

'And me? How does Ragener propose to punish someone who is already a prisoner?'

'You're not a prisoner, you are simply confined for your protection. You have just proved the wisdom of that. But the duke has asked to see you. You may find he intends to reward you for past deeds, not punish you for today's. He has asked me to escort you to his solar after the noon office.' The Vriesian court measured time by the bells of the Ischyrian temple.

'His solar?' She lifted an eyebrow. She did not want to be

alone with Ragener in his private quarters. Half the children in the castle were rumoured to be his bastards.

'Her Grace will be there also, and you may bring your woman. Duchess Severine has helped to choose the gift. It is something they wish you to wear at a feast tonight to welcome Jarl Magnus of Normark.' De Warelt's words were clipped and sharp. Adelais sensed that he didn't like her. 'And they ask that you also bring your sword.'

'Their Graces are too generous.' Her sword? To a feast?

'Save your thanks until you have seen the gift.' De Warelt looked down at her muddy boots. 'You may wish to prepare.' He paused, as if readying himself to say something unpleasant. 'Duke Ragener has asked me to be your guide in the affairs of the court, should you choose to avail yourself of my help.'

'That would be most welcome, Seigneur.' Adelais tried to sound as conciliatory as possible. By the gods, she needed some help.

'Then understand that *everyone* at Duke Ragener's court falls into one of three groups, as far as you are concerned. To those who follow the old gods, you are a saviour. You may even be the *örlaga vefari*, the one who is prophesied to unite the north against the foe.'

'I make no such claim, Seigneur.'

De Warelt ignored her. 'To some Ischyrians, particularly those who desire an independent Vriesland, you are an instrument of divine wrath against the greed of King Aloys and the high priest. And lastly there are other Ischyrians who wish Vriesland to be part of Galmandie. To them you are an evil sorceress. They desire your death.'

Adelais swallowed. 'And to which group do you belong, Seigneur?' If de Warelt was going to spend time in her company, she needed to know, even at the risk of offending him.

He snorted. 'You will remember that I took part in the raid on your sisterhouse. For that, my life would be forfeit in

Galmandie. It also means, mistress, that I may be the only Ischyrian at court you can trust.'

Adelais took a slow, measured breath, wishing she had just one honest friend to guide her at court. De Warelt clearly saw the task as a duty. She needed an Agnès de Fontenay, who'd been her protector in Galmandie. Someone she could laugh with. Drink wine with. Be herself with. A mentor she could really trust, especially when she was invited to a meeting with the duke.

To which she was expected to bring her sword.

CHAPTER TWO

2.1 TAILLEFER

Taillefer de Remy's *diakonerie* encompassed a rich province of thirty temples, in towns that lay in a fertile swathe to the north and east of Galmandie's capital of Villebénie. It was lush, prosperous and just far enough south of Galmandie's northern border to have been little troubled by the wars with Vriesland. The people had good cause to thank Ischyros for his bounty, yet after the noon office in Taillefer's temple at Harbin, he dismissed his congregation with a sense of unease. It was not just that the numbers of worshippers were falling in this, the foremost fire temple of the diakonerie, it was the look in their eyes. Once, their faces had shone with the light of Ischyros, the joy of believers who know they will be accepted into the arms of the God. Now, they sometimes looked back at Taillefer with hope, but more often with bewilderment, as if they had lost something precious and didn't know how to find it. It was not only Taillefer who saw this; subordinate priests from across the province came to him with their concerns, even the skilful orators who knew how to make a crowd weep with love for the God.

Ten years before, when Taillefer first became a priest, the

world had been a simpler place, as black and white as an anakritim robe. There was the faith of Ischyros, as revealed by His prophet Salazar, and later by the Blessèd Tanguy, who had brought the faith to Galmandie. Anyone who undermined the works of Ischyros, the Creator God, must be a servant of Kakos, the Destroyer. To the priesthood was granted the sacrament of pardon, that the faithful might be unburdened of their sins and cross the bridge of judgement. The unfaithful and the unpardoned would fall from the bridge into the eternal fires of the pit. It was written.

There had been four pillars to the temple: the faith, the priesthood, the Order of Guardians and the Order of Anakritim. The Guardians were the faith's own warriors, holy knights whose banner had struck fear into unbelievers, from the infidel Saradim of the east to the pagans of the north. They were beyond reproach; they were the Lions of Ischyros, who desired only to defend the faith or die in the attempt. The Order of Anakritim were priests who codified the writings of Salazar and Tanguy, defining what was holy and what was heresy. The people feared them, rightly, but it was a fear that kept the faith pure.

Then King Aloys accused the Guardians of heresy and foul perversions, and the anakritim's torturers had wrung enough confessions for the high priest to suppress the Order. Any who recanted their confessions were burned at the stake as relapsed heretics. One of the great pillars of the temple crumbled to dust. Taillefer bore a heavy burden, for he was one of the few who knew for sure that the Guardians' only significant crime was their affluence. The Order had vowed personal poverty but became rich with endowments; so rich that Aloys craved their wealth to fill his empty treasury. Anakritis-General Ghislain Barthram had wanted ever more power for his anakritim to rule the faith, power that came from enriching a secular king and eliminating the spiritual opposition. Barthram and Aloys had been a partnership forged in the pit, and Taillefer's own brother Othon, the chancellor, had helped them. Truly, as Othon once said, the pinnacle of power is slick with blood and shit.

If Othon knew that he, Taillefer, was aware of these terrible crimes, would he too be killed? Probably. Neither his priesthood nor his family connections would protect him if he were known to harbour such a secret. Yet Taillefer had performed King Aloys's deathbed unburdening; he had heard the truth from the king's own lips. He'd even pressed the sacred ash of pardon into the king's forehead, granting him passage over the bridge.

Yet the rumours persisted. Some said the king had been struck down by an avenging angel for his sins against the God.

Then the anakritis-general himself, who should have been an exemplar of the faith, had been tried for sorcery. Tried, found guilty and burned at the stake by his own tormentors. Was it any wonder that the people were bewildered? Their heroes were fallen, their zealots dishonoured, and their king was dead. Now they doubted, and found excuses to miss the holy offices. And all the while the realm stood on the brink of civil war, with neither Aloys's son Lancelin nor his brother Gervais of Delmas having the support of enough nobles to be acclaimed king.

Taillefer looked up, seeking wisdom. Above him the dome of the temple arched in a curve as perfect as the heavens, its blue surface painted with stars. He sighed and closed his eyes. By letting Adelais de Vries escape, had he served Ischyros or Kakos? What was she? He had no answer. He'd thought she was a page boy at that first encounter as he rode beside the king; a noble's son who sat astride a magnificent black destrier; a fine-featured, blue-eyed boy with high cheekbones and a small mouth; the disturbingly beautiful face of an angel. Then she'd swept her hat from her head, not in deference but in defiance, letting bright yellow hair fall to her shoulders. '*I am Adelais de Vries, whom you call the Vriesian Witch.*' She had handled that destrier like a knight trained to war, kicking the king from the saddle and riding him down without mercy.

Yet, after Taillefer had heard the king's unburdening, he could believe she was the instrument of the God's vengeance. He'd let her escape with the de Fontenays. It was only later that he remembered the wolf that had herded him and the king into Adelais's path, delivering her that moment alone.

He sighed. A moon of prayer and he still did not know.

The last few worshippers were filing out. One remained, watching him from far back in the temple. She was cloaked and booted as a noblewoman, with an escort of two men-at-arms waiting by the doors. Her head was covered, as was proper within the temple, and it was not until she lifted one hand and pushed her hood back from her face that Taillefer recognised Agnès de Fontenay.

He was unnerved to notice a lightening of his spirits, a quickening of his blood at the sight of her. But he was a priest. It was not proper. More than a priest, he was a diakonos, with fifty priests looking to him for leadership. Taillefer composed himself, dampening his smile even as hers blossomed. His pulse took longer to obey.

They met beneath the dome's edge, where the stars might fall. 'My lady de Fontenay.' No touch was appropriate.

'Excellency.' She held eye contact with him, a half-smile on her lips as if they shared secrets. Which, he supposed, they did.

'I had heard that you and Lord de Fontenay were in Delmas, with the duke.' He kept his tone formal.

'I am here at my husband's request. May we talk? Somewhere a little more private, perhaps?'

At her husband's request. Taillefer stifled his curiosity while he signalled for his cloak. How very appropriate that his assistant priest that day should be Malory d'Eivet, who bundled the cloak in his arms and rushed forwards in his eagerness to pay his respects to Lady de Fontenay. Of course. They had travelled across Galmandie together. D'Eivet, who so firmly believed that Adelais was a Blessèd One of Ischyros.

'My office, then? Perhaps Pateras Malory might join us?' He should not meet with a woman alone.

Agnès paused for perhaps three breaths before she nodded, a little reluctantly it seemed. 'I am sure Pateras Malory's discretion is assured.'

They stepped out together into the town, a little procession of priests, lady and men-at-arms, exchanging pleasantries as they walked. No, Agnès had not heard from Adelais, and she had not trusted anyone with a message. She might visit her one day soon. Yes, Pateras Malory now served Ischyros by ministering to the poor of Harbin. The God had been kind.

Lady Agnès slipped a little as they crossed Harbin's square. There had been snow early in the day, a late bite of winter in the fasting moon. It had not settled but the road was slick, and Taillefer offered her his arm. That much must be permissible, here in the open, with another priest and two men-at-arms following at a respectful distance. She rested a gloved hand on his forearm, squeezing her thanks. The last time this lady had been in Harbin there had been a fight here, between the castle's walls and the river. Broken bodies had lain where market traders now cried their wares, and rivulets of blood ran between the cobbles.

The girl Adelais had fought at the heart of that melee. She could have been any valiant man-at-arms with her dead sprawled around her until she let out that final, visceral cry. It had been half-scream, half-roar, both a cry of triumph and a challenge, an animal sound that could only have come from a woman's body. Or a beast from the pit.

Taillefer stole a glance at Agnès and knew that she too was remembering.

'What was she, do you think?' He did not need to say her name. 'Angel or witch?'

Agnès did not answer him immediately, but there was a slight pressure on his arm to show that she had heard and was considering her reply.

'I think...' Agnès spoke quietly, looking downwards, watching her path as the road rose onto the bridge over the Fauve. 'I *believe* she is neither. We will talk more anon.'

Beyond the bridge, the palace of the diakonos, *his* palace, spread eastwards along the river bank. Westwards, to their right, lay an open, muddy meadow. Its wet, winter grass still bore yellowed scars, for on the day of the fight it had been brilliant with nobles' pavilions and banners. Half the court had come to dance attendance on King Aloys. Within a day of his death, the factions had formed. That fight in the square had been just the beginning. Now nobles were assembling all over Galmandie, calling their knights and men-at-arms to prepare for war on behalf of Delmas or Lancelin. And now one of Delmas's principal supporters had sent his wife as an emissary. But why here? Why to him? Why not directly to the court of Prince Lancelin in the capital? Yet with this lady's hand on his arm Taillefer felt a lightness of spirit; a robin sang in a hedgerow and the trickling gutters promised the coming of spring.

A good fire blazed ready in Taillefer's office, and he and Agnès stood a while in front of it, warming their hands in a pleasantly domestic moment. She smiled at him, and he turned his head away; those wide, green eyes had already filled too many thoughts. The men-at-arms had been sent to enjoy whatever food and drink the buttery could offer, but Pateras Malory remained. He poured Agnès and Taillefer wine before settling a little apart, still cloaked against that corner's chills. Taillefer waved Agnès to a chair by the fire where, out of politeness, he had to look at her; she sat poised and upright and her face shone in the firelight. A priest should not notice how her travel-stained gown was tight-laced to her figure.

Agnès rested her wine on a small table at her elbow. To business.

'Lord Leandre sends greetings. He regrets he is unable to have this conversation in person.'

Taillefer inclined his head, understanding. Any noble who fought Lancelin's troops in Harbin's square that day would be arrested if they entered land controlled by the prince's faction, and brought to trial for killing royal soldiers.

'Do you speak for Duke Gervais, my lady, or Lord Leandre?'

'Lord Leandre. He believes there is a way both of unifying Galmandie,' Agnès continued, 'and of strengthening the faith. Very significantly.'

'One imagines that Lord Leandre's vision is not of a realm united under Prince Lancelin.'

'His message touches more on the spiritual than the secular realm.'

Taillefer said nothing. He had a sense that both he and Lady Agnès were swimming out of their depths.

'Let us be candid, Excellency. Each of us in this room, including Pateras Malory, helped Adelais de Vries. If that were known at court, neither your priesthood nor my nobility would save us. We are already in each other's trust.'

'And I sense you are about to burden that trust with something more.'

Agnès sipped wine and replaced her goblet with precision, frowning slightly. 'You asked me whether Adelais was an angel or a witch. I believe she is neither. I think she is a courageous but innocent young woman who has been caught up in great events.'

'I saw her kill the king. I saw her fight here. She is hardly innocent.'

Agnès shrugged. 'Do you know why the anakritim and the king's men pursued us across Galmandie?'

'There were rumours that a relic had been stolen from the Guardians' temple, but nothing was found. After the high priest died, people were more concerned with finding the "witch" they claimed had killed him.'

'As you know, my escort was led by Humbert Blanc, who had been the Guardian Grand Commander of Arrenicia. Four other Guardian knights were with us, all of whom died to protect that which we carried.'

'Which was?'

Agnès breathed deeply, composing herself. 'Hundreds of years ago, when Salazar himself walked this earth, there was a great battle on the shores of Alympos, before the land of the prophet was lost to us.'

Taillefer nodded. This was one of the founding narratives of the faith. It was written that a Saradim sword cut off the left hand of Salazar. When the battle began to go against the Ischyrians, the prophet seized his own severed hand, held it aloft, and only then did the army of the God prevail.

'After the battle was won, Salazar fainted from his wound, and two disciples bore him away on a boat. It is written that he lives still on the fabled Isle of Elisium, from whence he shall come to lead the faithful in the final battle against Kakos.'

Taillefer coughed in gentle reproof. A diakonos did not need a lecture on the faith's history.

'Two brothers fought alongside the prophet that day,' Agnès continued. 'Bayard and Jovan de Fontenay. Jovan went on to found the Order of Guardians. Bayard is Lord Leandre's ancestor.'

Taillefer straightened slowly in his chair. His mouth was suddenly dry; his lips and fingertips were tingling. His vision seemed newly sharp and his hearing so fine that he heard the rustle of Malory's robe as he too stirred. 'By the God—' Taillefer swallowed '—you have the Hand of Salazar?'

'It was kept in a golden reliquary in the Guardians' temple

at Villebénie, known only to the grand master and a trusted third degree of knights. It was thought to be too holy for common gaze.'

'But why did the Guardians keep it from the rest of the faith all these years?'

'Each grand master swore to protect the Hand until the faith could receive it with pure reverence, open to *all* the faithful—not just those with enough gold to buy access. It could not become tainted in the way that Tanguy's skull is tainted.'

The skull of Tanguy, the First Disciple, was encased in a golden head in the fire temple of Villebénie. Pilgrims paid so heavily to touch the reliquary that it was said their donations had built the city.

And if a mere disciple's head could found a city, then a relic of Salazar, the *only* relic of the prophet Himself, would forge a nation. Taillefer pushed that thought aside. It was unworthy. Venal.

'She touched the Hand of Salazar.' In his shadowed corner Malory was also on the edge of his chair, wonder in his voice. 'When the high priest asked how Mistress Adelais lived after being struck by the crossbow bolt, Humbert Blanc said she touched the Hand of Salazar!'

Agnès nodded. 'Yes, she touched the Hand.'

'And the Hand is now with Lord Leandre?'

'Hidden by him.' Agnès's smile was almost flirtatious, despite the gravity of their talk. 'Even I do not know where.'

'And if the Hand were to be revealed, how would we know that it is indeed the relic of the prophet?'

'Before the Order was suppressed and the Guardians' temple fell into the king's hands, the Hand was removed from its reliquary and hidden. As he was martyred, the last grand master signed its hiding place to Humbert Blanc, who was probably the last Guardian officer alive and free. He was also my uncle. Lord Brother Humbert agreed with my husband to recover the Hand and to bring it to safe keeping at Fontenay, hidden within my baggage train.'

Taillefer believed her; she was speaking with palpable honesty. He closed his eyes, thinking. Such a relic would relight the fires of the faith. He felt a great yearning grow within himself, like a starving man who glimpses a feast.

'Why are you telling me, Lady Agnès?'

'The country is divided. It is losing its faith.'

'This we know. Again, why me?' Had she read his mind that morning?

'The higher echelons of the faith are corrupt. They would exploit the Hand for personal gain.'

'Do you not think I would be tempted?' Taillefer almost growled the words at her. He did not desire the wealth, but the one who brought the Hand back to the faith would rise far and fast. There would be so much opportunity to do good.

If he remained uncorrupted.

'Perhaps it is time for the faith to rediscover the simple principles of Salazar, Excellency.' Malory spoke softly from his corner. Oh, that was real temptation.

'Are there no others?' Even as Taillefer spoke, he knew the answer. There were many good people serving Ischyros, both men and women, but the ones who climbed the ladder needed too much ambition to be pure.

'Lord Leandre knows you are an honourable man. You did not betray us. Trust is crucial in so great a matter.'

A more secular, cynical thought occurred to Taillefer, burning through his initial wonder. 'The higher echelons of the faith also support the established order. Lancelin.'

'And you, the brother of the chancellor, are ideally placed to bridge the two parties. Duke Gervais desires reconciliation with his nephew Lancelin. He wishes to move freely about the realm without fear of arrest. He wishes once again to lead the army. He also, by the way, speaks highly of you.'

'And if Delmas has the Hand, support for Lancelin would evaporate. Clever. How does Lord Leandre reconcile such a secular outcome with the pure teaching of Salazar?'

'The most precious relic in Ischyrendom has secular implications. That is inevitable. It will also need protection. However, Lord Leandre wishes simply to return the Hand to the faith, with two conditions.'

'Which are?'

'One, that no money is ever charged for pilgrims to see it.'

'And?'

'Two, that you become its spiritual custodian, ensuring it is always treated with the pure reverence that the prophet would have wished.'

Taillefer's heart thudded in his chest. His head rang with the sound of his own pounding pulse. *The Hand of Salazar*. In his divine agony Taillefer understood the wisdom of the grand masters who had chosen to keep its existence secret.

He swallowed enough wine to enable speech. 'Once the Hand's existence is known, every episkopos in Ischyrendom will want to control it, and they are all my superiors in the faith.'

'It falls to you and me to suggest how the Hand might always be treated with reverence. Lord Leandre suggests that the Order of Guardians be reformed to protect it. Would you like some time alone to consider the matter?'

'Thank you. I must take this to the God in prayer. He will guide me. Meanwhile, I will have the steward arrange suitable rooms for you in the guest quarters.'

Yet he knew it would be hard to find the calm he needed, even in prayer. *The Hand itself*. It would light such a fire in the faith that unbelievers would be swept into the sea.

2.2 ADELAIS

Adelais paced the battlements between the towers, buffeted by the wind, as she waited for de Warelt to take her to Ragener. She didn't know who she was any more, or rather what she was meant to be. All year she'd dreamt of being free in Vriesland, a free *woman* in Vriesland, able to walk tall and openly among her own people in a kirtle or gown, and with no need to hide under a man's cote-hardie. Now it was clear that people wanted to kill her. She'd wanted to be free to study the healing lore of the old gods; herbs and runes rather than the blood-letting and prayers of the Ischyrians. But since the purges, there wasn't even a *seidhkona* in the castle who could instruct her in rune lore. Her grandmother's staff lay against the wall in her chamber, unused.

Below her ran the mighty Schilde, grey and white-capped in the aftermath of the storm. Three hundred paces away a line of ships had been drawn up for the winter on the far bank, their masts unstepped and their hulls covered with oilcloth. They looked like the teeth of a saw. Only a fool of a mariner would risk the Saxen Sea in winter. There was a settlement there, undefended by any walls; a place where travellers from the north might stable their horses while they visited Vriesland's capital on foot, and inns where they might rest while they waited for a ferry. The sprawling mass of Siltehafn lay south of the river, behind her, unseen, not even smelt while the wind blew from the north; there was only the sharp tang of salt.

Perhaps they'd let her take Allier and ride north to find a *seidhkona* who'd teach her rune lore. She might even find friendly company, away from Ragener's court.

That was another thing she'd yearned for– the chance to grow her hair long enough to wear the braids of an unwed girl. One day she might find a man for whom she'd comb them free. Now she didn't even feel female any more. A year before, she'd been learning to be a healer in a sisterhouse; imprisoned far from home, perhaps, but a woman among women, caring for the sick. In the spring she'd been a fugitive, disguised in men's clothes but still a woman among men. She'd even had a lover, and in the silken coupling of their bodies she felt more a goddess than any mortal girl.

But she'd killed people. After her mentor Humbert had died, choked on a rope's end by an Ischyrian priest, it no longer mattered to her that men died. At the time she'd felt no guilt. Worse, she'd been filled with a murderous joy, balanced and poised on Allier's back, woman and destrier in perfect harmony. *Unnatural* harmony. He'd spun to the lightest touch of her spur, kicking, biting, until a litter of broken men lay around them. She and Allier had been of one terrible mind, and together they were invincible; she'd fought better than any knight trained to battle from boyhood, but that was not *her*, surely? Some gods-given skill had come with the humming of rune song, and turned woman into warrior.

She closed her eyes, remembering one soldier's snarling face as he came charging at her with a spear in the glorious chaos of her last fight. She hadn't consciously asked Allier to sidestep the man's thrust in a way that positioned her so perfectly for her response, nor had she told him to make that surge towards the enemy that added momentum to her strike. Then, she'd felt a warrior's triumph at a skilful blow. But afterwards?

Oh, the afterwards. Afterwards came the self-loathing and the waking horror. A moon later that man was still looking at her along the shining line of her sword, his eyes wide with shock, and on the battlements Adelais shook her wrist as if she could flick away the memory of the jolt as her sword's point broke through lips and teeth, tongue and skull.

She'd fought her way back to Vriesland but she'd left her caring, coupling, female self on the bloody fields of Galmandie. That Adelais felt like an old friend who'd gone far away and might never return.

A ferry had set out from the northern shore, one of the larger boats, with four oars a side, although the oarsmen were letting a triangular foresail do much of the work; it was bellied full by a following wind, hiding the cargo or passengers until the boat neared the town and the captain turned alongside the castle's private jetty, spilling the wind. Fifty paces from Adelais, where a river gate gave access directly to the castle's outer court-yard, the boatmen threw ropes to the shore.

The boat's turn revealed a huge man standing by the mast, dressed in the northmen's style with woollen trews pushed into heavy boots just below the knee, and a fur cloak so thick that his shoulders seemed as broad as the hairy aurochs cattle that could live the whole winter in the snow. If the cloak had not been open, revealing the man beneath, he might have seemed more of a standing bear than a warrior. His left hand rested on a sword hilt in the way of a chieftain accustomed to command, and his right cradled an ornate helmet against his body. A grey beard streamed away from his face, fluttering in the wind like the ferry's masthead pennant. His entourage crowded the waist of the vessel behind him: servants; four escorting warriors; and a younger man, also richly dressed and thickly furred, who stood head-and-shoulders above the others – perhaps the chieftain's son. Behind them all a sharp-featured, older woman huddled on the stern bench, alone and apart, even in the crowded boat. She looked up at the battlements as if she was aware of Adelais's scrutiny. Adelais knew that the woman's cloak would be cat skin, in honour of the goddess Freyja, for cradled between her legs, with its carved head resting against her shoulder, was the staff of a *seidhkona*.

As the boat brushed the jetty, the sun lanced under a cloud, and the chieftain was turned to gold; gold arm-rings where his hand rested on his sword hilt, a gold buckle on his belt, and a great golden brooch that pinned his cloak at the shoulder. But most of all, her eye was drawn to the crest of his helmet, wondrously formed so that the beak and head of a bird formed the nose guard, and drooping wings framed the dome, hunched as if spread over a grounded kill. A raven, she guessed, to honour Odhinn, or perhaps an eagle; it was too far to tell, even though the sun had turned the golden bird to fire. The chieftain had become a walking echo of her nightmare.

Adelais turned as the tower door creaked open, was caught by the wind, and smacked stone. Ulfhild struggled with its ring, loose strands of blonde hair streaming past her face.

'It is time, mistress.'

De Warelt made a slight nod of approval when he met her in the guardroom below. He gestured towards her waist. 'Your sword? Their Graces requested you wear your sword.'

'Ulfhild will bring it.' The girl was clasping the sheathed weapon to her chest, beaming with the honour. Adelais had decided that a knight's sword was too alien for her gown's finery, especially now the mud was newly brushed from the hem.

'Very well. Come.' With unexpected courtesy, de Warelt offered Adelais his arm. 'Jarl Magnus has arrived. Tonight there will be a feast in his honour. As we walk I will tell you of the great nobles that you will meet this evening.'

Adelais tried to concentrate. She wasn't much interested in politics. She'd rather learn rune lore, somewhere safe. Build a life where she wasn't the court's pet curiosity; two liveried servants stared at her as they passed, as if she were an exotic animal that had escaped from a menagerie.

'Vriesland is an alliance of three counties, plus the northern jarls. Duke Ragener is also count of the largest county, Votlendi, in the valley of the Schilde. South of the river are the counties of Sjóland to the west and along the coast, and Theignault to the east.'

'I have some knowledge of my nation, *mynherra*.' She resented his patronising tone.

De Warelt snorted; a noble's contempt for a low-born woman. He continued as if she had not spoken. 'The counts of Sjóland and Theignault are both Ischyrian, though many of their people secretly follow the old gods. Both will be at this evening's feast. North of Votlendi, between the mountains and the sea, is Normark, whose jarls support Ragener because he is a barrier between them and the expansion of the new faith.'

De Warelt walked quickly, despite the courteous arm. Ulfhild trotted to keep up, the scabbard rattling in her arms, as de Warelt led them through the arch into the ducal apartments.

'So what is my role in this, Seigneur?'

'His Grace will explain.' De Warelt paused at a set of ornately carved double doors, where a retainer knocked and announced them. *Still nothing useful.* Adelais gritted her teeth in annoyance as she was ushered into the chamber.

The duke's solar smelt of woodsmoke and beeswax, and was dark even in the middle of the day, shuttered against the cold so the light came mainly from a fierce open fire and thick, guttering candles clustered on stands. The corners were shadowed but

Adelais had the impression of tapestry wall hangings rippling in the draughts. Ragener stood hatless with his back to the fire, warming his hands behind him. The posture made his paunch look bigger; he reminded her of the draper's child's stuffed bear. Adelais motioned to Ulfhild to wait by the door, took a deep breath and stepped out, with her feet sinking into thick, luxurious furs that lined the floor. She made her obeisance, waiting for the tirade, wondering why she could not take this moment more seriously; her earlier nervousness had turned to belligerence. What the *fjakk* did he expect, cooping her up like this?

'I hear you had an exciting morning.'

Adelais looked up, surprised. The duke sounded almost amused. Ragener was an outwardly affable man of perhaps fifty summers, with haystack hair and a face of two halves; clean shaven below, a little jowly, often smiling. Above, close-set, poignard-sharp eyes held her gaze unblinkingly, as if the moving mouth beneath belonged to another man.

'More interesting than I would have wished, Your Grace.' Adelais spoke in the Galman of the court. One did not play language games with the duke. She stood, risking a wry smile. This might be easier than she'd thought.

'Then perhaps you have learned a lesson.' Ragener turned to de Warelt. 'Still nothing?'

'Nothing, Your Grace. We found the weapon, that's all.'

'What about the people who live there?'

'The house was thought to be empty, Your Grace. We suspect the ambush had been long planned, just waiting for the right moment.'

Ragener snorted. 'Search all buildings on the approaches to the castle. Look for other empty buildings. Pay particular attention to those who wear the hand.'

'It is being done, Your Grace.'

'And you, young woman. What are we to do with you?'

'Send me north, Your Grace. Let me find a *seidhkona* who will teach me rune lore.'

Ragener looked surprised. He probably had not expected her to answer. 'Oh no, no. You have a much more important role to play.' He stared into a shadowed corner. 'Master Knud, open that shutter so we can see. You know my master armourer, mistress?'

Adelais had not realised there was another man in the room, and turned to see the armourer's squat outline. Her eyes were adjusting to the light, and, as the man moved to obey, Adelais stifled a gasp, almost a scream, for her eyes saw a cloaked, head-less woman standing upright beside him, even while her mind told her that such things were impossible. Her shock faded as the opening shutter spilt a milky, yellow light and she realised that the body was standing on a single pole, not motionless legs; the cloaked form was no more alive than the wooden dummies that the duke's knights used to practise their sword skills.

Ragener crossed to stand behind the figure with his hands on its shoulders and a boyish smile on his face that this time reached his eyes; they sparkled at her in the new light.

'Aloys would have fought until all Vriesland was under his boot. I have a gift for you as my appreciation for stopping him.' He pulled off the cloak with the flourish of a fair-ground mummer.

Adelais gasped again. The armour he'd just revealed must be painted leather, even though it had the appearance of gilded metal, for not even the finest armourer could hammer iron to look so like a woman's body. It was made in two halves, a front and a back, forming a torso as moulded as a gown. But what a gown; the duchess herself might wear this to display her figure at court. Adelais circled the dummy, her mouth open in appreci-ation. The front half swept smoothly beneath the neck and looped over the shoulders, leaving half-sleeves of mail hanging to protect the upper arms. Full-length sleeves of a gown in a soft

golden cloth hung within. Only the buckles joining the two
halves interrupted the lines; no lacing here that could be sliced
by a sword cut. There would be a coif of mail to protect the
neck, she knew, and perhaps a bascinet, but such things were
not marvellous. This body, though – this was armour such as the
goddess Freyja herself might wear to war.

Would it allow enough movement to fight? The waist was
quite narrow, flaring over the hips to emphasise a woman's
shape. Thigh-length curtains of chain mail, slit front and back
to allow for riding, hung over the gown's skirts. She completed
her circuit, still speechless at the perfectly moulded female
form; the flat stomach was slightly ribbed to hint at muscles
beneath and even had a dimple to imitate a belly button. The
lower rim with its chain-mail hangings dipped seductively at
the front; this armour was designed to allure, as well as
protect. Adelais lifted her hand towards it, glancing at the
duke for permission before she let her fingers rest on the
chest. It felt as cold as her scabbard and, like that, had probably been shaped then boiled until it was iron-hard. She
looked down at her own slender figure within the duchess's
gown, and smiled to herself; this armour had been made for a
woman with much fuller breasts. The curves she'd always
wanted were now sculpted in rigid, unfeeling, nipple-less
leather.

'It will not stop the lance of a charging knight, nor a windlass crossbow.' Master Knud spoke from behind her in a thick
Vriesian accent. No *gyke* courtier, this one. 'But it will turn
most blades unless the strike is hard and square.'

'You made it?' Adelais managed to find her voice. The
armourer was short, with the hammer-wielding muscles of his
trade packed into a square frame, like a walking barrel. He
stared back in a way that made her uneasy, as if he knew some
intimate secret. She turned away to touch the armour. 'How?'

Ragener answered. 'You recall that the duchess sent her

seamstresses to measure you so that her gown could be altered for you?'

Adelais nodded. She was wearing that gown. The seamstress had been meticulous.

'Those measurements were sent to the finest craftsman in Vriesland for him to carve a mould for the leather. I left space for this gown,' the armourer added. 'The fabric is light, for summer work. I also added an extra layer of protection to the chest.' He smirked as he touched the breastplate. 'Will you try it on, mistress?'

They both seemed disappointed when she asked for privacy, but they let her change in an antechamber, with just Ulfhild to help. The armour fitted close to her body, leaving space only for the thin gown, and no shirt. It was heavy, but not excessively so. Most of the weight would be in the chain mail, not the leather. When they'd buckled the two halves together, she turned to Ulfhild and lifted her arms from her sides.

'How do I look, Ulfie?'

Ulfhild's grin was wide. '*Fjakkinn* magic, mistress!' She tugged at the collar of the gown, arranging it to frame her neck and face within the armour. 'Can you breathe?'

Adelais inhaled. 'Very well.' With each breath her body stretched to fill any looseness. She flexed her shoulders, then her back. Her arms moved naturally, but it was harder to twist her body. 'I don't think I'll be doing much dancing in it, though.'

'It needs this the way a gown needs jewels, mistress.' Ulfhild buckled Adelais's sword around her waist. It hung naturally on her hip, reassuring in its familiarity. Adelais took a deep breath and stepped back into the solar.

'By the God!' De Warelt's shock softened into honest appreciation.

'Excellent!' Ragener made a circular motion with his finger, inviting her to turn. As Adelais completed her circle all three men were eyeing her in a way that made her glance downwards.

She was revealing no more than many ladies at court, less perhaps, yet the thickened leather made her feel as if her chest was pointing at them, almost aggressively. She hid her blush with a curtsey. 'Your Grace is too generous.'

'Wear it tonight, if you please, at the feast. Jarl Magnus has heard of your deeds and wishes to meet you.'

Adelais found herself staring at the leather breasts as much as the men. *Why make me what I'm not?* 'My deeds, Your Grace, such as they were, were done in man's attire. I spent most of the year trying not to be noticed. This,' she gestured at her chest, 'demands attention.'

'But you have become an emblem, like a banner. And like a banner, you must be seen. You must inspire awe.'

'There is no "must", *mynherra*. I am a weaver's daughter who wants to live in peace, not a flag to wave.'

'We all want to live in peace.' Ragener's voice tightened in irritation. He gestured to a stool. 'Sit, girl. I will explain.'

Adelais waited until the duke was seated before she settled onto the stool. It was short-legged; the tops of her thighs lifted the armour's lower edge so her breasts were pushed uncomfortably upwards and a rim of hard leather pressed into her armpits. Her sword now trailed at her side, twisted in its belt. She was aware of the armourer walking around her, inspecting his handiwork.

'War is coming,' Ragener continued, 'even with Aloys dead. His son Lancelin is a weak fool, but Aloys's brother Gervais of Delmas is strong and his mind is set on conquest. If the Galmans come, those who follow the old gods will be burned as heretics. Would you fight against that, girl?'

'Aye, Your Grace.'

'Good. To defend Vriesland I need the jarls of the northern marches and their men. If Magnus pledges support, the others will follow. He also claims descent from Odhinn himself and has no love for the hungry god.'

'And what role could I have in that?' She'd seen enough killing.

'You must have power, for you killed both their king and their high priest. There are tales told about you in the taverns, and they grow wilder with every telling. It is said that you ripped a crossbow bolt from your own belly and lived. The people want a heroine.' Ragener gestured at her armour. 'And now you look the part. Men will follow you.'

'My grandmother cast the runes for me. She said I was like a tall tree that draws men to its shelter, but also draws the light-ning, and those around me will die. I have no wish to lead more to their deaths, Your Grace.'

'So you would flee? The lands north of the Schilde will not feed all my people. We must fight. There are no alternatives.'

'I will answer Jarl Magnus's questions honestly, Your Grace. He must make his own decision. I will tell no lies to lure men into battle.'

'Good.' Ragener nodded, though his eyes held a warning. 'He has a *seidhkona* with him. She will smell any falsehood. Now come and look at yourself.'

Ragener stood and led Adelais to an alcove where he pulled the cover off a framed mirror on a stand. Adelais did not know how such a wondrous object could be made; it was almost the length of her body and half as broad, and so smooth that she could not tell whether it was a single sheet of polished silver or steel, or even glass. She only knew that the image reflected within it was almost true, with only the slightest ripples of distortion. Her hands flew to her mouth, laughing with wonder, and a terrible beauty laughed back at her. The goddess standing before her was only a little fogged, and slightly greyer than life, but clear enough to show the shining excitement in her eyes.

'How is the fit?' Knud asked.

'Not too restrictive.' Eyes still on her own image, Adelais crouched into one of the guard positions for sword and buckler work, still marvelling at how the image moved with her. She'd never seen her whole self, let alone dressed like this; she'd seen only fragments of her face in small, polished-steel hand mirrors. And the fit? It would be hot and sweaty but her arms moved well enough. She tore her eyes away and looked down to where the ankle-length skirt was now folding onto a fur rug as she crouched. 'Though the hem will need to come up to just below the knees, or I will trip in a fight.' She straightened, realising she'd spoken as if she was already leading men into battle.

The armourer nodded. 'The seamstresses will have it done immediately and we'll deliver it to your chamber before the feast.'

'There is one other finishing touch.' Ragener lifted the lid of a storage chest and pulled out a scarf of golden silk. 'The gift of the duchess.' He arranged it around her neck.

Adelais backed away from his lingering fingers and moved her cheek against the material. She'd never felt silk against her skin before, soft and sensual, like a lover's caress. She wished her village could see her now. And all those she'd loved. Arnaud, who'd been her lover. Humbert Blanc, who'd been so much more than a father. And above all, Agnès de Fontenay, the dearest friend she had ever known. Agnès, the chatelaine of great estates who held her nobility so lightly that she could call a weaver's daughter *kjúkling*, chick, in that awful accent that Adelais had never had the heart to correct. By the gods, she missed her.

'*Mistress?*' The urgency in Ulfhild's voice shook her from her reverie.

Ragener was shooing de Warelt and Knud from the chamber. Ulfhild remained, with Adelais's blue velvet gown billowing over her arms, openly defying her duke. Ragener gestured again and said, 'Go, wench.'

Adelais took a deep breath. If she ordered Ulfhild to stay,

the girl would suffer for it. Perhaps lose her position. 'Wait outside, Ulfie. *Right* outside.'

Ragener closed the door behind Ulfhild and ran his fingers through his mop of blond hair. It was a strangely boyish mannerism for one who was probably intent on seduction. Adelais wished Agnès was with her. Agnès would know how to turn a difficult moment with a jest, and how to swim in the currents of a ducal court.

Ragener poured a generous measure of wine for them both from a side table, handed her a goblet, and toasted her across the rim. *A duke, serving me with wine.*

'To victory!'

'If war comes.' She drank.

'Quite. Do you like it?' He nodded at her goblet. 'It comes from Galmandie's far south, near the Alympian Sea.

'Very much, Your Grace.' The wine was better than anything she had ever tasted. 'You honour me.'

'I could do more, you know.' Ragener adjusted the hang of her sword belt, settling the scabbard at a new angle on her hip. When his hand slipped inside the riding slit at the back of the chain-mail skirt she was not surprised, just *fordæmdur* angry.

'You realise what I'm offering you, girl?' His face was very close. He was only a little taller than her, so her eyes were at the level of his nose. He had a fleshy lower lip that sagged forwards to expose teeth swimming in saliva.

'I thought this fine armour was a reward, not a purchase price.' His breath smelt of spices and wine. *Please, someone knock at the door.*

'Of course a reward! And richly deserved. I could reward you even more.'

'If I let you *fjakk* me.' Adelais spoke as bluntly and crudely as she could.

'So much more than that.' His hand now cupped one cheek.

Adelais tensed, clenching. 'I am asking you to be my... companion.'

Adelais managed to bring up her spare hand and rest the palm against his chest. 'I am indeed honoured, sire, but this is an invitation I must decline.'

'You would refuse your duke?' Ragener's look was mock-affronted.

Adelais thought hard. This was a threat that would not go away. Even if she rebuffed him now, he'd try again. Unless...

'Do you believe I can weave magic through runes, sire?' Adelais managed to keep her voice level, almost conversational.

'Of course.' The hand on her backside resumed its stroking.

Adelais took a swig of wine. His smile broadened, perhaps in anticipation.

'The *thurs* rune,' she spoke as sweetly as she could, 'is ideal for love magic.'

Ragener's grin became lascivious.

'And *kaunaz* can fire a man's potency.'

His fingers moved a little higher.

'Inverted, they have the opposite effect.' She could tolerate this for just a few moments longer.

Ragener frowned, not understanding, and Adelais hardened her voice.

'So if you touch me again I will shrivel your *fjakkinn* balls.' The shock on his face was sweet to see, the immediate recoil a relief.

She pushed past him, draining the goblet on her way out; it was far too good to waste. At the door she turned and gave him a respectful curtsey.

'Your Grace.'

2.3 GAUTHIER

Gauthier sat with his back against a cold stone wall, listening to Ragener's feast. He waited in a narrow minstrels' gallery, safe from all except accidental discovery, for today the duke followed the northern custom of having minstrels stroll among the guests, like the skalds of the pagan lands. Gauthier wondered who had made that suggestion, so apt for their guests, so convenient in leaving this space empty. Muted candlelight squeezed through a hand's-breadth gap in the heavy curtain that screened the gallery. A hand's breadth was all he needed.

The waiting was always the hardest. He craved activity, but he couldn't risk the movement. In actual combat, or in those heart-pumping moments before a blade struck home, he'd find a strange, calm energy that was not so much fear as anticipation. But the empty times before action were hard, and he'd been waiting since the temple bells had rung for the Lighting of the Lamps.

He'd watched the daylight fade, and listened to the hall filling. Now the hum of a hundred voices rose like swarming bees, and still she had not come. Had plans changed? She was to be paraded, he'd been assured, dangled before this heathen jarl to persuade him to make war. Yet the first meat was already served. Gauthier swallowed, again, wishing he had brought a skin of water to slake his thirst. Wishing too that he could have bolted the door to this gallery. He'd jammed a wedge of wood underneath that would stop a child, but it was hardly secure.

He stared at the crossbow in the shadows. It was another heavy windlass war weapon, and, like the previous bow, the maker's craft-mark had been chiselled from its stock. It was untraceable, and he wondered which noble was paying for this. It was also ready-spanned so that not even the slightest noise might betray his presence. He'd known it would be waiting for him, hidden under a pile of old sacks, with a single bolt beside it; a wicked, flesh-biting hunting bolt, like the day before. His master said it would be a fitting death; she who was said to have ripped a crossbow bolt from her own belly and lived would now die with one in her back. And, like the day before, Gauthier should have time to run clear, empty-handed save for a priest's leather satchel with the box of sacred ash, wearing the passport of robes. Their rough wool was coarse against his legs and he scratched while he mentally walked his escape.

Passageway outside. He'd be gone before revellers worked out whence the shot had come. *Then walk.* Steps up; the searchers would come from below. Another passageway. Steps down to a discreet door into the inner courtyard near the gate. If the alarm was already sounded and the gate shut, there was a tower chamber where a devout noblewoman was conveniently sick and in need of prayer, and who would vouch for his presence.

Gauthier heard the creak of the hall's great doors opening below him, even above the noise of fifty shouted conversations, and knew it was time. He stood and picked up the crossbow, cradling it gently as he placed the bolt into the groove. His heart was pounding, but at least this time his breathing was slow. He held his fingers clear of the release lever as he peered through the gap in the curtains, pushing his nostrils into a scented wall of rich food, spilt ale, and bodies. Candles guttered in a draught; a window had been opened to let the evening air cool the heat from massed candles and food, the fires in the hearths, and the press of people. At the far end of the hall the duke and duchess sat at the high table, flanked by the jarl and his son, and the Counts of Theignault and Sjóland; the greatest nobles of Vriesland. Their conversation seemed to be faltering; something was attracting their attention at the doors beneath Gauthier's feet.

The rest of the revellers had not yet noticed. They sat at two lines of trestle tables stretching down each side of the hall to leave a central passageway between. Guests were hunched over steaming plates of food, gesticulating with their drinking horns, and their talk made a single, deep roar like a torrent falling into a pool. Immediately below Gauthier, the axe-heads of two pikes advanced into the hall, their bearers wearing bascinets and draped in the ducal livery. The pikes were lifted and their butts rammed down together into the boards in a booming command for silence. The noise fell. Heads turned towards the door. Again the pikes fell. Now there were gasps. Fingers pointed. *And again.* The noise sank to whispers, like the hiss of wind through trees.

The woman had come.

2.4 ADELAIS

Adelais waited by the doors into the feasting hall, trying not to let her nerves show. The moment was wrong; she had no wish to be paraded. The armour was wrong; she was fully covered but *by Freyja* those leather breasts made her feel naked. The host was wrong; Ragener would probably never forgive her for not letting him shaft her. And at her ear Everard de Warelt was muttering instructions. He was richly dressed in a velvet, fur-trimmed cote-hardie. A trace of his scent sweetened the smells flowing from the room. *Gyke!*

'You will be expected to swear fealty. Do you understand?'

No, she did not understand. Ragener was Duke of Vries-land. Why swear fealty to someone who was already your ruler?

'It means you must obey his commands. You will be granted lands in return for service.'

'I don't care what he makes me swear, I'm not going to let him *fjakk* me.'

She'd told de Warelt, who'd seemed unconcerned.

'Not that kind of service.'

Two pikemen in the ducal livery were pushing open the doors, releasing rich smells of meat and mead. Adelais was surprised to find she was hungry. Tables of feasting nobles stretched away on either side. At the far end of the hall, the greatest in the land sat on a raised dais. Their heads were starting to lift, looking at her. Beyond the doors two pikemen were beating for silence.

'You show them, mistress!' Ulfhild squeezed Adelais's arm from behind. Ulfie would not be allowed into the feast, alas.

Adelais looked down, aware of how assertively female she must seem. Dangling between her moulded leather breasts was a charm on a thong, a gift from Ulfhild; a pear-shaped pendant of polished wood. Only *seidhkonur* knew the full richness of rune lore, but many people carved runes to invoke a blessing, and Ulfhild had cut the *perthro* rune.

Perthro, the most enigmatic of runes, the rune of fate and of *harmingja*, which the Ischyrians might call 'luck' but which Adelais knew to be a gods-given blessing, so much more than pure chance. A good choice.

At the third blow of the pikes, de Warelt waved her forwards. Adelais made a token dip of respect and offered him her arm.

'No. On your own. I will follow. Your woman stays here. Walk to the duke and duchess, and make your obeisance.' He shrugged. 'After that, do as they say.' Beyond his shoulders, heads were turning, staring at her, or rather at the walking statue of her body.

Adelais squared her shoulders and stepped out into the whispering quiet of a hundred faces, mostly male. She steadied her sword against her hip with her left hand, swaggering a little, acting the part, knowing she was not so much being presented as being displayed. Serving thralls, mostly women, backed against the walls, clasping jugs and salvers to their chests. They too stared, round-eyed with wonder. *Fjakk*, she was thirsty. She'd happily drink some of that ale straight from a pitcher. Near her feet two dogs fought over discarded scraps, growling, ignoring her. The *perthro* rune knocked against her armour.

How would she be received, now she'd threatened to shrivel his balls? Ragener was smiling affably enough; perhaps he took rejection in his stride. On his left sat his duchess, Severine, a gaunt woman in her middle years whose lips seemed always to be pursed in disappointment or disapproval. Adelais had been told she was the daughter of a Galman count, married off to Ragener as a peace-weaver before Adelais was born. That hadn't stopped King Aloys invading, twice. Duchess Severine had not produced an heir. Her main legacy had been to make the worship of Ischyros fashionable among the nobility. On Ragener's right was Jarl Magnus, in whose honour they feasted; a big man with a bristling, grey beard. Further down the high table sat a man who could only be his son; they shared the same strong jaws and faces that looked as if they had been moulded out of lumpy clay, like unfinished statues.

It was a long room and a long walk, with every head turning to watch her. Their eyes on her back felt menacing, as if she should arch away from some threat. De Warelt walked at her shoulder, whispering introductions for her ears only.

'The Count of Theignault is on the duchess's left.'

Theignault. South and east. A devout Ischyrian. The count wore a high-nosed sneer and a dark, pointed beard that sharpened his face.

'Beyond him is Sjóland.'

The grey-haired Count of Sjóland was bright-eyed and round-shouldered. He wore his years like a too-heavy stole.

So what would they all expect her to do? Sing rune song? Unthinkable. Adelais swallowed again, forcing moisture into her mouth.

A fluttering made her look up. A bird about the size of a thrush darted between the rafters. It must have flown in through the open window and was now trapped. It flew over the heads, wings whirring, low enough for guests to turn their heads and watch it. Adelais thought again of the seagull, and ran her fingers absent-mindedly through her hair. A strand fell free, spoiling Ulfhild's fragile attempts at a crown, the nearest she could manage to maiden's braids. The bird bashed against the window behind the high table and fell away, fluttering, panicking, before coming to rest on a roof beam. There it lifted its tail and squitted over the Count of Theignault's shoulder. Laughter spread through the hall, and her carefully planned entrance descended into chaos. Adelais put her head back and laughed with them, delighted at the easing of tension. She turned to share the moment with de Warelt, and was met with a scowl. Beyond his shoulder, the curtains of the minstrel's gallery moved slightly. She hoped that Ulfhild had found a place to watch.

But de Warelt was waving her forwards. Around them, thralls were opening more windows and chasing the bird towards them with brooms.

Adelais let her giggles subside into a sigh, and stepped out once more towards the high table. The unsmiling nobles looked like a bench of magistrates sitting in judgement. Theignault was glowering at her as if the bird *skit* on his shoulder was her fault.

And she still felt as if she had a knife to her spine.

2.5 GAUTHIER

At first, she was just a plaited crown of pale gold hair beneath his feet.

Gauthier breathed deeply, lifting his crossbow, taking care not to disturb the curtains. The angle was still too steep; he'd have to lean out, betraying his presence. Besides, a moving head was too uncertain a target; the body would be a surer kill.

He let his fingers rest on the release lever, sighting down the arrow into her neck. A long neck, he saw, richly wrapped in yellow silk. Two more paces.

Armour! No one had warned him about armour, even though this was surely only moulded leather. A windlass crossbow would punch through that, but it might deflect a glancing blow or weaken its impact. A hit on a shoulder blade might not be mortal. Gauthier paused, thinking furiously. He could hit, of that he was sure, but would the shot kill? He would let her take two, perhaps three more paces to be sure of a square strike.

A squire walked behind her. It had to be now, before his line of fire was blocked. Gauthier's finger tightened on the lever, and the girl took a step *backwards* into the squire's path, looking

upwards, laughing at some bird in the rafters. She turned, and
for a moment he felt a rare pang of regret as he glimpsed just a
laughing girl. The sort of girl he would once have enjoyed
unburdening. *What a waste.*

She was waved forwards and he took aim again, watching
for a clear line through the swaying backs. Her laughter had
been infectious; her procession now held little more pomp than
that of a mummer's, come to perform for the great ones.

Yet there was movement in the corridor outside his gallery;
someone was testing the latch. It triggered a dry-mouthed pulse
of panic around his lips. The door opened a finger's width and
jammed against his wedge. Wood rattled with the gentle thump
of a hip against the door; it was enough for the wedge to slide
back another handspan. It found a lower floorboard and moved
more, almost enough for a body to squeeze through the opening.
By then Gauthier had snatched the bolt from the groove and
returned the crossbow to its hiding place beneath the sacking.
He stood in the shadows in front of it, heart pounding, hoping
the door's creak had masked the sound of the crossbow sliding
against the boards. He held his arms behind his back, feeding
the bolt into the sleeve of his robe. A woman's head appeared
around the door; loose strings of a servant's plain linen cap
trailed over lank, blonde hair.

''S'all right,' the woman hissed over her shoulder. 'No one
'ere.'

She was no more than an underfed girl, he saw; tall and
thin, all elbows and knees. She stepped into the gallery, and put
her eye to the gap in the curtains. Another serving woman
followed at her heels, this one fatter with the smell of food upon
her. The gawky one was peering through the gap. 'Ooh, isn't she
lovely! She's messed her hair, though. Took me *fjakkinn* ages to
do that.'

'Gizza peek then, Ulfie!' The fat one nudged for a place.

Gauthier cleared his throat, and the women squealed.

'Beggin' your pardon, Pateras,' the one called Ulfie said, gulping as her hands flew to her face. 'We didn't know you was here!'

'Hello, girls.' Gauthier offered them the most affable smile he could manage. 'I'm just watching the feast.' He felt like a boy caught stealing food and inventing excuses.

'Only, we wanted to see Mistress Adelais.' The lure of the view was overcoming their fear of a priest, if they ever had any. The curtains had been pulled further apart, framing their heads, and they were ignoring him.

'Can she really throw thunderbolts, Ulfie?'

Gauthier clenched his fists, enough for the pressure to push the bolt up his sleeve until the tip pierced his bicep. He almost welcomed the pain. *Twice!*

'*Fjakkinn* right she can! And kill her enemies with a look.'

'She's a lucky, God-cursed *bitch*!' He spat out the words as his frustration took over. His vehemence surprised even him. The women pulled their heads back from the curtain and stared at him. It took him several breaths to master his anger and unclench his empty hand. The girls' fingers remained gripped in the curtains. After one more breath he could even lift his hand in benediction as he turned for the door. He could trust others to recover the crossbow. His chance would come again. His professional pride now demanded that he succeed.

2.6 ADELAIS

Adelais tried not to think of the power staring at her as she approached the high table. Vriesland. Sjóland. Theignault. The northern jarls. And underneath her leather tits and swagger was a weaver's daughter who didn't want to be there. From his seat on the dais, Ragener's eyes were on a level with hers and she stared back, refusing to be cowed, giving them the warrior they wanted. The armour helped.

She stopped two paces from the table and made the most feminine curtsey she could manage with a sword at her side.

'Your Graces.' A strand of hair came loose and flopped across one eye as she straightened, spoiling her poise. She finger-combed it behind her ear. The younger version of Jarl Magnus grinned at her, revealing a gap between his two front teeth that was half as wide as a missing tooth. His beard was red and silky, while his father's was bristly grey and full enough for him to be wiping food from it with a napkin. They were both big as bears. The duchess looked as if she'd just sucked a sour fruit. Beside her, the Count of Theignault lifted his nose, his oiled beard directed at her like a spear point. Sjóland looked half asleep. Only Ragener smiled benignly, like a justice inclined to mercy, and held up his hand for silence. Once again the spear butts rammed into the boards.

'Adelais Leifsdottir, also known as Adelais de Vries!' Ragener addressed her in a booming voice for all to hear. 'You have achieved as much alone as my whole army did at Pauwels.'

Behind Adelais someone thumped a table in approval. The sound became a drum roll as others joined in. Again Ragener held up his hand.

'And single-handedly you slew King Aloys of Galmandie, delivering justice for his lies and corruption.'

The table thumping was more muted now; Ragener had accepted Aloys as his liege lord after Vannemeer. This was open rebellion.

'Through you, Ischyros has shown his distaste for greed.'

Adelais's mind raced. By linking her to that god, Ragener was pronouncing an interpretation of events, even the death of the high priest, that might be acceptable to Ischyrians. He was trying to reconcile her with both factions. The hall fell silent. The tension was palpable, until a slow smile spread across Ragener's face and he lifted his arms as if appealing to his court.

'You are clearly a woman to have on our side in any future conflict.' He spoke lightly now, jesting. Polite laughter rippled around the hall. She looked him in the eye, glaring, because she knew this was all for show.

'So we are minded both to reward you and to bind you to us in the granting of lands from our own demesne.' At his signal a servant in the ducal livery rushed forwards with a small stool that he placed in front of Adelais. Another unbuckled Adelais's belt and took her sword. As Ragener walked out from behind the high table to stand in front of her, de Warelt held her elbow and whispered in her ear. 'Kneel.'

She obeyed, tilting her head to watch the duke. A second chin now framed his face as he looked down.

'Adelais Leifsdottir, do you accept us as your liege?' Ragener's voice had hardened.

'Aye, Your Grace.' Who else could be her ruler? And why did her answer seem to have such meaning?

'Then in return for your fealty we grant you the manor of Aldingardhur, together with its rents and produce...'

Adelais rocked back on her knees. Was she being made a noble? And where in this world was Aldingardhur? But de Warelt was whispering again.

'Put your hands out. No, like this.' He pushed her palms together and lifted them until Ragener could hold them within his own. His skin was surprisingly soft against her knuckles, but the pressure was strong.

'Repeat after me,' de Warelt murmured in her ear, 'but loudly.'

'I, Adelais Leifsdottir, also known as Adelais de Vries...'

'Swear fealty to you, Ragener, Duke of Vriesland.' The words sounded weighty. How, then, could they soar to the rafters?

'I will pay homage to you and your lawful successors...' They should have explained this before the feast. Told her the implications. One thing was sure, if she refused to swear, in front of all these people, she was dead.

'And will be your true and faithful liege woman...' But why would she not swear? She was a loyal Vriesian.

'And will render obedient service to your will...' Beyond Ragener's right shoulder, Jarl Magnus watched intently. As she knelt she was low enough to see the jarl's woollen trews and fine, soft boots beneath the tablecloth.

'For as long as my life shall last.' And beyond Ragener's other side, the jarl's son's eyes showed pity. *Pity?*

'All this do I swear, upon my life and honour.'

'Rise, Adelais.' Ragener released her hands, lifted her to her feet, and kissed her on both cheeks. His lips did not linger, thank the gods. The table-pounding began again, heavily now, and the duke was smiling at her, though it was without warmth. *What have I just done?*

Ragener beckoned another servant who brought forward a cushion bearing a folded yellow cloth. The duke lifted the cloth in front of her, sending its folds tumbling to the floor to reveal a knee-length surcoat. It had been woven from the finest linen, shot through with silk and perhaps even golden thread so that it reflected the candles in rippling sheens of light. Stitched onto this wondrous cloth was the black silhouette of a she-wolf with an open, snarling mouth, in the rampant shape it might make in leaping at its prey. The beast's eyes and tongue had been embroidered in red, making it more menacing than any heraldic device Adelais had ever seen. Ragener lifted it over her head, still talking in a voice that filled the hall and silenced the gasps of wonder.

'Furthermore, you are hereby granted arms. The device of the she-wolf shall be yours and your successors' in perpetuity. Bear it with honour.'

The servants lifted her arms and began lacing the front and back of the surcoat together around her armour. Adelais realised that the cloth had been cut to fit tightly to her armour so that it displayed rather than concealed her artificial curves.

The hall approved. The chaos of sound rose to a rafter-shaking height and settled into a rhythmic pounding. In between the blows came cries in Vriesian of '*hún úlfur*', she-wolf, and '*örlaga vefari*', fate-weaver. Adelais knelt to show her thanks, bowing her head in case Ragener saw the doubt in her mind, and the niggling suspicion that the ones making those calls had been told to do so. Her mind was in turmoil. She was honoured; the weaver's daughter with lands. And she was trapped; labelled as the fate-weaver whether she fitted the prophecy or not. She let Ragener lift her to her feet and found herself looking at Jarl Magnus. He and his son were tight-lipped as Ragener turned, flourishing a hand in front of her as if she were a prized mare and he the horse merchant.

'Jarl Magnus, may I present Adelais of Aldingardhur?'

That sounded well in her ears. Adelais de Vries, also known as the Vriesian Witch, was now Adelais of Aldingardhur. Did that mean she was now a noblewoman? She hoped the manor was as pleasant as its name; *aldingardhur* meant 'orchard' in the Old Tongue. She made another curtsey, and lifted her hand to push her hair back into place. Again. The jarl's son grinned at her as if they shared a joke, but Magnus stared at her with eyes that were the grey of moons-old ice, calculating but not unkindly. A seat was found beside him and he waved her to it. *Why did everything seem so planned?* Two seats; the son came to sit on her other side, and for a moment between their over-sized bodies she felt like a child between adults; her eyes were at the level of their shoulders, even though she sat very upright to avoid her armour digging into her chest. Their upper arms within their tunics seemed thicker than her thighs. A thrall offered her mead and she drank silently, unsure what to say.

'Congratulations.' The jarl's son toasted her, his silver goblet almost lost within his fist. 'My name is Hjálmar.' He spoke Vriesian with the lilt of the north, like her grandmother had done, and he sounded friendly.

'Adelais,' she added, unnecessarily, and drank again to cover her lack of words.

'That was a surprise, no?'

She nodded.

'So did you really kill the high priest of Ischyros, girl?' Magnus twisted in his seat to watch her face. He also spoke in Vriesian. It may have been intended as a private question, but beyond him Duke Ragener, lowering himself into his seat, glared at her.

'No, *mynn drottinn*.' My lord. She would not lie, even if she had just been clad in cloth of gold. That earned a sharp intake of breath from Ragener, and tension radiated out into the room the way a stone sends ripples across a pond. Everyone seemed to be listening; even the dogs stopped fighting. 'I was trying to frighten him. I sang the rune song of Thor and thunder came. The lightning did not strike him, but he died just the same. Whether that was by Thor's hand or Ischyros's, or his own fear, I do not know.' She shrugged. 'I did not intend him to die.' She kept her eyes on Magnus's, ignoring the murmuring that swelled around them.

Magnus held her gaze until he began to chuckle, and the chuckle grew until he threw back his head and released a great bark of laughter. He slapped the table with his palm as he straightened, his beard tufting like a boar's bristles as he grinned at her.

'And the King of Galmandie, did his death also just "happen"?'

'No. I meant to kill him. I rode him down with my destrier.'

'The king was unguarded?' Magnus sounded as if he did not quite believe her.

'There was a priest, a diakonos, but they had become separated from the rest of the hunt.' Adelais eyed the meat piled on platters before them. Her belly was growling with hunger and she was already feeling the first effects of the strong mead.

Hjálmar grabbed a bread trencher, heaped steaming pork onto it with his knife, and handed it to her. That was thoughtful. She smiled her thanks. 'So why did you kill him?' he asked.

'I got angry. He had caused the death of good friends. And my man, whom I loved.' She took a delicate bite and spoke as she chewed. *Fjakk* courtly manners; she was hungry. 'Others who I held dear were not safe while he lived.'

Magnus let out another of his barking laughs. 'Half the world was angry with Aloys. Yet you're the one that killed him.'

'I did not plan to. Not at first. He drew his sword to kill me.' Adelais shrugged, lowering her meat as the moment came back. 'I did not think much after that.' The memory of that cold, killing fury still frightened her. How could she be like that? She hadn't just killed the king, she'd *executed* him. Even if he deserved it more than any man on this world, she winced at the thought of how easily, how unthinkingly she had slaughtered him. She hadn't even sung rune song, she'd just been angry. Adelais shifted on her seat and reached for her mead as if the memory was a bloody taste she could wash away with strong liquor.

'Are you comfortable?' Hjálmar was more softly spoken than his father.

'This armour is designed for fighting, on foot or in the saddle, not for feasting.' That was no lie; the lower rim of her breastplate was digging into her thighs, pushing a hard line upwards under her breasts.

'Why not take it off?' Hjálmar gestured towards her chest, a graceful motion with a mighty hand. 'I am sure Duke Ragener would understand, now the fealty ceremony is done.'

'I fear Their Graces would be upset.' She glanced at the jarl's son. He had the same grey eyes, surprisingly gentle for a towering man-mountain. 'Besides,' she added, 'the gown beneath is so light as to be almost transparent.' *Am I flirting with him?*

Hjálmar had the same laugh as his father. She sensed he laughed easily. They both had broad, slightly upturned noses that made them look like boars when their heads went back. Further down the table Ragener visibly relaxed and began talking to the duchess and the nobles ranged beyond her.

'So are you the *örlaga vefari*, the one prophesied to unite us all?' Magnus's question came surprisingly quietly. Ragener had not heard it.

Adelais closed her eyes and breathed deeply. *Sætur Sif, sweet Sif, grant me the words.* She answered in the same, quiet tone.

'My grandmother, Yrsa Haraldsdottir, was a *seidhkona* from the Wolf People of the north. She believed I might be the one foretold. But I swear to you, *mynn drottinn*, I do not want to be. I have seen enough killing in the last year and have no wish to lead more men to their deaths.'

Magnus snorted. 'What you want, girl, may be irrelevant.'

'What *do* you want?' Hjálmar asked, interrupting his father.

'I believe there is power in rune song. Things happen when I sing. I would like to learn to channel that power for good. I want to heal, not hurt.'

'That too may be possible.' Magnus spoke in a low rumble, like a purring cat. A very dangerous cat. 'The question is, what you are fated to be.'

'And how, *mynn drottinn*, are you to know that? I might just be Duke Ragener's creation to entice you to war.'

'We will not answer that question tonight. Tonight is for feasting. Come to me in the morning, after those *fjakkinn* bells have rung a second time, and meet my own *seidhkona*. She will cast the runes and help me decide.'

'And what if I am simply a weaver's daughter who's destined to find a husband and raise babies in this Aldingardhur?'

'The runes will not say that.'

'You sound very sure, *mynn drottinn*.'

'I am. Because if you are not what Ragener needs, he will strip you of those lands as fast as he gave them, and throw you to the Ischyrians. He might let you keep that fine surcoat, though only so they can be sure which woman to aim at.'

Adelais stared at her cooling meat, feeling her hunger fade. Hjálmar nudged her with his arm, quite gently, so it was only a little like being barged by a horse. 'Don't let my father spoil your big moment, mistress. Hey, if Ragener throws you out, you could always come north. You'd make a fine shieldmaiden!'

She was warming to this Hjálmar, even if he did look like a troll.

CHAPTER THREE

3.1 TAILLEFER

Taillefer had not slept. He spent much of the night in prayer, on his knees in the temple, but his mind raced the way a mountain stream flows over rocks; tumbling, churning, too full for any peace. *The Hand.* A carved effigy of the hand of Salazar was lifted in benediction above every temple in Ischyrendom. A gilded version had been raised above the armies of the faithful in every battle with the infidel, more potent than any royal banner. And now Agnès de Fontenay said the Hand itself existed.

His instinct told him to believe her. And not simply because she was offering him a role as its custodian.

He was not worthy of that. Merely to imagine himself in the role was such arrogance, such hubris, that he felt the need to unburden his thoughts.

And as soon as the Hand's existence was known, or even believed, the great powers of Ischyrendom would manoeuvre to possess it. Some might even go to war for it.

Daybreak came slowly, even in the lightening days of the fasting moon. It would be a still day, with the calm that comes after the last blusterings of a storm are spent, but his mind tumbled like a leaf on the wind. He knew now how Adelais had survived and escaped; she had touched the Hand of the prophet. She truly was blessed by the God.

But that did not make her a Blessèd One, the God's instrument on earth.

And Adelais's role in this was insignificant in comparison to the great, emerging truth, that the Hand of Salazar existed and was being offered, unbelievably, into his care. In his sleep-deprived delirium, his soul was climbing the dome of his own spiritual temple, where all around him lay impenetrable depths, while before him, on the shining pinnacle, was the true Hand. But in his striving for this wondrous relic he might fall all the way to the pit if he reached for it with anything but humble purity.

The windows were paling when a subordinate priest stumbled sleepily into the temple to conduct the dawn office, and stopped in surprise at the sight of his diakonos already kneeling before the sanctuary. Taillefer knew that his lack of sleep was all too evident; he stood, ceding the place before the sacred flame, and rubbed his hands over his face as if he could wipe away the exhaustion. Stubble rasped against his fingers. Beside him, Pateras Malory's red-rimmed eyes shone with a new light; Malory saw only the prospect of a divine relic, not the burden of carrying it.

After the office they left the temple swaying like drunkards as cold, fresh air filled their lungs. Taillefer would not reveal his doubts to Pateras Malory; he was Malory's superior, his diakonos. He could only talk about practicalities as they walked back towards his palace.

'If this Hand is revealed—*if*—there must be a clerical court to judge its authenticity.' Taillefer paused on the bridge, wrapping his cloak more tightly about him. He did not wish to return to the everyday demands of his role.

'You will recall that my uncle is the Episkopos of Villebénie,

Excellency.' Malory stopped beside him. 'I believe he would understand the need for discretion until the Hand is attested.'

Of course. Villebénie was only a day's ride away, and until a new high priest was appointed there was no more senior cleric in Galmandie. No doubt the Episkopos of Villebénie would think he could host the Hand in his fire temple alongside the skull of Tanguy, and see the revenues from pilgrims soar beyond his most avaricious dreams.

'Only an inner circle of Guardians were permitted to see the Hand.' Taillefer did not let his cynicism of the episkopos's motives show in his voice. 'We must find some former members of this third degree to give evidence of its existence.'

'Most of them died in the persecution, Excellency, but there was a priest at the Guardian's temple who survived. He helped Humbert Blanc escape when I was leading the search.' Malory ducked his head in the way of one who remembers a past sin. 'At the time I thought we were seeking an idol that would be proof of the Guardians' heresy.'

'Good. But let us be sure ourselves before we constitute the court.' Taillefer walked on to the summit of the bridge over the Fauve and steadied himself with a gloved hand against the parapet; there had been a frost overnight and the footing was treacherous on the downwards slope. A cart carrying early vegetables for the market was stuck at its base; the farmer tugged at his donkey's bridle while the beast splayed its hooves against the ice. Its raucous braying reminded Taillefer of the everyday world beyond their planning. Downriver to the west, thin sunlight touched the treetops and he was suddenly hungry.

'Perhaps Lady Agnès would like to break her fast with us?'

Agnès had sprung into his mind, as fresh as the new day. The 'us' was an afterthought, for propriety's sake.

.   .   .

Apart from the sacrament of unburdening, he had not been alone with a woman since he entered the priesthood. Protocol was observed with Agnès, of course. They ate in his office, with the door open; they could be seen from the doorway but not overheard. Pateras Malory chose to sit outside at Taillefer's secretary's desk, still empty before the start of the working day. Taillefer did not protest at this chance to talk privately. He had servants move the table closer to the newly lit fire, for the room was cold. It was also a little more out of sight.

He was awkward, at first, solicitous about her health and her night in the guest quarters; his staff were not used to caring for a fine lady. She had bound her hair in a golden net, a little messily as if she was used to being dressed by a servant. This small detail somehow compounded the enormity of her news; to deliver it, this great noblewoman had risked travelling without staff, before winter had fully released its grip.

'You brought no attendant?' he asked, and immediately feared his question would be interpreted as a comment on her appearance. Exhaustion had dulled his manners.

Lady Agnès shrugged. 'Last year I was chased halfway across Galmandie by the king's men and the anakritim. I can look after myself. Besides, servants gossip.' She leaned back in her chair and smiled at him under slightly hooded eyes. She wore one of the newly fashionable gowns that were tight-laced across the stomach and open at the neck, emphasising her figure. 'We wouldn't want gossip, would we?'

Taillefer looked down, forcing his eyes away from the plunging neckline of her shirt and gown, that together so exquisitely edged the curves beneath. He broke bread and offered her half, lifting his eyes directly to hers. They were green, wide and mischievous. *This is folly. I am a priest, for the God's sake.*

'Especially when we can offer no plausible explanation.' Taillefer dreaded some cleric pushing his way past Malory.

'Quite.' Again that teasing smile. 'I suggest this is the last time we meet here, so openly.'

She was right, but he was disappointed. 'What alternative is there, my lady?' That sounded stiff. She had dropped the 'Excellency' honorific after their first greeting.

'I have lands at Molinot, on the banks of the Gaelle, north of Villebénie. I came that way from Lord Leandre and Duke Gervais in Delmas; there is a ferry there across the river. From there it was just a day's ride to Harbin, even on winter roads. If we were to meet again, I could ask the manor's staff to lodge in the village. They have served my family for generations and would be discreet.' Her slow-spreading smile was infectious. 'They'd probably think I'd taken a lover.'

Taillefer straightened, crumbling his bread. 'I have given much thought to your news.' He spoke formally, as a diakonos, dipping a piece of bread into the dish of butter to give himself time to compose his words. 'Let us assume that the relic is accepted as the Hand of Salazar. Both the faith and a future king would exploit it for gain, so I propose it is safer to stay initially within de Fontenay custody. De Fontenay is the only noble I would trust to fulfil his own conditions. I agree that a new order of knighthood should be founded to protect it.'

'Like the Guardians.' There was an edge to Agnès's words.

'If any survive, they would be ideal candidates.' Taillefer would not be drawn. 'But the greatest risk would come after the Hand has been announced or attested and before such an order was in place.'

'Agreed.' Agnès frowned a little, staring at him, all flirtation gone.

'And the attestation must be by a properly constituted cler-ical court under an episkopos. I think it would be easiest, and safest, to bring the Hand here to Harbin, but secretly.' Taillefer knew that to take an episkopos and his entourage to Château Fontenay, plus witnesses, he'd have to explain too much, too early. Prince Lancelin might have laid siege to Fontenay before the episkopos arrived.

'Then I think we are going on a journey.'

'We?' Taillefer lifted his head. A long curl of dark hair had escaped from Agnès's golden net and flopped onto her shoulder. She ignored it.

'I must go, not Leandre, because he is in Delmas and will be seized by Lancelin if he travels through Compeigne. Those who guard the Hand at Fontenay will require my personal authority to release it. I suggest you should also go—talk to the priests who guard it and satisfy yourself that you truly believe it to be the relic of Salazar, not some bones that a woman has just dug out of a grave. But if you come, perhaps the scarlet robes of a diakonos might attract too much attention?'

Taillefer closed his eyes, overcome by the sensation that he was falling. It would take a moon to reach Fontenay and return. A moon in this woman's company, and stripped of the visible signs of priesthood. When he looked up she was still staring at him, a half-smile on her lips.

'Lord Leandre places great trust in you, Lady Agnès.' A return to formality.

'Of necessity, since he cannot travel outside Duke Gervais's domains.'

'And...' He fumbled for words.

'As a woman, you mean?' That smile was provocative. He had heard that some women desired priests; they hungered for the unattainable.

'In all things. The Hand could alter the fate of nations. But yes, also as a woman. He sends you on this mission with an escort of just two men-at-arms, and in winter.'

'The travel does not worry me, and I have further yet to go.' Agnès looked away towards the fire, as if considering how much to say. 'And as for my womanhood, Leandre does not think as other men. Our union is more of an alliance than a marriage.

We respect each other's strengths. The respect borders on friendship.'

'But you are beautiful,' he protested, speaking truth before he thought to temper his words.

This time her smile was wry and tinged with hurt.

'He is comfortable in the company of his knights, and in the warlike arts. He values my ability to manage his estates. He can be amiable company.'

She finished with enough emphasis to hint that she wanted more. Taillefer glimpsed a yearning sadness that told him she was neglected in other ways. Was she talking to him as a priest or as a man? There were times, during an unburdening, when he'd learned intimate details; a priest usually heard more about why a man or woman had sinned than about the sin itself. But here? Now? Taillefer rose to his feet and paced the room, breaking the moment.

'I have two challenges for Lord Leandre, my lady.' Again the stiff episkopos. 'Would he accept my suggestion of a new Order of knighthood?'

'I think you will find he is already thinking along those lines. *Excellency*.'

'Then how does he propose to protect the Hand before that Order can be constituted? And how can we ensure it is not exploited for political gain? Let us agree that before we go further.'

Agnès also stood. 'I shall pass on your questions. Let us meet at Molinot. Shall we say the tenth day of the lamb moon?'

Half a moon away. It seemed like a long time, on so pressing a matter, for a woman who merely had to make the return journey to Delmas, and back to Molinot.

Agnès de Fontenay left promptly after they had eaten, while the rest of Harbin was still easing its way into a working day.

Later he was told that she and her escort had taken the north-
ward road, to Baudry, rather than the westward road to Molinot.
His niggling curiosity at that was soon pushed aside by the
certainty that the Hand would change the world. Perhaps he
had been blessed to live in the age when all people would know
the God's love, and when Kakos would be defeated in the final
battle. He prayed that he would be equal to the task that
Ischyros had set him.

3.2 ADELAIS

'So you are the granddaughter of Yrsa Haraldsdottir.'

It was a statement, not a question. The *seidhkona* stared at Adelais from behind a table in the rooms Ragener had allocated to Jarl Magnus's group. The woman's long, bony fingers were wrapped around an earthenware beaker and her elbows rested on the table in front of her. Sharp, intelligent eyes examined Adelais through steam that smelt of hot milk and honey. Jarl Magnus and Hjálmar sat a little apart, watching from stools either side of the kind of fire that only an honoured guest would be allowed. It was actually warm in this turret room, with woven hangings masking cold stone, and narrow, horn-glazed windows to keep out the wind.

'Yes. I am Adelais.' She wore a plain kirtle rather than the duchess's gown or the duke's brazen armour; she wanted them to see her as she was. She felt very alone at the centre of their scrutiny, despite Hjálmar's gap-toothed grin.

'I am Revna Friggisdottir.' Revna nodded at the bench opposite her. 'Sit, child.' She had a voice like crusted bread. A chain of bird skulls around her neck moved as she lowered her beaker, making a faint rattling like a dropped handful of pebbles. Each skull was about the size of a raven's and they had been bound, beak to nape, with silver wire. Adelais found their empty sockets more intimidating than Revna's bright-eyed stare. She forced herself to look at the face above the skulls; lean, lined like old leather, and of an age when some women begin to look like beardless men. Revna also wore a simple, belted kirtle; her cat-skin cloak was draped over a bench and her staff rested against the wall as if she had no need of the outward trappings of power.

Except those skulls.

'Yrsa Haraldsdottir went south when I was still a child. It was said she could have been a great *seidhkona*, but chose a man instead.'

'She was a healer, and well loved.'

Revna snorted. '*Seidhkonur* should be respected, not loved.'

'She was both.'

'So what did she say of you, child?'

'That I had the power to weave destinies with runes, and it would be both a blessing and a burden. This I believe. I have sung rune song, and things happened. Perhaps they would have happened anyway, but people died. That weighs heavily upon me.'

'And what state were you in when you sang rune song and "things happened"?'

'State?'

'Calm? Happy?'

Adelais closed her eyes to think. 'I was angry. Each time, I was angry. It was like I forgot myself and became someone else.'

She looked up to see a meaningful look passing between Magnus and Hjálmar. Perhaps they were hoping she would say more. *Fjakk* them.

'Yrsa Haraldsdottir taught you?' Revna drew her attention back.

'Of runes, very little. When I was a child, she said it would be like giving an infant a sharp knife. When I was older, after the defeat at Vannemeer, it was forbidden. A wise woman in Galmandie taught me a little. She said I had power but no learning. When we were escaping she taught me the runes to carve for concealment in a bind-rune; *ísa, naudhiz, reido*, and *bjarkan*. She was angry when she learned I had added *thurs*.'

Revna snorted, setting the bird skulls rattling. 'And did your enemies find love?'

'Not that I have heard.'

'Where is Yrsa Haraldsdottir now?'

'She is *fylgja*.' Adelais held Revna's stare, watching for the impact of her words; *fylgjur* were guiding spirits in animal form. Revna straightened, her fingers splaying on the table top.

'How do you know this?'

'In my village they say she willed herself to die, on the night before the anakritim came for her. She sang rune song until she could sing no more. Last year, a wolf came to me as I wandered, far to the south. A wolf with my grandmother's eyes. It led me to food and water.'

Revna breathed deeply, her eyes narrowing.

'Moons later a she-wolf tried to warn me of danger,' Adelais continued. 'A good friend died when I did not follow her.'

'It is rumoured,' Hjálmar added from beside the fire, 'that before King Aloys died, his horse had bolted at the sight of a wolf.'

'I was led to him by a wolf. He was alone except for a priest when we met, and certainly their horses were badly blown.'

Revna watched Adelais for the space of several breaths. Her look was calculating but not without kindness.

'What did your grandmother say about the *örlaga vefari*, the fate-weaver?'

'The prophecy is that a woman born of wolf-kind and of mud would unite the peoples of the north and push back the bounds of Ischyros. And I tell you now that I do not want to be that woman, even though Duke Ragener tells the world that it is me.'

'When Ischyros fights Odhinn, Thor, and Freyja, child, your desires are of no consequence.' Revna sounded irritated. 'Whose side will you be on?'

Adelais touched Ulfhild's rune-carved pendant hanging round her neck. 'I stand with Thor. He sent the thunder when I faced the high priest.' And her Amma Yrsa used to call her '*mynn litla Sif*' after the golden-haired wife of Thor.

'Why would you not wish to be the *örlaga vefari*?' Hjálmar leaned forwards. Of them all, he seemed most keen to understand her. 'You would be favoured of the gods.'

'Things happen around me. People get hurt, even those I love. Now I fear friendship, for what my friendship may cost.' For a moment Adelais wondered what had made her reveal so much. 'I don't want to be the cause of any more deaths.'

'What *do* you want, child?' Magnus watched her levelly. Now that she had declared herself, she no longer felt threatened by that stare.

'To walk openly, as a free woman, without wondering if there will be another assassin in the shadows. To find love without fear that I will cause my lover's death. Perhaps to learn to be a healer and *seidhkona*, and use what power I have for good.'

Revna leaned forwards and Adelais caught her scent: washed wool and candles, woodsmoke and sweat. She might have seemed homely but for the faint rattle of bird skulls. 'The runes may foretell a different fate.'

Jarl Magnus shifted impatiently on his stool. 'They say you ripped a crossbow bolt from your own belly and lived, with no sign of a wound. Is this true?' His stare was intense.

Adelais saw no point in lying. 'I was disguised as a youth. I'd tied a stone low, down there,' she gestured where, embarrassed, 'to give me a man's shape. The bolt hit the stone.'

Hjálmar snorted, and leaned forwards. 'But there was blood?'

'The stone was driven deep into my body.' She glared at him as her emotions welled to the surface. She turned them to anger before they became tears. 'I was with child.' That was almost a snarl, and she watched him flinch. *Good.* 'I lost the child and nearly died from the bleeding, but a wise woman sang the songs of healing over me.' She closed her eyes, mastering herself. Arnaud l'Armurier had died in that skirmish, hacked to death for trying to save her. He had never known he was to be a father.

'It seems you were not fated to die that day.' Magnus glanced at his son. 'I think we can keep the stone a secret. A little mystery might be useful.'

Hjálmar nodded, his head still bowed. Had she already passed their test?

'I also carried a *taufr* that my grandmother had carved.' Adelais touched her belt bag where the protective, bind-rune talisman had been hidden. She still missed that little hardness within the leather. 'The fate Yrsa carved was to bring me home.' And she'd burned it in Yrsa's hearth when that fate was fulfilled.

'And so to runes.' Revna lifted a small linen bag onto the table from the bench beside her. Its contents rattled like her necklace as she set it down. 'I think it is time for them to tell us what fate has been woven for you.' She began taking pieces of flat, polished bone from the bag and setting them face down on the table until twenty-four identical, blank ovals lay there, each twice the size of a thumbnail. Both Magnus and Hjálmar left the fire and came to stand behind her. Adelais would rather they had not been looking over her shoulder; her life was about to be laid bare.

'There are different methods,' Revna explained. 'I use the nine-rune boat.'

'That was Yrsa's method too.'

'Then, for the benefit of the men, know that each rune is only an indication of a greater mystery beyond.' She took one piece at random and turned it over.

'*Sowilo*. It represents the sun, but this rune-stave sheds no heat. It merely tells us of a life-giving mystery, and speaks of empowerment. Runes are but a window into the web of fate that surrounds us.' Revna chose another.

'*Bjarkan*, the birch-rune. It whispers to us of the music of the wind through the branches of the sacred grove, for runes are a song as well as a mystery. All runes are connected, like all life; *bjarkan* needs the warmth of *sowilo* and the water of *lægr* before it can be the rune of becoming.' She turned the runes over again and mixed them until they were lost within the rest. 'Now, girl, take one, and put it in the centre. This is your essence; you as you are now.'

Adelais closed her eyes and let her fingertips find a rune. She let it click onto the table before she opened them again.

Úruz, for the mighty auroch cattle. She knew it to be a strong, masculine rune that spoke of health and a free, warrior spirit. But this was upside-down, so the meaning would change. A lot. Weakness. Fatigue. Confinement. She looked up at

Revna for an explanation, but the *seidhkona* merely tapped the table to the right of the rune.

'Now three more, here in the realm of Urdhr, who weaves that which has become. Show us how you came to be trapped and sick.'

'I am not sick,' Adelais protested.

'In your body, no. But in your spirit? Now choose.'

Adelais took three more and laid them in an arc to the right of *úruz*.

ᚠᛗᛁ

Ansuz. Ehwaz. Ísa. Adelais paused. Revna was nodding to herself. She seemed pleased.

'*Ansuz* is the god-rune, the rune of Odhinn. It gives strength to the galdrar-magic that is in rune song. This tells me much. Most *seidhkonur* are able only to *see* the fates in the runes. You, I think, can *sing* the fates and so change them. The threads of fate run strongly through you.'

'As others have said. Does that mean I am the *örlaga vefari*, the fate-weaver?'

'Not necessarily. It merely says you have power. Perhaps much power, even though now it is untrained. Rune lore is like playing a lute or a harp. When first you learn, it is just noise. After much practice you can make music that the gods themselves delight to hear. In time, you *become* the music. This one,' Revna pointed at the next rune, 'is the horse-rune, *ehwaz*. As a rider forms an unbreakable bond with a horse, this speaks of trust and friendships.'

'There were friendships on my journey.' Adelais thought of Agnès and Humbert, Elyse and Arnaud. 'There is also a bond with my destrier that goes beyond all training. Before battle I sang rune song, and it was as if we danced together. We felt invincible.'

'*Ehwaz* is also the rune of *fylgjur*. *Ansuz* tells of your own power, but *ehwaz* tells of others. Friends, horse, *fylgja*.'

'And *ísa*?'

'*Ísa* is the ice-rune. You are locked in this place as the land is locked in winter. But be patient—the ice is melting.' Revna reached across to tap the table just in front of Adelais, beneath the arc of runes. 'Now Verdhandi, who weaves that which is becoming. Three more.'

Ingwaz. That could mean a sudden release of power, or energy, or new beginnings, but the crucial thing was the combination with other runes. Adelais simply didn't know enough to interpret them. *Tiwaz*. Sacrificial victory, or oaths fulfilled. *Odhala*. The hearth-rune of ancestral right, or justice, or inheritance. As Adelais laid *odhala* down, building the arc to the left of *úruz*, Revna made a sharp intake of breath, enough for Adelais to pause and look up. She earned another, impatient tap on the table.

'Two more, girl. You are entering the realm of Skuld, who weaves that which may become.'

Perthro, and it was back to front. Adelais suspected that was bad news. *Perthro* was the rune of *harmingja*, of positive chance. Inverted, it spoke of betrayal.

Only one space remained; this would complete the shape

and form the point or bow of the 'boat' of runes that had her, as *úruz*, within it. This was the direction of her fate.

Dagaz, the rune of light. Dawn. Beginnings. Was that better than an inverted *perthro*? Adelais looked up, waiting. The pattern was now complete.

Revna stared at the pattern of runes, her eyes darting between each, making connections. The silence stretched between them, broken only by a log falling within the fire.

'Are you going to tell me?' Adelais asked.

'Well, for one thing, child, you are not fated to be *seidhkona*. At least not for many years. You have too much need to love and be loved.'

'Then I am not your fate-weaver.' In a way, Adelais was relieved. She was also disappointed; if she could not use rune lore for good, as *seidhkona*, what was she to do?

'I did not say that. The *örlaga vefari* need not be *seidhkona*. The time for that is when you are old and dried up. You have much life to live before then, and too much passion to give. If the gods allow.'

'If?' There had been a weight to those last words.

Revna dropped her eyes to the runes again, tilting her head as if to view them from a new angle. 'Assuredly, if.' She sighed.

'So what do you see, *mynn frú?*' Adelais did not like the meaningful look Revna made towards Magnus. Hjálmar swung his leg over Adelais's bench and sat an arm's length away. His weight made her body dip. Magnus sat opposite, beside Revna. She too bounced from his weight.

'War is coming.' Magnus looked at her intently, grimacing. 'It will be a war between gods as well as men.'

'Like Ragnarök?'

He shook his head. 'This is not Ragnarök, not the end of all things. But if Vriesland falls again, the Galmans will wreak a terrible vengeance, and their Ischyros will push the domain of the old gods back towards the Ice Sea.'

'My grandmother called Ischyros "the hungry god".'

Revna smiled thinly. 'It is a good name. He will tolerate no other. He is like an eagle who allows no other bird in the sky, be it falcon, swan, or songbird. Any who do not follow him are called heretics and are burned alive.'

Magnus leaned forwards, resting his arms on the table, and held her gaze. 'So when war comes, mistress, will you fight, or run, or pretend to believe in the hungry god?'

Adelais did not answer the question directly. 'Am I your *örlaga vefari?*'

Magnus looked sideways at Revna. 'Her bloodline is right.' His intonation turned that into a question.

Revna shrugged. 'In truth, I am not sure.'

Adelais realised that it would take confidence, perhaps courage, for Revna to have admitted that.

'The gods have a way of playing with us,' Revna explained.

'They let us think our destiny lies down one path, only so that they can fool us into a different destiny of their own devising.'

'If I am the *örlaga vefari* of the prophecy, then I can weave fates. The fate I choose to weave for myself may be to live quietly in Vriesland...' She stopped, aware of how discourteous that must sound.

Beside her, Hjálmar laughed but Magnus merely snorted. For a moment he looked as if he was going to cuff her round the ears like a precocious brat, but, though his hands fisted, he merely grimaced before he spoke.

'Some fates cannot be set aside. What matters is how you live them.' He made a gesture of dismissal. 'Now I would like to talk with *Frú* Revna quietly. And remember that in killing a king, and a high priest, you also killed your chance of living quietly.'

CHAPTER FOUR

4.1 ADELAIS

'I was told I could find you here.'

Adelais turned at the sound of Hjálmar's voice. She wondered if he'd come to tell her more about Revna's predictions; since the runecast, she'd spent two days wondering *so what now?* and wishing she could take Allier out. There was a smell of spring in the air and the earth was thawing as the worm moon waned. There would be good ground for a gallop.

Adelais ran a brush down Allier's neck. 'This is the most groomed, least ridden horse in the stables.'

'He's a fine animal.' Hjálmar moved away from the door. Two guards waited outside. The set of their shoulders told Adelais they still resented her escape.

'He's a good friend.' Adelais kept her hand on Allier's neck. 'And there's something healing about horses.'

'What ails you, lady?'

Adelais shrugged. 'I have a way of upsetting everyone.' Hjálmar wore a thick fur cloak and towered over her like an amiable bear, but she felt relaxed in his company. She sensed that emotions would show clearly and honestly in his face, not like *gyke* courtiers who hid their sneers behind sugared smiles.

'Anyone in particular?'

'Your father. Probably *Frú* Revna. Certainly Duke Ragener, before the feast.'

'Do not worry about Father. He needed to see you as you are, not how Ragener wishes us to see you. And how did you upset our illustrious duke?'

'I refused to sleep with him.'

A slow smile spread across Hjálmar's face. 'Brave. But not unknown. I am told he tries to bed every pretty woman in his court.'

Adelais ignored the compliment. 'But not every woman threatens to shrivel his balls with rune magic.'

Hjálmar threw his head back and let out a great bark of laughter. His father laughed the same way. When Hjálmar looked at her again his eyes were shining.

'Adelais, I respect you even more.'

She liked that he'd used her name. 'I don't even know if I could. Work that magic, I mean.' She found herself smiling; Hjálmar's laughter was infectious. 'And now I've angered the most important man in Vriesland. My benefactor.'

'Don't worry. He needs you.' Hjálmar paused long enough for his chuckles to subside. 'He is keen that we should know you better. He has offered me and my men horses, that we might escort you on a ride this afternoon. Would that be agreeable?'

'I am allowed out?' Adelais's heart leapt. 'Even after someone tried to kill me?'

'You will have a close escort—my men and his—and we are to take the sally port. I am told the exercise ground leads directly into open country.' Hjálmar described a field outside the castle walls, used for jousts and to exercise the horses; cart-loads of coarse sand had been raked into its surface so that it was useable even in the frozen depths of winter. 'Though you might want to wear your new armour, just in case?'

Adelais's heart leapt. She brought her hands together in the universal sign of pleading. She knew her eyes would be shining.

'And I have a proposal to make,' Hjálmar added. 'Don't worry, it is an honourable one.' The twinkle in his eye suggested it could have been otherwise.

They passed through the sally port without incident, perhaps without Adelais even being recognised outside the walls; cloak-wrapped, with her hood pulled forwards, and the scabbard of her sword hanging beside her, she must have seemed just another man-at-arms. Six men rode with them – four of Jarl Magnus's berserkers and two of Duke Ragener's household guards. The berserkers formed a protective ring around Adelais and Hjálmar, while the guards were sent forwards to clear the road. All held their shields on their arms, ready to fight, not slung on their backs.

Once they were on the open road, their escort spread out, giving them space but still alert. Allier danced beneath her, begging to run, and she touched his neck. 'Steady, my friend,' she gentled him, 'not until we're sure of the ground.' The road had been trampled into mud but the day was cold enough for ice to rim the puddles in the shadows, and she had no wish to lame him.

'You ride well.'

Adelais glanced at Hjálmar, wondering how to return the compliment. The castle's stables had loaned him a lumbering giant. It still looked like a pony beneath him. In fact, none of the northerners seemed comfortable on their borrowed mounts.

'We are used to smaller horses,' Hjálmar answered her unspoken question. She was surprised at his intuition. 'Smaller and hairier. Not so fine as yours, but better at surviving the winters.'

'They can carry the weight? Oh, gods, I'm sorry, I didn't mean...' He wasn't fat. Far from it. Just big.

He frowned at her, mock-offended. 'They manage. But our style of warfare is different to the Galmans. The core of their army is the armoured knight on his destrier, willing to charge into the enemy. In the north, a jarl fights on foot in a shield wall, shoulder to shoulder with his men. His horse need only carry him to war, not bear him in battle.'

'My brother fought at Vannemeer.' Adelais smiled at the memory of Svend, now five years dead. 'He said a charge of Galman knights broke the Vriesian shield wall.'

'Aye. They call it the war-hammer formation. They ride knee to knee so that the horses in the centre cannot turn away even if they do not want to run onto the shield wall's spears. Many of the front rank of the charge will die, but their momentum will smash the wall for the second line. If the enemy has enough brave knights, it is hard to beat.'

'And destriers like this one do not evade.' She remembered her friend and mentor Humbert Blanc charging headlong into the enemy on Allier. Shortly after that, she herself had killed a young soldier, almost by accident; he'd slid down a bank and onto her lance. She flinched at the memory and turned her head away.

'Why are you sad, Adelais?'

She didn't answer at first. She needed to prepare her words, even for this man that she instinctively trusted. She stared at the patchwork of fields. Farmers had begun the first ploughing of the thawing earth, making the mounded field strips look like ribs on a skeleton.

'I do not like killing. I do not like myself for having killed. At first it was horrible.' After that first kill she'd shamed herself by running from the fight to try and wash the blood off her hands in a lake. 'Later I was even proud of my prowess. Now I remember them all. I don't want to do it again.'

They were silent for several squelching strides of their horses. She sensed that he too was assembling words. When he spoke it was quietly, for her ears only, though his eyes were on the rump of the next horse, ten paces ahead.

'Seven summers ago my father thought me old enough to join him when he marched south to help Ragener stop the Galmans. I was in the shield wall at Pauwels, when their heavy cavalry became mired in mud and could not press home their charge.' Hjálmar paused, remembering. 'A gang of berserkers is a fearful thing. They *want* to die in battle, so they might be chosen for the *einharjar* in Valhalla, and the *Valkyrjur* choose only the bravest. In their company I felt invincible. We ran among their staggering horses, hooked the Galmans out of their saddles, and smashed their armoured skulls with axes or clubs. Five hundred knights died that day.' He flexed his hand in front of him, as if he were gripping and releasing an axe. 'Afterwards, I found a quiet place to be sick.' He looked at her directly. 'And I remember, like you.'

Adelais was humbled that he should tell her that, confidence for confidence. 'Yet you would go to war again?'

'Sometimes I do not know whether the Ischyrians want our souls, or whether they use their god to justify taking our land, but I do know they must be stopped.'

'Were you at Vannemeer?'

Hjálmar shook his head. 'Father didn't think the Galmans would come back so soon. When they came north we were away raiding the coast of Saxenheim. Five longships, near two hundred men. We did great scathe and came home laden with silver and thralls. By then Ragener had been defeated and had signed his treaty banning the old gods.'

'Only south of the Schilde,' Adelais corrected. 'And did King Aloys really think a piece of parchment could kill Odhinn or Freyja?'

Hjálmar grinned at her mischievously. 'Perhaps we should

not tell the Ischyrians about the thralls we took on that last raid. They make good thralls, the men of a brotherhouse; they think their god is punishing them for their sins.'

'Don't you think that taking Ischyrians as thralls might provoke them to war?'

Hjálmar shrugged. 'What we do is no different to them. We take silver and slaves, where we can, and call it fate. They take land, and say their god demands it. At least we are honest about it.'

It was good to talk; Hjálmar was the first person since she'd escaped from Galmandie who'd talked to her as an equal rather than a curiosity. Or a witch. Or, like Ulfhild, as some sort of goddess.

'You mentioned you had a proposal,' she asked, when they had been silent with their own thoughts for a while.

'Going to war against the Galmans is a great matter. So is assembling an army in case of war; men must be taken from their farms and boats. My father has called a meeting of the jarls at Heilagtré. The passes through the mountains should be open soon. We would like you to come with us.'

For perhaps five paces of their horses Adelais was too surprised to react. *Heilagtré.* It was a name whispered in awe among those who followed the old gods; the most sacred site on this world, hallowed to Odhinn, Thor, and Freyja. Her grandmother Yrsa had journeyed there once as a young woman to learn at the feet of the greatest *seidhkonur*. She had spoken of a blessed island with a mighty tree that was as old as the gods. Some said it was a shoot of the world tree Yggdrasil itself, and that the three Nornir wove fates among its roots.

'I am honoured,' she stuttered. You didn't refuse an invitation to Heilagtré. She was also a little frightened. There she would be seen by *seidhkonur* who had spent their whole lives working *seidhr* and runecraft. She would be a child among giants.

'And it might be safer. At least it will keep you out of Ragener's clutches for a couple of moons.'

Hjálmar grinned, exposing the gap between his teeth. She suppressed a smirk, thinking his red hair and beard made him look like a giant squirrel.

'We will leave as soon as we have confirmation that the pass is open through the mountains,' he continued, 'but your horse will need to be shod for ice. Do you have winter rugs for him? And he must be taken by barge across the river. You too will need warm clothing...' Hjálmar rattled off a list of requirements, most of which she forgot instantly. *Heilagtré.*

'May I bring Ulfhild?' Adelais spoke the thought as soon as it occurred to her. If Adelais left, Ulfhild would be returned to her life of drudgery.

'Who?'

'Companion.' Adelais stopped herself saying 'servant'.

Hjálmar shrugged. 'Of course.'

Adelais felt a grin spreading across her face. It would be the greatest adventure that Ulfie had ever known. And it would take them both away from Siltehafn with its enforced inactivity and *gyke* courtiers and assassins in the shadows.

Heilagtré!

The light was fading as they made their way back to the city; a flat, grey, early dusk beneath a low sky. Their escort moved into close formation around them as they approached the jousting field, their shields ready. A company of strangely dressed cavalrymen were exercising; they wore cloth-wrapped, conical helmets, light, quilted armour of an exotic style, and were armed with short, recurved bows hanging in wide sheaths from their saddles. A line of onlookers watched from beneath the castle's walls, and a gaudier knot of nobles from the battlements. One of the riders was galloping his horse past a leather dummy in the centre of the field. He rose out of the saddle and put two arrows in quick succession into the dummy's chest. It was a demonstration of superlative archery; nocking, drawing, and firing from the back of a charging horse.

'What are they?' Adelais asked, as another rider launched into his run.

'Tarrazim.' Hjálmar loaded the word with distaste. 'Sell-swords.'

The next rider shot his first arrow further away from the target, another when he was nearly level, and twisted in the saddle to fire a third over his horse's quarter, earning himself a cheer from his friends and shouted comments in a language Adelais did not understand. The dummy now had a fan of arrows radiating from its chest like splayed fingers.

'Where do they come from?'

'From grasslands far to the east, I am told.' Hjálmar sounded as if he did not want to know.

'And whom do they serve?'

Hjálmar snorted. 'Whoever pays them.' He looked up towards the nobles on the battlements. 'They are blown in by rumours of war, like flies around dead meat.'

'You do not approve of them,' Adelais prompted. The sight of the tarrazim had clearly lowered Hjálmar's mood, but Adelais found it impossible to be unhappy; she'd ridden out of the castle for the first time in nearly a moon, apart from her brief escapade, and she was going to Heilagtré.

'A man should fight his enemies face to face. You don't send assassins. I hope Ragener would not stoop so low.' Hjálmar frowned thoughtfully. 'I also hope they are still trying to sell their skills, and have not already been hired. Once they have taken gold they will achieve their contracted task or die in the attempt.'

'They ride so well.' Adelais was impressed by the tarrazim's horsemanship; they had controlled their mounts by legs and weight alone, and stayed balanced enough to shoot arrows into a target.

'They bond with their mounts.' Hjálmar nodded at Allier. 'Like you.'

Allier was still dancing. She'd had to contain him throughout their ride, knowing that he would have outrun Hjálmar's horse and any of their escort with ease. But yes, she felt Allier's happiness. They were of one mind. *Hey, my friend, we're going north!* She vaulted from Allier's back outside the stables, where Ulfhild stood waiting. Adelais enveloped her in a hug, unable to contain her excitement.

'You should smile more often.' Hjálmar towered over Adelais, still on horseback. 'It lightens your face.'

She stretched, still grinning, locking her fingers behind her neck so that her cloak slipped back over her shoulders, and Hjálmar's eyes dropped from her face to her armour. She made a small, mental shrug. They were only leather.

Another party of riders was coming through the main gate: a lady and two men-at-arms. The escort were well equipped but wore no distinguishing livery, yet there was something impossibly familiar about the cloak-wrapped lady urging her horse across the yard directly towards them, and at least one of her escort. *Can that be Guy?* Guy Carelet, who'd escaped with her from Villebénie the year before? The lady's horse was clearly exhausted and its rider mud-spattered, but even before she pushed her hood back from her face, Adelais knew who it was. Only Agnès could finish what must have been a great journey sitting that erect in the saddle, with her cloak fanned so perfectly over her horse's rump. Adelais could feel her mouth moving, but no words came. Agnès looked down at her with those familiar, green, shining eyes.

'Hello *kjúkling*. Love the new tits.'

4.2 GAUTHIER

Gauthier stood beneath the castle wall, watching the girl and her escort ride past the exercise arena into the castle. With all those guards there would have been little chance of a kill, even if he was equipped, and even less of escaping afterwards. And soon, according to Roche, she would be taken north with Jarl Magnus, leaving, no doubt, by the castle's own protected jetty. Gauthier sensed events slipping away from him.

She must disappear on the journey, Roche had said. His master required it.

Gauthier had snorted his derision. She would be too well protected. One man could not fight his way through that escort, and he'd be killed if he fired at them from the roadside.

So they must all die. The calmness with which Roche had spoken was chilling. This was no quiet killing in a back street, this was eliminating one of the most powerful men in the land, and his whole entourage. Vriesland would not only be fragmented, but the north would be leaderless.

Roche's lord was playing a game of nations.

Tarrazim would be ideal, Roche said. Ruthless. Efficient.

Sure. And untraceable. No tarrazim were ever captured alive. It was part of their code. And Gauthier was to arrange a meeting.

So Gauthier stood beneath the castle walls, watching them perform and waiting to catch their leader's eye. There was one warrior, more richly dressed than the others, who did not show off his skills but merely observed. He scanned the crowd for just the kind of almost-imperceptible nod that Gauthier gave him. A brief flash of gold in a cupped palm; an invitation to talk. There was an equally slight lift of the head in acknowledgement.

Gauthier pushed himself away from the wall and walked out into the countryside, knowing his path would be noted. Five hundred paces away was a small barn where he could wait.

Roche was already there.

'He'll come,' Gauthier announced, watching the path from the door. 'So where does this leave me?' He too had this assignment.

'Oh, you're going with them. Make sure they get the right girl.'

'I prefer to work alone.'

'You had your chance.'

It was almost dark before the man arrived, moving silently. He stood outlined against the last of the light, with his arms held away from his sides, letting himself be seen. Gauthier waved him into the barn, where Roche unshaded a lantern and gestured an invitation for the tarrazim to sit. Gauthier stayed by the door, his attention flicking between the twilit path and the two men eyeing each other across the lantern; Roche on a log, the tarrazim cross-legged on the dirt with his sword across his lap. The tarrazim was short and wiry, with skin like old leather. Gauthier guessed that he could unfold from the floor and have his sword in his hand in a heartbeat. There were no pleasantries and no introductions.

'You have gold?' The words seem to come from a dry place at the back of the man's throat.

'My lord has gold.'

The tarrazim grunted. 'Must know lord.'

Gauthier understood. The tarrazim would not work through intermediaries. That too was part of their code. But they would never, under any circumstances, reveal the identity of their employer.

'We do deal, you meet lord.'

Gauthier listened with interest. He would like to meet Roche's lord as well.

'How many you want kill?' The tarrazim's accent was harsh. The 'kill' sounded as if he was hawking to spit.

'Eight. Six men. Two women. In mountains. No trace. Want disappear.' Roche used the same pattern of broken language.

'Six warrior?'

'Six warrior. Girl fight too.'

'Girl.' The tarrazim snorted dismissively.

'How many warrior you have?'

'Fifty.' He held up both hands, splaying five times. 'How many you want?'

A pause. 'Twenty.' Roche's hand stretched into the lamp-light and opened four times. 'Sure kill. How much gold?'

The tarrazim held up a single finger. 'One man,' he showed a gold crown in the other hand, 'ten gold.' He splayed his fingers twice, counting. 'Twenty man, two hundred gold. Half now. Half when kill.'

Two hundred gold crowns! It was wealth beyond Gauthier's imagination.

'How long? Stay how many moons?' Roche leaned forwards into the lamplight.

'Short kill, long kill, all same. Stay till dead. Who you want kill?'

Roche pointed at Gauthier. 'This man show. You take him.'

The warrior turned to Gauthier. 'You ride? You fight?'

Gauthier snorted. 'I fight.'

Gauthier's eyes narrowed as a leather purse was laid in front of the warrior. 'Ten gold today. You come tomorrow. After dark. Here. Ninety more. Meet lord.'

Roche had been walking around with ten gold crowns on his belt! Half of Siltehafn would kill for ten gold! Gauthier eyed the purse being hefted in the tarrazim's palm.

The tarrazim leaned forwards, folding over the purse, until his face was over the lantern. For the first time, a hint of a smile appeared, a killer's smile that did not reach the eyes. His teeth were very white. 'Take gold, they dead. Sure. Lord no pay rest, him dead. You both dead.' He pointed at Roche, then at Gauthier. 'Sure.'

4.3 ADELAIS

At first, there had been no time to speak in the bustle of ostlers and servants that surrounded Agnès; the de Fontenay name was renowned even in Vriesland. Duke Ragener's steward himself led Agnès to rooms that were kept constantly in readiness for visiting dignitaries, having sent servants ahead to light fires and lay fresh linen. For once, Adelais left Allier to a stable boy and followed, listening. His Grace was otherwise engaged this evening, *shafting some poor wench, no doubt*, but would be pleased to see Lady Agnès on the morrow, when she was rested. Meanwhile, a meal would be sent to her. And wine, perhaps?

'Wine would be most welcome.' Agnès turned in the middle of the chamber she'd been shown, smiling her dismissal. 'Perhaps enough for two?'

'Two, my lady?' The steward frowned his puzzlement.

'Mistress Adelais and I have much to discuss.'

Adelais pushed past him into the room, grinning. 'And for once I need not have a clear head in the morning.'

When the steward had gone they looked at each other, laughing for no more reason than the joy of the moment. Agnès opened her arms and they crushed each other in a hug;

Adelais's unfeeling leather against Agnès's softness. That prompted more laughter, and a pretend-saucy cupping of Adelais's armoured breasts.

'Take it off! Let's hold each other properly.'

'The gown underneath is really thin!'

'So? I've seen it all before.'

Those had been happy days, when Agnès had sheltered Adelais in a hunting lodge during her escape from Galmandie. Happy days, and happy nights of wine and easy friendship. They'd talked late into the evenings then lain in the same bed – until the night when Agnès had drunk too much wine and a boundary was almost crossed. It hung between them like an old, unresolved argument, making Adelais hesitant as Agnès tugged at the armour's buckles with something like a lover's urgency. Yet the embrace that followed was the crush of deep friendship, nothing more, and it lasted until they had to pull back to arm's length to draw breath.

'I've missed you.' Adelais blinked away the dew in her eyes.

'And I you.'

Words tumbled over each other, bubbling, unfinished, until a knock announced a servant, bringing wine and a platter of cheeses to sustain them while their meal was prepared.

'There are guards outside! Am I a prisoner?' Agnès spoke to the servant's back, watching him leave.

'No, my lady!' The man seemed affronted and looked to Adelais for help.

'They're my shadows,' Adelais sighed. 'Duke Ragener insists. People are trying to kill me, even in Vriesland.' Though she didn't want to talk about the attempt with the crossbow. She wanted companionship and laughter.

Agnès looked hard at her, her smile fading. 'It seems we have much to tell each other.' She poured wine. They touched goblets and drank deeply, looking at each other over the rims.

'You're a long way from home, my friend.'

'So's this wine.' Agnès drank again. 'Jourdainian. Rather good.'

'Aren't you going to tell me why?'

'I missed you.'

Adelais stared at her, a little hurt by the flippancy. It would take more than friendship to bring Agnès to Vriesland in the worm moon.

'Sorry.' Agnès waved towards the fire. 'Let's sit.'

There were high-backed chairs, but that would seem too formal, like an audience with the duke, so they pulled the pillows from the bed and sat cross-legged on the floor, staring into the fire. After the first gush of welcome, there was an awkwardness between them; too many matters that would not be spoken of until the wine was lower in the jug; barriers greater than an almost-indiscretion. The woman beside Adelais was outwardly the same: wasp-waisted, dark-haired, green-eyed, and beautiful in the long-cheeked way of Galman women. But there was a tension about Agnès, an edge that Adelais had never felt before in her company. Adelais rested her chin on her knees, staring at the flames. Agnès had a purpose, an agenda, and she wasn't talking about it. Their talk was all of journeys and of people they both knew – Guy Carelet, Elyse at the hunting lodge – easy questions and easy answers that skirted and mapped the hard places, and led naturally to Adelais asking after Agnès's husband, Lord Leandre de Fontenay.

Agnès sighed and swigged wine. 'Leandre is not secure.'

'I thought he was with the Duke of Delmas, and under his protection. He fought alongside him at Harbin.' Where Adelais had also fought, as a de Fontenay man-at-arms, with her face concealed by a chain-mail aventail.

Agnès was uncharacteristically hesitant. 'I'm afraid it's all about you, *kjúkling*.' She made an embarrassed little smile. They had come to one of the hard matters that lay between them; as hard as Adelais's armour yet not so easily set aside. 'For every Ischyrian priest or noble who says you're an angel, there's another who says you are a witch and the spawn of Kakos. You were captured at a de Fontenay lodge, and you found sanctuary on his lands. That much is known. He is also suspected of helping you escape to Vriesland.' Agnès paused again, as if wondering how much to say. 'He needs to prove that he is a good Ischyrian.'

'I had not realised that our friendship would cost you so much. I'm sorry.' Adelais did not know what else to say. The silence between them lasted for several sips of wine. 'What do you think of me, Agnès? Do you think I'm evil?'

Agnès looked down. 'I know your heart to be good.'

'But?'

'When we were fugitives together, we were just girls caught up in great events. Then you killed the high priest...'

'I didn't mean to kill him. I just frightened him and he died.'

'And I believe that. But then you killed the king as well, and I saw you fight at Harbin. Better than any knight. Things happen around you, *kjúkling*, that are beyond explanation.'

Adelais took another pull of wine. They'd nearly finished the jug.

'They do. And I can't explain them either.' But she'd tell Agnès what she could. She owed her that much, and it might break down this barrier between them. Adelais took a deep breath. 'I was raised by my grandmother Yrsa. She was a *seidhkona*, a healer and what you would call a sorceress. She was respected, in the days before the conquest, before the old gods were proscribed. She taught me a little about runes, but then I was sent away to a sisterhouse and forgot much of the lore while I learned to be a good Ischyrian.

'When Humbert Blanc and I were taken in front of the high priest, I knew they were going to kill us. Torture us to death. So I sang the rune song of *thurs* under my breath and the lightning came. I only meant to frighten him into letting us go. I didn't mean it as a spell, it was a song to give me courage, almost like you'd say a prayer, but there was a *fordæmdur* great clap of thunder and he died.'

Agnès let out a long, slow breath. 'And the king?'

'I just got angry. No runes. No magic. But I sang rune song at Harbin and felt invincible. *Was* invincible.' Adelais swigged again. She could feel the warmth spreading within her, loosening her tongue and will. 'So that's me. Things happen, usually when I get angry and forget to be a good little woman. But I wish the nobles would let me go and be a healer. Maybe one day I'd find a man and raise cattle and babies.'

'You're being used.' Agnès looked hard at Adelais. 'When Ragener's got what he wants he'll throw you away. We hear in Galmandie that he's wrapping you up like a holy icon.' Agnès nodded towards the breastplate, propped against the wall with its mail skirts trailing across the floor, almost as if a third woman sat there, listening. 'Farmers' wives don't wear armour.'

'I think you might be right.' She reached for Agnès's hand and squeezed. 'I don't want to go to war.'

'You could refuse?'

'If Ragener withdrew his protection, I'd be killed. Someone tried three days ago. One of the jarls has invited me to go north, where it should be safer for a while, but everyone talks of war.'

'Stay there, *kjúkling*. Stay north, where you're safe.'

'I might.'

'Don't get pulled into the games of nobles.'

'Is that why you're here, Agnès? The games of nobles?'

'I am just a messenger, really. Emissary. Ambassador. Call it what you will. Neither Duke Gervais of Delmas nor my husband can risk travelling outside Delmas's lands, but a woman can pass safely. I carry letters from Gervais for Ragener so that he knows I speak in his name. I bring messages that are for his ears only.'

'That tells me nothing.'

'Because I can say nothing, *kjúkling*. Just stay out of it. Please, for friendship's sake.' Agnès reached for the jug and peered into its depths. 'We need more wine.'

So that was one barrier they wouldn't cross. Adelais sighed and went for more.

When she came back, Agnès patted the cushion beside her. She'd moved them closer. They sat with their hips and shoulders touching, reaching for each other's hands as if they were lovers making up after a quarrel, and Adelais wondered if they'd ever sit by a fire like this again. If war came, they'd be on opposite sides. Beside her, Agnès sighed, her eyes on the flames.

'I hope you find your man, if that's what you want.' Agnès sounded wistful. Adelais sensed there was something she wanted to share.

Good. We're talking as friends, now.

'De Fontenay does not please you?' Adelais knew there had been difficulties. She gave her friend the opening to speak.

'We are an alliance between two noble families. He entrusts me with great matters, but he prefers the company of his knights to the marriage bed.'

'Still?'

'Still.'

'Oh, I'm so sorry my friend. I do not understand. You are beautiful...'

'It is a matter he will not discuss.' Agnès made a humourless little laugh. 'Perhaps I should take a lover.'

'Ragener will probably offer. He'll listen to your embassy and then try to bed you.'

'Is he beddable?' There was a glint in Agnès's eye.

'I think you have better taste, my friend.'

'Is there a man you'd like? Around Ragener's court?'

Adelais shook her head. 'It's like a nest of snakes, this place. The courtiers smile their compliments, then sneer when my back is turned.'

'Learn to play them at their own games. It's the only way.'

'Inside the castle, the men are all courtiers, soldiers, or prattling servants, and I'm not allowed out somewhere I could meet an honest man.'

'Maybe you'll find one in the north.'

Agnès fell quiet, staring at the flames, and Adelais let the silence stretch. She sensed that Agnès had more she wanted to say.

Eventually Agnès sighed and spoke. 'It pains me to say this, *kjúkling*, because you're one of the few friends I trust, but don't come back. Please. I think things are going to get very nasty.'

'War, you mean? Because we'll be on opposite sides?'

'War. And when wars go wrong, whole armies die. The nobles would be ransomed, but you? They'll blame the whole war on you and your sorcery. Make an example of you. They'll flay you alive. Literally.'

As the sun rose, Adelais paced the battlements above 'her' tower, trying to clear the previous night's wine from her head; chill, fresh air blew from the west, sharp with salt. She put her face into it, letting it lift her hair, while she watched a fat-bellied cog blow in from the sea under a bulging sail. It was one of the first to brave the voyage from Saxenheim after the winter, and it was probably loaded with wool. Soon, weavers like her father would come to buy so that they could blend the wool's warmth with local linen. The life of the city hummed beneath her, beckoning; the ride with Hjálmar had reminded her how much of a prisoner she had become. She'd spent a year wanting to come north to Vriesland, but now part of her wanted to ride south with Agnès. It would be quite like old times. Agnès even had Guy Carelet as her escort.

Impossible, of course. She did not even know if they were fated to meet again, but at least she could give Agnès a gift to remember her by. A charm, perhaps, to bring Lord Leandre into Agnès's bed. She'd have to be swift; Agnès would spend the morning with Ragener, and would leave on the morrow when her embassy was done. Adelais fingered the new belt around her waist, thinking. This belt would be ideal. It was new. It was of good quality. And a little bind-rune cut into its reverse would be discreet.

Adelais sent Ulfhild to the kitchens to beg the loan of a sharp cook's knife, and began work. Ulfhild watched her, entranced, believing utterly in Adelais's power. Adelais wanted to tell her it was only a charm, like the Mjölnir pendant around Ulfhild's neck.

First, the arrowhead of *kaunaz*.

Kaunaz, the rune of creation and of fire, beloved of metal workers but also the rune that could light another kind of fire, deep in the loins. Adelais sang the rune's song in the Old Tongue as she worked. *Kaun er barna böl, ok bardaga för, ok holdfúa hús...*

But *kaunaz* must be balanced; lust must be tempered with love, so two mirroring cuts added *gebo*.

Gebo, the rune of giving and receiving, of hearts willingly exchanged. The rune of lovers.

A single upright line to the left added *thurs*.

Thurs had brought the thunder when she faced the high priest, but when bound with *gebo* and *kaunaz* it should yield prowess of an earthier kind, and Agnès so deserved joy in her bed.

But Adelais knew too little about binding runes. Their individual meanings, yes, but the infinite ways in which they might work together? She wished Yrsa was here to teach her. And *thurs* was dangerous; it was also a rune of wild power, even rage.

She cut anyway. She had the complete pattern of a bind-rune in her mind.

Thurs er kvenna kvöl, ok kletta búi, ok vardhrúnar verr...

A final upright line to the right added *dagaz*, the rune of dawn and light.

Dagaz was a rune of beginnings; the dawn of a new time, the end of unhappiness and darkness. And Agnès deserved to find laughter.

The runes must be painted with blood, but if she simply smeared it over the cuts, the stain would spread across the leather. Ulfhild came up with the idea of cutting a small tuft of hair from her own braids and binding them into a tiny brush with a thread. It worked well enough when soaked with blood that Adelais cut from her thumb.

Adelais sat back, satisfied with her work. More than satisfied; she had channelled all her intent, all her wishes, and created a bind-rune to bring love and the joy of a lover to her friend.

It was risky. Only a trained *seidhkona* should cut a bind-rune, and Adelais knew so little. But surely if her intent was good, no harm could come?

·   ·   ·

The bells of the Ischyrian temple in the city had rung the noon office before she and Agnès could meet. Agnès was still richly gowned for her embassy with Duke Ragener, her hair held in a net of fine gold. She pulled Adelais through the door of her chamber and folded her into a tight embrace.

'Oh *kjúkling*, Ragener told me about the crossbow. What happened? Tell me all about it. You said people were trying to kill you, but I had no idea they'd got that close. Why didn't you say? You're not hurt?' Agnès's questions gushed into Adelais's shoulder. When she pulled back, her eyes were full of concern.

'I think something was looking after me.' As Adelais began to tell her, the warmth of Agnès's embrace unlocked emotion that had been bottled within her ever since. The nearness of death came back to her and she felt suddenly, unexpectedly close to tears. Agnès pulled her to sit on the bed and held her, rocking her gently until the moment passed.

'Sorry.' Adelais took a deep breath. *Oh, to have a friend nearby, all the time.*

'I'd probably be the same if someone tried to kill me.'

'It was so *fordæmdur* close. *That* close.' Adelais held her hand in front of her face. 'I spend so much time having to be strong. Be the image they want to create. I think you're the only one I can be myself with.'

'The same goes for me. In Delmas or Fontenay, I'm surrounded by nobles with honied smiles and sharp knives.'

'You know, Agnès, there's something about you that makes me cry.' Adelais's humour was coming back.

'And there's something about you, *kjúkling*, that makes me drink. Let's share a flagon. By Salazar, I'm going to miss you.'

'I made you something, but I don't know if you will want to wear it.' Adelais unbuckled the belt from around her own waist, and showed Agnès the bind-rune near the buckle, on the inside. 'Think of it as a lucky charm. These are runes, though they just look like a pattern. If someone asks, tell them it's the craftsman's mark. Wear it low, over your hips, so it hangs just so.'

Agnès looked slightly unsure but let Adelais arrange the belt around her, fastening it loose so the buckle angled downwards as if pointing the way for a lover.

'And what are those runes supposed to do?' Agnès smiled uncertainly.

Adelais pushed the belt into Agnès's belly above the womb, gently, the way a lover might touch. 'They're love-runes, to help you find passion and friendship, and all the joy in a man that I wish for you. But beware, these runes are for true love; you will give yourself to your lover as much as you receive the gift of his heart. They are runes to bind souls.'

'If you believe in rune magic.' Agnès leaned into the intimacy, her smile now mischievous.

'If. If not, accept it as the gift of a true friend, to remember me by, whatever happens.'

Agnès opened her arms, her eyes shining. 'I think our souls are already bound.' They hugged fiercely, her breath warm against Adelais's neck. 'Stay out of this, Adelais. Stay north. Stay safe.'

PART TWO

THE LAMB MOON

CHAPTER FIVE

5.1 FYLGJA

Awareness returns to her like the slow awakening from a long sleep; that soft confusion when dreams and reality blend. She remembers a time before, a soaring time in which the dream of flying is so powerful that she lifts a foreleg as if it were a wing, and the impossibility of that movement shakes the dream into fragments, like feathers in the wind. They flutter across another memory, more real, for she is wolf-kind now; a bounding, hunting, baying time when the pack flows across the snow as one, divides, out-flanks, and rejoins in a great, collective *yes!* She remembers the joy of the kill; the hot blood on fangs and tongue, and the tearing, ripping end to her hunger.

This wolf within her tenses, newly aware of her presence in its mind, and lifts its head. The pack sleeps around her, sheltered beneath a great pine tree where the snow has not settled. A thick layer of dry needles lies between their bodies and the frozen ground; it is a good place to rest. Their pelts blend with the leaf-litter; browns, greys, charcoal, the occasional splash of white. The wolf growls, not knowing why or at what, and she speaks to it in the wordless way of wolf-kind, building acceptance, letting herself be known as one of them, dominant, non-threatening so long as she is obeyed.

She remembers other beginnings. Birds that had been too unthinking for any purpose save mindless sacrifice, but it had been the only way. A wolf would not have been tolerated among the dwellings of people.

Wolves recognise her. Accept her. She has done this before and knows their fierce intelligence. They know her lineage, for once she was a woman of the people of the wolf, but now she is spirit. She is *fylgja*. The gods have enabled her to enter the wolf and possess it, to impose her will upon it as a rider directs her horse.

Yet like a spirited horse, the beast's own will remains. There will be challenges.

Her purpose is still unclear, the way a new day's plans can be unclear on waking; there is only a sense of momentous events building, beyond the horizon of her understanding.

Yet there must *be* purpose. A *fylgja* cannot be summoned by the living, and yet she has woken. Has *been* woken. The threads of fate that bind her to the girl are trembling.

Fragmented at first, a pattern takes shape, as the leaf speaks of the tree. The girl. She rides into danger the way she might ride under a cliff that will fall. There is a tug towards a place the *fylgja* does not know, like a lodestone that points always to the north star, and it is a summons to protect. How, and from what, she also does not know. She accepts that she is only one piece on the board in the games of the gods.

A little further away, on open ground, a smear of pink across the snow marks the place where they brought down the elk; its body lies broken and dismembered, legs splayed like fallen branches.

She rises to her feet, crosses to it, and feeds again even though her belly is full. She has far to go. The warp and weft of fate that has summoned her now calls her to climb higher, above the treeline where there will be little game to hunt.

The meat is still warm. She rips it from the bone until her belly will take no more. She turns to leave, ignoring the *why?* within as the wolf fights this leaving of the pack. Yet in truth there is no choice. The pack will look into her eyes, see the change that has happened, and know that she no longer belongs. Even her own whelps would tear her apart if she stayed.

There are no farewells. When she pauses at the edge of the pack, fighting to dominate the wolf, a young male bares its teeth at her, its hackles rising. She understands; she has done this before. There can be no pack for *fylgja*.

And now she must run, towards a menace that will be revealed, somewhere beyond the high peaks. The ground is frozen but her path is clear as a scent trail on warm earth.

5.2 ADELAIS

Four days out from Siltehafn, they stopped at a wayside inn, set in its own clearing at a fork in the road. Here they would replenish their stores for the crossing of the mountains, and eat their last good meal before Heilagtré. There had even been a half-barrel of warmed water to wash away the day's dirt, and space for Adelais to change from leather armour into a warm kirtle for the evening. While the innkeeper's wife cooked, Adelais walked up a low, rounded hill near the inn. She was tired but relished the freedom to move and the whispering peace of the forest; the air was clean with the chill of distant snow, and sharp with the tang of pine.

She stopped at the summit, awestruck at the sight of the mountains. They had seen them in the distance from the road for two days, at first like low clouds on the horizon. For most of this day they'd only been glimpsed through gaps in the forest, but now they rose impossibly high to the east, as sharp and jagged as shards of glass. The setting sun turned their snows pink. Adelais turned, scanning the view. To the west, undulating, forested hills stretched to the horizon, grey-green, broken only by the clearing around the inn, where their horses grazed in a paddock. A small field was striped by new ploughing. And much closer, Hjálmar climbed after her, leaning into the slope, his thighs like moving tree trunks. She was not upset that he'd followed; she found him easy company. And he didn't begin by admonishing her for walking off on her own.

'Where is the pass?' The line of mountains looked impenetrable to Adelais.

'There.' He pointed with a sausage-thick finger. 'Between the one that looks like a broken tooth and the arrowhead.'

Adelais had to stand close to sight down his finger. His bulk made her feel childlike.

'You know the road?'

'My father's hall is two days' ride to the north, on this side of the mountains. The innkeeper is his man. I have been to Heilagtré two, three times.'

'Is it far?' Those mountains were beautiful, but forbidding, like a castle wall.

'One day's ride to the top of the pass. There is a shelter there. Four days ride beyond to Heilagtré, if the roads are good.'

Adelais swallowed, wondering how to ask. 'What can I expect there, Hjálmar?'

'Our *örlaga vefari* is nervous?' He made round, mock-shocked eyes at her.

'I don't want to be your *örlaga vefari*. But everyone's talking about war and saying I have a part in it. What will they do to me? How will they decide?'

'First you will meet the *gydhjur,* the priestesses of the sacred isle. That alone is a great honour. Then the jarls will talk.'

'But what should I say? How should I behave?'

'Just be yourself. They'll like what they see.'

His tone suggested he liked what *he* saw, and she flinched. Men who grew too close to her died. Arnaud. Humbert. All the others who'd died around her in the past year. She didn't want Hjálmar to die. She turned away, not knowing how to keep him at arm's length. Agnès would know; the polished courtier who could turn awkwardness into laughter with a jest. By the gods, she missed her friend already.

At the bottom of the slope, Ulfhild was wandering between the trees, stiff and saddle-sore, gnawing on a heel of bread. The girl was rake-thin and always hungry.

'Ulfie!' Adelais beckoned. 'Come and look at the mountains!'

Beside Adelais, Hjálmar sighed at this gentle shutting of a door. In another world, one where she did not fear friendship, she might have kept it open. Perhaps even met him on the threshold.

5.3 GAUTHIER

Gauthier watched from a distance as Jarl Magnus and his party left the inn, soon after sunrise. He waited for the sun to climb two finger-widths into the sky before approaching, alone, leaving the tarrazim in the forest behind him.

He hated working with tarrazim. He preferred to work alone, and he didn't like playing nursemaid to outsiders who together were being paid many times what he would have earned for the same task. His resentment was made worse by the knowledge that his own failure had handed them this rich opportunity. By Salazar's wounds, for two hundred crowns he'd have found a way. Taken more risks. Just ten crowns Roche had offered him for this journey; the same as any of them. Yet his local knowledge was crucial.

He'd had to endure them for six days now, since they'd been ferried across the Schilde upstream from the city, away from prying eyes. At first they'd ridden in small groups, heavily cloaked, their weapons unstrung and wrapped, but after two days they left the farmlands behind and entered the vast forests of Normark where there were few settlements and fewer travellers. The tarrazim probably disliked having an outsider in their midst as much as he disliked them. Their overnight camps were awkward; they shared a fire, but not food, and there was no invitation for him to share the shelter of one of their leather tents. The winter snows had melted from the foothills but the nights were bitingly cold and he had only a fleece-lined bedroll.

On the fourth day he'd found them a place to camp in a hidden valley beneath the mountains, about a league from the inn. He'd summoned the tarrazim leaders, smoothed a patch of ground, and drawn a map with a stick as he outlined his plan. He remembered this road. Just. He'd ridden it in the years after he was thrown out of the priesthood, during the lean years when he'd stolen a sword and found employment escorting travellers. He could remember several places ahead of them, up in the pass, that would fit their needs. On the fifth day he'd led an advance party to the pass road, moving through the forest around the shoulders of the mountains to avoid the inn; the kind of stealth that is feasible for a few but not for a war band as large as the one waiting behind him. Beyond the inn, the pass road climbed up a steepening valley and concealment would not be possible. Nor, indeed, desirable.

Now it was time to make sure that no one lived to tell of how Jarl Magnus and the woman Adelais had journeyed into the mountains, followed by tarrazim. Anyone who had seen the jarl's party, or who might see the tarrazim, must also disappear, and Gauthier had waited long enough to be confident that there were no other travellers at the inn. The paddock was empty, save for two heavy nags that probably drew a plough or a cart. Beyond the house a broad, bosomy woman walked a field strip, scattering seed from a sack on her hip. Gauthier remembered a laughing, flush-cheeked young mother with children old enough to help. They'd probably be wed and gone by now. No sign of other youngsters.

Good.

Gauthier nudged his horse forwards. He'd shed his priestly

garb in Siltehafn and rode in the simple cote-hardie and cloak of
a tradesman. No one would know how well he could use the
sword at his side. The woman turned at the sound of Gauthier's
horse but did not come back to the house. Shadowed inside the
doorway to the inn, a man cradled a crossbow, watching
Gauthier scrutinise the woman.

'Greetings, friend.' Gauthier swung out of the saddle, his
smile open and friendly. He even unbuckled his sword belt and
hung it over the pommel to show his peaceful intent, and the
man relaxed. 'I bear a message for Jarl Magnus Finehair.'

'He left here at first light.' The man lowered his crossbow.
'If you ride hard you will reach him before noon.'

'I was told I might buy supplies here.'

'That you can.' The innkeeper turned away. 'What do
you—'

He gasped as Gauthier's knife, the one he kept hidden in his
sleeve, slammed into his back, slicing upwards into the heart.
The man's knees buckled, but the crossbow hit the floor first.
The snap of its release ended in a louder thump as the bolt rico-
cheted off the boards and buried itself in a barrel. Beyond the
door, the woman called her man's name, an edge of concern in
her voice.

Fuck. This will be messy. Gauthier retrieved his sword,
stepped over the body, and strode out towards the field.

He'd make it quick.

5.4 ADELAIS

'We are being followed.' Hjálmar halted his horse where the road climbed around the shoulder of the mountain, and stared back along the way they had come. Adelais turned with him. Mounted, their heads were almost on a level; she on the mighty Allier, he on a shaggy-maned, squat horse that seemed to carry his weight with ease.

She didn't see the danger at first. The road snaked down the open mountainside for half a league before it straightened and ran between scattered pine trees. At this distance the trees were like fine ink marks upon white parchment, but the forest thickened as the road dropped, gradually hiding it within its solid, charcoal mass. Further away, the mounded hills of Normark stretched into the distance, towards the Saxen Sea, which would be far beyond their sight to the west. Somewhere in that forest was the inn where they'd spent the night.

Two warriors paused with them, also scanning the edge of the trees. Both led packhorses. The rest of the group rode by, with the two other warriors leading the way and Jarl Magnus and Revna following, all on horses that were as small and hardy as Hjálmar's. Each rider hunched against the cold within heavy, fur-lined cloaks. Ulfhild, bringing up the rear, was on a larger but ploddingly safe mount. She was looking about her with such wonder that the hood of her new cloak had fallen backwards and her blonde maiden's braids shone in the sunlight. Ulfhild was unused to riding, but the aches and the sores had not damp-ened her excitement. She had never seen mountains before. Never been more than two leagues from Siltehafn. She grinned at Adelais as she passed, a toothy beam of happiness.

Bringing Ulfhild had been a good decision. She was tireless and keen to please, and she was finally realising that Adelais really needed her company more than her service.

'There!' One of the warriors pointed.

Adelais resisted the urge to stand in her stirrups. It might be the lamb moon, with the ground thawed enough for ploughing in the lowlands, but here in the mountains their water skins froze unless they rested against the warmth of their horses. Allier had a thick woollen rug draped over his quarters against the cold, and she'd pulled its front edges forwards over her knees, wedging them inside her legs. She was comfortable enough, if she kept that rug in place. Her armour might not leave enough space for a thick gown beneath, but she wore a fur vest over it, and thick woollen trews like the northern men. She also wore her sheepskin-lined bascinet, more for warmth than protection, and had her cloak wrapped tightly around her until only a small gap was left for her gloved hands to hold the reins.

'I don't see anything.' Adelais scratched Allier's neck. The great destrier seemed tucked into himself, tight against the cold, and it hurt her that she could do nothing more for him, not until they reached the refuge and stables she'd been told were beyond the pass. She was glad he'd been fitted with studded shoes to give him grip on the ice.

'Watch the treeline.' Hjálmar did not point. He too wanted to keep his cloak tight about him.

The road followed the bank of a stream that had been

almost a river when they first came upon it, near the coast. In the foothills it flowed fast and full, tumbling stones in its bed, but in the heights it merely trickled. Full or faint, they'd been drinking its icy purity for days.

There! Movement among the trees, black against white, so tiny that it might have been a fox, but that outline could only be a mounted man. And others. Many others, emerging onto the snow in a wide line that was slowly converging as the valley narrowed and the road climbed towards the pass. Adelais counted fifteen before Hjálmar wheeled his horse around and trotted after the others.

She fell in behind Hjálmar and Magnus, alongside Revna. Jagged peaks scraped the sky ahead of them, dazzling white in the sunshine, so high that their summits trailed faint streamers of blown ice, though here in the pass it was still. Beyond the mountains, she'd been told, the land fell away towards the great Ice Sea and Heilagtré.

'How many?' Magnus had not paused his horse. 'How armed?'

'About fifteen.' Hjálmar's breath fogged the air. 'I think they are tarrazim. Too far to be sure. Some were spread out either side of the road, others riding along it.'

'So their intent was to prevent us turning back.'

'If we are their target?' Hjálmar challenged.

'Men who ride in peace would use the road. And if we were not their target, I would have heard of a reason for fifteen armed men to ride my lands.'

'Then why have they not attacked earlier, Father? We have been on the road for five days.'

'Too many people on the road from Siltehafn, even in the lamb moon. They do not want witnesses.'

'Isn't it lovely?' Ulfhild came alongside. She was staring up at the majesty biting the sky around them, her mouth open in wonder, and clearly did not realise their danger.

Adelais had been among mountains before, in Galmandie's far south, but that had been in summer and the mighty peaks had seemed benign, smiling in the heat until their summits blended into the blue. Here, in early spring, the mountains were aloof, unforgiving, and hard-edged. Yet the scene had such awesome beauty that it was easy to forget the threat behind. It was a place, a moment, to share with a lover. They rode beneath a great cliff of snow and the sun reaching into the valley made the white wall shine hard enough to hurt the eyes. Adelais wondered what it would be like to stand on top of that cliff and look down on the world. Below them, the stream was burbling over its stones, fed by a sheet of water that leaked from the base of the cliff.

'How far behind us?' Magnus's question brought Adelais back to the urgency of the moment.

'Half a league, as the eagle flies,' Hjálmar replied. 'Thrice that on the road.'

'They will attack in the pass, I am sure.' Magnus gestured to the banks of snow beside the road. 'Before the summit, where we cannot escape. We will choose the ground for battle, in the narrows where a few can face many. Let us make haste.' He spurred his horse.

'They might also be ahead of us,' Adelais called after him.

'She's right, Father!'

Magnus slowed, looking down at the road's surface. It had been newly swept, probably with fir saplings dragged behind horses to keep the way clear. The brushed snow showed no fresh tracks. 'Maybe. What we can be sure of is that there are at least fifteen killers behind us, and we are but six.'

'Seven,' Adelais corrected him. 'Seven with swords.'

'They are still too many. And if they are tarrazim they will have bows. We ride on.'

But Magnus did send two of his warriors ahead, telling them to keep within sight.

Half a league later, the leading warriors' horses shied, spinning and trying to bolt back towards the group until their riders brought them under control. They had come to a place where the track broadened for perhaps a hundred paces before narrowing to pass around a rockfall. A great, flat-topped boulder was embedded in the valley floor to their left, diverting the trickling stream around its base. And at the far end of the open space, where the track curved around the rockfall, a great she-wolf stood motionless, staring at them. Staring *past* the warriors, still fighting their mounts, towards Adelais. One of the warriors dismounted, swearing, handed his reins to his companion, and hefted his spear into the overarm throwing position.

'No!' Adelais's scream cut the air. The man had turned and shrugged his incomprehension before the sound echoed back to them from the ice cliff. Adelais nudged Allier forwards, ignoring Magnus's growl that they could not delay. She could feel Allier's tension; that quivering, ears-pricked dance a horse makes when all its instinct is to run but its rider's legs squeeze him towards danger. By the time they reached the warriors, the fear was like a wall against Allier's chest and she could force him no further. Adelais dismounted and walked towards the wolf.

'Don't be a fool. It'll rip you apart.' The man grabbed her trailing reins. She ignored him. He could not have known that Allier would never run, not while she was there.

The only sound was her breathing, rasping a little in the cold, and the crump of snow beneath her boots. Twenty paces from the wolf she paused, sensing tension in the animal as if it too fought the need to run. Or perhaps to fight. Its hackles had come up. No closer.

She opened her arms wide, hip-high, non-threatening, and dropped to her knees, submissive.

'Amma?' There had been another wolf, far away. Different patterning. Different wolf. Same eyes. They too had reflected the blue of the sky. They too had reminded her so powerfully of her grandmother. 'Amma Yrsa?'

The animal relaxed a little, and Adelais rocked back onto her heels and stood. Her trews stuck to her knees, two patches of chill wetness. One step forwards, and the she-wolf growled, baring its fangs. The warning could not have been clearer.

'What should I do, Amma?'

The wolf began to paw at the snow, steadily, rhythmically, at the speed a *seidhkona* might pound the beat to rune song, and Adelais understood. She backed away, facing the wolf, only turning when she was almost level with Allier.

'What was that about?' Magnus seemed irritated by the delay.

'It is a warning. We must go no further.'

He snorted. 'We're not going to stand here and wait for fifteen warriors to catch up with us, just because a tame wolf likes your face.'

'She is *fylgja*. The last time I ignored her many people died.' Adelais pulled her grandmother's carved staff from the straps of a packhorse. 'I think this is a time for rune song, not swords.' *Though which runes?* She had no idea.

'I agree. We have been given a sign. We stay.' Revna climbed stiffly out of the saddle. 'Hjálmar, help me onto that rock and pass me my staff.'

'This is madness,' Magnus raged. 'You trust our lives to an animal and the whim of a girl!'

'I trust our lives to the gods.' Revna put a foot into Hjálmar's cupped hands and let him heave her upwards until she could use his shoulders to scramble onto the rock's flat top. Hjálmar grinned nervously at Adelais as she followed. There was a strange intimacy in using him as a ladder. Revna called down to Magnus as Adelais crawled over the rim. 'If this is your dying-day, Magnus Finehair, then at least you can die with a sword in your hand.'

Is this really our dying-day? In this icy silence? Not if I've interpreted the wolf's sign correctly.

Adelais stood, precariously, and looked around her. The valley wound its way westwards, sinking towards the forested foothills. The great ice cliff rose to her right, shining in the sunlight and so high that she had to crane her neck to see its peak. There was no sign of pursuit; the men were probably in one of several bends in the road. Behind her rock, two warriors were tying horse lines between boulders. The others were preparing for battle, donning helmets and wrapping hard leather greaves around their legs. Ulfhild stared up at her, as if she'd finally realised the gravity of the situation and was looking to Adelais for help. There was no sign of the wolf. Beside her, Revna was kicking at the snow, clearing a space.

'What are we going to do?' Adelais asked, quietly. She'd been so sure, a few moments before.

'I thought you were the one with ideas.' Revna's bitter grimace may have been the closest thing to a smile Adelais had seen on her face.

'*Ísa?*' she guessed. The ice-rune was said to constrain opposition, and they were surrounded by great cliffs of it.

'Nay, child. Exactly the opposite. *Sowilo*, I think, the sun-rune. It is a rune of bright energy and hope.' Revna closed her eyes and lifted her face to the sun. 'Do you not feel her warmth upon you?'

Adelais shivered. The first of their pursuers appeared around a bend in the road, perhaps eight hundred paces away. They were walking their horses, unhurried. Adelais jumped as Revna rammed her staff into the rock, making a sharp crack that rattled around the valley and came back to them in a miniature thunderclap. Revna let her staff fall again, lightly now, as if she were practising. 'Some say *sowilo*—' another echo '—is a rune of victory, though I find *tiwaz* more effective for that. Join me.' She gestured to a cleared space on the rock beside her.

'Then why not *tiwaz* now?' Adelais remembered the rune of Tyr, the one-handed god. 'Or *thurs?*' She'd murmured the rune of Thor before the Ischyrian high priest, but then the thunderstorm had been building for days. She could not have called the lightning. She had not willed him to die. And now? Did she really believe rune song could alter fates? When overwhelming numbers of tarrazim were coming at them?

'*Sowilo* is energy itself. It calls the gods to our aid. It is power. It is protection. It is life. Now, together!' Revna struck the rock with the base of her staff, hard.

And the two of them were perched on a rock, like targets on a post for the archers.

'With me! *Sól er skýja skjöldr...*'

The sun is the shield of the clouds.

Revna's voice was high and grating, the noise a child might make with a reed flute. With her next blow, timed to hit as the echo returned, Adelais was with her, driving Amma Yrsa's staff downwards.

'*Ok skínandi rödhull...*'

And shining ray.

They sang together, the hard cracks of their staffs melding with the echoes and echoing back again, redoubled.

'*Ok ísa aldrtregi...*'

And destroyer of ice.

Far away, the line of ant-like warriors had paused. One may have been pointing a lance up the valley towards them. No, not a lance, a bow. Tarrazim, for certain, and they had seen them, high on their rock. And heard.

'Harder,' Revna shouted between lines of the chant. 'Invoke the power of the gods!'

The line moved again, trotting now. Two in the lead began to canter.

'*Sól er skýja skjöldr...*' The line disappeared behind a bend like a snake sliding into a hole.

'*Ok skínandi röðhull...*' The staffs and their echoes, multiplied and remultiplied, were as loud as warriors' fists beating on the tables at a feast.

Not long now. Revna had closed her eyes to focus her intent. Adelais couldn't. She stared at the bend where the road first curved out of sight, three hundred paces away.

'*Ok ísa aldrtregi...*'

'... and destroyer of ice.' The first two pursuers rounded the bend, cantering over compacted snow, riding one-handed with bows ready in the other.

'Oh, *fjakk!*' Adelais forgot the chant and forgot the rhythmic pounding as she looked up. The side of the mountain above the ice cliff had changed from sunlit white to the grey of bare stone. It was soundless; a slab of pure snow three hundred paces high slid towards the valley, pushing a tumbling ice-cloud at its base, a cloud that burst in an almighty, silent eruption of white as the whole cliff began to crumble.

The roar of the avalanche arrived several breaths after it began, and it was as if all the gods had been woken in Asgard and were bellowing their anger, thundering into Midgard on icy, iron-shod steeds to wreak retribution. The mountainside appeared to be sliding in a single, cloud-fringed sheet until its lower edge hit the bank above the stream, and the valley disappeared.

The whole world was disappearing. Frozen clouds filled Adelais's view, blotting out everything except their shining tops and their rolling, shadowed bases. They rushed towards them, a thunderous charge of celestial cavalry that came faster than any horse could run.

As a child she had watched storm-driven waves crash onto a beach. This is how a crab must feel, looking upwards at a wall of water, thinking this must be the end. She knelt, holding her staff futilely upright before her, as if that could give her any protection, and bowed her head against the impact. Beside her, Revna had done the same, either in defence or in obeisance to whatever god was descending upon them. Below them on the track, Hjálmar, Magnus and his men had formed a shield wall and crouched, braced. Ulfhild must be behind, with the horses.

The horses. *Allier.* Her heart reached out to him, though her eyes looked upwards. She thought the moon itself must have fallen to earth and was rolling up the valley towards them, vast, vaporous, wiping away both sky and mountain.

'I'm sorry,' Adelais murmured, just before the clouds hit. She wasn't sure if she was apologising to her friends or to the divinity that must live within this fury.

5.5 GAUTHIER

The man the tarrazim had left with Gauthier was not happy, and had maintained a stream of invective as they buried the bodies of the innkeeper and his wife. At least, Gauthier assumed it was invective. He shut the man up with two words.

'Ten gold.'

That, he understood.

They made good time afterwards. By the time the road was switching backwards and forwards in the climb to the pass, Gauthier could see the rest of the tarrazim from the outside of the bends, when his line of sight allowed.

He did not understand the sharp crack that echoed down the valley, leaving no clue to its source. It sounded like the single, fracturing rap a sheet of ice makes as it breaks. Others then followed, folding over the first until there was a confused rhythm, the way two horses cantering together create a rhythm. It was eerie; the shining silence of the peaks now rattled loudly enough for Gauthier and his companion to crane their necks to see where the noise might come from.

'Bad *sakhar.*' The tarrazim warrior paused as they approached a bend, falling behind. He looked spooked, as if he feared the spirits of the mountains were angry. 'Bad, bad *sakhar.'*

The noise stopped. Suddenly. No fading, just stopped. On its heels came a thunder louder than anything Gauthier had heard, and around the next bend in the valley came a rolling torrent of snow. As both his horses screamed and spun, scrambling at the icy track, Gauthier looked up at the tumbling wall of white, higher than any castle, and knew that this was the moment of his death. Though his body still moved franticly to gather reins and fight for control, and some part of his mind screamed his denial – *this is not real, this is not happening* – that deeper acceptance of death brought a moment of calm, and a sadness more profound than he had ever known.

The impact swept him from the saddle, tumbling him over and over, smothering him in white then stifling grey. He was held fast, twisted, his feet higher than his head.

Silence. No, there were still rumbles, as much felt as heard. *Can't breathe!* He struggled against this icy prison, but only one leg moved, from the knee downwards.

A hand gripped his ankle. *Get me out of here!* Reached along his body, scooping, but he was breathing snow before the hand reached higher than his waist and a choking blackness began to claim him. He was only half aware of being dragged into a place where he could take shuddering, retching gasps of air so cold that it burned his lungs. He lay helpless as a baby while a fiery liquid was tipped into his mouth, making him cough and gag. He opened his eyes, staring upwards at a sky that shone with dazzling specks of floating ice. The tarrazim warrior knelt beside him with a flask in his hand. Gauthier groaned and rolled over, slowly piecing together what had just happened. What had been a deep valley was now a chaos of lumpy snow. There was no sign of the road nearby, but a horseshoe curve appeared around the inside of a side valley a few hundred paces away; he and his companion had probably been sheltered from the avalanche's main force by an arm of the mountain.

'Thank you.' Gauthier looked the tarrazim in the eye.

'Ten gold.' The man grimaced.

'Horse?' Gauthier made riding motions with his hands.

'No horse. No *kaws*.' The tarrazim made bow-pulling motions with his hands. He spat another, monosyllabic word, rose to his feet and staggered uphill over the snow. Gauthier managed to roll onto his knees, stand, and follow. They stopped where they could see directly up the valley. A thousand paces away a great, grey sheet of bare rock scarred the mountain on the northern side. All else was an impassable chaos of snow.

The tarrazim fell to his knees, spread his arms wide, and began to sing in a high, ululating voice that Gauthier guessed was a chant of mourning for his brothers.

Gauthier spat his own expletives. He had no way of knowing whether the avalanche had also killed Jarl Magnus's party and the witch Adelais, but he and the warrior could not go on, even if the path had been open. They had no horses, no food and no means of shelter. No weapons save the swords that had been buckled to their bodies. And if they did find the girl alive, they would probably be outnumbered. It would be a long walk back to the inn.

At least the advance party would still be in place. The role of the larger group had only been to push the girl and her party forwards, and prevent escape.

Perhaps the avalanche had done the task for them.

5.6 ADELAIS

Adelais had braced herself against the boiling wall of ice, expecting to be hit by a crushing brutality, but the reality was more like kneeling under a waterfall, as snow and ice thumped into her back, wrapped itself around her, and held her. It became a suffocating pressure as light turned from white to grey to a luminous dark. The cascade may have stopped, or it may have been so far above her that she could no longer feel it. The cold gripped even her head until it would not move, not even a finger's width, but she could bite and found her mouth filled with ice and a fold of her hood. She tried to flail, to swim upwards through this weight, but only the arm that had been high on her staff moved. That now gripped nothing, but her forearm was only lightly held and could wave, widening the gap, until a column of air reached her face. She took a great, shuddering gasp and rocked her shoulder side to side until she'd shifted enough snow to stand.

Powdery ice was still falling, thick enough to narrow her world to an arm's length. The edges of the boulder were barely visible, merely darker patches in the cloud. Adelais left her staff upright in the snow and dug like a dog, hand over hand, at the swelling beside her in the snow that must be Revna. The ageing *seidhkona*'s eyes were closed but she coughed through blue-tinged lips when Adelais cleared her face.

'Got to get up, *mynn frú*. Help me dig the others out.'

The fog was thinning. Enough to see the edge of the rock clearly, and a virgin surface beyond. The road had disappeared and was just a snow-filled gully, humped above the place where the shield wall had formed, with a lone spear spiking upwards. Beyond it a snow mound heaved as Hjálmar erupted through, gasping. He stared at her, chest working, before he dived back at the snow, feeling his way to the others. Adelais slid off the rock and used her staff to probe for Magnus.

He was alive; his shield had created a pocket of air around his head. His eyes darted around him wildly after they'd cleared enough snow for him to stand. Three of his warriors lived as well. The fourth had been closest to the boulder, where the ice seemed to have fallen most thickly, like a drift. Adelais thought it strange that his body should still have enough heat to melt the snow on his face, even though no breath misted the air in front of his mouth. The avalanche had crushed the rim of his shield against his head, leaving a slightly curving furrow across his cheek that did not fill, like a lopsided smile. Would he spend eternity with that mark on his face?

'*Fordœmdur* girl!' Magnus had recovered enough breath to swear at her. He knelt by his warrior's body. 'Forty winters I have known him. He'd be alive now but for you and your *fjakkinn* notions!'

'Would he, Father? Fifteen bows against seven swords?' Hjálmar waved downhill at the nightmare jumbling of snow-slabs emerging like miniature mountains through the thinning fog. The main impact seemed to have been several hundred paces below them; the road and their pursuers might never have existed.

'At least he would have died facing the enemy, with a sword in his hand.'

'He did, remember?' Adelais had seen them kneeling behind their shields, swords drawn. She was too tired to argue. A great weight of exhaustion had settled on her like a second icefall. At least she could breathe. She turned away, looking up the valley for Ulfhild and the horses.

The ice had not covered Ulfhild, but the horse lines had broken; their tracks churned through the fresh snow towards the rockfall where Adelais had seen the wolf. Ulfhild had managed to hold one; it was dragging her away, bucking, but the girl was refusing to let go. Only Allier stood facing her, trailing reins, quivering in his fear, his nostrils so flared that they shone pink; two snorting dots of colour against the snow. Of the other horses there was no sign.

Adelais walked up to Allier, slowly, arms wide until she could gather the reins and wrap her arms around his neck.

'Oh, my brave boy.' What it must have taken for him to master his instinct to flee, the whole herd's instinct to flee, just to wait for her. Her eyes prickled, dewing at the horse's courage, humbled by their bond. She could have stayed there, with her cheek against his warmth, and slept on her feet, but Ulfhild's struggles brought her back to reality. The girl had no idea how to calm a horse. Adelais helped her, and with that gentling they found a moment's peace, a strange harmony of two women and two horses. Adelais looped Allier's reins over her shoulder and pulled Ulfhild into a hug. She wasn't sure which of them needed it more. It lasted until the crump of boots in snow told them Hjálmar was coming, and Ulfhild pulled back. She managed a nervous smile, wide enough to show those slightly splayed teeth. Her eyes shone with wonder.

'Did you just do that, mistress?'

Adelais shrugged. 'The gods did it. Only Revna knew how to call them. I...'

What had she done? Many men had just died. She should feel something. Guilt. Triumph. Anything but this numb tiredness.

'Come, *kjúkling*.' Adelais used the same, affectionate word she'd taught Agnès, *chick*, and saw Ulfhild's face brighten. 'You did well.' She gathered the reins and prepared to mount. 'Now let's go and find their friends.'

'Not on your own.' Hjálmar put a great, fur-gauntleted hand on her arm to stop her. 'Just in case this is not finished.' His beard was dusted with ice that had become tiny droplets of water near his mouth.

'But they're all dead.' Adelais waved down the valley.

'You yourself said they might be chasing us towards something. An ambush. A battleground of their own choosing, perhaps. We go together, armed for battle.'

Adelais looked down the valley, now filled with a new, smaller mountain of snow. Icy slabs of it projected into the air like pieces of broken pottery. 'Well, we can't go back.'

'And if any of them still live, beyond that fall, they can't follow.' Hjálmar lifted a hand as if he wanted to make some gesture, but let it drop. 'What my father said—'

'It does not matter.'

'You did well.'

'Revna knew which runes to sing.'

This time his fingers touched her shoulder, though she could not feel it through the armour. 'Now let us find the horses, or we have a long walk to Heilagtré.'

Adelais pulled herself into Allier's saddle, wishing they could just stay where they were, light a fire, and sleep.

They heard the first of their other horses before they saw it. Beyond the rockfall, one horse had fallen in its panic and lay on its side, screaming, with one leg clearly useless. Two others were still entangled with it by a trailing line and were trying to pull free, tugging it over every time it tried to rise. Hjálmar killed the injured animal swiftly, with a single blow of a war hammer. He handed the reins of the other two to Magnus and Revna. He had to help Revna to mount; she seemed close to collapse. Adelais understood that exhaustion; her grandmother and Elyse had been the same. So much effort, so much intensity went into rune song that it had left them as tired as a warrior after battle.

'If they were planning any more surprises, it will be soon.' Magnus rocked in his saddle, frowning as he scanned the path ahead. 'It is where I would choose.'

'Why, *mynn drottinn?*'

'This stretch of the pass is called Thor's Footsteps.' He nodded uphill, where the road climbed towards the saddle between two mountains. Two hundred paces of gentler ground rose to a low cliff that had been cut into a gorge where the road passed on to the next level. 'There is another like this beyond. After that the land falls away more gently towards Heilagtré. If I wanted to make sure none escaped, I'd block the road and put archers on the cliffs while my main force came up the road.'

Adelais scanned the skyline along the next cliff. She saw no movement.

'I'm sorry I shouted at you.' Magnus met her eye as she turned. 'He was an old friend.'

'I understand.' She was too tired to think of a more polished answer.

'Stay near me, *mynn frú.*'

Adelais was as surprised by Magnus's honorific as she was by the apology.

Magnus sent Hjálmar and his surviving warrior ahead, on foot. No one spoke as they watched them walk up the gorge, their shields held high before them and their necks craned towards the cliffs above. There was a collective sigh when

Hjálmar waved them to follow, as if they'd all forgotten to breathe.

Another cliff lay across their path about two hundred paces ahead of them, though they could not see where the road cut through to the next level; the valley broadened and curved around the last shoulder of the mountain, making a pattern like a footprint. Above them, on each side, bare mountainsides offered no cover for archers. Ulfhild's horse pricked its ears and trotted forwards, responding to the high whinny of a horse from around the bend.

'Stay back!' Hjálmar bellowed at her.

But Ulfhild did not have the skill to contain her horse. 'He can hear his friends!' She turned in the saddle, grinning over her shoulder at them, not realising the danger.

And then Adelais knew a terrible sense of impending doom; her thoughts outran the pace of her mortal body and she was condemned to watch while still filling her chest to scream. She knew she would remember the moment for evermore; the girl who idolised her, all teeth and laughter, with her golden maiden's braids shining in the westering sun as the first arrow hit her full in the chest. It struck with the noise of a stick beating dust out of a carpet, and its impact slammed Ulfhild back in the saddle. She was held there by the high cantle, even as the horse spun, so their eyes met. It was only an instant, but long enough for Adelais to see the pleading disbelief in Ulfhild's eyes and the flowering of blood between her teeth. Even as Adelais let out a silent *no!* a second arrow struck Ulfhild between arm and breast, tumbling her sideways to the ground.

Three tarrazim came galloping around the bend in the road; two archers in the lead, both already nocking another arrow to their strings, and, at the rear, one with a lance – a captain, perhaps, more richly dressed than the others. A calm, detached part of her mind admired the effortless way they controlled their mounts, but her overwhelming reaction was sheer, elemental fury. Her scream as she drew her sword came from deep inside her, from gut and heart and soul. It did not occur to her that it was brave or foolish to charge the nearest bowman; it was the natural eruption of raw anger, and if she heard Hjál-mar's shouts to come back, form a line, they did not matter. These men had killed Ulfie. There was the briefest of moments when she saw her assailant draw, turn his body to aim at her, and she realised her own madness.

She had begun to twist in the saddle, trying too late to dodge the shot, when the arrow punched into her own right breast, pinning her fur vest to her armour and kicking her backwards, unbalancing her so that her sword's point dropped. Allier jumped beneath her, correcting her balance as a trained and loyal warhorse, though still galloping towards the enemy. The pain as Adelais straightened told her that the point had penetrated the leather, into her body, but perhaps not mortally; she was able to bellow an obscenity and was close enough to see the man's eyes widen in shock that she had not gone down. He had no time for another arrow and was still reaching down to draw his sword when Adelais spun Allier, riding without thought, all instinct, but an instinct that unleashed both his hind hooves into the other horse's shoulder. She continued the turn, swinging full circle with her sword raised, but the tarrazim horse and rider were falling. They hit the ground in a flailing tumble of limbs and with a noise like a miniature avalanche. The rider rolled free, but Hjálmar was running towards him, hefting his war hammer. His eyes flicked towards the arrow embedded in her chest.

It hurt. A lot. A sharp, cutting pain, as if someone had pushed a knife into her breast, hard enough to break the skin but probably not enough to punch through the ribs. Adelais owed her life to an armourer's lustful fantasy, and perhaps to the arrow striking at an angle rather than square, but the point had still passed through her fur vest and the thickened leather beneath. She hunched over, making space between the razor-sharp tip and her softness, and tugged at the shaft with her left hand. It would not move.

Behind her, Magnus and his surviving warriors were trying to surround the other archer. She heard the *thunk* of an arrow striking a shield, and Revna chanting.

'*Týr er einhendr áss...*' The rune song of Tyr, the victory-rune.

Allier began to dance beneath her, tuned to the sounds of combat, until she could hardly contain him. *By the gods, that arrow hurt.* Better to sit straight and endure the point in her breast than to hunch and let herself move against it.

'*Ok ulfs leifar...*'

Some instinct made her look up. Fifty paces away the captain still blocked the road, but his skywards-pointing lance began to drop as he began his charge. At her.

'*Ok hofa hilmir...*'

The world seemed sharper and clearer than she had ever known. High mountains, shining snow. A fog of breath under the nostrils of the charging horse, whipped away and lost. The man's face grimacing with determination, eyes focused on the point where his lance would strike her body. The hammer-on-anvil sounds of combat behind her, and the thunder of hooves in front. And a lance tip that fell so gracefully towards her. Her own sword upright before her eye, its edge a line of shining light. A warm, spreading stickiness inside her armour. The lance now couched across the charging horse's neck in the way of knightly combat, shield arm to shield arm. Adelais touched her spur against Allier's dancing side, a warning not a command. *Be ready. We will go left, the other way. Wait. Wait.*

Now! Adelais put her right spur into Allier's flank and the warhorse leapt sideways, across the path of the charging man-at-arms. She twisted in the saddle to let the lance pass in front of her chest and felt the arrow tip carve her again. She recovered, ignoring the pain, and swung her sword in a flat, scything blow at the man's face.

'*Thurs er kvenna kvöl...*'

It was not a heavy blow. She expected the scoring pain across her breast from the arrow's tip, but it was still enough to make her wince so that she felt rather than saw her sword's edge bite into the bridge of the man's nose. A jarring impact twisted her body as his momentum wrenched her blade backwards and dragged it across his eyes. The arrow sliced her again and she screamed, folding over in the saddle. The tarrazim also screamed, a high note of agony. Over her jolting shoulder she saw he'd dropped his lance and had both hands palmed to his face. Hjálmar and one of his men were running forwards, hefting weapons.

Adelais knew she was spent. She barely managed to bring Allier to a halt before she folded over, slumped in the saddle, her sword trailing towards the ground. There was no blood on her body that she could see; the arrow pinned the fur vest to her chest, but the bleeding was all under her armour. Its stickiness spread down her belly, reached her hip, and made little runnels down her groin between thigh and saddle. If she didn't know better, she'd think she'd pissed herself. She blinked, trying to stay awake. *Mustn't fall. Might push it in further.*

In front of her, the cliff had been cut into a narrow defile where the road passed through to the top of the pass. This narrow gorge had clearly been blocked with fir trees, newly pulled aside to let the tarrazim through. The remainder of their own horses milled around the open space between her and the defile. The clatter of combat behind her had ended, but there were running boots coming up behind her. She ought to look. Ought to be worried. But she could barely sit to Allier's dancing. Could no longer straighten even if she wanted to. Could not lift a sword. Running boots and the drumming of hooves.

Hjálmar appeared by her side, war hammer ready, shield up, positioning himself between her and a galloping horse; the last of the bowmen had broken off combat and was fleeing. Her head swaying with exhaustion, she watched him reach the point where the track entered the defile. When he'd gone, perhaps she could sleep.

A snarling blur of white and grey detached itself from the rim of the defile and took the bowman in the throat, sweeping him out of the saddle to lie in a kicking, yet strangely silent, heap on the track. The loose horses scattered, panicking. Adelais blinked and the patterns snarling over the fallen man resolved themselves into the wolf, now sending the fallen man into a final spasm with a vicious wrench that sprayed blood on the snow.

The she-wolf's forepaws were either side of the man's shoulders, pinning him to the ground. She looked up towards Adelais, panting, blood on her muzzle. If Adelais could have mustered the energy to lift her sword, she'd have saluted the beast, but all she could do was stare and mutter 'Amma'. The she-wolf made no acknowledgement, but limped unsteadily up the track, leaving her own trail of blood.

'She's hurt.' Adelais tried to point after the wolf, but lifting her arm would have taken too much effort.

'So are you.' Hjálmar sounded quite tender. She liked that. He stood by her knee, though he was big enough for his head and shoulders to be above the level of Allier's withers.

'Can't get off.' She managed a weak smile. If she tried to dismount, she'd fall. Might fall anyway.

'Lean on me. Come on, brace your head against my shoulder while I pull that thing out.'

She let her sword drop. She might have toppled over onto the ground if Hjálmar hadn't braced her. He pulled her gently forwards, lowering her shoulders until her head rested in the angle of his neck. She could feel the heat of his body and wished she wasn't wearing a bascinet. Her body moved painfully against the arrow tip but with a downwards jolt the sharpness was gone, leaving the stickiness of blood pooling inside her armour. She let Hjálmar gather her into his arms and lift her off Allier's back. For a moment she liked that; it made her feel female and vulnerable and protected, but her body moved within her armour, twisting the cuts, and she yelped like an underfoot puppy.

Hjálmar laid her on a fur that Revna spread over the snow. She was a little disappointed to hear him sent away while Revna arranged a tent of cloaks over lances above her, and unbuckled her armour. Inside, her gown had been shredded where the arrow's point had carved a criss-cross pattern of cuts between her nipple and her breast bone.

'Drink.' Revna held a leather flask to her lips. The liquor inside made Adelais choke. Revna trickled some of the spirit onto her wounds, causing Adelais to growl like the wolf that had saved them, her fingers clenching at the cloak that had been laid beneath her.

'The wolf is hurt. *Fylgja*. Amma.' Adelais had been light-headed even before the spirits spread their fire though her belly. Now she was finding it hard to talk clearly. She gasped again as Revna daubed at the wounds with a spirit-soaked rag. Adelais grabbed the flask out of her hands and swigged again, wondering why Revna was looking so hard at the cuts. Adelais formed the bizarre impression that some of the bird skulls on Revna's necklace were staring at her too.

'What's the matter?' Adelais peered downwards. The wounds were all in the soft flesh of her breast, none deep enough to reach the ribs, but they were bleeding steadily. Adelais wished Revna would just cover them and stop wiping them with the rag. *Sœtur Sif*, that stung. It was pulling at the lips of the cuts and soon she'd start whimpering with the pain.

Perhaps she had some salve? No *seidhkona* would travel without a small stock of cures.

'*Ansuz.*' Revna traced the lines of cuts with her fingertip, not quite touching the flesh, pointing out the rune of Odhinn. 'You are rune-marked.'

ᚠ

Ansuz, the god-rune.

Adelais shook her head. 'Nah. If I were to be rune-marked, it would be *thurs*.' The rune of Thor. She'd sung it in front of the high priest and the high priest had died. 'My Amma used to call me *mynn litla Sif* after the wife of Thor.' Adelais thought she might be muttering nonsense. Why was she so tired? Not just blood loss, though her shirt was saturated. Always tired after rune song. And battle.

Revna began smearing a paste onto the cuts, her touch feather-light but still enough to bring Adelais back from the edge of sleep.

'I danced to rune song again, didn't I?' She tried to sit up, against the pain. There was something she needed to do. 'Must help the wolf.'

Revna pushed at her chest, high on the unwounded side, forcing her back onto the cloak and making shushing noises.

Adelais let her head fall backwards. *So tired.*

The cold woke Adelais; it seeped through the layered cloaks and furs beneath her, touching her backside and shoulders with ice. At first she was disoriented; she could see nothing above her, nothing that would tell her where she was, or whose snores were rumbling gently beside her. She turned her head to look, and that slight movement dragged pain across her breast, sharp as fishhooks, and she remembered. Men's voices murmured nearby, too low for her to hear their words. A fire burned beyond the tented cloaks; flashes of red light flickered through a gap and showed Revna's face beside her, slack in sleep, mouth open.

Adelais pushed back her coverings and eased her way out of the tent, cradling one arm lest she pull the skin around her breast. Cloak-wrapped, still booted, she stood and breathed a crisp, windless night, beneath a shining canopy of stars.

She had not slept for long; the lamb moon was still rising over the mountains, silver as the snow beneath. A few paces away Magnus and his warriors sat on logs around a fire, looking at her, a new respect in their eyes. She smelt roasting meat and burning pine. Their horses stood in a silent huddle a little further away, sharing warmth, a many-legged mass against the white. One, larger than the rest, lifted his head and looked at her. Allier. Two other tents had been set up beneath the cliff; proper tents, leather over willow. She did not recognise them. A pile of scavenged weapons lay outside: swords, a lance, tarrazim bows, quivers of arrows. She'd take one of those bows when they left.

'Come. Eat.' Magnus lifted something towards her. 'It is only horse, but it is fresh.'

Adelais sat, gratefully. Magnus had laid a bloody, scorched slice onto waybread, the thrice-baked rations of the road. She realised she was ravenous, even for horsemeat.

'Where is Hjálmar?' she asked, chewing.

'He took the first watch. Up there.' Magnus lifted his chin towards the road where it cut into the cliff.

Adelais straightened. In the starlight she'd just seen the carcass of a horse further back down the track, and beyond that a line of six bodies lying in the snow. Two lay a little apart, arranged with honour; one had a sword clasped in dead hands on his chest.

'Six?' She mentally counted: their own warrior; the tarrazim with the lance; two archers. Ulfie. She shouldn't be lying in the snow like that. She'd be cold. Adelais still couldn't think of her as dead.

'There was another, waiting above. Your wolf had been busy.'

'Where is she?' The she-wolf had been limping the last time Adelais had seen her.

'Nearby.' Another jerk of the chin. 'She is badly hurt. She will die, I think. If she cannot run, she cannot hunt.'

Adelais stood. 'Give me some of that horsemeat.' She wasn't going to let the she-wolf die without trying to save her. She also took a stoppered bottle of Revna's salve from inside their tent.

The defile had been blocked by fir trees. That must have been what was fuelling the fire, and why their horses had not bolted further. She realised that this ambush had been planned days in advance; even in summer nothing grew up here but grasses. Someone had scouted their route, chosen their ambush site, and dragged the trees for several leagues. Hjálmar and Magnus must have brought the enemy's tents down to the shelter below the cliff.

Hjálmar sat on his shield where the track levelled above the cliff. When he saw her, he stood, fur-wrapped and massive against the mountain.

'How are you feeling?'

'Better. I needed to sleep. I'm always tired after rune song.'

'You did well.'

'Revna knew what to do. I just got angry.'

'But you did well, just the same. I only had to run after you and sweep up your mess.' Hjálmar spoke lightly, teasing her. 'May I offer you a throne, princess?' He made a courtly gesture towards his shield.

She shook her head. 'Is that the wolf?' A black hump lay in the snow, fifty paces away.

'She will let no one come close.'

'Will you stay here? Please?' Adelais stepped towards the wolf, ignoring Hjálmar's whispered pleas to take care. Her boots crumped in the snow.

The wolf's ears twitched towards her. At twenty paces it let out a low growl of warning and she stopped. The ears had gone back, flat to the head.

'I have brought you food, Amma.'

The ears swivelled forwards. Eyes glinted. In daylight, they would be blue, impossibly blue, like her grandmother's. In the semi-dark they were points of starlight in the blackness. Adelais sensed a tension within the wolf; that which was wild, and that which loved. The wildness was trapped by the will of the other, and was therefore dangerous. The loved and the wild were both warning her not to come closer. She laid the meat on the snow and backed away. Only when she was standing by Hjálmar did the wolf rise to its feet and stagger over to the meat, sniffing it before snatching it away and limping back to its bloodied snow hole.

She let Hjálmar give her the shield. He tucked his cloak beneath his backside and sank into the snow beside her. It seemed strange for their eyes to be on a level.

'They were waiting for us. Knew we were coming.' She hunched further into her cloak. The betrayal must have begun in Siltehafn, even before they set out.

'And whoever planned this had money. Money and influence.' Hjálmar spoke towards the wolf, now holding meat between its forepaws and tearing it with its teeth.

'Were there really only four of them?' Adelais looked around at the empty mountainside. They were at the crest of the pass; she sensed the land falling away beyond a near horizon.

'They wouldn't have needed any more, with the road

blocked and others following us. But for that wolf, this would have been our slaughter ground.'

'Then why weren't they waiting up here?'

'They will have heard the avalanche and seen our riderless horses. They probably came down to investigate.'

'They might have been after Magnus, or you.'

'No. When they came upon us, they ignored armed warriors and fired at a golden-haired girl, the least threatening member of our group. You were their target. When the leader realised their mistake, he charged you, even though he was outnumbered and should have run back to safety behind his barrier. That took courage. And commitment.'

'They too were people. Maybe even with families.' Adelais felt the sick guilt that came after killing.

'Their families will receive their gold. Half the fee, for men who died with their target still alive. Double for the man who makes the kill. It is the tarrazim way.'

'And if whoever hired them does not pay?'

'They kill any client who defaults. Always. That too is their way.'

Adelais felt a little less guilty. Just an aching sorrow at the thought of Ulfhild, lying cold in the snow.

'You have powerful enemies, princess.'

'So who would have the money to hire tarrazim?' If she ever went back to Siltehafn, she would need to know.

'Only the great nobles. And perhaps the Ischyrian temples. It is easier to say who would gain from your death. And, incidentally, mine and my father's.'

The wolf finished the meat and looked up, expectantly. Adelais stood, awkwardly. 'I'll fetch her more. Then you can tell me who that might be.'

This time the wolf allowed her a little closer.

Adelais settled back on the shield. 'So who?'

'I've been thinking. Two possibilities. One is an agent of Galmandie itself. That noblewoman who visited...'

'Agnès? Impossible!'

'Then someone close enough to the court to know that you were being sent north. The greatest Ischyrian nobles in Vriesland are Theignault and Sjóland, though it would be a brave man that accused either of them of treachery.'

'Or?'

'The duchess herself.'

'*What?*'

'I think you threaten her. She will have seen how Ragener looks at you.'

'But I threatened to shrivel his balls.'

'You're young. The people love you already. She's barren. And she knows that saying no to Ragener will only make him want you more. What if he offered to divorce her and make you his duchess?'

'Nothing would be worth having that lump of pork fat rut on me.'

'She doesn't know you feel like that. There wouldn't be many weaver's daughters who'd turn down a duchy.'

'*Skit.*' Adelais hugged her legs and settled her chin on her knees. The wolf watched her across the shining snow. Hjálmar bumped her with his shoulder.

'Is there room on that shield for two, princess? I can't feel my *rass.*'

She laughed, glad for the lightening of the mood. There was barely enough space; they had to sit back to back, she perched on an edge, he overflowing the rest. It was companionable. And in a way they'd made a team during that skirmish; she toppling them, him finishing them. Him being there, protecting her when she couldn't fight any more. Adelais passed Revna's leather flask of spirits over her shoulder with her left hand, the one that didn't hurt to move.

'Here. Drink. Warm our watch.'

Hjálmar uncorked it, sniffed, and swigged.

'Why do you call me princess?' She took back the flask and sipped. *Sætur Sif*, that was good.

'My father says you could be the mother of kings. I think he rather likes you too.'

Adelais groaned. Not another ageing noble who wanted to *fjakk* her.

'Well, a mother of kings could be a queen,' Hjálmar continued, 'but I don't want you to get ideas above your station.' Hjálmar held up his hand for the flask.

'I'm no more a princess than you are a troll. And I'm flattered. But Jarl Magnus is really old.'

'I'm not.' He spoke in the same, teasing tone.

'Don't get ideas yourself, troll-man.'

She felt his laugh as much as heard it; a rumbling chuckle where their backs touched.

'Besides...' Adelais paused. She wondered how they could laugh. Friends lay dead by the road below them. And she'd killed again. She'd promised herself she'd never do that.

'Besides?'

'Every time I grow close to someone they die.' Arnaud. Humbert. Ulfhild. Her mood was swinging. Now she was closer to tears than laughter.

'So if you're unkind to me, I shall take it as a great compliment,' he said.

There was still a little laughter left within her, like the dregs of wine. She let her head fall back against his shoulder. His slow breathing rocked her.

'*Sætur Sif*, I hate killing.'

'Sometimes it is necessary.'

'When we're fighting I feel proud. Invincible. So tuned with

Allier that we are one being. Afterwards, I feel dirty beyond all cleaning.'

'Today they were trying to kill you.'

'And Ragener still wants me to lead men to war.'

'Then stay behind the shield wall, princess. It will spare me having to clean up your mess.'

She thumped her head backwards into his neck.

'*Fjakkinn* troll-man.'

CHAPTER SIX

6.1 ADELAIS

Adelais tied one of the tarrazim bows to her saddle on the morning after the skirmish. Its broad scabbard hung behind and to the left of Allier's saddle and was balanced by a capacious quiver on the right that she filled with arrows. When her chest was healed she'd teach herself to use it. Meanwhile, it was both a trophy and a statement. *Even the tarrazim failed.* Once in a while she felt she'd earned the right to be defiant.

When they first left the pass, dropping down towards Heilagtré, Adelais looked over her shoulder, reluctant to leave Ulfhild's body behind. They'd laid the dead together in one of the leather tarrazim tents and made a snow-cairn over it to keep out carrion birds and wolves. Magnus said he'd send men and a sled from Heilagtré, but it still felt wrong.

The wolf kept pace with them, half-seen through the trees as it lurched on three legs with one forepaw lifted high. It rested nearby when they stopped each evening in one of the empty wayfarers' cabins beside the road. Their stocks of waybread and dried fruit were shrinking, but they had plenty of horsemeat. Adelais took some to the wolf each night, approaching slowly and carrying her grandmother's richly carved staff, not as a weapon but as an emblem of the bond she felt between them. On the second night the wolf allowed her to smear salve into the cut, a deep knife or sword slash across one shoulder. She sang the rune song of *Úruz* as she worked; a rune of strength and healing, of endurance and power. *Úr er skýja grátr, ok skára thverrir, ok hirdhis hatr.* It seemed to calm the beast, which made a low, half-threatening growl as she worked, and a single yelp as her fingers probed, but did not bite.

She too began to heal, but she didn't like the way her scabs made a crusted representation of the *ansuz* rune. She'd always been embarrassed by her small breasts, and now she'd have an additional shame if she ever bared them to a lover; she'd look as if Odhinn had branded her. That would be enough to put off any man. She moved carefully lest she open up the wound, and smeared Revna's salve onto the cuts night and morning. By the fourth day they were starting to itch, and it took willpower not to scratch.

By then the wolf was putting all four paws to the ground. Low, freezing cloud had blanketed them all day, but Adelais could see it limping through the trees, about fifty paces from them.

'It is wild,' Magnus grumbled beside her, 'and to the wild it must return. It frightens the horses.'

'She saved our lives,' Adelais replied. 'I will not let her die.'

'Soon you must let it run and hunt.'

'She is free to go, but I think it is too soon. And while she stays, I will feed her.'

'And at Heilagtré? Among people? We will be there before nightfall.'

As Adelais watched, the wolf stumbled badly on its injured side, and her heart went out to it. 'I will leave it more meat. Perhaps it will be enough until she can hunt.'

. . .

As Magnus had predicted, before dusk the road had dropped down a hillside and delivered them below the cloud. Winter still lingered on this side of the mountains; trees spiked the snow above an expanse of water the colour of polished armour. The shoreline curved away on either side; it might have been a bay of the Ice Sea or a vast lake. The horizon was indistinct, mere shadings of grey. A wooded island perhaps half a league long lay at the centre of this great bowl, connected to a sprawling settlement on the land by a wooden bridge broad enough for two carts to pass. The smoke of its hearths made a darker layer of haze beneath the cloud.

The settlement was the size of a town, but made of a small cluster of houses and an outlying rim of guest halls, all with paddocks that were trampled brown by horses and spotted yellow with mounds of winter forage. A city like Siltehafn was a place where many lived and some visited; Heilagtré was a place where few lived but many visited. A line of ships had been drawn up on the strand, their masts unstepped, their black oilcloth winter coverings patterned with snow so they looked like roosting seabirds. A few were moored to jetties in the water, their masts bare and upright, their sails rolled and laid fore to aft along their decks. Hundreds of people milled between the halls and the strand, and a crowd was gathering to watch their arrival.

Adelais reined in on the last slope before Heilagtré, taking in the scene. Of their party, only Hjálmar stayed with her, but she was too nervous for their usual banter. Here she would be tested, and she did not know how. Ragener had turned her into a figurehead, the *örlaga vefari*, the fate-weaver, when all she wanted was to live peacefully. And was it time to say farewell to the she-wolf? She turned in the saddle, looking for it.

There, on the fringes of the forest; a pattern of grey, brown, and white that blended with the trees behind. The wolf was watching Adelais the way Allier sometimes watched her from pasture; ears pricked, focused, as if waiting for her call.

'Goodbye, Amma.' The moment was strange and Adelais's cry was gentle, slightly disbelieving of this unearthly communion she felt with a wolf and which no one else would understand. Beside her Hjálmar also twisted to watch. At least he did not laugh.

But the wolf came towards her, one paw at a time, and the link between them told Adelais of a battle between that which was wild and that which was *fylgja*; to enter the world of men or to run. There was another battle, but purely of mind and muscle; the battle to dominate the pain and conquer the limp, and to show no weakness even though the walk was too stiff to be natural.

As the wolf came closer, Hjálmar's horse snorted and wheeled away. Only Allier would accept its presence within ten paces, though Adelais sensed that they did not like each other; they were too much predator and prey for anything more than tolerance. When the wolf was close, Allier would dance under her, curved on the bit, needing her reassurance.

Thus Adelais entered Heilagtré like a true princess, with Jarl Magnus, his three warriors and Revna riding before, and Hjálmar behind. She rode alone in their midst, drawing stares; a young woman on a mighty warhorse, with a knight's sword on her hip, the richly carved staff of a *seidhkona* slung from her shoulder, and a tarrazim bow behind her saddle. At her side a huge she-wolf walked with a broad-shouldered, stamping gait, exchanging snarls with the settlement's dogs. Adelais could understand the stares. *But what if I'm not what they're seeking?*

Warriors in gilded helmets stopped them before the entrance to the bridge, and directed them away from the island. Accommodation would be prepared for them and their horses, they were told, and they would be presented to the *gydhjur* on the morrow. The word '*gydhjur*', for the priestesses of the sacred isle, was spoken with reverence. They should carry no weapons in their presence.

The guards turned from them, distracted, as the wolf walked on towards the bridge. It stopped in front of a young woman who had stepped into the road, almost as if she was greeting the wolf. She had the face of a girl new-grown to womanhood, younger even than Adelais, but her eyes held the wisdom of ages and she leaned on a staff like a crone. Despite her youth she wore the cat-skin cloak of a *seidhkona* around her shoulders. One of the guards half-drew his sword as if to protect her, but the girl-woman held up her hand to stay him.

No words were spoken, though Adelais sensed that much was understood. The girl merely nodded to the wolf, and gestured towards the island as if bidding her welcome, and the wolf went forwards alone. There was something in the beast's awkward gait, that determination not to limp, that evoked her grandmother as she had last known her, walking into the distance, leaning on her staff, willing herself to stay strong.

6.2 FYLGJA

The struggle to master the wolf within her is easier now. There was a time, high in the mountains, when the girl was too close, too trusting of this wildness. She, *fylgja*, had been too full of the joy of the girl's touch. So many moons, so many winters in the counting of men, since they touched. The knife wound in her flank was a tiny price to pay to hear the girl's voice singing the songs of healing, to feel her fingers smooth salve into the cut. But the wolf within almost broke free in that sweet moment when she forgot she was *fylgja* and remembered herself as one who had been woman-kind and loved. For several heartbeats she'd had to hold the beast's jaws shut by force of will, as though she were a master gripping the muzzle of a hound.

It has taken time to teach this wolf, whose whole life has seen people as the herders of prey and the killers of wolf-kind. People are the enemy, best avoided. Yet each night when the girl has brought food, it has been easier, and each day she has felt the pull of this place where the warp and weft of fate thrum so strongly. With her ears she hears no more than the natural sounds of wind through trees and hooves on frozen earth, but she *feels* the drumbeat of destiny more loudly than any staff on a *seidhr*-platform.

It is easy now for the wolf to follow the girl, for she is leading them into the homeland of Geri and Freki, the wolves of Odhinn. This is a mightier pack than ever hunted elk beyond the passes, and she knows herself to be welcome within it. There are more people here, and many dogs, and she forces herself to walk without sign of pain. It is the way of the wild; the weak and wounded are singled out and killed, the hunter becoming the prey, while the strong and whole run free. She hunches her shoulders and snarls at these dogs of men. They are right to fear her.

A figure greets her, outwardly of woman-kind, but one who shimmers with possibilities. From her hands, she trails the faintest threads that move like ribbons of silt in water; they have no beginning, and flow on to an unseen ending. She is the one who weaves that which may come into being. There is a bargain, unspoken but as real as those unseen threads. No, not a bargain, an offering. Of herself.

The girl will be tested. What will you give to save her?
My life.
So be it.

6.3 TAILLEFER

Taillefer de Remy reined in his horse on the crest of a low hill outside Molinot, planning his approach. The dome of a temple glinted in the distance, and temples had priests. Priests travelled, and although Molinot was beyond the borders of his province, the risk of his being recognised was real even though he wore a plain woollen herigaut beneath his cloak, not the scarlet robe of a diakonos. On his head was the unfamiliar weight of a broad-brimmed, oiled-wool hat, not the blood-red cap of a pardoner. He'd set out after the dawn office, fully robed and ostensibly on a tour of distant temples. But he had emerged from woodland before noon in the drab, winter clothes a petty official might wear; someone respectable but not affluent. The quality of his horse might give him away, but his love for this mare was too well known around his palace – it would have been most unusual had he ridden out on another. There were already enough questions about him travelling alone, without raising further suspicions.

He was doing the work of the God. So why did he feel so guilty? He had lies ready on the tongue; he could be a steward taking a message, using his lord's horse. What had started as an easy deception risked dragging him into ever greater sin. Thank the God he'd had no reason to use those lies. He carried a hunting sword on his hip; a short, broad-leafed blade that was permitted to the priesthood in the way that warriors' swords were not, and he was glad he had not had to use it; no thief had tried to take his lovely mare. He had broken no vows. Yet.

The River Gaelle lay in a shining arc across his path, winding its way towards the Saxen Sea. To the west it reflected the sinking sun, and to the north the sky's blue; the cold blue of a clear, lamb moon day when the hedgerows rang with birdsong. In front, the road ran downhill and joined a greater road that followed the river all the way from Villebénie, the capital, to the sea. This evening it was empty of traffic. A lesser track beyond the junction led through the newly ploughed furrows of arable fields towards an unfortified manor house, sitting on a slight rise before the river. The village lay several hundred paces apart; its houses followed a sharp line around the edge of another low hill, as if they had drawn their feet up above some earlier floods and had forgotten to put them back again.

He was growing whimsical. *She* would be in the manor. He would deliver his message, unwelcome as that might be, and leave the following morning. This was an interlude, nothing more.

A woman took his horse at the manor's door. She called him 'Excellency', and dropped a curtsey, and he looked at her sharply. He didn't recognise her at first, even when she lifted her eyes and told him Lady Agnès waited within. Yet there came a memory of that day at Harbin when this woman sat on a gelding with her hands shaking in fright, with the retainers of de Fontenay around her. One of them had been Adelais de Vries and in that moment he'd held all their lives in his hands.

'We meet again, Mistress...?'

'Elyse, Excellency.'

'Just "messire" today, Elyse. I am no one you need remember.'

She inclined her head, and as Taillefer walked into temptation he knew that she, at least, could be trusted.

The manor's solar was already shuttered against the evening's chill. A great fire splashed ruddy colour on plastered walls, and low beams trapped its heat in the room; he could feel it on his face. Agnès stood at a table, pouring wine, and something inside him turned cartwheels at the sight of her.

'I thought we'd talk in here. Much warmer than the hall.' She handed him wine, smiling. 'Cosier.' She made no other greeting. They might already have been together for some time.

Yet there had been the slightest shake to her hand. Questions followed about his journey, spoken too quickly. Her nerves calmed him; he felt more in control. He let her talk, trying not to feel guilty about his pleasure in the moment: cushioned chairs, fine wine, the flush cast across her cheek by the candlelight. It suited her. She had taken care with her appearance – a blue velvet gown, sapphires around her neck, and dark, lustrous hair that only a servant could have arranged so perfectly.

After that welcoming wine, Elyse showed him to a chamber where another fire burned, and brought him warmed water so that he might refresh himself after his journey. 'Dinner will be a while,' she announced, 'since I'm cook and stable boy and lady's maid today.' He took care with his preparations, taking fresh linen from his bags. It was a matter of respect, of course, not seduction.

It was an awkward meal, at first, at the table in the solar. The moment felt unreal; a priest and a woman. Alone. *This* woman, who made him feel like a moth around a candle flame. Conversations would start then stumble, interrupted by Elyse's serving or clearing. Yet in the silences there were shy smiles as if they already shared some secret.

They did. The Hand. Yet that was not why they smiled.

That, by unspoken agreement, was not mentioned until all was cleared away save a platter of cheese, a bowl of dried, sugared fruit, and another jug of wine.

'I have these figs sent from Fontenay.' Agnès nibbled at the delicacy. 'There are whole groves of fig trees in Jourdaine. It is one of the joys of summer.' She was bright-eyed and may have been a little intoxicated. 'There is something almost intimate about a ripe fig.'

Taillefer closed his eyes. This was dangerous. He knew exactly what she meant; that way the soft, purple inside of a fig could seem so like a woman's secret places. He was not completely without experience; there had been a woman, before he took the vows of priesthood...

'I have thought much about the Hand.' Taillefer straightened in his chair.

'Ah, to business.' Agnès could even make that sound flirtatious.

'I think it should stay hidden until it can be protected.'

'My husband has fifty knights sworn to his service in Jourdaine.'

'Then let it stay within Château Fontenay until the new order of knighthood can be raised. Any surviving Guardians would flock to his banner.'

'But only when the Hand has been attested by a clerical court.' Agnès sighed. 'You can't have the lamb without the ram, as they say.'

'As I said in Harbin, if the Hand is revealed before it can be protected, my lady—'

'Agnès, please.'

'Before it can be protected, then one of the warring factions will use it for their own ends. Agnès, I would be so honoured to be the Hand's custodian. I am not worthy. No man is worthy. But I can only fulfil the spiritual role if the Hand's temporal safety is assured. I must ask that Lord Leandre first raise the new Order. His family founded the Guardians, for the God's sake; surely within a year he would have enough good, Ischyrian knights.'

'Leandre may not have a year,' Agnès murmured. 'Powerful people say he is not a good Ischyrian.' She turned to him. 'Including your brother Othon.'

'Othon and I are estranged. I have no influence there. And it is better that the Hand stay hidden, than for the Hand to be used for base purposes.'

Agnès sighed, and the silence stretched while they found a way to move on to easier subjects, yet the silence was easy, more companionable now that the great issue was decided. Taillefer felt himself relax, willing to relish this unique opportunity to enjoy the company of a woman who seemed to take pleasure in his own. In time, their talk turned to other intimacies: their lives; their families, their dreams. By unspoken agreement they danced away from matters that might unsettle their new calm, such as Adelais de Vries or the Hand.

They stayed at the table. There would be a formality about the chairs by the fire, an unnecessary distance. Sitting across a corner they could talk quietly, heads close, and see the way their smiles reached the eyes. Their talk had all the excitement of a first encounter, and all the ease of a couple who have known each other for years. Taillefer watched her lips move, widening in laughter, narrowing in a playful moue at one of his sallies, and felt a sinful urge to kiss them. When she stood, crossed to the fire, and bent to feed it another log, Taillefer let himself watch the firelight caressing her gown. *This is wrong. I am a priest. But so delightful...*

Agnès stirred the flames for longer than seemed necessary, and Taillefer realised she knew he was watching. Welcomed him watching.

'Agnès, do you realise how rare this moment is?'

She straightened and turned, smiling at his use of her name.

'In what way?'

The belt around her waist hung loosely over her hips, so that the buckle hung low, in a broad, downward-pointing arrow-head that emphasised the flatness of her tummy. Taillefer rose to stand with her, carrying their goblets.

'Out there, we live by rules.' *What am I doing?* 'We survive through the judgement of others.'

'Out there, I have a husband I do not wish to hurt. A good man, even if he is not a lover.' She paused, and Taillefer feared this moment would slip away. 'But here, for this one night,' she continued hesitantly, 'we can set our own rules.'

They watched the fire together, sipping, and the not-touching between them was almost unbearable, as if his body was drawn to the lodestone of hers. She swayed a little closer. Did she feel it too? He glanced at her. Agnès stood very straight, shoulders back, her goblet clasped beneath her breasts. That downward-pointing belt seemed almost to be showing him the way.

'No one to judge us.' Taillefer swallowed, knowing what happened now might change his life forever.

Agnès turned to him, her eyes wide and clear and oh-so-green. 'Time out of time.' There was a half-smile of encouragement on her lips. He wondered again what it would be like to kiss them. She was close enough for him to inhale her scent – a floral summer-sweetness and a hint of rich earth.

Taillefer took the goblet from her hands, placed them both by the fire, and dared to touch her cheek with his fingertips. She leaned into him and he bent his head until their lips could touch. Hers were warm and soft, and tasted of wine and sugar-dusted fruit. Gently, hesitantly, he placed a hand on her breast. She leaned into that too, holding it there for several heartbeats before lifting it to her lips. Her eyes were shining as she turned and led him towards the stairs.

'Time out of time,' she murmured.

6.4 ADELAIS

The following morning, a silent woman in her middle years led Adelais, Magnus, Hjálmar, and Revna onto the island of Heilagtré. The woman wore a cat-skin cloak and carried the staff of a *seidhkona*, but Adelais sensed she was merely an assistant to the *gydhjur*, the priestesses of the sacred isle. Adelais had cast aside her fine armour and wore the belted kirtle and underdress of a Vriesian peasant. She was glad to be unremarkable, and dwarfed by Magnus and Hjálmar, who towered on either side of her. Their shield hands twitched against their thighs, instinctively feeling for the weapons they had been made to leave behind. She too felt strangely naked without her scabbard against her hip, without Allier, and even without the wolf. She carried only her grandmother's staff, looped over her shoulder on a thong. She did not feel she had the right yet to stride with it like their guide, not in the presence of those who have spent their lives in the study of rune lore.

The only temples Adelais had ever known were Ischyrian; all people knew that the old gods could not be confined to houses. When the gods crossed the rainbow bridge of Bifrost to walk this world of Midgard, they lived among people the way the eagle soars through the same air as the sparrow; worthy of awe but demanding no obeisance. To be sure, there were sacred places where the veil between worlds was thin, places that were made more sacred by generations of ritual; her grandmother's home of Freyjasoy was such. That too was an island, said to be on the edge of the world. Before the Ischyrians made them put their dead into the ground to rot, they'd burned them there, with mead and waybread for their last journey, before scattering the ashes on the tide. Couples had gone there to make their vows in the eyes of the gods.

Heilagtré was also a place where one trod gently, with respect. Adelais felt her palms turning outwards, opening, as she breathed a world of timeless peace. The gods were surely near, if only they chose to reveal themselves. Yet in a wide open space she saw great structures that might be meeting halls or feasting halls, and in a smaller clearing beyond were three totems, equally spaced, each carved from mighty trees whose roots still grasped the ground. Odhinn stood in a rune-trimmed cloak with two wolves at his side and two ravens on his shoulders, wisdom shining from his single eye. His fierce-bearded son Thor glared at the visitors, cradling his short-handled hammer, Mjölnir. Freyja stood in terrible beauty with a golden torc about her neck, bare-breasted in the cold, a cloak of feathers draped about her shoulders. The boar Hildisvíni had been carved at her side. Their guide led them to each in turn to pay their respects, ending at a narrower pathway that led further onto the island.

'Just you.' She pointed at Adelais. It was the first time she had spoken. 'Without your staff. Only the *gydhjur* weave fates on Heilagtré.'

Adelais looked back nervously as the path led her into the trees. Magnus did not seem pleased to be excluded. Hjálmar smiled encouragement. Revna cradled both their staffs. Their guide lifted her own, imperiously, to point the way with its tip.

The path rose towards the centre of the island. It was well

trodden, bounded in places by staked logs, and utterly silent;
the trees had kept the way clear of snow, and Adelais trod a
litter of fallen pine needles. Within two hundred paces it
curved around a dell that embraced a mighty yew tree; the
crown towered above her, and the trunk had hollowed and split
into a ring so that one vast tree grew from several lesser trunks.
Its roots were knotted into the dell's floor, twisted over each
other, knuckling the ground. Some roots had been worn smooth,
as if there were acknowledged pathways into the tree's heart.
Adelais sensed the peace of immeasurable age; this tree would
have been old when the gods were young. A small spring
trickled through the roots, falling in little steps towards the
shore. Three women waited at its base, each sitting on a root,
each dressed identically in grey, belted kirtles and cat-skin
cloaks. They watched her approach, on a curving path to the
base of the tree, until she stood a little below them, staring
upwards. They did not seem unkindly, merely curious.

'I am Adelais,' she announced, breaking the silence.

'And why have you come?' The one who spoke was old and
her face lined, though once, perhaps, she would have been
lovely. She stared at Adelais with sharp, watery eyes that had
sunk within high cheekbones. The hair within her hood was
thin and grey, and the way her jaw moved as she spoke
suggested few teeth within.

'I was asked to come, by Revna Friggisdottir.'

'You could have refused.' This one was straight-backed, full-
figured, and of an age where in another life she might have children at her knees and a man in her bed. She alone wore a
weapon; a wooden-handled, flaked-flint knife hung through a
loop on her belt. Her question held a tone of mild reproof.

Adelais swallowed and took a breath. 'I wanted to know my
destiny.'

'And what would you like your destiny to be?' the youngest
of them asked. This was the girl-woman they'd seen as they

arrived, the one who seemed a child until Adelais looked into her eyes and saw the weight of years. She thought men would find her disturbingly beautiful.

There was a flicker of movement behind the women, greys and browns against tree trunks, and the she-wolf appeared over the edge of the dell, stepping daintily over the roots until it settled near the matron. Adelais saw no sign of a limp. It settled its nose on its paws, watching Adelais.

She found the wolf's presence reassuring. It had warned her of danger before. Adelais found time to consider her answer.

'My destiny? I do not want to kill any more. I do not want to *have* to kill.'

'And how have you killed before?' The old one. Adelais felt as if she were talking to one woman, not three.

'With rune song.'

'Rune song does not kill. People kill.' The matron.

'When I sang, I felt invincible. I found a skill beyond all training. I sang rune song and men died, sometimes by my hand, sometimes under my horse's hooves.'

The three women looked at each other, their heads turning inwards as if of one mind.

'You are the Nornir,' Adelais blurted, as the realisation dawned; the women who weave fate at the base of the world tree, Yggdrasil. The old one would be Urdhr, who weaves that which has become, and the matron Verdhandi, who weaves that which is becoming. The girl must be Skuld, who weaves that which might become.

'They are within us, and we within them.' They spoke together, their voices overlapping.

'The tree under which we sit is an offshoot of Yggdrasil.' Verdhandi touched the root on which she sat.

'One tree becomes many.' Skuld waved at the fragmented trunks.

'Who can say which was the mother of them all?' Urdhr

cackled. 'Once I was as she.' Urdhr pointed at Skuld, the beautiful girl.

'And one day I shall be as she.' Skuld nodded at Urdhr. It was said without malice.

'Sing rune song for us.' Verdhandi interrupted them, looking hard at Adelais.

'Now? What rune should I sing?'

'As you wish. But beware. In this place, runes have greater power than anywhere in your world.'

Adelais breathed deeply, thinking.

Jera. The rune of plenty. It was a blessing-rune, a part of the cycle of the year. She called the image into her mind, closed her eyes, and chanted.

'*Ár er gumna gódhi, ok gott sumar, ok algróinn akr.*'

The ancient tree seemed to release the peace of centuries as she finished, like a blessing. Adelais looked up at the women, and saw them shrug. Skuld made a moue of disappointment.

'Nothing.' Verdhandi rose to her feet and placed one foot either side of the she-wolf's shoulders. Adelais was stunned that the wolf would tolerate anyone that close, in so threatening a position. It made no movement, but looked down at Adelais with a weight of sadness or farewell in its eyes.

'Not a ripple in the warp and weft of fate. You are a fraud.' Verdhandi tugged the flint knife from her belt.

'No!' Adelais could not believe what she was seeing. Verdhandi lifted the knife in an underhand grip, and brought it down in a scything blow into the wolf's neck.

'*Íss er árbörkr!*' Adelais bellowed the start of *ísa*, the ice-rune. The shout was instinctive, without thought; calling on the rune that binds an enemy or freezes aggression. Even to

Adelais's ears, it sounded like a thunderclap. Verdhandi flew backwards as if kicked by a horse, dropping the knife.

'*Ok unnar thak!*' Adelais took a step towards her, snarling her anger. The knife spun onto a rock at the edge of the stream and shattered. '*Ok feigra manna fár.*' She was beating the woman back with the force of her chant.

Urdhr, the old one, held up her hand. 'Enough!'

Adelais stopped, but only because the wolf had risen to its feet, apparently unharmed. It stared at her with those intense, blue eyes, swaying on its legs. The wolf's staggering exhaustion told Adelais it had accepted, even expected a sacrificial death, and that the blow had been launched with real intent. Only the force of her rune song had spared it.

'If that was a test, it was cruel.' Adelais was furious.

Verdhandi also stood, favouring one leg. 'Cruel, but needed.'

'You have power,' Urdhr explained, 'but only when you feel passion.'

'Think.' Verdhandi stretched away her pain. 'Think of when you unleashed the power of rune song. It will have been when those you love were threatened.'

Adelais thought, and knew the wisdom of the matron's words. She'd sung *thurs* before the high priest when both Humbert and Agnès were in danger. *Sowilo* before the walls of Bellay on the day Humbert died. *Thurs* again in the square at Harbin when everyone's life was in danger, including hers. *Sowilo* in the mountain pass before Ulfhild died.

'Once in a generation we see such gifts,' Skuld added. *Surely she is too young to speak of generations?* 'But few learn to unlock them.'

Adelais turned her back on them, sat on one of the roots, and stared downhill through the trees to where the water shone grey between the trunks. The wolf came to stand near her, but she made no move to touch it. This was no domesticated dog, to be petted. It was enough to be together. And what had happened here, to be so passive beneath the knife?

Skuld sat lightly beside her, holding out a wooden bowl of water.

'Drink,' she said, 'and be grateful. Odhinn gave his eye for that.'

The moment was unreal. 'Is this really the well of Mimir? The source of Odhinn's wisdom?'

When Skuld smiled, she could almost be truly young; fresh-faced and clear-skinned. Only the tiny lines around her eyes and mouth suggested a much greater age.

'You have a rare power, but you won't always find the passion to wield it. Those around you may depend upon it even when no one you love is threatened. To lead, you need wisdom. Drink.'

Adelais sipped. The water was crystal sharp, peat-flavoured, and cold. Just water.

'You said "to lead". What if I don't want to lead?'

'Few want war to come, but that will not stop it. This will be a battle between gods, but it will not be decided by Thor throwing Mjölnir and thunderbolts; it will be decided by armoured men. And perhaps by you.' Skuld's old eyes softened with compassion.

'Why me? Why can't I just find a man and a farm, and raise children?'

'Who knows why some run faster than others? Why some are blessed with great skill that sets them apart? That is a question for Urdhr, who weaves what has become. Your gifts were in your blood, through your grandmother Yrsa Haraldsdottir, but I think Urdhr added more. It's like your farmer, planting for the future, trusting that the seed will flourish. I fear, sister, that it is now harvest time.'

Sister. Adelais liked that. She sat companionably between a girl who might be a Norn and a wolf who must be a *fylgja*.

'Is that the great Ice Sea?' She wished this moment of peace could last, here where there were no demands, no threats, no wars. Even the memories of killing were less intrusive here.

'A finger of it. It is fresh enough to drink, and has no tides like the seas in the west. On its furthest shores lie Niflheim, the land of eternal ice, and Muspelheim, the land of fires.'

'Have you seen them?'

'I have seen rivers of burning rock that turn the ice to steam and make new mountains. I have seen ice bears and sea giants.'

Adelais was silent for many heartbeats, absorbed in the wonder of Skuld's words. Beside her, the wolf yawned and settled its snout onto its forepaws.

'Yrsa was born on the shores of the great Ice Sea.'

'I know. She was of the people of the wolf. That is why the she-wolf accepts her.'

'She is part of this too, isn't she?'

'"A woman born of wolf-kind and of mud". It is a good prophecy.' Was there a little pride in Skuld's voice?

'So are you going to tell me my destiny?'

Skuld stood. 'I weave only what *may* become. Perhaps even what *should* become. But your destiny is your own to make.' She held out her hand. 'Come. Let us see what you *might* do.'

Skuld guided Adelais back through the woods of Heilagtré, arm in arm. Adelais put her hand over Skuld's wrist, feeling for the warmth of living flesh.

'I am a woman, as well as a Norn.' Skuld understood her touch immediately. 'Just as you are both flesh and spirit, and the she-wolf is both wolf and *fylgja*.'

Adelais looked over her shoulder. Behind them, Verdhandi was also arm in arm with Urdhr, the matron helping the crone over the tree roots. The wolf followed them, among the trees. There was no sign of a limp.

'I could not feed her last night,' Adelais said.

'Fear not, she ate well,' Skuld replied. 'She will stay with you now, for as long as one of you lives. You are bonded.'

'Will she live long?' Adelais sensed that the wolf might be old.

'For now, she is strong, but she has already whelped many young. Your destinies are linked; perhaps neither of you are fated to live out your natural years.'

Adelais almost stumbled at the implied threat. 'If you are Nornir, you can weave fates.'

'We see where the gods' blessings may be best spent.' Skuld nudged Adelais along the path. 'And we weave the conditions for success or failure, but people make their own destiny. Give a man gold, and he may lose it all on dice or turn it to great profit. The art of the *spakona*, the prophecy-woman, is to glimpse what may become, for at the heart of the web of fate there is no past, no present, no future. All is one.'

They had reached the clearings and the carved representations of the gods. There was no sign of Hjálmar, Magnus, or Revna. Skuld led them towards a domed structure on the lake shore that appeared to be made of leather hides stretched over a wooden frame. Attached to it by an arched passageway was a smaller structure with a brick chimney and a leather entrance flap.

A wall of heat greeted them as they entered. Inside, two young women were using an iron stretcher to carry a large, hot rock from a furnace through another flap into the tent's interior. A third tended the furnace. All wore just loose under-dresses that were damp with their sweat. Verdhandi and Urdhr came in behind them, crowding the small space.

'Take off your clothes.' Verdhandi spoke as if this was the most natural of instructions. She swung her cloak onto a peg and unbuckled her belt. Skuld and Urdhr followed suit. Self-consciously, Adelais obeyed. When she turned back from hanging her clothes on a peg, they were all staring at her chest.

'What?' She lifted her hands to cover herself, but Verdhandi held her wrists.

'How did that happen?'

Adelais looked down at the wound on her breast, the sharp lines now well scabbed but edged in pink.

'An arrow stuck in my armour. Its point cut me as I fought.'

'*Ansuz.*' Verdhandi traced the cuts with a finger.

'The god-rune.' Urdhr nodded.

'Come.' Skuld, now naked, took her by the hand and led her through the passageway and into the domed tent.

The heat inside took Adelais's breath away. There were no windows, so the only light came from two small lamps. It was enough to show a pile of hot rocks in the centre, some still glowing from the furnace, and a ring of wooden benches around it. Skuld led her to a seat, where a cloth had been folded to protect her backside from burning; the wood was hot enough for Adelais to wince and pull her hand away when she touched it. Verdhandi and Urdhr followed them in, sitting on the benches around the stones. Like Skuld, they seemed unashamed of their nakedness. Verdhandi sat with her hands palm-up on her knees, strong-bodied, her full breasts lifting as she inhaled the over-heated air. Beneath her ancient eyes, shadowed in the lamp-light, Skuld had the body of a girl new-grown to womanhood. She smiled as she handed Adelais a wooden mug.

'Drink, sister.'

The water had a strong herbal taste. It was cold, and refreshing in the tent's warmth. When Skuld lifted her palm, encouraging her, she drank more deeply. Two more acolytes pushed through the flap, bearing yet another rock, still a dull red from the furnace. The iron stretcher was hinged along its length like double doors so the rock could be positioned safely on top of the glowing cairn in the centre and released when the doors were allowed to swing open. The acolytes wore thick leather gloves to protect their hands from the hot metal.

'So will you cast the runes to tell me my destiny?' Adelais could see no space where the rune-staves could be safely laid.

'No. *You* will tell *us* your destiny. We will sing rune song to bring us wisdom as we listen.'

'I...?' Adelais stopped as Verdhandi emptied a ladle of water over the rocks and a wall of steam hit her face and caught in her throat. She bowed her head, eyes shut. Sweat flowed from every pore, trickling down her back, forming a stream between her breasts and over her belly. The steam was earthy with the scent of mushrooms.

Each of the Nornir reached behind them, into the shadows, and pulled out a carved staff. Even Skuld's looked ancient, its runes smoothed by decades, perhaps centuries, of use; it had an open, carved top, like a distaff for spinning thread from wool. Together the Nornir let the tips fall onto the wooden decking beneath their feet, and began to chant in time with their beat.

'*Reidh er sitjandi sæla...*'

Raido, the rune of riding.

'*Ok snúdhig ferdh...*' but now they were riding into the spirit world. Adelais felt light-headed as she joined the chant. Threads of silk, fine as the first strand of a spider's web, began to flow from the distaff-baskets at the top of each staff.

'*Ok jórs erfidhi...*'

Raido, a rune with a beat as steady as a cantering horse's hooves, the drumbeat of the warp and weft of fate, the rhythm of this world. *Raido*, the rune to unlock the truth within her. The silk moved to their chant, finding other threads and twining with them like partners in a dance.

'*Reidh er sitjandi sæla...*'

Now Urdhr, the old one, lifted the chant into the high, wailing song of *galdrar*-magic.

'*Óss er algingautr...*'

She was singing the rune cut into Adelais's chest. *Ansuz*, the god-rune of Odhinn.

'*Ok ásgardhs jöfurr...*' Odhinn, who hung nine days upon Yggdrasil to receive the wisdom of the runes. The threads now made a veil around them, fine as morning mist. Adelais's skin burned in the heat, her head still swimming. Or was that the herbs? Or the mushroom-scented steam?

'*Ok valhallar vísi...*' The rune of the chanted spell, and the god's wisdom.

There were shapes beyond the veil, moving but indistinct. They were far away, almost beyond sight, but had colour: reds and a bright splash of gold. Urdhr's keening created gossamer visions of that which has already come to pass.

'*Óss er algingautr...*'

The reds became a line of Guardian knights riding towards her, all in white surcoats, with the red lion badges of their order emblazoned on their chests. Her heart lifted because Humbert Blanc had been a Guardian. His four companions who'd fled with her from Villebénie had been Guardian knights, and they'd fought the forces of King Aloys and the anakritim. She'd fought alongside them. They'd been good men and they'd died, bravely, every one, to protect the Hand of Salazar. And Agnès. And her.

'*Ok ásgardhs jöfurr...*'

Yet she saw them couch their lances at the shield wall of a Vriesian army, and she knew she looked at the field of Vannemeer. Her brother Svend had died in the aftermath of

Vannemeer. Skuld's words hummed in her mind. *At the heart of the web of fate there is no past, no present, no future. All is one.* Did that mean she could alter the past, or was she condemned to watch? The war-hammer formation, they'd called it. Four lines of twenty knights charging knee to knee, smashing the Vriesian line.

'*Ok valhallar vísi...*'

But how would she change the past? How could she weave another fate?

Verdhandi's voice now dominated, weaving that which is coming into being, and a golden hand rose high over the battle lines in the Ischyrian sign of benediction, but not over Adelais. Definitely not over her.

Now all Adelais could see was fighting. She found herself twisting on her bench, mimicking the combat she saw. A soldier fell onto her lance and she knew again the horror of her first kill. Every kill. The hunting lodge. Bellay. Harbin. She wove bloody fates as if her sword was a needle, and Allier's hooves the loom, and she knew the sick guilt of every death. *Please, no more!*

'*Óss er algingautr...*'

Skuld's voice, high and sweet, sang that which might become, and the beating of staffs became the pounding of a mighty, golden fist that crushed another line, on another field, smearing Vriesian blood. There were women and children there, as well as warriors; Ulfhild's face looked at her with pleading eyes from amidst the carnage. The fist lifted again and a woman who might have been Adelais's older sister ran from under it, cradling a baby, tugging a boy...

Adelais could stay passive no longer. She was mighty, she was a goddess, she was Sif, she was strong.

'*Thurs er kvenna kvöl...*' Adelais broke the chant, hurling *thurs* at the enemy.

'*Ok kletta búi...*' And rocks, the way Thor might hurl thunderbolts. Fiery rocks that she could lift one-handed from the cairn and which burst into angry flames as she flung them towards the enemy. They sailed through the veil and the golden fist did not fall. Yet. It poised over Vriesland while the people screamed.

'*Ok vardhrúnar verr...*'

But hands seized her, roughly, and held her arms. She was being tied to a stake, atop a pyre, naked before a seething mass of jeering people, and her greatest pain was the betrayal as Agnès herself leaned to light the fire of execution. Beyond her friend's back, the shining hand, poised to crush her people, began to drop.

She screamed and writhed against her bindings as the flames found her feet, and her scream sliced through the galdrar-chant, stopping it as cleanly as a swung sword.

She was being carried from the stake. *Sætur Sif*, her foot hurt. A blast of cold air on scalded skin, like the blessing of the gods, and then a moment of falling.

Icy water closed over her head, the shock paralysing her in the high-shouldered, hunched posture of a newborn babe. She took one half-breath of water but hands lifted her before she choked, holding her head clear in frosty air while she retched. Strings of drool trailed from her mouth onto the surface. She tried to lift her head, but the world was unfocused. Slabs of white over forest-grey must be mountains on the far shore. She squinted at regular shapes nearby that might be a jetty. Had they just thrown her in? But Skuld and Verdhandi were with her, holding her head clear of the water, their faces blurred, their bodies slippery as fish.

Adelais folded over as a spasm gripped her gut. She was cold now, shaking cold.

'Let's get you dry.' Verdhandi lifted her in her arms and waded out of the sea. The chill air cut at Adelais's skin but her sight was returning; there were screens along the jetty to hide the bathing *gydhjur* from prying eyes. An acolyte waited with drying cloths.

'What happened?' Adelais felt a juvenile comfort in being held against Verdhandi's softness. She almost forgave her for trying to kill the wolf.

'You ran onto the hot stones. You were going to pick one up.'

'Why?' But she knew why. She wanted to hurl fiery rocks at the forces of Ischyros.

'We gave you mandrake root, and a little opium.' Skuld, wading alongside, spoke as if that were the most natural thing in this world.

Adelais's head fell backwards and Verdhandi shifted her hold, squashing Adelais against her chest as if her weight was becoming a burden. Adelais reached for the Norn's neck, like an infant clinging to its mother. She could cry at the pain from her feet.

Verdhandi sighed as she set Adelais down on a stool in the furnace room. The smothering heat was welcome. Acolytes rubbed the wet from Adelais's skin, ministering to her as if she were a princess. Another dabbed at the sole of her foot, smearing ointment on the burns.

'I will bind that with birch bark, marked with healing runes. You must not walk on it for a few days.' Verdhandi was drying herself vigorously, a pink-fleshed goddess.

'What visions did you see?' Skuld knelt in front of her, the drying cloth around her shoulders left unashamedly open at the front. Her whole being radiated the lithe promise of youth.

'I was tied to a stake, the way Ischyrians execute witches.'

Adelais drew back her feet, remembering the agony. An acolyte pulled them forwards again, smoothing balm over them.

'And before that?' Urdhr was hunched into a blanket, her eyes bright and inquisitive. She had not come into the water and her face was glowing with recent heat.

'Vannemeer. The Guardian charge that broke the line at Vannemeer.'

'That which has come to pass,' the crone grunted.

'And that which is coming into being?' Verdhandi pulled an underdress over her head.

'A golden hand. Huge. It crushed people.' Adelais closed her eyes and swallowed. It had been so real.

'Why did you walk into the fire?' Skuld squeezed Adelais's thighs to call her back. She was still kneeling in front of her, still showing the promise of that which might become.

Adelais frowned, trying to separate vision from reality.

'I can hurl fire.' She spoke as if this was a perfectly reasonable explanation. Surely they must know this? 'I stopped the hand with fire.' Or was that a dream she'd had in Siltehafn?

'And were burned.' Skuld's look was touched with sadness. How could a face that young, that fresh, have eyes that have seen generations?

'So what did you see? Are you going to tell me my destiny?'

Skuld took Adelais's hand in hers. 'A famed *spakona* once told a man that he would soon die by an arrow, so he refused to follow his jarl to war even though that betrayal cost him honour and lands. He was killed by his own son, hunting in thick cover, when the boy mistook his footsteps for a boar and shot his bow into the bushes.'

'So you're not going to tell me.'

'The gods have a way of making men run into their fates when they think they are running from them. Sometimes it is better not to know.' Skuld squeezed her fingers, smiling. Adelais hoped she would come to know this unfathomable woman better; she felt the first tugs of friendship.

'Some advice, though.' Skuld held eye contact to emphasise her words. Her eyes were the same blue as Yrsa's had been. 'Beware of *thurs*. Use it only in extremes, for in you it becomes a rune of wild rage that could cause irreversible harm. Beware also of *tiwaz*, that some call the victory-rune. You have been marked with *ansuz*.' She placed her fingertips on the wounds on Adelais's breast, as gently as a lover. 'It is the rune of enlightenment, of wisdom, and of magic. *Tiwaz* may win you one battle, at a cost, but only *ansuz* will win you the war.'

'It is to be war, then?'

'Between the gods. Ischyros makes war on the gods of Asgard. Men are just their agents, and the outcome is uncertain. If we lose now, a new generation may carry on the fight, but with each generation the fight will be harder. You—' a slight pressure of the fingers '—have been chosen because you may make a difference. Now.'

Adelais sensed a yearning within this young-old woman. Whether Skuld's life was measured in decades, or centuries, or aeons, if she was a Norn it would be lived as a virgin.

'One gift I can give you.' Urdhr lifted a claw-like hand from beneath her blanket and placed it on Adelais's head. Her touch was warm on Adelais's chilled skin. 'That which has already come to pass has left wounds that show no scar. We saw your pain. We will not unpick that which is already woven, for it has shaped what you are, and what you may become, but we can make those memories fade.'

Adelais jolted as a soldier's face flashed into her mind, screaming as he fell backwards under her sword. Backwards, backwards... and faded, never hitting the ground.

She blinked, unsure what had just happened.

Urdhr lifted her hand away. 'You will carry those scars always,' she said, 'but they will be like an old wound, healed, no longer raw. There will be times when they ache, but they will no longer frame your life. That which may yet become may still haunt you, so listen to your dreams.'

Adelais muttered her thanks, unsure how much to believe. It had felt like the time Humbert had placed his hand on her head after she killed the soldier in Villebénie, like an act of pardon after the Ischyrian rite of unburdening. Cleansing. She hoped it would last.

'When you are dressed,' Verdhandi hinted that they had already delayed too long, 'we will call that man-bear that you travel with to carry you to your lodgings. The jarls will meet tomorrow, but you are welcome to stay in Heilagtré until you are healed.' She tightened her belt around her kirtle.

'The avalanche will have closed the pass, anyway.' Adelais liked the thought of staying in Heilagtré. She liked the peace and the sense of immense age beneath that ancient yew.

'There is another, two days' ride to the south.' Skuld stood, perhaps reluctantly. 'And this is not your home. Your destiny lies far away.' She rested her hand on Adelais's shoulder; she was a woman who touched a lot. Woman? Goddess? Adelais still did not know. Her vision was still a little blurred. As Skuld took her hand away, it seemed to trail gossamer threads, and when she spoke her voice seemed to come from far away.

'Above all, sister, remember the god-rune.'

6.5 TAILLEFER

Taillefer woke with the first glimmerings of dawn and a chorus of joyous birdsong. Agnès was warm beside him, her head haloed by a great fan of hair, but the chamber's fire had long since burned out and the air was cold on his face. Taillefer slipped out of the bed as gently as he could, but he heard her stir as he lit kindling from the all-night candle, and blew it into a fire. He knew she was watching, but he made no move to cover himself. Feeding the flames was primal; he felt lithe, stallion-strong, ready to prance and cover.

'Good morning.'

Agnès lay on her side, appraising him. Her smile told him she liked what she saw.

'There are better ways of keeping warm.' She lifted the covers, showing her curves. Now that their first urgency had been met, and met again, there was a more languorous hunger about her; a need that could take its time.

Later, much later, they sat cross-legged on the bed, facing each other across a tray of bread and honey that Elyse had left. He had draped his cloak around his shoulders, and she a long sable cape around hers; Agnès de Fontenay wore the worth of a small manor on her back, and nothing beneath. Her unashamed openness both shocked and enthralled him. If anyone had described such a moment to him, before this morning, he would have thought it brazen. Now he could only wonder at her body and know her to be magnificent.

'Do all women have this delight?' Taillefer fed her a morsel of bread dipped in honey. 'In bed, I mean?' Taillefer didn't realise he could still blush. Her joy had been real. Sensuous. At the moment of union her sigh had been the slow exhalation of one who has thirsted long and now drinks deep.

Agnès lifted one eyebrow, questioning. 'I do. In you.' She took the bread in her hand and his fingers in her mouth, sucking at the sweetness. Her hair cascaded onto her shoulders, just as dark, just as lustrous as the sable. Agnès drew her lips slowly backwards until she could speak again. 'You priests tell us that women must be dutiful wives and mothers or holy adeifes in a sisterhouse. Virgins, wombs on legs, or harlots.' She drew her tongue down the length of a finger. 'Is it so shocking to discover that women can also find joy?'

'It is wonderful. *You* are wonderful.'

She pushed his hand inside the cape and settled the weight of a breast into his palm as if it was the most natural act in the world. 'And the wonderful thing for me is to discover that in taking pleasure I give it, and in giving pleasure I take it.' She watched his face as he began to caress her. Her eyes were wide and green and clear as she said, 'I love you, Taillefer. Even if this moment has to last me a lifetime, I shall always love you.'

Around noon he stood at the window, staring out over the river between half-closed shutters. He should feel guilty, but he felt like a king. More than a king, when Agnès stood behind him and pushed her softness into his back.

'Do you really have to go today?'

Oh, she understood him too well. But a niggling sense of duty clawed at his pleasure.

'It can't last, can it?'

'I think you're lasting rather well, so far.' She reached around him and stroked approvingly.

'I am a diakonos,' he pleaded. 'I cannot just disappear. I must go. Today.' Yet he almost groaned aloud at the thought that he might never again know this melding of minds and bodies.

'Then come to Château Fontenay with me.'

'What?'

'Tell your episkopos about the rumours of the Hand. Swear him to secrecy. Tell him you're off to investigate, at the invitation of de Fontenay. All true.'

Taillefer could not just walk away from her. 'I'd have to go back to Harbin first. Make arrangements.' He swallowed. 'We'd have to be discreet.' His resolve had faded like dawn mist. He simply could not imagine climbing onto his horse and riding away, not without the certainty of seeing her again.

'Time out of time.' Agnès sighed her happiness, her breath warm against his back.

6.6 ADELAIS

Adelais jolted awake on a bench outside the furnace room as an arm like a tree trunk slid under her knees. She tried to cover herself, thinking she was naked, but her hands touched clothes, not skin. She had no memory of being dressed. Another arm went around her back and she was lifted high, infant-light.

'Come, princess!'

Was Hjálmar trailing threads too, like the Nornir? No, just a beard. A red, silky beard. He grinned at her and Adelais giggled. His squirrel look. He smelt of male sweat in a way that was mildly appealing, not rank.

'Hello, Thor.' That was a much better name for him than 'troll-man'. 'I'm Sif. *Thynn litla Sif.*' She put her palm against the slabbed muscle of his chest, curled a little closer within his arms, and winced as the movement pulled at the healing cuts on her breast. Not yet.

'You're giving me ideas, *litla Sif*. We all know what happened between Sif and Thor.'

They were on the bridge from the island; she swayed with the movement, her legs dangling. The road through the settlement seemed to be lined with people – chieftains, women, warriors. Very few children. They watched her curiously as if she were a messenger from afar.

Adelais had a moment of clarity and pushed again at his chest.

'Don't get too close, troll-man.'

Hjálmar held her out at arm's length. The muscles in his arms bulged with the effort. Impressive, but not what she meant.

'Not that sort of close. Lover-close. People I like tend to die.'

'Hey, you began this with Thor and Sif!'

'I know. Sorry. I'm not thinking straight.' She yawned. Why was she so tired?

'Am I keeping you awake, princess?'

'There's something about you that makes me sleep, troll-man.'

'Definitely not Thor and Sif, then.'

The following morning, Adelais was carried to the meeting of jarls in a chair, lashed to poles. She did not wear her armour; she felt safer in Heilagtré than she had in Ragener's castle, for all the walls and guards that had been around her, and she did not want to show herself in too martial a guise. Not when they were talking about going to war. She did carry her grandmother's staff, though; she could hobble around on it without putting her burned foot to the ground.

They left her on a raised dais, perhaps a *seidhr*-platform, at the edge of a great hall that was already crowded with men. A huge central fire cast a ruddy light on bearded faces, all looking at her; jarls and chieftains on benches near the flames, berserkers and retainers standing to the rear. A scattering of strong-looking women stood among them that Adelais guessed were shieldmaidens; some wore the arm-rings of warriors.

Magnus and one or two elders had stools; no thrones here, among equals.

Revna walked into the hall's open centre, near the fire, and held up her carved *seidhkona* staff for silence. She turned, glaring at them all, waiting for the noise to subside. Fierce faces turned away from Adelais towards Revna as the room quietened.

'You have all heard of Adelais Leifsdottir. Much is rumour. Her fame and her deeds grow by the day in the taverns of Vriesland, fed in part by Duke Ragener. The duke wants us to go to war for him, and he claims this Adelais is the *örlaga vefari*, the fate-weaver who is prophesied to turn back the tide of Ischyros. So let me tell you what I know to be true.'

Revna paused, circling the fire. Her voice was harsh and low for a woman, like a man's tenor, and she had the skill of throwing it to command attention.

'She has the power of runes, to be sure. She sang the rune song of *thurs* at the high priest of Ischyros, and he died on the spot. She rode down King Aloys of Galmandie and killed him. She sang the rune song of *sowilo* with me in the pass, and together we brought down an avalanche that killed our pursuers. She is rune-marked; she was wounded by an arrow in that fight, and the arrow carved the *ansuz* rune in her breast.'

Murmurs spread around the hall; heads turned sideways to speak to neighbours, and Revna held up her staff again until they quietened.

'And I have spoken to the *gydhjur*.'

Adelais was curious why she called them *gydhjur*. The three women were the Nornir, weren't they?

'They say her power is multiplied by anger, and when angry she could throw Verdhandi backwards with the force of her rune magic.'

The rumble of men's voices filled the hall, questioning,

wondering, and heads again turned in Adelais's direction until a voice called from a far corner.

'Yes, but is she the *örlaga vefari*?'

Others echoed the cry until the hall was a tumbling mass of men's voices, like a crowd before a riot. Adelais groaned inwardly, frustrated. What did it matter what *fordæmdur* label they tied to her?

This time, Magnus had to stand to quell the noise, bellowing in a voice that could command an army.

'Let *Frú* Revna speak!'

Revna waited until the noise subsided.

'The *gydhjur* say that war is coming, whether we go to meet it or let it come to us, and it is a war between the gods as well as between men. Adelais Leifsdottir's role in that war will be pivotal. However, they will not proclaim her the *örlaga vefari*.'

Another grumble of noise, silenced by a raised staff.

'They say that if they announced that fate, it would change it. The *örlaga vefari* must be revealed in the light of fates that have yet to come to pass. To bestow that title before it is earned would prevent it *ever* being earned.'

There were several heartbeats of quiet while the crowd digested that statement, until a greybeard called out from the back.

'Typical *fjakkinn spakonur*. They prophesy with so many twists they can never be wrong!'

Adelais looked up as the discussion raged. Above her, hammer-beam rafters hung in the gloom. A thick layer of smoke lay below the thatch, making the apex of the roof indistinct, like the beginning of her vision. Had she really seen that, or was it only the mandrake and opium? And where was the wolf this morning? Had the Nornir fed her?

Adelais was growing bored. She wanted to walk. Groom Allier. Laugh with Hjálmar. Anything but sit on the edges of a

debate where no one asked her opinion. Here she was useless.
And felt a fraud.

'Are we really expected to go to war?' One voice, more stri-
dent than the rest, cut through the noise. 'Because some chit of a
girl rides into Heilagtré with a tame wolf at her heel?'

Adelais's frustration boiled over. She seized her grandmother's staff at its middle and rammed it down on the boards
beneath, unleashing a thunderclap of sound into the hall. Even
she was surprised at the noise. Yet it was more than noise; an
unseen wave burst from her that rocked men on their seats or
feet the way that tall trees bend to a squall and recover. In the
awed silence that followed, she used the staff to climb upright.

What had she just done? Apart from striking a *seidhr*-plat-
form with a *seidhkona* staff. In Heilagtré. And after the pulse
that followed she no longer felt a fraud. Just a fool, a 'chit of a
girl' standing on one foot and facing a hall full of elders with no
clear idea of what she was going to say.

Remember the ansuz rune. The god-rune of Odhinn. The
rune of wisdom. She slipped a hand inside her shirt and
touched the scabs the way she used to touch her grandmother's
taufr.

'It is strange that none of you thought to ask what I think
about this great matter. You all seem to assume I want to be this
örlaga vefari and lead you to war. You assume too much.' She
had their attention. A sea of bearded faces watched her. 'I do
not claim to be the fate-weaver, and I have seen enough of
killing in the last year, done enough killing, to know that I won't
lead more people to their deaths.'

Adelais tried to read their faces. She saw a range of respect,
disappointment, disbelief, curiosity... And behind Magnus's
stool, Hjálmar's red beard might have framed compassion.

'But if you choose to go to war, I will come with you, and I
will fight. I won't fight for Ragener, even though he is my duke
and I have sworn fealty. I don't trust the man. I'll fight for the

memory of a girl called Ulfhild. She was an innocent woman, killed because she was mistaken for me. I will fight for Jarl Magnus's warrior who died defending us.' Adelais paused, leaning on the staff. She was in danger of becoming emotional. And toppling over. She struck out with the staff to keep her balance and another boom resounded through the hall, another shock.

Remember the god-rune.

Óss er algingautr, ok ásgardhs jöfurr...

She was calm now, and steady; she found she could put her toes to the ground on her burned foot.

'Because with the *gydhjur* I had a vision. I saw the Hand of Salazar that the Galmans put over their temples and hang around their necks, and it had become a fist that crushed Vriesian people as if they were insects crawling across a table. It will not stop until the hungry god is taught to feed elsewhere. So I will fight, if you go, for all the other Ulfhilds and for the right to honour our own gods. My vision did not promise victory. It may have shown me pain and fire,' Adelais gestured to her foot, 'but for me, it is a battle that must be fought.'

Adelais sat, elated but suddenly tired, and let her head fall backwards. A slow, approving stamping and pounding of benches began around her and swelled until the hall itself seemed to shake. Perhaps it was only the *seidhr*-platform beneath her. Above her, the smoke was twisting into tendrils that seemed to dance to the beat as they wound their way towards an opening at the southern apex. Galmandie would lie in that direction. Agnès. She'd seen threads like that flowing from Skuld's hands.

A moment of passion, or frustration, and she'd sent a shock wave through the jarls. She hadn't planned this. There would be more talk. That was inevitable. But the outcome was as sure as the threads of smoke dancing towards Galmandie.

She'd just tipped the balance into war.

6.7 TAILLEFER

Taillefer sat in his temple at Harbin, staring into the sacred flame, his mind in turmoil. He had not unburdened his sins, for he felt little guilt, but he could not have dreamt of such a conflict of extremes. There was such tension within him between the spiritual and the carnal. He craved to know the wonder of being in the presence of the Hand of Salazar. He could do such good as its custodian, and prevent such evil.

And he craved the company of Agnès de Fontenay. He wanted to hold her. Laugh with her. Break every vow with her. Was this what they called love? Whatever it was, it had ignited the first time he saw her, in Harbin; petite, green-eyed, with a figure that showed him the price of priesthood. Somehow, that spark of attraction had been fanned into a great fire of passion at Molinot. Now he felt like a man who has been blind from birth but who has been granted a day of perfect sight; a day of colour when the world sparkles with wonders. Already he missed her, raging against his blindness, truly knowing it for the first time. Even in this holy sanctuary he tortured himself with the memory of Agnès rolling onto her back to receive him, hungry for him, welcoming him into her heat. He could not feel regret, even though it was a sin that would push him from the bridge of judgement into the pit of Kakos.

And now the route to the holiest relic of Ischyrendom was in her company.

'You are troubled, Excellency.' Pateras Malory d'Eivet sat beside him, uninvited. 'You carry a burden.' He took liberties at times, this half-mad priest. But then, they shared the great secret of the Hand. Taillefer nodded, absent-mindedly.

'Before I came to your diakonerie, Excellency, I committed many sins. The worst were the ones I was required to commit as an anakritis; using torture to turn lies into truth, letting men die horribly when they would not confess to crimes that we ourselves had invented. My sins were like a cloak of lead around my shoulders, dragging me ever deeper into the pit. Then Mistress Adelais put the print of pardon on my forehead, even while the high priest and his temple burned beside us, and I felt those leaden sins become mere cobwebs under her hand. Since then I have tried to serve the God truthfully, with my whole heart.'

Did this talk of sin mean that Malory suspected? 'You are a good priest, Pateras.' Taillefer chose to divert the conversation. 'I am lucky to have you in Harbin. But this Adelais is said to be a witch.'

'She brought me the blessing of Ischyros. And she has touched the Hand of Salazar.'

'Ah yes, the Hand.' Taillefer looked up into the blue, star-spangled dome. Above that, outside, a carved and gilded hand would be shining.

'It will unite and strengthen the faith!' Malory's face shone with the light of a zealot.

'I am not worthy,' Taillefer groaned. 'Only those who are without stain should approach the Hand. The God will surely destroy any who use it for base purposes.'

'It would be a greater sin to know of the Hand and not let it be revealed to the world.'

They were silent together for several long, slow breaths.

Taillefer sighed, coming to a decision. 'I must visit Ville-bénie, and seek leave of absence from the episkopos. You are related, I believe?'

'He is my uncle. But for his influence I would have been executed after I let Mistress Adelais escape.'

'Perhaps that woman did the faith a favour. Only in the absence of a king and high priest can we hope for the Hand to be treated with the pure piety it deserves.'

'I have always said she is a Blessèd One of Ischyros.'

Taillefer lowered his head. He had his doubts.

'Will he be discreet, your uncle, until the Hand is proven?'

Malory made a rocking, ambivalent motion with his spread fingers. 'He will be discreet if it is in his interests.'

Taillefer sighed. So much venality in the faith's hierarchy.

'Will you come with us to Fontenay, Pateras?'

'Of course, Excellency.'

Taillefer wanted a priest with him on the road; his faith was wavering. No, not his faith, but his belief in himself, the sinner who yearned to sin again. But if he ever felt able to unburden his sin, it would be to Malory.

And of one thing he was sure: to be worthy to stand in the presence of the Hand, let alone be its custodian, he would have to make that unburdening. And to receive the ash of pardon he must be resolved to conquer the greatest temptation he had ever known.

PART THREE

THE FLOWER MOON

CHAPTER SEVEN

7.1 ADELAIS

It was over half a moon after the gathering at Heilagtré before the army of Normark had assembled and marched south to the Schilde. They reached the river when the flower moon was still full; four thousand men, in all, with a core of berserkers and house-guards to the jarls, and a mass of farmer-warriors who had reached for spear and shield when the spring sowing was done. Adelais rode in their midst, always protected by a ring of Magnus's berserkers. She rode in her armour – it had proved its worth in the pass – and the men looked at her as if she were some goddess come among them. She knew what they were saying. The girl who can rip a crossbow bolt from her belly and live. The girl who killed the high priest and the king. The girl who called an avalanche. The rune-marked girl whose rune magic could hurl a *gydhjur* across the sacred isle. The *örlaga vefari*.

She felt a fraud.

Ragener sent every available boat to ferry them across the bridgeless river, but it still took several days. It had taken one boat just to ferry Adelais, Allier, and the wolf; no other horse would come close, and the wolf would tolerate no humans but the crew. Since then the wolf had disappeared; she didn't like people. Adelais was not concerned; she knew she'd be close, and there would be food in plenty now the lamb moon was past.

Magnus sent across an advance party and made a secure encampment on the south bank, surrounded by a ring of trusted shield men. Adelais's tent was pitched in its centre, among the jarls' pavilions and beyond the sure range of any bowshot. There was even space for Adelais to practise her archery with the short, recurved bow she'd taken from the dead tarrazim. Hjálmar had nailed an old shirt to a tree as a target. A steep bank beyond, part of the dyke that protected the land from floods, would catch stray arrows.

Adelais doubted if she'd ever be able to fire from horseback. It was hard enough to hit a stationary target thirty paces away, even when she was standing on the ground.

Hjálmar interrupted her next shot. 'No, don't sight down the shaft. These are bodkin points, designed to punch through chain mail.' He held up an arrow, showing the head. It was slender, square, almost edgeless, and tapered to a sharp point. 'But to have the power to do that you must draw the string to the ear, like this.' He'd also taken a tarrazim bow. It looked like a child's toy in his hands. 'And aim off.'

He loosed. The *thunk* as his arrow struck the target was much weightier than hers had been.

Adelais winced as she drew the next arrow and felt the muscles across her back strain.

'How's your chest, princess?' Hjálmar smirked and raised an eyebrow, suggestively.

Adelais drew back further, just to show him, aimed off, and loosed. She missed the tree entirely, sending the arrow into the bank behind.

'Healing. Fortunately there are no muscles in tits.' She could be outrageous with Hjálmar.

He laughed, delightedly. 'If you want help applying *Frú Revna's* salve, just let me know.'

'Sorry. No trolls allowed in those hills.' The soreness of her wounds had faded since the scabs fell away. The cuts were now just red lines in the skin, with little puckering, thank the gods, though they still itched occasionally. Her dreams of combat had faded since Heilagtré, though she still had nightmares about being choked by a hand. Either that, or being tied to a stake while Agnès lit the fires at her feet. The *gydhjur* had said they could lessen the painful memories, but not the dreams of that which might still come to pass. That made them even more unsettling.

Adelais fired again. This time she hit the tail of the shirt. Close, but not a kill. She realised it was easier if she did not concentrate too hard. There was a flow about archery, similar to the staff-fighting she'd known as a girl. If she could only find that point of calm amidst all the straining, she'd be on her way to shooting well. At targets. The chaos of battle would be another matter, when it came.

Hjálmar said it was 'when', not 'if' there was a battle. This many men, and all the others massing from the other counties of Vriesland, would not go home without a fight. She looked at him. She'd expected a riposte to her 'trolls' sally, but he was staring across the encampment, frowning.

Adelais turned. Duke Ragener was riding through the protective perimeter, his mail-wrapped, gambeson-padded outline overflowing his saddle. Despite his escort of guards, and a squire following with the red eagle banner of Vriesland, he looked more like a mummer playing a knight than a leader of armies.

'Your Grace.' Adelais and Hjálmar made their obeisance.

'So, Adelais of Aldingardhur, if you do not come to me, I must come to you.' Ragener sounded petulant, like a fat little boy whose friend won't come out to play.

'Here I am safe, Your Grace.'

'I am distressed to know you do not feel safe in my castle.'

'Someone in your castle knew I was riding north.'

'Many people knew that.'

'Someone with the wealth to hire twenty tarrazim. Which of your nobles wants me dead, Your Grace? And were prepared to kill Jarl Magnus, Hjálmar, and all their party at the same time?'

'Sjóland and Theignault are joining us with every knight and man-at-arms they can muster. It will not be them.'

'Who then, Sire?'

Ragener looked uncomfortable. 'I believe it was agents of the Ischyrian faith. Their temples have that wealth. Or an agent of Prince Lancelin. It's the kind of underhand trick he'd play. Where is Jarl Magnus?'

'On the north bank,' Hjálmar answered. 'He expects all the men of Normark to be across the Schilde by the day after tomorrow.'

Ragener snorted. 'Here is a lesson for you, young Adelais. Rivers stop armies. It will take four or five days to bring the men of Normark south of the Schilde, and my capital is only two days' ride from the Galman border. And south of here we have the River Gedha to cross before we can fight. At least that one has a bridge.'

'Have the Galmans invaded?' Hjálmar frowned. 'Already?'

'Lancelin is gathering an army at Baudry. Our scouts believe he already has seven thousand men. And since Baudry used to be a Vriesian town, I would say they have already invaded.' Ragener looked at Hjálmar. 'Send a message to Magnus. The army will muster at Gedhabrú, on the south bank of the Gedha. There we will take council. March onwards as soon as you are able.'

Adelais watched Ragener leave, thinking that he could at

least have thanked Hjálmar for four thousand men, or thanked her for helping to persuade them.

The battle seemed suddenly inevitable. The day was fine, the country lush, and the air sweet on the riverside above Silte-hafn, yet their purpose was war. How many of the men around her would return home for their harvests? She turned, nocked an arrow, drew to the bow's straining limits, and loosed.

This time she hit. Square. The key was in the flow.

7.2 GAUTHIER

Gauthier had known for several days that the girl had survived the avalanche, ever since the northmen began arriving at the riverbank, demanding boats. He'd scouted the area south of the river where they'd put her, and knew that there was no way in. Not unless you were Duke Ragener. He stood on the dyke with Roche, watching the duke leave with his entourage.

'The northmen say she caused that avalanche,' Roche muttered. Gauthier's employer wore a plain cote-hardie and a sword, but no retainer's badge; he was an anonymous face amidst an army. Gauthier had reclaimed his priest's robe; priests could go anywhere, except that girl's camp within a camp.

'There were sounds just before it came, like someone was hitting the mountain with a hammer. I have no idea what that was.'

Roche snorted. 'I'm beginning to think you're unlucky.'

Gauthier didn't take the remark seriously. Men like them didn't believe in superstitious nonsense. They were practical men. An avalanche had wiped out the pursuit. End of that plan. What next?

'Our *friends* all died?'

'As far as I know, apart from the man who pulled me out. And if any of the advance party had lived, the girl wouldn't be carrying a tarrazim bow.'

'Do you know where the rest of the tarrazim are, the ones that didn't ride north?'

'I came back with the one who lived. We crossed the river a day's ride east. They're all there, waiting to know if you have any orders. I sense they would like to finish the job.'

As would Gauthier.

Roche turned towards that protected inner area. It was now a square of green open space surrounded by two thousand men. More were arriving with every boat.

'They'd never get to her, Roche. That ring of berserkers is tighter than a duck's arse. This is going to take stealth.' Gauthier wanted this job. It was personal now. No target had ever slipped away from him like this. His professional pride said she had to die.

'I can see that, you fool.' Roche paused, thinking. 'Go and find the rest. Tell them we will hire them all. Give them a chance for revenge. Then take them to the Forest of Liense on the Theignault borders. There is an abandoned tower overlooking the River Gedha, and I will meet them there with gold.'

Gauthier sighed. Roche was wasting his lord's money. 'And then?' He wanted a slice of it.

'Join me at Gedhabrú, where the army musters. Come as a priest. A priest can go where thirty tarrazim cannot. We'll watch for our chance. There will be battles, and in battles people die.'

'Just get me close, Roche. I'll do the rest.' *With relish.*

7.3 TAILLEFER

Taillefer and Agnès drew close to Fontenay when the flower moon was full. Taillefer rode with one of the escort, putting a public distance between himself and Agnès. It was hard to be together and not alone, and harder still to show no affection. Sometimes they rode together, letting their knees touch, and it was enough to be in each other's company. Of all the nights on their journey, staying in the manors and castles where Agnès claimed the hospitality of her class, they had risked being together only once. Spectacularly. Noisily. It was fortunate that their hostess had known Agnès since childhood.

Yet when he rode behind her, Taillefer could not help noticing how straight she sat; narrow-waisted, full-breasted, with her saddle cupping her backside the way he might cradle a goblet of wine in his palm. Was it a sin to want so badly, knowing so well what was possible, or a sin only to yield to such wanting?

The young man-at-arms beside Taillefer was pleasant, in a boyish way, and proud to reveal that he too had been at Harbin on the day the Duke of Delmas fought through Prince

Lancelin's troops. Taillefer remembered him. Guy Carelet. Like all the men-at-arms in their party he wore no identifying retainer's badge. Behind them in the party was Elyse, who'd been at Molinot. Agnès kept her trusted staff close.

Guy looked up at the sun, already past noon, and told Taillefer that it was only another four or five leagues to Château Fontenay. They could be there by dusk, if they pushed on.

Regret swelled within Taillefer. He knew that within her château Agnès would once again be a great lady, surrounded by courtiers and prattling servants. There he must become the scarlet-robed diakonos, and if the Hand of Salazar was indeed at Fontenay, then intimacy with Agnès would be unthinkable. He – they – could not profane its holiness.

Yet Agnès reined in at a fork in the road, where a lesser track led off into forested hills. She announced that there was a hunting lodge in the forest where she would spend the night, having sent warning of her coming ahead to Fontenay. All the men-at-arms of her escort were to ride on, and send messages to summon all her lord's knights, from every corner of his lands. They were to come prepared for a journey, and equipped for battle, with such of their own retainers as could bear arms. And they should come immediately. Guy Carelet and the other men-at-arms should return to the hunting lodge in the morning, in Fontenay livery, as her escort. She would enter Fontenay as befitted its chatelaine. For now, *Master* Taillefer, Pateras Malory, and Elyse would be sufficient protection.

They let Malory and Elyse ride ahead. Within the trees, Agnès's fingers brushed his thigh as they rode. Her eyes had a sparkle that promised much. It seemed their time out of time was not yet over.

It was further to the lodge than Taillefer expected. The sun was halfway to setting when Agnès reined in at a ford across a stream, staring up at the empty battlements of a fortified manor. Once, this small castle must have been significant; the disinte-grating ruins of a settlement lay outside the walls, clustered around a ruined temple.

Elyse seemed excited. She trotted her horse forwards, saying she'd hang some linen out to air. Two ravens circled her head, cawing raucously, as she disappeared around the curve of the curtain wall.

'This was her home,' Agnès explained. She spoke as if the place had deep meaning to her, as well. She nudged her horse forwards, waving towards a meadow that lay before the gates. 'This is where Prince Lancelin's men tried to seize Adelais.'

'Ischyros was with her that day,' Malory added. 'They all died. Seven of them.'

'Also Elyse's husband, who was castellan.' Agnès led the way beneath the portcullis, where one gate lay rotting against the wall. The courtyard beyond was weed-choked and empty apart from drifts of leaf mould in the corners. The windows of a hall gaped sightlessly beside a tower too small to be called a keep; it looked not so much a hunting lodge as a defensive outpost whose military use was long past and which had been abandoned. Taillefer swung out of the saddle and helped Agnès to dismount, a permitted intimacy, before leading their horses towards stables below the curtain wall.

'Where you stand,' Malory pointed to the spot, speaking in the reverent tones of one describing a wonder, 'six moons before the fight on the meadow, Mistress Adelais pulled the crossbow bolt from her own belly and lived, because she had touched the Hand of Salazar.'

Taillefer found the scene hard to imagine. There were just a few wisps of rotting straw and, across the courtyard, Agnès standing on the tower's steps, slowly turning, memories written across her face. 'You saw that too?'

'Indeed, Excellency. I would not believe it otherwise. I was an anakritis, then, before Mistress Adelais opened my eyes to my sins.'

'This woman is like a thread that ties us all together.' Taillefer and Malory pulled saddle bags from the packhorses. There were, of course, no servants. 'It seems we cannot escape her.'

'The heathens say she weaves the threads,' Malory grunted as he shouldered a bag. 'They call her the fate-weaver.'

'Yet you say she is a Blessèd One of Ischyros.' Taillefer lifted his own pack, and another. On the morrow he would be a scarlet-robed diakonos, dispensing blessings and pardons. Today he laboured, willingly.

Malory smiled, a man at peace. 'Those who know the God may interpret His works in different ways.'

Was it really so simple? Together they heaved baggage into the main tower's guardroom, where Elyse was fussing, leaking happy tears, and talking in a continuous stream. *There's dry firewood in the kitchens and the jars have kept the mice out of the oats. I've found some honey too, though everything else is mouldy. I left in a hurry, see? Oh, and there's linen in chests that will be better for an hour in the sun, though you may want to see if there's good straw still in the stable loft...*

Taillefer dropped his bags and climbed the stairs, exploring. Behind him Elyse was once again a castellan's wife, commanding Malory as if he were a servant. *There's meat and day-old bread in the saddle packs. Here's where I hid the cellar key; see if there's wine that's escaped any thieves. There's wrapped cheese down there to age too, where it's cool...*

He found Agnès in the hall, drawing her finger through the dust on a great table.

'We had good times here, Adelais and me.' That woman again. Agnès turned to him, rubbing the fingers of her glove against her thumb. 'There was a minstrel. We danced. We were happy.' She made it sound as if they were lovers. 'And now I must raise an army against her.'

That should not have surprised him. 'I thought we were here for the Hand?'

'Of course.' Agnès smiled, too brightly, as if she'd said too much. 'But if the Vriesians come, we will have word by messenger. Prince Lancelin's forces will be drawn north to defend the border, so it will be safe for lords loyal to the Duke of Delmas to gather. A truce between the factions must happen; the de Fontenay knights will be needed to repel any invasion. Lancelin could not do that alone.'

Taillefer frowned. 'Yet you have just summoned the knights. You must be very sure that there will be war.'

'Even if there is no war, a powerful escort must take the Hand to Harbin. Either way, we need the knights. And it will take some days for them to gather. I wish we could spend those days here.' She sighed wistfully. 'Molinot belongs to me. Fontenay is Leandre's. This is Leandre's too, but feels as if it is mine.'

'Would it be safe?'

'For one night. Two nights and there'd be talk. Elyse will have her old room off the kitchens. Malory will be warm in the guard room. The lord's chamber is just above, and there's a guest chamber for you in the tower.' Agnès put both hands behind her, displaying to him, her eyes saucy. 'That might be quieter...'

Taillefer yearned for the day to be done; the necessary eating and talking before everyone retired. 'It is almost time for the Lighting of the Lamps. Pateras Malory and I will rekindle the sacred flame in that ruined temple.' As they neared the Hand, his priesthood was starting to reclaim him. The conflict within was tightening.

.   .   .

He did not don his scarlet robes that night, even when he'd washed away the dirt of the journey; he was holding on to something that would be lost on the morrow. He and Agnès sat late in the hall, waiting for the sounds from the others to fade. They had arranged two chairs side by side in front of the fire, like an old married couple, and the silences between them were as eloquent as any sonnet. They had found a place of calm, on this their final night; a companionship that neither wanted to end.

'Is it a sin to love, do you think?' Agnès spoke towards the flames.

'I cannot believe that. Surely the God loves his creation?'

'I mean, just love. To be complete in someone's presence, even if they irritate one?'

'Do I irritate you so very much, Agnès?'

'So much I could hit you sometimes. All that stiff-backed piety. Lighting the Lamps when we could have just kissed. This night is so precious.'

Taillefer sipped a fine Jourdainian wine, supple as silk. He felt wonderfully mellow, staring at the embers. Unusually, she'd hardly touched hers.

'At first, I thought it was just our bodies,' Agnès continued. 'You gave me more pleasure than I had ever known.' She looked up, smiling wistfully. 'But after all these nights of unwanted purity on the road, I know I shall miss your company most of all.'

Taillefer took her hand and lifted it to his lips. 'And I know that there is something within me that will always turn somersaults at the sight of you, however pompous I may seem on the outside.'

'Though a little ploughing would never be unwelcome.' Her smile became mischievous and she opened her legs just a little, provocatively; enough for the buckle of her loosely fastened belt to drop into the valley.

Taillefer cocked his head to one side. Silence. 'Talking of which, I think the others are abed.'

'Then let me show you to your chamber.' She stood on tiptoes to kiss him, letting her body press against his before she led him towards the stairs.

At the door to his chamber they kissed again, and his body stirred in response. He made a small sigh of regret when she pulled apart, but it was only to push at the door, take his hand, and lead him inwards.

'Time out of time,' she murmured.

As dawn crept through the shutters, she took him, again, before he was fully awake, with a desperate urgency as if she needed to imprint his body on hers, and hers on his. She who had so often cried out with her own fulfilment now wept, quietly, when he was spent. She stayed straddling him as if to pin this moment to her soul.

Taillefer framed her face with his hands and kissed away her tears. 'Hush, my love.'

'But today you'll be a diakonos and I'll be a lady and we won't be able to touch each other ever again.' She sniffed.

He had no words for that. He could only stroke her back and crush her to him. She was right. Soon he would kneel with Pateras Malory, and he would unburden, for though he felt no guilt, he could not be in the presence of the Hand with this 'sin' upon him. And once he had unburdened, he would have to swear to sin no more before he could accept the sacred ash of pardon. Their 'time out of time' was over.

Agnès pushed away, sitting up. *By all that is holy, she is magnificent!* Taillefer reached for her.

'I must tell you something, my love, while we are together.' Agnès lifted his hand away from her breast.

'It is well over a moon since Molinot.' She pressed his finger-tips into the warmth of her belly, between her bush and her navel, in a way that was intimate but not seductive. 'And I have missed my courses.' She looked into his eyes, willing him to understand. 'I am with child, my love. Your child.'

7.4 ADELAIS

Twenty leagues south of Siltehafn, the main road towards Galmandie crossed a small river. Adelais knew this land; she'd ridden north up this road in the snow moon after her escape, a solitary figure in lordling's clothes. Now she was riding south with an army.

A small keep commanded the crossing from the crown of a hill on the southern bank; a single tower set in a curtain wall that might enclose the accommodation and stabling for a garrison of twenty men. Today this tiny fort flew the red eagle of Vriesland, for Ragener had made it his temporary headquarters. An insignificant cluster of houses lay beneath the tower, mainly catering for travellers. An inn. A cobbler. A blacksmith. An Ischyrian temple, beneath its pointing, carved hand. The village was called, she remembered, Gedhabrú: the bridge over the Gedha. Beyond the keep, the road followed the spine of a long, low hill that local folk called 'Nautshrygg', the bull's back. She remembered open fields stretching towards the horizon, where teams of oxen dragged ploughs for the first cut of the spring. There had been a smell of newly turned earth, the chill of late snow on the wind, and the cries of seagulls feasting in the ploughs' wakes. Today Nautshrygg was the gathering place for an army, its crops trampled before they could ripen, and the breeze stank of leather and latrines.

Adelais and Hjálmar had dismounted on the northern bank, thirty paces from the road, where a grassy slope gave their horses good grazing; there was no rush, and once the whole army had assembled they might have to range far for fresh grass. Below them, the river curved in a great, north-pointing loop around Nautshrygg like the moat around a castle, cutting the hill into slight river cliffs on each side. Too deep to ford and too shallow in places for river craft to come upstream, the River Gedha's main purpose seemed to be to water the lush country-side around it, now green with crops, and to choke their south-ward advance. The bridge was broad, but marshals were forcing men to cross no more than four abreast, or two carts at a time, lest the pounding damage the structure. Troops were backed up to the north as far as the eye could see.

They sat on Hjálmar's cloak, their horses' reins held loosely in their hands, watching the shuffling passage of men. Four of Hjálmar's men had halted with them as her guards. A young squire also waited nearby, holding Adelais's banner at an angle away from his stirrup so that her device of a black wolf on a golden field could be seen. Ragener's insistence on a standard bearer irritated her. That banner set her on a level with the great nobles; the blue chevron of Theignault or the green oak of Sjóland. Like her leather armour, it proclaimed her to be more than she was. The well-born lad who'd been given the task was puffed with self-importance at his role. Pompous little *gyke*.

A line of Jarl Magnus's berserkers was edging past, calling greetings to Hjálmar. A few of them lifted spears or axes and shouted '*hún ulfúr*,' she-wolf, laughing in a way that made her feel more of a mascot than a leader.

'They seem happy.' Adelais waved her acknowledgement.

'They just like your leather tits, princess.' Hjálmar spoke

quietly, for her ears only. He handed her a flask, and she sipped. Water, clean as snow.

'Would they fight better if I took off my armour?' She liked this easy camaraderie.

'They'd think the *Valkyrjur* had come to take them to Valhalla.'

'There's nothing much underneath, you know.'

'Enough, I think. But I want them looking at the enemy, not over their shoulder at you.'

'Sometimes I feel a fraud.' Adelais could let herself be vulnerable with Hjálmar. 'A bit like these.' She tapped her chest. 'All these men following me because they think I'm more than I am.'

'Princess.' Hjálmar turned to her, leaning on an elbow. He sounded earnest. He had one leg bent at the knee, and his chain-mail hauberk had fallen away to reveal a mighty, hose-clad thigh.

'Troll-man.' She imitated his tone, mock-frowning.

He ignored her. 'I know you well enough to be sure that, when the time comes, you will find strength. Revna heard that you threw a *gydhja* two paces with rune magic.'

'And the *gydhjur* told me that rune magic will win a fight, but only wisdom will win a war.'

'I think you are sharper than you know. And when it comes to what's inside the armour...'

'Yes?' She hoped he'd hear the warning in her voice.

'I've heard it said that anything more than a mouthful is a waste.'

She swung her fist back-handed into his shoulder. Even through a gauntlet, the chain mail hurt her knuckles.

'*Fordæmdur* troll.' She shook her fingers. She wasn't upset. Not really. And he knew it. The flirting made her feel good. Warm and wanted. But she'd never let it go any further.

Adelais closed her eyes, drowsy with the day's warmth. She

had not slept well; she'd had the nightmare of the choking hand and had woken with a loose corner of linen wrapped around her neck. The air throbbed with the tramp of feet and rumble of carts, and she tried to focus instead on the steady chomp of Allier's grazing. He was ripping the grass with the same rhythmic, methodical intent with which a woodsman might hew a tree. There was a backdrop of birdsong and the hum of insects. War could be far away.

Adelais wondered where the wolf was lurking. She would probably swim this river after dark. Adelais no longer feared for her; she would be close.

A new jangling of metal, unlike any armour, intruded into her thoughts. She straightened, looking for its source.

'What in the nine worlds is that?' Hjálmar lifted his chin towards the road, where a line of carts had appeared, each large enough to require ten oxen to pull them, yoked in pairs. Their slow, ponderous progress was a little faster than the men queuing to cross the bridge, who moved to the side of the road to let them pass. The first flat-bed cart seemed to be stacked with baulks of timber so long that their bouncing ends projected many paces behind. Others had reinforced sides and held great stones, two handspans across, that had clearly been quarried and roughly dressed until they were the same size and weight. And at the head of this procession, beaming with pride, strode Knud, the stocky armourer who'd made Adelais's moulded leather suit. She rose to her feet and crossed to meet him. Her guards pressed their horses forwards, flanking her.

'Well met, Master Knud.' She spoke without great warmth for the man who'd taken such delight in enhancing her shape. 'What do you carry?'

'Greetings, mistress.' The armourer swept off his hat and bowed, his gaze lingering too long on her chest on the way down. 'Meet Geri and Freki!' The first truck rumbled past as he spoke. It had the thickest wheels she'd ever seen, and was dragged not by conventional harness of wood and leather but by great lengths of clanking chain.

'The wolves of Odhinn, armourer? Are you planning to carve them in wood, as you carved my body?'

'I will assemble them, mistress. They are trebuchets!'

'What is a trebuchet?' Adelais sensed she was asking a stupid question.

'Mighty slings that will pound a town's walls to rubble!' He grinned at the prospect. 'Three hundred paces they will throw these rocks!'

'And these?' Adelais pointed to the next cart, stacked with rope-bound spheres and a line of barrels. Even above the stink of beasts and men she smelt the reek of oil.

'Fireballs, mistress. They goes even further. We soaks the rope outside in oil and put fire to it. The stone inside smashes houses, and *poof*! The town burns.' He lifted his hands, wiggling his fingers to imitate flames.

'And how does burning a town help us defend Vriesland from invasion?' she asked.

The armourer laughed as if she were a child, shook his head, and walked on.

'We are summoned, princess.' Hjálmar pointed out Everard de Warelt, the squire who'd been her mentor at Ragener's court. He stood on the far bank, calling to them across the now-choked bridge. His words were lost in the thunder of wheels and oxen crossing the wooden surface, but his beckoning arm was unmistakable. 'I suspect there is to be a council of war.'

Adelais sighed as they turned to remount. She was uncomfortable among the nobles, no longer trusting any of them. Which one of them had paid to have her killed? And not just her – Hjálmar too. And Magnus, with his warriors. Was it Sjóland? Theignault? Or Duchess Severine? Ragener still insisted it must be agents of Prince Lancelin. Who else, he said, would benefit from the collapse of the Vriesian alliance? At least there had been no sign of any more tarrazim.

But until Adelais knew who ordered her death, she stayed as much as she could amidst men she could trust. Magnus's berserkers. The northern jarls. And perhaps de Warelt.

Adelais took the short, recurved tarrazim bow from behind her saddle so that she could mount. 'Teach me some more, later?' She lifted it towards Hjálmar. Under his tuition she could now hit a stationary, shield-sized target at twenty paces, but only if she stood squarely on the ground. She had a whole new pattern of aches across her shoulders from the strain.

'Of course!'

They were both aware that being seen with tarrazim bows added to their mystique. Adelais had overheard the campfire talk. *Someone sent forty tarrazim to kill her, and she brought a mountain down on them!*

Adelais made a point of wearing it over her shoulder to the council of war, with a quiver of arrows on her belt, hoping that one of the nobles there would understand her defiance. She watched their eyes for signs, but saw only amusement. She took a seat against the wall of the tower room and watched. The key nobles hunched over the table, shoulders high, arms splayed around a map. The southern lords' surcoats trailed to their knees; Theignault's blue chevron and Ragener's red eagle dominating the discussion. Sjóland said little. Jarl Magnus, in chain mail and arm-rings, was also a listener, until it really mattered to speak. De Warelt and Hjálmar were there to observe, it seemed, like her.

'Twenty leagues to Baudry,' Theignault insisted. The count had the aloof manner of someone trying to ignore the smell of ordure. 'And the land is open all the way. The enemy is gathering to defend the city, but not with their full might—we believe about seven thousand, mainly foot.' He spoke in the clear Galman of the nobility and probably thought Vriesian was the language of peasants.

'Are we attacking Galmandie or defending Vriesland?' Adelais asked, thinking it was a perfectly reasonable question, but it earned her glares from around the table. De Warelt lifted a finger to his lips to silence her. No one answered.

'But what of our flanks?' Ragener drew his fingers over the map, ignoring her. As he bent, his sword belt curved under his gut, like a leather hammock. 'Our line of march is unprotected now we are south of the Gedha.'

'To the east is Theignault. My lands. I would know of any threat.' The count's voice around the table carried weight; a hundred knights and a thousand mounted men-at-arms owed him fealty – the bulk of the Vriesian cavalry.

'And my lands are to the west,' Sjóland made a rare interjection. 'I too would learn of any incursion. My scouts have ranged as far as the sea. There can be no force large enough to threaten us.'

'And beyond Baudry?' Ragener spoke as if he had already made a decision, but was seeking confirmation.

'Beyond the border with Galmandie we must be more discreet.' Theignault sounded as if Ragener's caution was testing his patience. 'I sent squires on fast horses, without armour, ostensibly as messengers. Again, they report no sign of the enemy in force as far as Harbin.'

Ragener straightened, a slow smile spreading across his face. 'It is as we were told. The Duke of Delmas and the warrior lords of Galmandie are letting young Prince Lancelin suffer alone. They are sacrificing Baudry to win a crown. My lords, are we agreed?'

Adelais wondered where that intelligence had come from. Around the table, several heads turned to Magnus, who shrugged.

'I have marched four thousand men south. I'm not going to

march them back without a fight.' His beard tufted around his mouth as his face split into a broad, rather evil grin. 'And perhaps a little Galman silver!' He too spoke Galman, but with the heavy, lilting accents of the north. Half of these lords probably wouldn't understand Vriesian.

'Then, my lords,' Ragener rapped the table with his knuckles, 'we shall accept the gift they offer and retake Baudry for Vriesland!' At his signal, servants appeared with jugs of wine.

Adelais stared into her goblet. She supposed that if she asked what happened after Baudry, it would be taken as another dumb question.

She sipped, enough to be polite, and left as soon as she decently could. Her ring of berserkers formed around her, shields outwards, and Adelais wished she could go for a quiet walk, alone.

Beyond the keep's curtain wall, the army was camped all along the hill of Nautshrygg, leaving only the road as a moving spine of men dividing a broad back of tents. The sun made their linen look like fields of dirty snow. Near the keep, a gaudy cluster of nobles' pavilions was being erected. One of those would be for her and Revna. Beneath the army's feet, a crop of wheat was being trampled back into the soil. Adelais trailed a crushed stalk through her fingers. She hoped the farmers would be compensated.

'You are troubled, my lady?' De Warelt had followed her out. Her escort looked to her for permission before letting him close.

'It's all pretence, isn't it?' Adelais straightened, breathing deeply. She was on dangerous ground, but just then she didn't care. Let Ragener throw her into a dungeon. See what happened to these berserkers who'd marched south with her and Jarl Magnus.

'And what are we pretending?' De Warelt sounded more amused than upset.

'To defend Vriesland. They were never going to invade this year, were they? This is all about grabbing more land, isn't it? Snatching Baudry while the Galmans are divided. We're no better than the Galmans when they came north and beat us at Vannemeer.'

'Ah, yes, the lesson of Vannemeer. How long will it take the army to cross that little river down there?'

Adelais shrugged; she didn't see the point of the question. 'A day?'

'Two days. And how long did it take Jarl Magnus's forces to cross the Schilde?'

'Five days.'

'And Siltehafn is just five days' easy march for cavalry from the Galman border. We lost at Vannemeer because the jarls' forces were all north of the Schilde, growing crops or raiding elsewhere. Our capital is vulnerable until we push them back. We are simply retaking what was stolen from us.'

'And what happens when the northmen go back to their farms, or the Galmans decide who's going to be their king?'

'We will have taught them such a lesson that they will think hard before attacking us again.'

'So we're punishing, not defending.' Adelais picked up a pebble and hefted it in her palm. She missed hunting; that carefree, earthy, solitary creeping along a riverbank, sling ready. No politics. No *gykes*. No killing except ducks or pigeons. 'Four thousand men came south because they thought they were defending their gods. They thought I was their *örlaga vefari,* the woman the *seidhkonur* prophesied would unite Vriesland and let them live their lives the way they wanted.'

'You heard Jarl Magnus. They came for glory and silver.'

'They didn't need me to do that.'

'A word of advice, my lady.' De Warelt's voice hardened. 'Don't let Duke Ragener think you have fulfilled your purpose. He might agree with you.'

Adelais threw her pebble at the curtain wall, hard enough for it to splinter against the stone. For a moment she felt light-headed and disoriented, as if she were once again standing on top of the boulder in the pass, and the crack of the pebble was the pounding of her staff. The avalanche when it began had been silent; a mighty slab of sliding snow, seen before its thunderous noise was heard. She turned, staggering a little at the sense that the fields of grey-white tents had begun to slip to the south, towards Galmandie. Soon there would be cataclysmic noise; of falling ice, of battle. She'd started the avalanche with a blow of her staff, and at least fifteen men had died. And she'd started this war when the jarls felt the power of another blow of her staff, at Heilagtré. How many would die now? Fifteen thousand?

7.5 TAILLEFER

Taillefer climbed the steps to the temple of Château Fontenay with Agnès distractingly, untouchably close beside him. The wonder and the sin of her body lay fresh as scent on his skin, and the turmoil of her news filled his thoughts. He glanced at her; she was moving with regal grace, head high, attendants in her wake, the returning chatelaine in a full-sleeved, silken gown that clung to her body like a sheath. Green today. Like her eyes. Her belt hung loosely over her hips with its buckle enticingly low over a still-flat belly. The glow of her skin would be taken as a sign of radiant health. It made him want to hold her again.

And he was entering a temple. Behind them walked Malory, the priest who had just unburdened him for this sin. Yet Taillefer felt no guilt. Agnès had become a part of his soul. He felt he should be more anxious for her – the child could not be her husband's, and soon she would show. Why, then, did he feel such joy? They had done this; it had been formed in something wonderful, even if the consequences were unimaginable.

He knew immediately that the priest waiting to greet them was a holy man; there is a calmness that comes to people, whether they are religious or lay, when they are certain of their passage across the bridge of judgement into the arms of Ischyros. It is a humble confidence rooted not in the shallow zeal of a convert, but in long years of great piety. Pateras Bardolph was short, with the lean frame of an ascetic, and a fringe of fine, grey hair beneath his red pardoner's cap. He limped; one sandalled foot was disfigured and missing a toe.

Taillefer could reach much from a person's eyes. Usually it was deference for his scarlet robes, even if only a facade. At other times it was timidity. Today his priesthood, his morality, seemed worthless, yet Bardolph regarded him with gentle grey eyes full of compassion. If they saw failure, it was through a veil of mercy. This was a man at one with the God, a worthier man than Taillefer would ever be.

'Pateras Bardolph was a priest to the Order of Guardians.' Agnès finished her introductions with a gracious gesture of her arm, trailing green silk. She looked towards Malory in a way that invited him to speak.

'And I was once of the anakritim.' Malory bowed humbly. 'A persecutor who will spend his life in atonement.'

Bardolph's eyes flicked towards Malory; a moment's tension before he relaxed.

'And I unburdened King Aloys on his deathbed,' Taillefer added. 'I know the wrongs that were done.'

Bardolph took one of Malory's hands in his, and reached up to place his other hand gently on Malory's head. 'Your contrition is sincere, so the God will already have pardoned you, Pateras. Who am I to harbour grievances for that which the God has already set aside? With my whole heart, I forgive you.'

Malory fell to his knees and kissed Bardolph's hand as if he were a diakonos. His eyes had filled.

Agnès diverted attention away from them by turning to the ladies and men-at-arms following her and dismissing them. 'I will meet with the priests alone.'

There were times when the command in Agnès's voice

reminded Taillefer that the soft, passionate woman he knew also ruled great estates. By the God, he loved her.

They were alone by the time Bardolph had lifted Malory to his feet.

'I bear a letter from Lord Leandre.' Agnès held out a small, sealed scroll.

Bardolph waved them to seats near the sanctuary while he read. When he had finished he knelt in front of the sacred flame, held the letter to it, and bowed his head in prayer while the letter burned.

'So the time has come,' he sighed. 'After two hundred years.'

'Lord Leandre believes the Hand will restore the faith.' Agnès still spoke with authority, even on this clerical matter.

Bardolph rose to his feet, still staring at the flame. 'I pray that is his only motivation, my lady. I hope this decision was only taken after great prayer. I wish I could have supported him in that.'

'Perhaps you could tell us of your association with the Hand, Pateras?' Taillefer needed to be sure. Provenance was all-important with relics.

Bardolph turned. 'I served Ischyros in the citadel of the Guardians in Villebénie, where the Hand has been kept since the great battle when the Blessèd Salazar was wounded. It was brought there, we are told, by Jovan de Fontenay. It was wrapped in silk and kept in a gold reliquary in the form of a hand, which was only ever shown to the third degree of Guardians, the great officers of the Order whose faith and courage were beyond question.'

'And how did it escape the searches of the king's men?'

'The Hand itself was hidden among old vestments by the last grand master. I believe the gold was thrown into an armourer's furnace. The king's men and the anakritim were searching for a golden idol, not a relic.'

'Pateras Bardolph endured great torture, but did not reveal the Hand.' Agnès nodded towards Bardolph's foot.

Malory hunched in shame. One of the anakritim's methods was to smear a victim's foot in pig fat and hold it in a fire until they talked. Taillefer started to offer stuttering praise for his courage, but Bardolph lifted his hand to stop him. 'Lord Brother Humbert Blanc took the Hand, by agreement with Lord Leandre. By the God's grace, Lord Leandre recovered it at a hunting lodge before it could be discovered by the anakritim.'

'I was there, to my lasting shame,' Malory added.

'After that, Lord Leandre invited me to come to Fontenay from Villebénie. There are too few of us who can be trusted with such knowledge.'

'Indeed.' Malory and Taillefer spoke together.

'And now Lord Leandre has chosen to reveal the Hand to the world.' Bardolph sounded doubtful.

Agnès shifted on her seat. 'The faith has suffered much through the Guardian persecution and the mistakes of the anakritim. Lord Leandre believes that the Hand will breathe life into the people of the God.'

Bardolph inclined his head. 'It is his decision to make, though I do not believe any mortal truly owns the Hand. We are merely custodians. But I will warn all of you, and Lord Leandre: the Hand will punish anyone who uses it for base purposes. I cannot say this strongly enough. It is not a curiosity. It is the holiest relic on earth.'

'The Hand must be attested by a clerical court, as you know.' Taillefer tried to sound reassuring. 'This will be held in my own temple at Harbin under the direction of the Episkopos of Villebénie. I hope you will come with us and give your evidence. If attested, Lord Leandre hopes to re-establish the Knights Guardian as the Hand's protectors.'

Bardolph stood. Only the movements of his hands, working over each other as if washing, showed his distraction. 'All my life I have held this precious secret. I have endured much for it. I feel rather like a father sending their child out into the world, not knowing how they will fare.' He limped to the sanctuary and stood with his head bowed in prayer before turning towards Agnès. 'My lady, if you will forgive us? This is now a matter for the priesthood.'

If Agnès felt any resentment at being dismissed from her own chapel, she hid it behind a graceful inclination of the head. Bardolph bolted the doors of the temple behind her and returned to the sanctuary. He knelt at a tomb set into the floor, decorated with a brass engraving of some long-dead de Fontenay in the armour of an earlier age. Bardolph took a knife from his belt and prised off the name plaque, revealing a small cavity. The plaque had been flush with the rest of the brass lid and was not immediately apparent as a separate piece. He reached inside and tugged at some hidden bolt or catch. There was a snap as it was released, and the entire brass cover of the tomb could be lifted and tilted onto its side. A square recess had been cut into the capstone beneath, about the size of a man's forearm on each side, and half as deep. Within it lay a small, oaken chest, of the kind a lady might use to keep her jewels.

They all made the sign of the God.

Bardolph gestured towards the box. 'Beneath here is the tomb of Aramis de Fontenay, who was father to both Bayard and Jovan de Fontenay, the brothers who fought beside the prophet at the great battle. Bayard is the ancestor of Lord Leandre. It is said that this tomb was where the Hand lay until Jovan founded the Order of Guardians and wrote the rule by which we lived.' He bowed his head in another brief prayer, lifted out the chest, and placed it with great reverence before the sacred flame. 'Our Order not only guarded the faith and the faithful, it guarded the most sacred relic on earth.'

Taillefer knelt beside him, staring at the oak box. It was

completely plain, under a coating of dust, without lettering or adornment.

It did not need lettering. Taillefer could feel its power. He took a deep breath, trying not to weep. He had to swallow before he could speak and even then it was with hushed tones.

'Why was it kept secret for so long?'

'Jovan de Fontenay lived long enough to see the wealth that was made from the relics of Tanguy, the First Disciple. And Jovan held to a simpler faith. All Guardians swore a vow of poverty; they had no interest in personal wealth. Jovan and his successors as grand master chose to wait for a less venal time. Pray the God that it has come.'

Bardolph reached forwards and opened the lid. There was no lock. The chest was lined with padded satin that might once have been white but had faded to ivory, and on a cushion of the same material lay a neatly-folded parcel of ancient silk, yellow with age, and stained with blotches that had faded to a thin, rusty brown; the blood of the prophet. The ridges and furrows in the wrapping might be stones or sticks, not the bones of Salazar Himself.

Taillefer made a choking cry and threw himself prostrate on the floor, feeling no shame at the tears flowing so freely down his face. *Beneath the Hand of Salazar, the God will prevail.* Thus it was written. Thus a carved hand was raised above every temple in Ischyrendom. At the great battle on the shores of Alympos, when all seemed lost, the prophet himself had lifted high his own severed hand and turned defeat into victory.

He did not need to look further, within the wrappings. He knew he was in the presence of divinity, and knew himself blessed beyond measure. This would change the whole world.

'I am not worthy,' he sobbed.

Bardolph gently touched his shoulder.

'None of us are.'

7.6 ADELAIS

The lush birdsong of the dawn chorus lifted Adelais from sleep; it fluttered upwards through the tent lines from the bushes down by the River Gedha. She slipped from under her covers and dressed quietly in the simple kirtle and underskirt of a peasant; Revna still slept, deeply and noisily. Adelais fished her sling out of her baggage, gathered her bow and quiver, and slipped out of the tent into a morning laced with blossom, male sweat, and the charcoal of old fires. Around her, eleven thousand men snored like a single, rumbling giant. The guard leaning on his spear outside nodded but, by agreement with Hjálmar, did not follow. This morning just Hjálmar would be her guard. It was a risk, but worth taking. She could not hunt within a ring of shields.

Adelais rapped on the pole of Hjálmar's tent and grinned her greeting as he ducked under the flap; she felt as if they were two children slipping away from their chores to steal apples from an orchard. He too was dressed for a hunt in a simple cote-hardie, though he'd belted on a sword.

Naturally, they were seen. No one can move through a camped army without being seen. But perhaps they were not

recognised in their drab clothes; she'd wrapped the bow in a
cloak, so she might be mistaken for a camp follower. She was
not the only woman with the army. As they scrambled down the
river cliff to the banks, more than one soldier was pissing away
the previous night's beer. She and Hjálmar must have looked
like a man and his maid, creeping away for private time in the
bushes; one soldier called out a ribald question, and muttered
'lucky bastard' when they didn't answer. She fingered her hair;
not yet long enough for full maiden's braids, but it had grown
enough to be plaited and pinned, almost like the real thing. She
wished she could brush them out, just for the freedom of it,
though that would have been indecent; only husbands should
see a woman's hair loose. Yet to walk free, without armour or
banners, made her feel like a real woman, not an icon on a
warhorse.

Thank the gods, no one came after them to demand she take
a larger escort. She and Hjálmar followed a path going
upstream on the river bank, stooping to pick up smooth stones
when they spotted them. A light, early mist lay over the water,
quickly clouding the view over their shoulders to the tented hill
of Nautshrygg. She and Hjálmar were quiet as they walked – as
quiet as it was possible to be with Hjálmar crashing through
bushes like a lumbering ox – while the sounds of the waking
camp slowly gave way to birdsong. Several times he startled
ducks into the water before she could come within slingshot
range. She'd have no hope of hitting them with an arrow.

Yet. Soon they would find a tree for target practice.

'You are thoughtful, princess.' They'd reached a meadow
where they could walk side by side. The river flowed quietly
beside them, trailing waterweed, disturbed by the occasional
swirl of a rising trout. Armies and war might belong to another
world.

Adelais ran the thongs of her sling through her fingers,
thinking.

'In Heilagtré I felt close to the gods. There was an ancient peace, a strength about the place. I felt the power of rune magic. My *own* rune magic. The *gydhjur* convinced me that we were going to war to defend the ways of our ancestors, so that we and our descendants could honour the old gods as we have always done. They told me I had a part to play. An important one.'

'Do you doubt you have a role?' Hjálmar's voice was gentle. He was truly listening.

'I *had* a role. I helped convince the jarls, and four thousand men marched south. But there is no Galman invasion. Was never going to be an invasion, not this year. It's all about conquest, not defence. Ragener's ambition. Land, not beliefs.'

'Half the Vriesians south of the Schilde are Ischyrian. The Counts of Theignault and Sjóland are Ischyrian. They would not fight just to let us worship Odhinn. They too fight for lands and glory, and the right to be a sovereign nation.'

'And the jarls' men?'

'Most of them planted their crops, left their wives and children and old folk to tend them, and marched south because their jarl told them to. They want to go home loaded with Galman silver in time for the harvest.'

'Most of them? What of the others?'

'The berserkers are different. They are as feared on the battlefield as the Guardian knights used to be, because they want to die gloriously. They believe that if they die valiantly in battle, the *Valkyrjur* will take them to Odhinn's hall in Valhalla. They also know that you are rune-marked. To them, Odhinn has claimed you as his own. They will take your words as if they come from the lips of the All-Father himself.'

'*Skit!*' Adelais threw a stone into the river. She seemed to be throwing a lot of stones near Gedhabrú. A duck she hadn't spotted squawked and flapped out of the reeds, its wings spreading overlapping rings across the water.

'Don't scare the game!'

She pushed him, hard. It was like barging a tree.

'But if you don't give them the chance to die with a sword in their hand, they'll settle for Galman silver. And maybe a few stories to boast about in the feasting halls, of how they fought the Galmans alongside the *örlaga vefari*. What they can't do is go home empty-handed and without a fight.'

The duck she'd startled came edging back across the river, trailing an arrowhead wake. Adelais loosed her sling at it and missed. Too much anger.

'Talking of going home empty-handed...' Hjálmar teased.

She stuck out her tongue at him.

'Why can't my fate have been to have a farm and raise crops and babies?'

'Maybe you will.' Hjálmar paused, as if choosing his words. 'I like babies.'

Adelais turned to look at him, lifting an eyebrow. He grinned evilly.

'But I couldn't eat a whole one!'

It was good to laugh. She felt her cares slip.

'Do you want to try again? Ducks. On the bank.' He nodded upstream, where a pair were huddled on a sandspit on a bend in the river, fifty paces away, their beaks tucked under their wings.

'Stay here.' Adelais signalled to Hjálmar.

'Woof!'

Sætur Sif, it was good to play. Adelais dropped her bow and stretched out the thongs of her sling. She wasn't going to waste a precious arrow shooting over water. She edged around the birds, ensuring her silhouette would always be against the trees and hill behind. Slowly, slowly. Forty paces. Thirty. She slipped a stone into her sling's pouch and pulled the thongs out to their full length. Twenty, in range. One duck lifted its head, looking at her. Aim small, miss small. *That* feather, high on the wing. She swung.

Yes! She'd hit the head. The bird made a single flap and

rolled, thrashing, at the water's edge. Its companion took off in a clatter of wings and Adelais ran forwards, whooping, but the dying bird's struggles had carried it out, into the water. She threw herself down on the bank and pulled off her boots, watching the bird spiral away on the current, twitching. She gathered up her skirts, kilting them over her belt as she waded out to catch the body before it was carried away. By the time she waded back out, triumphant, she was soaked to her thighs and elbows. Hjálmar stood on the bank above the spit, looking at her in a way that was fond and serious at the same time, and she threw him the now-dead bird. She made a little dance to shake out her skirts, scattering a ring of droplets onto the sand.

Adelais found a moment of pure, irresponsible happiness, and laughed aloud for the joy of it; the rising sun, low and indistinct through the haze, sand that squeaked beneath her feet as she bounced, even the tiny caves of old sand martins' nests in the bank. She sat on its grassy edge and unrolled saturated hose from her legs, not minding if Hjálmar saw. She even threw them at him as she stood and turned. She missed, but he growled in mock anger, and bent to offer her a helping hand up the bank. One hand became two; he lifted her lightly and easily under the arms, swung her into the air, and kissed her full on the lips. For a heartbeat, just a heartbeat, she melted into him. Wanted to wrap her legs around him. But her hands came up, between them, pushing him away.

'No, Hjálmar.'

He put her down but still held her, letting his hands slip down her body so that his thumbs brushed her in a way that was dangerously welcome.

'Why?' Those huge hands now rested at her waist, almost encircling it. 'What we have... it is more than friendship.'

A stupid, rebellious part of her wanted to yield to the warmth within her, but she pushed harder against his chest, leaving damp patches on his cote-hardie. He let her go.

'When I grow close to someone, they die.' Adelais breathed deeply, wishing she did not have to sacrifice this moment. 'I don't want you to die.' She reached up to touch his cheek, intending it as a gesture of apology. His beard was soft under her fingers. 'I like you too much to let myself love you. To let you love me.'

Hjálmar stroked his cheek against her palm.

'In that, my princess, you have already failed.'

7.7 FYLGJA

The *fylgja* watches the girl and the man from within the woodland's margins. They play like cubs, these two, batting each other with sheathed claws, and growling in a way that has no menace. She wonders if they will mate.

She does not approach. There are many men nearby; so many that the wolf within tugs at her, wanting wilderness, not this land of tended fields and woodlands. Here she can feast on lambs, but there are dogs, and with the dogs are more men with bows and slings; there is good reason why she does not encounter other wolf-kind. Besides, the girl is not in danger, not in this moment.

Yet there is a heaviness to the morning that belies the dancing dragonflies and the glow of sun through mist, for an ending is coming. Her own ending. She feels it in the warp and weft of fate, and she feels it in this place more than in any other.

There have been endings before, in the realm of that which has come to pass. None were easy. Once she was *seidhkona* and chose her ending that she might become *fylgja*. That was hard; she had had to fight her own inner being, much as she now has sometimes to fight the wolf. No matter how much her mind and

her heart wished to make that step, her wild, animal self had
clung to life, refusing to let her spirit leave her body. She had
worked *seidhr* until her strength was utterly spent; only then
did her ageing heart stop.

There was another ending that was more a letting-go;
another wolf that had accepted her readily and served her well.
The bond had been strong. From another forest margin, by
another river, they had watched the girl fight, and win, and she,
fylgja, had known that her task was done. Releasing that wolf to
her reward of pack and wilderness had been like falling asleep,
a long expiring of breath. All was endings and beginnings, the
cycle of renewal.

The gods would not give such choices for love alone. The
gods take little interest in the affairs of men, until the affairs of
men threaten the gods themselves. The girl must be given her
chance to fulfil her destiny; the gods need their fate-weaver,
even though she may not be enough. She is a roll of dice, a
casting of runes.

A bird swoops low over the water and she remembers
another life; so brief, so tenuous that it is like a dream, half-
forgotten with the dawn; a slicing pain and a brief, fluttering
fall. That too she chose.

Now there will be another ending. Whether in days or a
moon, she cannot tell. She senses it being woven into that which
is coming to pass, for this world is changing. It is like the tilt of
the year when rich summer slides towards an iron winter.
Somewhere to the south and east, a terrible light has risen. It is
unstoppable. Even the gods could not stop it. She can guide, she
can warn, but she has no more hope of resisting this icy sun than
a leaf would have of holding back autumn.

The wolf within her senses this ending. It wants to run. If
this ending must come, then let it be among its kind, among the
pack that might accept her back. But the *fylgja* knows that she
cannot run from this destiny. Flee death here, and it will find

her half a moon later when the pack tears the wolf apart for the difference it cannot flee. Herself.

The *fylgja* reads the threads of fate the way the wolf reads a landscape, with sight and smell and instinct. She questions, she listens.

Will we be together, at this ending?

Yes. That fate is already woven. The answering voice in her mind is Verdhandi, the Norn who weaves what is coming into being.

Will she have an ending too?

All mortal creatures have an ending. Urdhr now, her old voice dry as bones.

But when?

There was a pause, as if the Nornir were consulting one another, before the girl-woman Skuld spoke of that which may become.

That fate is being woven.

PART FOUR

THE STRAWBERRY MOON

CHAPTER EIGHT

8.1 ADELAIS

Adelais was sweating in her armour; the impossibly early sun of the strawberry moon was barely halfway to noon and already it was hot. In front of her, beyond a shallow valley, the Galman army sat in companies four or five men deep as if they were spectators at some vast tourney, not participants. Their line stretched for a thousand paces, and at a distance their mail-clad bodies merged into dull grey blocks laid on green wheat. Their captains walked among them in bright surcoats, conferring, pointing. Water carriers staggered along the lines, hunched under their burden of skins. A squadron of cavalry defended each of the Galman wings, gaudy with heraldry. A bouquet of banners in the centre must be Prince Lancelin and his nobles. Beyond the army, the walls of Baudry crusted the skyline, flags flying from its towers.

Hjálmar seemed nervous. The nose guard of his helmet made small, swift, side-to-side movements like a hawk on the fist, waiting to be launched. He'd fixed a horsehair plume to the crest, once white, now a dirty grey. It wasn't vanity, she knew; this was to help his men know him in the confusion of battle. He stood in his stirrups to survey the rolling grainlands around them, and his chain mail rippled like a metal waterfall. He had a circular shield slung over his back, a sword at his side, and a war hammer hooked to his saddle. That poor horse was carrying a lot of weight. Around them lay a wide, open landscape of gentle hills, patterned with field strips; some growing wheat, others fallow, all green. All empty, like the farms they had passed. No cattle. No farmers. Two armies.

It was unreal, like some vast dance for which they'd donned the ritual dress of chain mail and armour. If Adelais looked up she could almost forget the tramp of feet around her, and the shouts of the marshals as the last Vriesian companies were ordered into their positions; the rumbling thunder of feet on the road became the swish of boots through wheat as another swathe of crops was trampled into the ground. A skylark trilled above the battlefield, swooping, hovering, and swooping again as if stitching its song to the sky.

Allier fidgeted beneath her, breaking her reverie; the warhorse knew better than she what was coming. Across the valley, an order had been given and the breeze now brought the sound of many windlass crossbows being spanned on the far slope, their *click-click-click*s overlaying to make the noise of a swarm of crickets.

'Where is the rest of their cavalry?' Hjálmar threw the question at no one in particular. 'You could hide half an army in one of these folds of ground. Can we be sure they will not surprise us?'

'Their cavalry is with Duke Gervais in Delmas,' Everard de Warelt answered. 'Lancelin has few mounted troops, apart from nobles and their retainers. What you see is what he has.'

'And where is our cavalry?' Jarl Magnus looked pointedly at the Count of Theignault. A single squadron of barely fifty Vriesian knights clustered on the right of the Vriesian army.

'Making sure the Galman cavalry has stayed in Delmas,'

Theignault answered drily. 'Though if His Grace wishes, I can order them back? Of course it will take time...'

Ragener tilted his head at Magnus, questioning. In the absence of cavalry, Magnus's men would bear the brunt of this battle.

Magnus scratched at his beard, watching the Galmans, whose rearmost lines were leaking men uphill towards the walls of Baudry in the way a dandelion puffball will leak seeds on the wind.

'No need. They will break and run.' Jarl Magnus sounded confident. 'Use what men you have to harry them when they do.'

'Why is he so sure?' Adelais whispered to Hjálmar.

'We know how to fight in a shield wall.' Hjálmar nodded towards his own men, then pointed at the enemy. 'And they do not. See how we are arranged. Shield men to the front, spear men behind, whether in attack or defence. Half the shield men will have an axe or war hammer, the rest swords, and we fight as a team. Axes and hammers hook the enemy's shields away from their faces, so spears and swords can kill. It is how we fight. But those Galmans are trained to follow a cavalry charge.' He stared at the enemy line, nodding slightly as he counted companies, guessing numbers, sending the horsehair plume on his helmet bouncing. Between the nape of his helmet and the top of his hauberk there was a band of bare skin, fuzzy with ginger neck hair. Vulnerable.

'And we have more men,' Hjálmar finished.

'Then why does Lancelin meet us in the open,' Adelais asked, 'when he has a walled town behind him?'

De Warelt, waiting on Hjálmar's other side, looked at her sharply and inclined his head, honouring the question. 'He could probably fit his eight thousand within the town walls, but he may not have enough food to feed them if we laid siege.' De Warelt sniffed the breeze. A faint smell of roasting meat carried to them, even across half a league of country. 'Though I suspect they are cooking every cow within ten leagues.' Smoke clouded the battlements and drifted high over the waiting armies, hazing the sun.

Ahead of them, Jarl Magnus spoke quietly to Duke Ragener and wheeled his horse away. Hjálmar turned to follow and touched her on the arm before he left. His helmet's nose guard and cheek pieces hid most of the tension in his face. Not all.

'A jarl fights with his men. We must join the shield wall. Stay safe, princess.'

He was telling *her*? Her place, she'd been told, was with Ragener in the rear, watching.

'The gods be with you, Hjálmar.' Too much unsaid. Too much armour between them. Too many people around. She allowed her fingers to trail along his arm as he spurred his horse away. They touched only the hardened leather vambraces strapped to his forearms.

De Warelt edged his horse alongside her, into the void of Hjálmar's absence. Had he seen those small signs? Did it matter?

'I think this is all about pride.'

'What?' Adelais glared at de Warelt. What had friendship to do with pride?

'You asked why Lancelin fights in the open, rather than hides in Baudry. It's pride. There's a river in the valley beyond Baudry. The Dalsven. Before King Aloys invaded, it marked the boundary of Vriesland. If Lancelin was a good war leader, he'd have let us retake Baudry, but would defend the crossings where he could be resupplied from Galmandie. But there are no war leaders with him, nobody of the quality of Delmas or de Fontenay. He has only lesser captains and the politicking Othon de Remy.'

Adelais was only half listening. Magnus and Hjálmar were

dismounting behind the line, leaving their horses with the army's baggage.

'But Lancelin wants to prove himself,' de Warelt continued, 'especially with an audience lining the walls of the town.'

A steady pounding of shields marked the place where Magnus and Hjálmar were striding into the midst of their men. A chant began: *'fínt hár! fínt hár!'* Fine hair. It faded as they took their places. Adelais forced herself to look away from Hjálmar's plume. Two hundred paces away it looked curiously like a wolf's tail.

She hadn't seen the wolf for half a moon, and then she'd only glimpsed it in the distance. Perhaps that was a good sign. If she was riding into danger, then surely the wolf would come?

She could not see Revna, either, though she'd been told why. Half the army was Ischyrian, and would not welcome a *seidhkona* singing rune song. That would be happening discreetly, behind the baggage lines.

Richly caparisoned heralds rode forwards from each side, timing their advance so they met midway between the armies, their destriers dancing beneath them as unheard words or challenges were exchanged. With the parley ground established, Ragener and Lancelin rode forwards; the red eagle of Vriesland greeting the golden sun of Galmandie with elaborate courtesy. One portly duke, one effete prince, neither of them a warrior, though each would send many men to their deaths. The armies watched; a thousand muted conversations blended into an insect hum. The smell of sweat and leather grew stronger than the cooking meat.

No agreement. Naturally. Ragener lifted his hand before he had even returned through the Vriesian line, and a squire dipped the ducal banner to start the advance.

They went quietly, at first, or as quietly as ten thousand marching men can be; captains walked in front with arms stretched sideways, keeping the line. Hjálmar was one of them.

The body of the army followed, still well spaced, a single mass of men over a thousand paces wide. The skylark dropped almost to the ground and danced over the grass, trying to lead twenty thousand tramping boots away from its nest. Two hundred paces from the Galman line, the captains halted the army, and the shield wall formed. Shield men, spear men, interlocked. Two lines now, each two deep. A third line, further back; reserves. There was a single cry of *Vriesland!* from the centre, and a rippling thunderclap sounded along the line as weapons struck shields.

The thunderclaps became rhythmic, like a drum, keeping the pace. With the beatings came the call from ten thousand throats, a repeated cry of *hoo!* as men stamped forwards. The line became as unstoppable as a water wheel, clanking its slow progress, one sideways step, one intimidating blow, one shout at a time. The first volley of crossbows rained on them in a rattle of bolts on shields, and almost as one the line ducked. Some fell. Not many, but as the lines advanced, the front rank left bodies behind, some kicking, some still, some crawling. She looked for Hjálmar's plume, dreading to see it among the fallen, but he was lost in the press of men.

Click-click-click. The Galmans were respanning their crossbows.

Hoo! Hoo! Hoo!

Another volley at fifty paces. Another drum-roll rattle. More men went down. Many more. Some pinned through their shields. Replacements rushed forwards from the second line and were absorbed. The crossbowmen turned and ran through the Galman lines, which opened to let them through and closed again into a solid wall.

And the business of butchery began. Spears flattened, held overarm, stabbing downwards, and the noise became a continuous, thunderous cacophony of blows and cries. The shield walls ate each other and crept up the hill, shitting men. So

many men that they made midden heaps around which the
lines buckled, flexed, and straightened again as warriors
pushed into gaps, probing, hooking, killing. The positions
locked; the only movement became the flicker of short, wicked
blows where men strained and died, screaming. The smells
drifted downwind; the tang of blood, the sickly stench of guts.
Skit.

Adelais felt detached; here among the nobles she was an
observer. Useless. Down there in the din it was bloody chaos.
The rigid battle lines bowed now, as if some vast metal snake
writhed slowly where the armies met. A bend bulged into the
Galman centre, near Hjálmar, slowly swelled, and the Galman
reserves began to run. Their cavalry were already ahead of
them, cantering towards the gates of Baudry.

Ragener turned in the saddle and bellowed at the Count of
Theignault.

'Theignault! Cavalry, now! Cut them off! I want ransoms!'

'I will send what I can, Your Grace.'

De Warelt did not wait for the order. He had already taken
his great helm and lance from his attendant, and cantered
towards the waiting Vriesian knights. They needed no further
encouragement, and advanced with him, in trot now to save
their horses for the charge. Ahead of them the foot battle on the
far slope was disintegrating. Some Galman companies retreated
in good order, stepping backwards behind their own shield
walls, but others simply ran. They seemed to brush Lancelin
ahead of them; the blue banner with its golden sun moved faster
than any running man. The knot of nobles around the prince
were soon barging troops out of the way in the press around the
gates.

'Congratulations, Your Grace.' Theignault bowed in the
saddle. 'The day is yours.'

Ragener turned in the saddle. He did not seem pleased. 'If
your cavalry had been here, it would have been decisive. We

might even have taken Lancelin himself. Now we must starve them out.'

'Remember, the Galmans can field four times the men that faced us today, Your Grace, and ten times the cavalry. If my men had been here rather than hunting the enemy, we might have been badly surprised.'

Beyond the arguing nobles, the battle was coming to a stand-off. The bulk of the Galman army was wrapping itself around the walls of Baudry. Crossbowmen on the battlements were firing down into the attacking Vriesians, so the two sides faced each other across a hundred paces of open ground while the Galmans slowly drained through the gates into the town.

'At least Lancelin has been humbled!' Ragener forced a smile.

'One imagines that is why Duke Gervais of Delmas did not engage,' Theignault sneered. 'He has let you humiliate his rival for the crown.'

'Then I shall accept his gift.'

Gift. Adelais looked at the bodies littered over the far slope. Now the noise of battle had faded, the cries of the wounded sounded like a herd of bleating sheep. She nudged Allier down the slope, angling across to where she'd last seen Hjálmar. Her guards and standard bearer began to follow, but she sent them to the baggage lines saying they needed bandages, not banners, and they should bring as many as they could carry. Oh, and wine to wash the wounds. Two escorting berserkers refused to leave her, so the three of them worked their way up the far slope. She dismounted by the first body. He wore simple armour so it could not have been Hjálmar, but she heaved him onto his back to see if she knew him.

And threw up at the sight of the crossbow bolt in his eye. Adelais wiped her face with the back of her hand and walked on, towards the tidemark of men where the lines had first clashed. Here, the stench was overpowering; blood so strong it was like metal in her mouth and nostrils. Piss and *skit*. The sheer scale of slaughter rocked her. She began to sob. Her escort watched.

'What do you do?' Adelais waved a hand, uselessly, at the carnage. She'd had to gulp air before she could speak.

'Well, if they wear a hand, we bury 'em,' one of them answered. 'And if they wear a hammer, we burn 'em.'

'Can't just leave 'em, see?' his companion added. 'Not when we're going to be here a while.'

Most had head wounds, but they weren't all dead. One of Magnus's berserkers was struggling to stand, holding one arm across his body with the other. The mail of his hauberk shone in a bright line where an axe had smashed his shoulder. Another crawled, trailing blood from where a blade had scythed under the shield wall and found his leg. She ripped a surcoat into strips and made a tourniquet.

Other people were moving across the battlefield: camp followers seeking loved ones or coin among the dead, scavengers seeking weapons or armour or valuables. Three Ischyrian priests, their grey robes soon bloodied at the knees where they knelt to pray and press ash into the face of any body that wore a hand. One of them, sandy-bearded, smiled at her as if they were friends. Another glared at her as if this were all her fault. Perhaps it was. Adelais pushed that thought away, deep inside her, losing it in a frenetic rush to save those she could.

By the time Hjálmar found her, she'd organised an impromptu hospital on the hillside. Some could stagger to her. Others were brought by her guards on makeshift stretchers of shields laid on spears, so she could make terrible, god-like decisions; this one has no hope, put him over there. This one she might save. She had her standard bearer running back and forth with supplies. Take the horses. Bring more linen, more wine. Take an axe to that spear shaft and make a splint. Bring *Frú* Revna with her salves. She needed Revna's skills. When she'd worked at the infirmary in the sisterhouse, there had always been Adeifi Elodie to advise her. Now she must decide alone. At least here she could chant rune song.

Úruz, the healing-rune. *Úr er skýja grátr, ok skára thverrir, ok hirdhis hatr...* *Úruz*, that carried the strength and endurance of the auroch cattle. It gave heart to the men who still had their wits. She could see it in their eyes. One or two touched her arm as she worked, and whispered '*örlaga vefari*' in reverent tones. She grimaced. She didn't want to be their *fjakkinn* fate-weaver if the only fate she could weave was death.

Adelais looked up, wiping sweat from her face, and Hjálmar was standing nearby, his helmet under one arm and a well of tenderness his face. He looked tired but the blood spattered over him did not flow from any visible wound. She sensed he had been there a little while, watching. Behind him, the jarl's men were filing down the hill. Some of them carried friends between them to join the queue for her attention. She wanted to run to him, hug him with relief, maybe cry a little more. Instead she wiped an arm across her face, again, smearing her sniffles and gore; she was bloodied to the elbows. Her priceless cloth-of-gold surcoat was brown with it.

'Hello, troll-man.' Was that really all she could think to say?

'Princess.'

If he looked at her like that any more she'd crumble.

'What can we do to help?' Hjálmar's war hammer danced from his wrist as he gestured.

'You've done your job. Today it's my turn to clean up the mess.' How could she joke amidst all this death? 'But you could find me Revna and her salves. And doesn't Ragener have any surgeons or apothecaries with his army?'

She worked late into the long evening, until Hjálmar came back for her. He'd been nearby as the day waned, talking to those of

his men that were wounded, ensuring their dead were treated
with respect. They spoke from time to time. Revna sent salves.
She was busy elsewhere, also with wounded. When it was too
dark to see, Hjálmar led her away, one arm around her waist
and the other holding aloft a flaming torch. The torch blinded
her rather than helped her see her way, but she sensed other
carers still around her on the field: friends of the fallen; a few
Theignaulters; the kindly, bearded priest.

Hjálmar set her down on a stool outside a tent, knelt in
front of her, and pushed the torch into the ground beside them.
He wiped her face and hands with a damp cloth, as a parent
might clean a child before a meal. Now the torch helped; she
could see his face, folded with exhaustion, but with that tenderness in his eyes that made her weak. Around them was the hum
of an army drinking, boasting and retelling deeds. Further away,
the wounded bleated in the darkness.

Hjálmar put a goblet of wine into her hands and she drank,
greedily, emptying it.

'This is all my fault.' Adelais held out the goblet for more.
She wanted to sleep and forget.

'The battle?' His voice was gentle, like his eyes.

'The war. Without me, or what the *gydhjur* said of me at
Heilagtré, Jarl Magnus would not have marched south. Without
the jarl's men, Ragener would not have made war. It's all my
fault.'

Hjálmar shook his head. 'I tell you what you *have* done,
princess.' He squeezed her thigh with a great paw, a gesture of
reassurance rather than intimacy. She didn't mind that. She
wouldn't mind a hug, either. Just a hug. Between friends.
'You've made them love you.'

'What? Who?'

'The men saw you, after the battle. The nobles went off to
feast the victory, but you knelt in your finery among the
wounded. You bound their wounds and sang the songs of heal-

ing. That will not be forgotten. You blame yourself for costing lives, they praise you for saving them.'

Adelais began to cry. Hjálmar put his arms around her and she wept into his neck. It was an awkward hug, him kneeling before her stool, both of them still armoured. She moved one hand up to the back of his neck where she could feel warm skin, not cold chain mail. His head moved, brushing his beard against her cheek, and she straightened, pushing him away. She must not love this man.

'Is it over, Hjálmar? Have we won?'

He shook his head. 'There will now be a siege. Sieges can go on a long time. And this was too easy.'

'*Easy?*' Adelais had come from a slaughterhouse. *That was easy?*

'We have defeated no more than a quarter of the forces Galmandie could put in the field. I think this was the appetiser before a very bloody feast.'

8.2 GAUTHIER

Gauthier did not mind acting as a priest. It kept him clear of the fighting, and there was a wonderful power in the ritual of unburdening. Believers look at priests in such a pleading way when they feel their lives slipping away. And a priest, of course, can ask for more detail of the sins, stringing out the moment when he granted pardon and pressed the sacred ash into their forehead. Sometimes he may have left it too long, but unburdenings happened in private, so there was no one but the sinner to object.

He'd be expelled from the faith if he was caught, of course, but he never really believed in that. Most who did were a bunch of weakling fools. Besides, he was doing the men a favour. There were never enough priests to go round after a battle. The ones he blessed weren't to know he'd been thrown out of the priesthood.

He might well have been able to kill the girl, if Roche hadn't stopped him. That shocked him. All this gold, all these moons of effort, and just when he was close he was told to let her be. For now. He didn't understand.

He'd been working his way towards her along the battleground. Even got close enough to smile at her. Her guards were getting careless, fetching and carrying for her. He thought when it was dark he might have a chance. One quick slice with his knife and away into the night before anyone realised what had happened. With the cut he had in mind, she wouldn't even be able to cry out. He just had to wait for the right moment, if it came. Then there was a touch on his sleeve and Roche's voice in his ear. 'Not now, Gauthier. Let her be.'

Gauthier spun to face him, stunned. Roche's head was hooded, his face unrecognisable in the darkness.

'Why the fuck not?' Gauthier was angry. He'd worked himself up to take the most delicious risk. It was heroic, almost. 'I've been waiting for a chance like this for four, five moons, and now you tell me to let her go?'

'We've had news. Things are changing to our advantage. Kill her now, and you'll make her a martyr. A moon from now she'll die anyway, but by then these northerners will know she's a worthless fraud.'

'But...'

Gauthier's protest died on his lips. It was pointless asking for more information. He hated not knowing the plan. It made him feel out of control.

But he knew the identity of Roche's lord now. It's hard to disguise who you worked with in an army on the march, and Gauthier had been keeping a close eye on Roche. This might be useful information. And very dangerous information.

8.3 TAILLEFER

Taillefer found peace, of a kind, while Agnès waited for her knights to gather at Château Fontenay. They reached a balance; intimacy had become unthinkable when the Hand was nearby. Desire was so easily set aside during the day, robed in his scarlet, praying in the temple that held it. In that holy place, his desires were so mild that they were no test of his resolve.

But there were moments in the dark of the night, alone in his chamber, when a terrible need came upon him and he'd torture himself thinking about her. It was not simply a need for her body; he yearned even more for that easy company, the intimacy of shared laughter, the joy of knowing and being known, of loving and being loved. Their coupling, at Molinot and for that night in the hunting lodge, seemed an expression of that love, the way a smile is the product of happiness; a consequence not the cause.

Ah, consequences. So much to be resolved.

Taillefer spent a great deal of time with Pateras Bardolph, his junior in rank but his superior in holiness. Bardolph's manner was one of gentle sadness, perhaps concern. Understandable, of course; his role as custodian was being taken from him, though Taillefer did his best to assure him that he would always have a role to play in the Hand's care. They were standing together on the temple's steps when a line of knights rode up the central street within the château.

Knights had been arriving every day, in ones and twos, from the furthest corners of de Fontenay's lands, but this was a file of ten, and they wore the identical blue hand on white surcoats of a military order; the order, Taillefer had heard, that had sheltered Humbert Blanc after he and Adelais de Vries had escaped from the anakritim. They were equipped for war, with shields on their backs and lances rising from their stirrups, and they had the travel-stained look of men who have come far; their mounts' heads drooped wearily even though the knights sat tall in their saddles. Each led a spare mount whose baggage had been loaded in the precise manner of the proscribed Order of Guardians: a leather-wrapped roll of chain mail across the withers, bedding roll behind the mail, a great helm tied to its straps. Saddlebags for horse feed and clothing.

They halted in the small square between the temple and the great hall, and looked around them in the way of strangers, yet Bardolph gave a small cry of recognition and limped down the steps towards their leader. He moved among them with the light of brotherhood shining on his face, reaching up to clasp hands, calling them by name, and Taillefer realised that these knights were not simply *like* Guardians, they *were* Guardians. Their leader dismounted, spun Bardolph to him, and embarrassed the little priest with a bear hug. All was smiles and laughter until Bardolph called Taillefer over.

'Excellency, this is Brother Thanchere, a dear friend and once among the most trusted of the Guardian knights.'

So he was of their inner circle, the third degree as they called it. Taillefer held out his hand. 'And I am Diakonos Taillefer de Remy...'

The smiles faded and tension spread through the group like

ripples across a pond. One even reached for his sword until he remembered he was facing a priest.

'The same who pronounced the expulsion of Lord Brother Humbert Blanc.' Thanchere's stare was icy.

'An expulsion I lifted as soon as I knew the injustice that had been done.' Taillefer bowed his head. 'As soon as was possible, the Lord Brother was buried with honour in the temple of the Guardians at Villebénie.'

The glare did not soften, even when Bardolph tugged at Thanchere's sleeve. 'Come, Brother, there is much that you cannot know. Shall we meet once you are refreshed, just the three of us, in the sanctuary?'

There could be no strong words in that sacred place. Thanchere, Bardolph, and Taillefer knelt on the sanctuary steps, staring not at the flame but at the tomb, united in their knowledge of what lay beneath.

'The Lord Brother said that prayer would tell us when to come.' Thanchere broke the wondering silence.

'The God sent you at precisely the right time,' Bardolph assured him. 'Lord Leandre has decided the time has come for the Hand to be revealed.'

'But why did you come *here*, Brother?' Taillefer asked. 'Lord Leandre is in Delmas.'

'We heard that Pateras Bardolph was here, so the Hand would likely be here too. Our allegiance is to the Hand, not to any temporal lord, even one so esteemed as de Fontenay.'

'Lord Leandre proposes that the Order of Guardians is reformed to protect the Hand. He has assured me, through Lady Agnès, that he does not wish to retain control.' Taillefer sighed, feeling unworthy even to speak of his own possible role. 'He has asked me to ensure it is not used for gain, in the way that has debased the relics of Tanguy.'

Thanchere turned his head, a flicker of irritation on his face. 'Pateras Bardolph is a good and worthy custodian.'

'But I am a humble priest, Brother. I must obey the commands of superiors in the faith. A diakonos could stand firm.'

'And a de Remy.' Thanchere shifted on his knees. 'Is your brother still with Prince Lancelin, *Excellency?*'

'Yes. But he does not direct me and never will.' Yet Taillefer could not say why he and Othon were estranged. The secrets of an unburdening were sacrosanct. Especially King Aloys's.

'And Lord Leandre is with Delmas.' Thanchere made the sign of the God and rose to his feet, grunting slightly as he straightened his stiff limbs.

And if Delmas triumphed over Lancelin, his brother Othon would fall. It was inevitable. 'We have a tight line to walk, Brother.' Taillefer also rose. 'You have just ten knights?'

Thanchere looked at him cautiously, still clearly suspicious. 'We are emissaries. Forty others would come to our call.'

'Then I suggest you send for them, Brother Thanchere. Send for them all.' Taillefer closed his eyes, praying that what he was about to say would find favour with the God. 'There is no high priest, so let us take clerical law into our own hands. Ask your knights to gather at Harbin. We will reform the Order of Guardians. You can make your oaths in the presence of the Hand itself. I fear it will need your protection, and soon.'

That evening, Agnès feasted her knights and the ten former Guardians. She sat Taillefer in the place of honour on her right hand, and Brother Thanchere on her left. Before them, almost fifty de Fontenay vassal knights sat at benches, all with their squires and some with their ladies, though this was primarily a gathering of warriors. The Guardians sat together, with Bardolph. After much initial suspicion they seemed to have accepted Malory d'Eivet into their circle. He'd found willing ears for his version of the Adelais story; the Lions' Claw, the avenging angel for the wrongs perpetrated by both king and high priest.

Agnès touched Taillefer lightly on the wrist, interrupting his thoughts.

'I had a messenger this morning.'

Taillefer knew. The Vriesians were invading. Yet he sensed she had more to say.

'Adelais is with them. While Pateras Malory has been telling everyone that she's a Blessèd One,' she lifted her chin towards the priest, 'she has raised four thousand heathens against us.'

'And she is your friend.' Taillefer sighed.

Agnès's fingers fretted with the belt in her lap. There was little other sign of the distress she must feel within. 'I warned her to stay north. I fear she is being used. And now we will face each other across the battle lines.' Agnès looked fragile, as if all that outward serenity was just an over-starched gown, and the woman within was about to fold. She pulled herself together with visible effort and signalled to her steward. 'Now it is time to let them all know.'

'You will not tell them of the Hand?' He had an instant's alarm; the Hand was not yet attested – it would be premature to proclaim it.

'Of course not.' Agnès tone was sharp.

Taillefer winced inwardly. He'd seen Thanchere raise an eyebrow at that flash of anger, and perhaps at the fingers so quickly withdrawn from Taillefer's wrist; the manner and the gestures were a little too intimate, too familiar. She should mask her feelings.

Agnès stood. Her steward pounded the heel of a staff into the boards, demanding silence. A trio of troubadours, strolling between the tables, stilled their lutes and voices. Fifty shouted conversations faded away. A hundred and fifty faces turned towards the high table.

'My lords, a messenger arrived this morning from Baudry, in the north. Duke Ragener, that most perfidious of nobles, has broken the Treaty of Vannemeer and his oath of fealty to our late king. Ten thousand men are marching on Baudry, which may by now be under siege or taken.'

A rumble of talk spread around the room. The news was not unexpected. Why else would they have been gathered?

'My lords, now is not the time to let our enemies exploit our differences. Lord Leandre sends you word, calling on your oaths; Galmandie is at war. The army will gather at Harbin. We ride tomorrow.'

The hall erupted into a din of table thumping. The troubadours abandoned their song of courtly love and launched into a martial air that was only half heard in the surge of voices.

Agnès sat, and Thanchere leaned in to speak to her quietly. 'And will you be taking a certain artefact, my lady?'

Agnès nodded. 'Discreetly. That is Lord Leandre's command. A clerical court will be convened to rule on its authenticity.'

'And is he seeking to reinvigorate the faith or to unify Galmandie under Delmas?'

Agnès breathed deeply before she answered. 'Why don't you ask him yourself, Brother Thanchere? You will have your chance at Harbin.'

Where the Hand's appearance, Taillefer knew, would absolve de Fontenay of any taint from his family's association with Adelais de Vries.

But by the time they reached Harbin, or soon afterwards, Agnès's pregnancy would become apparent. Taillefer tried to imagine Leandre de Fontenay's reaction. Rage? Certainly.

Violence? Probably. And he'd demand to know the identity of the father. And if Agnès was cast out, would he, Taillefer, have the courage to admit his part and stand with her? Would he have to choose between his love and his God?

8.4 ADELAIS

The frame of the trebuchet towered into the sky, a broad-based arrowhead five times the height of the men that worked around it. A metal axle ran through its apex, and on this the arm could rotate, though at this moment it was held upright by a cart-sized, soil-filled box that swung at its base. The trebuchet's tapered arm soared like a lance for a further thirty paces above the axle. Around Adelais, perhaps a thousand soldiers had come to watch both trebuchets fire.

One of the crew climbed up a ladder on the side of the frame, all the way to the apex, and then swung onto rungs on the arm itself to scramble up to a dizzying height. He trailed a line that he passed through a ring a mere ten paces from the tip. On the ground, the crew heaved on the line to haul the heaviest rope Adelais had ever seen up to the ring. It had an iron hook bound to its end, which the climber secured to the ring. There were cheers at this achievement, and jeers at the crew of the other trebuchet one hundred paces away where the crew were still filling the counterweight. There was competition between them, and Geri was beating Freki.

Beneath each trebuchet, outside the frame, were two wheels

about four paces across that served no purpose of movement that Adelais could see; their lower rims did not even touch the ground. She was bemused as two men climbed into each of Geri's wheels and began walking up their inside slopes. Slowly, the great arm began to lower, pulled down as the rope wound around a third axle, between the wheels, and the counterweight rose at the other end. A ratchet clicked within the frame and Adelais realised that the wheels served the same purpose as the windlass that spanned a crossbow.

'Come, mistress!' Knud the armourer was like a boy with a special toy. He'd been working as hard as his men and was stripped to the waist with his shirt knotted around his belt. His sweaty torso was stocky, with slabs of fat laid over muscle. 'I offer you the first shot!'

Adelais moved closer, ignoring the way the man's eyes still flicked over her body. She wore a simple kirtle and underskirt, loosely belted, but still he stared, undressing her with his eyes. His crew were better behaved to her face, though there were comments behind her back that ended in dirty laughter. Perhaps she should have worn her armour, but the day would be warm and a washerwoman was trying to clean blood from her surcoat. Her guards gripped their swords and snarled at the crew to show more respect. Adelais ignored them all.

She wouldn't fire the shot. To them, this was a game. They were almost dancing with excitement, pushing a heavy iron hook over the arm as it came horizontal, and uncoupling the cable that had pulled it down. Now the arm was straining on its axle, weighed down at the front end by enough soil to fill a cottage, and held at the other by this iron hook. The wood was groaning so much that she feared it might snap and cut them all to pieces with its splinters.

A slide like a long cattle trough ran lengthwise through the frame. Two of the crew were greasing it 'to make the shot run smooth'. Adelais sighted along its length; it pointed directly at one of Baudry's gatehouse towers, two hundred and fifty paces away. Two other men were carrying a rounded boulder on an iron stretcher that reminded her of the acolytes and the heated stones at Heilagtré. They dumped it at the front end of the trough, into a leather pouch that must have taken the hide of a whole cow to make, and ran ropes from the pouch to the end of the arm. The giant slingshot was ready.

'Stand clear!' The armourer stepped back, trailing a rope attached to the restraining hook. He offered it to Adelais but she shook her head. This was being fired at people.

She was glad she'd refused; it took two big men to drag the hook off the arm. Had Master Knud been planning a joke at her expense? She would have been left tugging ineffectually, the useless woman, while they laughed.

Unleashed, the arm bowed as it felt the weight of the stone, which thundered along the trough and was swung high into the air like an overarm throw. Two nearby horses panicked at the sudden noise, bucking and throwing their riders, while the pouch threw its load, like a slingshot of the gods. The rock seemed to hang in the air, gradually shrinking, so that by the time it dropped it was as tiny as a speck of bird *skit*. It bounced ineffectually on the turf thirty paces in front of the walls, and rolled to a stop. The other trebuchet team jeered. Far away on the walls, Galman soldiers made obscene gestures.

The armourer seemed unconcerned. 'Fifteen more soil bags in Geri's counterweight. Make sure the stone is the same weight. And grease the top axle again!'

Adelais spun as another snap and rumble announced the firing of the second trebuchet. This one hit the base of the same tower, and the watching crowd cheered, almost drowning the crack of the impact coming back to them several heartbeats later.

'Five more bags on Freki!' The armourer made a

triumphant, underarm fist. 'And a barrel of ale to the first team that lands one on top!'

Adelais settled onto the grass to watch. She had never thought of warfare being like this. She'd seen the courage of armed combat, one-to-one or one-to-many. She'd fought too, delivering death with her sword or her warhorse's hooves. But never this casual hurling of death towards people she could not see.

'You are pensive, my lady?'

De Warelt sat beside her. He too was unarmoured, wearing a cote-hardie, hose, and fine leather boots. They might have been a couple enjoying their leisure at a tournament.

'Where is the honour in this, messire? Hurling rocks from far away?'

'The honour will come when the trebuchets have punched a hole in those walls and we have to fight our way through. Many will die. Many more would die if we had to use scaling ladders.'

'When I was a child, Baudry was Vriesian. Are the townspeople enemies or the duke's subjects?'

De Warelt laughed. 'You are such a dreamer, Adelais.'

That irritated her. She didn't like being patronised, and she didn't like him using her given name without permission.

'So how long will this take, *Everard?*' She let her anger show.

He sat more stiffly, rebuffed. 'It depends how thick the walls are. They will reinforce overnight, and we will knock down during the day. When one tower is untenable, we'll probably switch to the gates or the other tower. Half a moon? Who knows?'

Adelais snorted. This was going to be tiresome. Already detachments were being placed opposite every gate of the town to prevent supplies entering. A series of miniature forts, mere palisades of stakes, were springing up around them in case of sorties. The largest of them had been built around the trebuchets. Duke Ragener's army was settling in for the siege.

'Why are they soaking their sling?' Adelais pointed to the crew around the Geri trebuchet, who were throwing buckets of water over their sling and the surrounding woodwork.

'Fireball,' de Warelt answered. 'It's a lighter shot so will go further, but they don't want to burn their own weapon. This way they might win the ale without taking the time to load more soil into their counterweight.'

The master armourer watched his crew, fists on hips, an amused smile on his face. This wasn't what he'd asked for, but he'd see what happened.

The game of war. Geri's crew lifted one of the rope-bound fireballs out of a half-barrel of oil, laid it in an iron stretcher, and put a torch to it. They let it burn until the fire was well established, staggered with it to the sling, and fired before the flames could ignite the trebuchet. The shot soared, trailing oily smoke, a line of fading ink against the sky. It curved downwards like a shooting star, and the trebuchet crew cheered it on. *Yes! Yes! Yes!* They punched the air as a ball of flame burst on the parapet, engulfing the whole top of the tower; the impact had spattered burning oil over a wide area.

Adelais stood, a physical reaction to her mental turmoil as memories of her nightmares came flooding back, hurling firebirds at a disembodied hand. They'd been happening more often recently. She was also filled with a cold fury.

'Master Knud!' They were of a height, she and him, and as she looked into his greasy, sweat-streaked face in her peasant kirtle she felt like a duchess.

'Mistress.' He sketched a bow that held more mockery than respect.

'There are Galman soldiers on the walls.'

'Of course.'

'But Vriesian people in the town.'

His smile faded.

'If you burn their town, Master Knud, which king do you think they will want to follow when the armies go away?'

They held each other's eyes and his jaw tightened. His crews were watching. Many soldiers were watching. Not all could hear, but they would be able to tell by the set of her shoulders that this *woman* was reprimanding the armourer. Adelais could almost see him think; confront her, or make light of the moment. He breathed deeply and turned away, forcing laughter.

'Very well, the Geri crew earn the ale. Now load up that counterweight and put a stone in the same place.'

She didn't stay to watch, but strode back towards the tent lines, knowing her guards would follow. Today, she resented them; how the *fjakk* did they expect her to be natural with people if she had to be protected in their presence?

De Warelt fell in beside her and she groaned inwardly. The last thing she wanted was to exchange pleasantries with a *gyke*. Maybe she'd take Allier for a gallop. That was always good for the spirit. Or fire arrows at a target. She was better when she was angry. Quite good, these days, though she still couldn't shoot from the saddle. But de Warelt was persistent. 'Armourer Knud may not be the best man to upset, mistress.'

Adelais rounded on him. 'And one day, *mynherra*, he may discover that I am not the best woman to upset.' She put such fury into her glare that the *gyke* backed away, making a placating gesture.

She rode out with Hjálmar. She wished he had a better mount; his shaggy, compact horse might be able to carry him over great distances, but it had little speed under his bulk. And she wanted to run.

'What ails you, princess?'

'I just got angry. Again. With de Warelt and the master armourer, this time.'

'I'm told the armourer deserved it. Yes, I heard. Word travels fast in a camp.'

'I seem to upset people. I can't stop myself.'

'You don't upset me.' Hjálmar grinned at her.

'Perhaps I haven't really tried.' Throwing words at Hjálmar was like punching a pillow. Or was she really calmer with him?

'And what are you angry about, Adelais? I mean really angry, deep down, not the day's trivia.'

Hjálmar could be so perceptive, sometimes.

Adelais twisted to watch her two guards, riding fifty paces behind. Out of earshot. She settled back into her saddle.

'I don't believe in what we are doing.' There, it was said.

He too looked behind, his brow furrowed in thought.

'There is a word in the Old Tongue that we don't use much. *Vápnadómr*. It means the judgement of arms. The wise ones say that the threads of fate favour those whose actions have been rightful and honourable.'

'There's no honour in burning a town that was Vriesian for generations.'

'I agree. Perhaps in preventing that today, you have gained more power through honourable action. The gods must decide where justice lies. And *Frú* Revna says this is a struggle between the gods as well as between men, so they may choose to be involved.'

Adelais wished things were simple. Easy choices like good and bad. And in that moment she wanted to forget all choices and just gallop.

The sun was sinking, but still two handspans above the horizon when they crested a low hill and saw the track stretch half a league to the next hill; grassy, straight, and fast. Allier danced beneath her, reading her mood, also wanting this moment. Adelais did not ask permission, just followed her instinct and touched her leg to Allier's side, releasing his power into the evening. As he surged into a gallop she folded over his neck, her chin close to his mane, relishing the drumming of hooves and the eye-watering wind in her face, knowing she would let him run as far and as fast as he wanted because all her cares were being blown from her, streaming out behind, and their void was filled with laughter. Perhaps one day Hjálmar would have a big, fast horse and they could race. Perhaps he would be the one for whom she unbraided her hair and let it fly in the wind. But this day it was just her and Allier, two bonded beings, confident in each other, happy with each other, and if horses could laugh, he too would be whooping with joy.

Allier came to a snorting, heaving, blowing halt at the next crest and Adelais leaned forwards to scratch his neck with both hands, low near the shoulders where he liked it, to show her gratitude. He began to crop the lush grass beside the track, still blowing, and she straightened to survey an empty landscape of unspoilt fields. Almost empty. On two distant hills she could see Vriesian patrols, and on the track behind her, still four hundred paces away, was Hjálmar. Her two escorting guards were a little in front of him, pushing their blown horses as they tried to catch up. She spread her arms wide as if she could touch the horizon, enjoying the moment of being alone.

The guards weren't happy, but Hjálmar grinned at her when they finally caught up. By then she'd recovered her breath.

'We're going to have to find you a bigger horse, troll-man.'

'I like this one. He's sure-footed, even in ice.'

Adelais shrugged. 'I suppose I quite like being able to look you in the eye.'

'Wait.' Hjálmar put a hand on her arm, then pointed forwards, a look of awe on his face.

The she-wolf stood at a meeting of tracks, fifty paces away.

She seemed distressed, running a few paces down a track to the north, towards Vriesland, before returning. And again.

'She's asking us to follow her!' Adelais had seen another wolf behave like that, warning her. Friends had died when she hadn't followed.

And in the mountains this wolf had prevented them running into a tarrazim ambush.

Adelais nudged Allier onto the track northerly after the wolf, but one of her guards caught her bridle. '*Mynn frú*, I must insist. We are already far from camp, and the day is ending.'

'But she is warning me! We must go!' Adelais looked at Hjálmar, hoping for help.

'Princess, I must agree. Even if you had provisions, night is falling.' The three of them boxed her in, turning her towards the camp. Adelais twisted in the saddle, looking at the wolf, furious with her escort. And Hjálmar. She glared at him. 'I thought you of all people would understand.' She was truly hurt.

Hjálmar leaned close. 'If you left, so would half the men from Normark. The army would fall apart. And besides, remember you swore fealty to Ragener. You *cannot* leave without his permission. And that he will never grant.' He put a hand on her arm, gently, but she shook it off, too angry to speak. To think that she had imagined unbraiding her hair for him, giving herself to him. They rode fifty paces in silence before he spoke again.

'Whatever our fate, princess, we face it with honour. We do not run from it.'

Behind them the wolf howled.

PART FIVE

THE HAY MOON

CHAPTER NINE

9.1 TAILLEFER

When Taillefer and Agnès returned to Harbin, early in the hay moon, surrounded by a protective guard of former Guardians, the town had been transformed into the hub of the world. The Duke of Delmas himself had come with the nobles of his faction, now that Prince Lancelin and Othon de Remy were safely trapped in Baudry. All were drawn by the promise of war and the chance to humiliate both Lancelin and Vriesland.

From the hill above the town, Harbin looked as if some multicoloured fabric had wrapped around the axle of its walls. Squadrons of grey-mailed cavalry exercised their horses in the fields, so many that at a distance they looked like flocks of starlings, swooping in unison. A tent city had sprung up in the meadows by the river; nobles' pavilions near the bridge, common soldiers downstream lest they piss in the town's water. A harassed quartermaster despaired of finding either accommodation for the column of de Fontenay knights or forage for their horses.

Leandre de Fontenay greeted them warmly, and Taillefer had his first twinge of guilt. Leandre was not tall, but well muscled, as a man who had worn mail and wielded a sword for much of his life. He was old enough to have threads of silver over his temples. Grey eyes smiled at Taillefer, holding his gaze. This was a man that veteran knights would follow. He welcomed Agnès as if she were a trusted lieutenant returning from a successful mission.

Within a day of their return, Episkopos Juibert of Villebénie arrived at the head of an entourage of priests, lured by Taillefer's insistence that the Hand was found, and in Harbin. Taillefer led him into the temple, knowing the likely impact of what his superior was about to see. Like every senior priest, Taillefer understood the power of pomp and theatre, and enough of Brother Thanchere's Guardians had arrived for them to stage a scene that would take the visitors' breath away.

Six fully armed knights of the banned Order of Guardians stood sentry around the sanctuary in their forbidden red lion on white surcoats. Their bowed heads faced outwards and their hands rested on the pommels of drawn swords, held point-down before them. Twenty more Guardians knelt in an outer half-circle in an attitude of prayer or adoration, facing inwards through their armed brethren towards a low, linen-covered table beyond the sacred flame. On that snowy square lay the plain, oak casket that held the Hand; it drew the eye even more than the forbidden panoply of red and white.

Every one of the visiting priests gasped audibly as they entered the sacred space. The gasps became a continuous sigh as more clerics pushed through the doors. No more blatant statement was possible; the surcoats were redolent of a time when the faith was pure and honourable, and they shouted to the episkopos that they, the survivors of a persecuted Order, had already made their decision. Here stood, or knelt, holy warriors who were sure enough to defy the edict of proscription and the risk of expulsion from the faith. These were the Lions of Ischyros, who would accept being burned as heretics rather than deny whatever lay beneath that linen.

None would ever implement that law, not now, not since
the death of King Aloys and the proven sorcery of the anakritis-
general. The mood changed within the temple; before, it had
been filled with a quiet holiness. Now, as Delmas and his nobles
spread out behind Episkopos Juibert and his entourage, it was
awe, for the Guardians spoke of a time many thought lost; a
time of certainty, a time of heroes. They all fell to their knees,
making the sign of the God, the way a crested wave breaks upon
a beach.

The clerical court to validate the Hand was a formality. Pateras
Bardolph, Brother Thanchere, and Leandre de Fontenay spoke
of its provenance. Agnès de Fontenay spoke of its journey from
the Guardian's temple to Château Fontenay. Pateras Malory
told them of the miracle it had worked, when a woman was
healed of a crossbow bolt in the belly by its touch. All this the
episkopos *wanted* to believe. Afterwards, he conducted an office
of thanksgiving and spoke eloquently of the miracle of the
Hand's revelation in their hour of need, and of his hope and
belief that it would ignite the fire of Ischyros throughout the
world. The heathens, the spawn of Kakos, would not prevail.

Taillefer hosted a dinner that evening for an ill-matched
gathering of dignitaries. Delmas was bluff, hearty, and a little
too smug. Leandre de Fontenay was quiet, saying little; perhaps
he doubted the rectitude of the great events he had set in
motion. Taillefer saw no tension between him and Agnès, who
was radiant, her skin shining and clear. She had laced her robe a
little more loosely than normal; she would not keep her condition quiet for much longer. He saw the strain of worry in the
tightness around her eyes; she was like a rose that has spent too
long between bud and bloom.

Another confrontation was about to happen, and Episkopos
Juibert may have been the only person in the room who did not

see it coming. He was in great humour, eating and drinking his fill; a jowly man whose purple robes mounded over his belly. The family resemblance with Malory was strong. Perhaps, as some said, he was indeed Malory's father, though if so Taillefer could no longer condemn such a 'sin'. The moment of confrontation came when Juibert began quizzing Brother Thanchere about how many men he had at his disposal, because 'a guard will be necessary when I take the Hand to Villebénie', and silence spread around the table.

'The Hand will not be going to Villebénie,' Leandre de Fontenay said quietly.

'Of course it must!' Juibert frowned, more irritated than concerned. 'Until we have a new high priest who can decide, the natural home for the Hand is the fire temple of Villebénie.'

'With respect, Eminence, that is not your decision to make,' de Fontenay growled, his hand fisting. Like Delmas, de Fontenay had left his sword outside with his squire, but his body was as tense as one of the siege engines they were reportedly using around Baudry, ready to fling violence.

'Then whose decision is it?' Juibert was affronted.

'Mine. The Hand came to my family after the battle when the prophet received his wound. It was merely entrusted to the Order of Guardians by their founder, Jovan de Fontenay. That was why they took their name; the Guardians of Salazar's inheritance, both spiritual and physical.'

'But the Hand must be housed where it can be properly revered. A mere provincial temple is inadequate. It must be taken to Villebénie while discussions continue.'

'Fifty de Fontenay knights disagree with you.'

'As do fifty Guardians,' Thanchere added.

'And two hundred of mine.' Delmas gripped a goblet and swigged.

'I have asked Diakonos Taillefer of Harbin if he will be the Hand's spiritual custodian.' Leandre still spoke quietly.

'But I have already commissioned a pure gold reliquary to house it,' Juibert blustered. 'It will cost a whole year's profits from the pilgrim trade!'

'You have just demonstrated, *Eminence*, why the Guardians refused to reveal the existence of the Hand.' Thanchere sighed.

Juibert swallowed, wide-eyed. Taillefer brushed aside the irreverent thought that he looked like a purple frog.

'So what do you plan to do with this most holy of relics?' Juibert glared around the table.

'Inspire an army.' Delmas lowered his goblet and belched.

'Of one thing I am sure, Highness,' Taillefer cast around for the right words, 'the Hand will punish any who exploit it for gain, whether that is personal enrichment or temporal conquest.'

Delmas snorted. 'Repelling heathen invaders is hardly personal gain.'

'But half the Vriesian army are Ischyrian,' Thanchere said.

'No devout Ischyrian will stand against the Hand of Salazar. There will be no one left who deserves the God's mercy.' Delmas slapped the table as if he'd just made a huge joke. 'And they certainly won't get mine.'

9.2 GAUTHIER

Gauthier, in his priestly guise, had a lucrative business going with unburdenings. It was not unknown for priests to request a 'gift for the poor', though reducing the penance as the generosity of the gift rose had no part in Salazar's teaching. But it didn't look as if he was going to collect any gold for killing the girl any time soon, and a man had to live somehow.

He was not surprised to see Roche in his queue of penitents; it was the perfect excuse to visit.

Gauthier had already guessed why Roche's lord desired a Galman victory: he aspired to be the next Duke of Vriesland. But Gauthier hadn't worked out why Roche expected the tide to turn against Ragener, not until Roche told him the Hand of Salazar had been found and was with a gathering Galman army. That rocked him backwards.

Now was the time, Roche said, for Gauthier to earn his keep. And for once it would be by persuading people, not by killing them. Go, tell every Ischyrian knight, man-at-arms, and soldier he could find that the world was about to change, and change gloriously.

So that evening Gauthier sat around a campfire with a squadron of Sjólander men-at-arms. They were all strong Ischyrians; he'd seen them go to the camp's makeshift temple when less godly men were carousing. Gauthier knew how to charm people. All it took was a smile and an easy manner. He could watch people's faces and slide words into their fears as easily as he could put a knife into their backs, and he had the passport of his priestly robes. The Sjólanders willingly shared their fire and a mug of ale while he rehearsed the words he would use many times that night.

There is wonderful news, he said, radiating happiness. *The Hand of Salazar is found!*

There was disbelief at first, even among such men.

It was hidden by the Guardians, and has been revealed by Leandre de Fontenay.

It would take more than words to persuade these men, even words from a priest.

It has been attested by the Episkopos of Villebénie and the Diakonos of Harbin. It is the blood and bones of the prophet himself.

That was more convincing.

It has been encased in solid gold, and all Galmandie unites beneath it. The faith is triumphant!

The brightest of them saw the risk. 'All Galmandie unites? What if they march on Vriesland? What if the whole Galman army comes to lift the siege?'

Each man must look within himself and pray that he makes the right decision. All our lives we must choose between doing the works of the God Ischyros or the Destroyer Kakos.

Then would come the inevitable question to which he had been leading. 'I am a loyal Vriesian and I hope a good Ischyrian, Pateras. Should I fight?'

I too am a loyal Vriesian, and I thank the God that my priest-

hood forbids me to fight, for I do not think I could take up arms against the Hand of Salazar.

When he left them for another fireside, their faces were slack with doubt.

9.3 ADELAIS

Rumours spread through the army faster than disease through a slum. It was de Warelt that brought confirmation. He'd taken a mounted troop south towards Harbin. They'd been lightly armed for speed, and had scouted the land from hilltops rather than pressing down the road.

'At least a thousand horse,' he told the war council in Ragener's pavilion, 'and ten thousand foot. More joining daily so their column stretches for leagues, back to Harbin and beyond. And at their head there are priests, singing as they march, with a golden hand held aloft.'

Adelais winced at his words. A golden hand. Her nightmares were coming to life.

'There is an episkopos with them,' de Warelt continued. 'I saw the banners of Delmas, de Fontenay, and many of the warrior lords.'

'This story of the Hand is true, then?' Ragener's shoulders slumped. He'd spent two days trying to stamp out the rumours and reassure his men.

Adelais rarely spoke in the war councils. That morning she wished she had something better to say. 'De Fontenay has custody of the Hand. This I know. If an episkopos walks beneath it, we have to assume it is the true relic.'

Theignault tugged at his beard, sharpening its oiled point. He did not seem surprised. 'Delmas has turned this into a holy war. No good Ischyrian will fight the Hand.'

'Does that include you, my lord?' Ragener's stare was intense.

'It certainly will include many of my men.'

'We must lift the siege.' The Count of Sjóland sighed and spoke what many knew to be the painful truth. 'Even if we could depend on the whole army, we could not let ourselves be trapped against hostile walls.'

'But we are so nearly through!' No one answered Ragener. The siege engines had slowed their rate of fire in recent days after all the cut stones were shot. Teams with wagons were scavenging the countryside for rocks, whose variable weight had limited their accuracy, but the pounding had reduced the gates of Baudry matchwood and their towers to rubble. The great assault was planned for the morrow.

'He promised!' Ragener's anger spilt over and he pounded his fist into the table.

'Promised what, Your Grace?' Sjóland motioned to him to continue.

'Delmas promised me Baudry so I could humiliate Lancelin.' Ragener swung an accusing finger towards Adelais. 'That was your friend Agnès de Fontenay's message.'

Adelais closed her eyes as a great sadness overcame her. This war was all a bloody game of kings and lords. She now knew it had all been engineered to put a triumphant Delmas on the throne of Galmandie. Cheating within deception.

'So what about your famous prophecy, hey?' The duke was shouting at her now, sending flecks of spit over the table. 'The *örlaga vefari* who'd unite the peoples of the north and roll back the borders of Ischyrendom?'

Adelais shook her head. 'I never wanted this, and I never made that prophecy.' *But why were the gydhjur of Heilagtré so sure that I am pivotal in this?*

'So weave some fates! Send their Hand back to Villebénie.'

Her anger boiled over. 'What do you want me to do? Throw thunderbolts at them? *Your Grace?*' she bellowed.

'Careful, girl,' Magnus cautioned.

But Ragener's anger seemed spent. 'How long before they are here?' His voice was gravelly with exhaustion.

'We will see their outriders tomorrow, Your Grace,' de Warelt answered, 'and the main force the day after.'

Ragener stood and paced the room, striking the knuckles of one hand into the palm of the other behind his back. All eyes watched him as he turned and faced them.

'Then we will pull back to north of the Gedha. Sue for peace from a position of strength. Theignault, have your men destroy every bridge over the Dalsven. Burn the timbers. That will delay them. Then throw a mounted screen behind and around the army, lest Lancelin is tempted out of Baudry to attack our rear. We will march in good order.'

As the meeting broke up, Jarl Magnus looked long and hard at Adelais. She could not read his look, but interpreted it as disappointment. She glared back at him. So why was everyone blaming her? She wished she hadn't fallen out with Hjálmar, but the wolf had been right. He, if anyone, should have understood. There was something about that amiable giant that allowed her to be soft and vulnerable in a good way, and to talk about anything. And right now she needed to be held and told that it wasn't her fault and that everything would be well.

She lay awake late into the night. There was always noise in the camp of an army, but she sensed more movement than usual; furtive shufflings that were more alarming than honest footfalls.

At times there were sounds of blows and screams, and running feet that faded out of earshot. She fretted on her bed, her sword within reach, for once glad there were guards outside. She was not aware of falling asleep, but suddenly knew with crystal clarity that the hand was coming for her. It was only bones and scraps of skin, but it walked across the ground on its fingertips, like a spider. For some reason she did not understand, she could not run; she was as fixed as she would be if chained to a stake, and knew that when it reached her that putrid-yellow obscenity would climb up her legs and her body, and fasten those fingers around her neck. The furnace of the *gydhjur* was beside her and she seized burning rocks to fling at the hand; they filled her hands with flame but did not burn. For several heaving breaths the bounding rocks held back the Hand of Salazar, but Agnès offered it a pole to grasp, and then carried it towards Adelais. Adelais threw another rock, this time at Agnès, screaming, '*I thought you were my friend*', but Agnès thrust the hand on its pole at Adelais's neck, saying, '*sorry, kjúkling*', and the skeletal fingers leapt the gap and tightened around Adelais's throat.

Adelais heaved herself out of the nightmare, gasping for breath. She had to touch her neck to be sure that it had been a dream. Around her, the camp was stirring in the early dawn of the hay moon. Everyone was keen to put some leagues between them and the Galman cavalry.

9.4 TAILLEFER

The office of the Lighting of the Lamps, in the temple of a small town on the south bank of the Dalsven, attracted a modest gathering; the bulk of the army had crossed the river and were pursuing the Vriesians northwards, beyond Baudry. Taillefer thanked the God that he and the Guardians had persuaded de Fontenay to keep the Hand safely in the rear once the army had crossed the Dalsven and entered enemy territory. Taillefer had found the sight of it being marched to war on a pole, like a banner, inexpressibly sad, even sordid.

So did Thanchere and the former Guardians. Their resentment simmered, but it had not yet become open opposition to de Fontenay and Delmas. In revealing the Hand, de Fontenay had wiped away any lingering concerns about his association with Adelais de Vries; if Delmas became king, de Fontenay stood to become the most powerful noble in the land. The Guardians were but fifty, and many of those had been through torture and were not fit for battle. They had only just begun to wear their banned red lion surcoats again, and seemed nervous of any further challenge to authority. Their presence in the army was more symbolic than practical. They always stayed close to the Hand, and at this office they formed the bulk of Taillefer's congregation. With them were some local people, come to hear an office with a diakonos, plus a few de Fontenay knights and Malory d'Eivet.

And, he saw with a lurch of his stomach, Agnès de Fontenay. She asked to unburden afterwards, dropping to her knees at the sanctuary steps when the temple was empty. He knelt beside her, knowing this was a pretext.

'I heard you would be with the army.' Taillefer kept his voice even. Having her so near, and making no sign of affection, was hard.

'Delmas thinks I might have a role as an intermediary. I met Ragener, you see.'

'And lured him south.' Taillefer wondered how much of Delmas's plans she had known. Could she really be so devious?

'I only delivered a message.' Agnès answered his unspoken question. Sometimes they didn't seem to need speech. 'I didn't know what would happen afterwards.' Agnès fingered the belt at her waist. 'And I didn't plan to fall in love.'

Taillefer sighed, savouring those words. 'You also know Adelais,' he prompted. Why did that woman come into his mind?

'Delmas insists he'll never talk to Adelais himself. Calls her "that fucking witch".'

The obscenity was all the more shocking for dropping from her lips, in a temple, when she was in an attitude of prayer. It was almost erotic.

'But he'd send you.'

'And Leandre agrees. He knows, by the way.'

Taillefer masked the jolt of shock by bowing towards the flame. 'Just about the child, or about my... involvement?'

Agnès made the sign of the God, as if she had finished her unburdening. 'Just the child,' she whispered.

'And what was his reaction?'

'He is angry. Hurt. He is like a cornered boar who does not know which way to charge. He has not denounced me. Not yet. He'd have to admit that he does not lie with me. His pride and honour would be hurt either way.'

Taillefer looked over his shoulder. The temple was empty.

'It is hard, having you close. Not being able to talk. Touch.' He turned back towards the sacred flame.

'And for me.'

'And it will be hard to watch your child, knowing...'

'We have to stop torturing ourselves.'

'I cannot deny my feelings. You are part of me.' Taillefer opened his box of sacred ash and made the ritual motions of unburdening, lingering as he touched his thumb to her fore-head. Skin. Contact. Warmth. She leaned into his hand, smiling.

'By the God, it is you!' Leandre de Fontenay's hiss from the back of the temple made them both spin. He was armed for war in a suit of mail, gaudy in his red surcoat with the golden flow-ers. He'd left his sword in the porch, as was customary, but he was striding through the temple, boots thumping the boards, his eyes blazing fury, his fists flexing into violence.

Taillefer rose to his feet, turning to face him, readying himself for a blow. Beside him Agnès had also stood, a rustle of silk. Should he stand between them? That would probably make it worse.

'You're a priest! A diakonos!' De Fontenay was pure, coiled anger that could be unleashed at either Taillefer or Agnès by a single word or gesture. 'How could you?'

Taillefer looked down. He had no words. If his guilt had not been written on his face before, it certainly was now.

De Fontenay's blow landed on the back of the chair for the officiating priest, sending it clattering over the flagstones. Taillefer glanced towards the door, wondering if people had stayed close enough to hear.

Agnès looked calmer now, even serene. Perhaps relieved.

'I'll tell you how, husband. We fell in love.'

De Fontenay breathed like a bull about to charge, but even in that appalling moment Taillefer was warmed again by her words. *We fell in love.*

'I wish I could have spared you this, husband. But you lay with me once. Just once. We both know it is not in your nature to share my bed, so which is the worse sin? Your neglect, or our love?'

'I'll bring you both down!'

And he could. Taillefer was no better than all the other diakones and episkopes who preached purity and kept a mistress. The difference was that *they* found a common woman and kept it discreet. Transactional.

'You could do that.' Taillefer glanced at Agnès, drawing such strength from her that he thought his heart would burst. 'But I counsel you to consider the effect on your honour and your cause.' Taillefer squared his shoulders, finding the courage to defy one of Galmandie's finest warriors.

'Tanguy's bones, priest!' De Fontenay's hands grasped Taillefer's robes over the chest. His twisted face was close enough for Taillefer to smell his breath.

Taillefer kept his voice as calm as he could. 'Will you call into question the purity of those who instigated your holy war? You cannot shame Agnès or denounce me without casting doubt on the origins of the Hand.' Taillefer glanced sideways. There was such adoration in Agnès's eyes that he felt invincible.

Leandre shook him, pushed him backwards with a growl, and turned away. He looked up at the dome above the sanctuary, his chest heaving, his hands clenching at his sides.

'I offer you a choice, my lord.' Agnès still looked at Taillefer. In a way, this was like lovemaking; the giving, the taking, the togetherness. In adversity as in passion.

'*You* offer *me* a choice?' De Fontenay's jaw was so clenched that he might have been grinding the words with his teeth.

'Today, you can dishonour me, destroy Taillefer, and shame yourself on the eve of war.'

'Or?' De Fontenay closed his eyes. Taillefer and Agnès's eyes were still locked onto each other. She toyed nervously with the belt that hung low on her belly, and in that moment Taillefer wanted her so very badly.

'Or you can keep your honour intact, husband, and the purity of your cause, and raise an heir to the de Fontenay lands. Which will it be, my lord?'

9.5 GAUTHIER

Someone had taken Gauthier's horse in the night. He'd kill the fucking thief if he could find him. Now he had to tramp the road north, carrying a back-aching pack of baggage, no better than the foot soldiers around him. Like them, he'd pulled his hood over his head and tied a cloth over his face against the dust. Clouds of it were turning them all powder-grey until only weapons distinguished soldiers from priests.

He looked back at the top of a hill and saw Roche a few hundred paces behind. He only recognised him by his horse. He waited, pulling the cloth from his face, and fell in beside him. Roche dismounted; they could speak privately within the thunder of a moving army.

'Somebody stole my horse!'

'My horse, you mean.' Roche shrugged. 'And before you ask, I can't spare another one.'

'I've served you well, messire.'

Roche's cold eyes stared sideways at Gauthier. Sweat cut glistening slug-trails down the dust on his face. 'Now just what have you done for me, *Pateras*? You've missed, once. You've failed to fire, once. You've turned back, once. Why should I be grateful?'

'I told hundreds about the Hand, like you said.' Gauthier was irritated.

'Good. Worthier men than you did just the same.'

'And I'd have killed her outside Baudry if you'd let me.'

'There will be a battle. It will serve our purposes better if she is crushed by the Galman army. I'm beginning to think you've outlived your usefulness.' Roche retied a cloth around his face.

'And what if she survives the battle?'

Roche sighed, puffing silk. 'She and Ragener will be defeated. Humiliated. But if you can ensure that she does not survive the battle, and does not escape, that could be useful. We don't want to leave the rebels any figureheads.'

'Same terms?'

'Just make sure you earn them.'

Oh, he would. Once Gauthier had taken an assignment, his professional pride demanded that he see it through. He was like the tarrazim in that respect.

Just a whole lot cheaper.

CHAPTER TEN

10.1 ADELAIS

The army was bleeding troops; at least a thousand men had already taken what they could carry and fled towards their homelands in Theignault or Sjóland or Votlendi. The marshals posted extra guards around the horse lines at night, but not enough; the previous night they'd hung two thieves and lost thirty mounts. Some cavalry patrols, particularly the Ischyrian Theignaulters, simply did not return. The mood on the march was sombre; even the berserkers who had laughed with Adelais on the way south avoided her eye on the way north. It had not rained for several weeks and they tramped through a fog of dust, heads down, eyes half-closed, shoulders slumped, faces covered. In the mid-afternoon, Adelais rode among the northmen, seeking Revna, who was swaying along on the little mountain horse that had carried her to Heilagtré and back. Riding beside her on the mighty Allier, Adelais had the height of a mounted adult beside a child on a pony.

'Where is the *gydhjur*'s prophecy now, *mynn frú*?' Adelais asked. 'Duke Ragener used me, now he blames me for his failures.'

The linen covering Revna's nose and mouth moved. She

may have grimaced. 'The gods are playing with us. Let us wait and see what fate has been woven.'

'But what of me?' Adelais insisted. 'You cast the runes for me, once. Was my fate only to launch men into this useless war?'

'You are marked with *ansuz*, the god-rune. I think the gods believe in you, even if you do not believe in yourself. Do you remember the runes I cast for you?'

Adelais closed her eyes, reaching for her mental picture of the reading. The image was still clear.

'At the centre, *úruz*, upside-down.'

'You were trapped and sick. True?'

'True.' Perhaps she still was. Trapped in fate. At least the dreams of killing had faded since Heilagtré.

'*Ansuz. Ehwaz. Ísa.*' Adelais described the right-hand arc of three.

'God-rune, horse-rune, ice-rune. *Ansuz* told me that your own power over rune magic had brought you to that point, for the threads of fate run strongly through you, perhaps more powerfully than in anyone for generations. The horse-rune shows that you are able to inspire close bonds with people, as well as your horse. People would die for you.'

'They have.' Arnaud. Humbert. Ulfhild. Now she was frightened to love.

'*Ehwaz* is also the rune of the *fylgja*. That too is an unbreakable bond.'

'She tried to warn me. Hjálmar wouldn't let me follow her. I have not seen her since.'

'Have no fear, the she-wolf will still be nearby. The ice-rune told me you were trapped. That ice has now melted. What came after *ísa*, in the realm of that which is becoming?'

'*Ingwaz. Tiwaz. Odhala.*'

'These three are linked. *Odhala* is the rune of ancestral right, while *tiwaz* speaks of sacrificial victory. *Ingwaz* is a good rune, a rune of ideas and resolution. One day we will look back and see how these are linked. It is always easier to look back and understand than to look forwards and interpret.'

Adelais growled inwardly at Revna's vague response. 'But you saw something that made you take me to Heilagtré.'

'*Tiwaz* and *odhala* linked. A victory, at a cost, for the old ways.'

Adelais snorted. 'It doesn't look like it now.' They rode in silence. Far ahead of them, where the road rose up a hill, the vast wagon-train of the dismantled trebuchets had stopped and the crews were putting their shoulders to the wheels. Half the army had slowed to a shuffle behind them.

'There were two more runes, *Frú* Revna, in the realm of that which may become. *Perthro* inverted and *dagaz*. What of these?'

Revna looked up at her. 'Do you really want to know, girl? Is it not better to live happily if you can, while you can? Remember the tale of the god Baldr, whose dreams of his own mortality brought about his death. Sometimes it is best not to ask.'

'Tell me.'

'*Perthro* inverted warns of a crushing blow, perhaps a

betrayal. *Dagaz* is where opposites meet and become one; light and dark, pleasure and pain, life and death. There is no life without death, no death without life, and in *dagaz* they become one. It is timeless. It is a mystery. It is beyond our comprehension.'

Adelais frowned. She didn't understand, and didn't know how to question that.

'And thinking of living happily,' Revna added. 'Wouldn't it be sad on your dying-day to know of great happiness that might have been, but which you did not accept?' She pointed forwards, to where Hjálmar was working his way back along the line, sending men on to help with the wagons.

Adelais would not respond to that. She was still cross with Hjálmar. 'Why do you tell me my fate now, *mynn frú*, when you would not tell me before?'

'Because that fate is now set. You cannot run from it. The only question is how you face it.'

Hjálmar turned his horse to join them. Adelais kept her eyes on the road ahead, and ignored his greeting. Out of the corner of her eye she saw Revna reining back, leaving them together. *Not fair.*

'Princess?'

She looked at him, despite herself, and looked away quickly. He'd pulled down his dust mask and was imitating her, with his nose in the air, mouth pursed into a cat's-arse circle of disapproval, reins held high and central like a noblewoman displaying her breeding more than her riding skills. She tried very hard to stifle the instinctive giggle at the sight of this hairy warrior pretending to be a grand lady, but failed, and it came out as a strangled hiccup that she smothered with her hand. She kept her hand there, glaring at him over her thumb and not breathing because if she drew in air it would come out as laughter.

Hjálmar lifted his nose further in the air and sniffed, and she failed.

'*Hálfviti!*' Idiot.

'That's better. I love you too, princess.'

Adelais filled her chest to retort, knowing that their reconciliation would come through play-fighting, but she twisted in her saddle at the sound of a rider barging his way through the troops. The road was filled verge to verge with men, all shuffling forwards at the pace set by the ox-wagons, and de Warelt was trying to canter past them, forcing them out of his way, leaving curses and shouts of '*fjakkinn gyke!*' in his wake. He paused as he drew level with Adelais and Hjálmar.

'Have you seen the Count of Theignault?' De Warelt was more distressed than she'd ever seen him. All that aristocratic calm was gone.

Adelais shrugged. 'Not since first light. Might he be with the duke?'

'He did not burn the bridges. Galman cavalry is already over the Dalsven, half a day behind.'

Adelais was too stunned to respond, but Hjálmar muttered '*fordæmdur bastardhur*' under his breath. He too twisted in the saddle, eyes scanning the line. 'Have you seen *any* Theignaulters today?'

She looked around them. 'Actually, none since we broke camp.'

There was no fixed camp that night. Men marched long into the evening until small groups settled by the roadside to share what food they carried. Some, exhausted, rolled themselves in their cloaks and snatched a little sleep, others tramped on. Adelais stayed with a group of Jarl Magnus's men, who chose to light a fire in a field, cook their food, and sleep through the darkest hours. Cavalry, after all, would not attack at night; they'd lame half their horses on unseen obstacles. It was also a chance to rest Allier. She and Hjálmar sat away from the fire in grass so dry they needed no cloaks between them and the earth. They kept their weapons beside them and cradled mugs of the herbal broth in which the night's dried beef had been boiled. There had been waybread and honey too; these men were practiced campaigners.

The road was now just a chalky stripe in the darkness, and they listened to the sound of the trebuchet wagons in the distance; the crews were taking advantage of the clearer roads to push them onwards. Armourer Knud had ignored calls to abandon them. His crews spoke of their machines the way others might describe their wives; they would probably have refused such an order, anyway. The high music of the chains lingered after the rumble of the wheels had faded to silence.

'It's a night for lovers.' Hjálmar craned his neck backwards. Above them, away from the glare of the fire, uncountable stars shone.

'I've only just forgiven you. Don't push your luck.'

'But this might be our last night.' His bantering, teasing tone made light of the words.

'If I let you love me, it probably *will* be yours. The men I love have a way of dying.'

'I'd take the risk!' Wide-eyed and soft-bearded, in the starlight he looked like an overgrown dog waiting for her to throw a stick.

Adelais pushed his shoulder. 'Get some sleep, troll-man.'

They were on the road at dawn. Soon after sunrise they saw the first cavalry riding the skyline a league to the west. A mounted patrol of Sjólanders confirmed they were the enemy; their leader flew the blue pennon of Galmandie from his lance. By the time the sun was a handspan higher, a similar line of

mounted men-at-arms shadowed them to the east. A larger force
followed along the road, their numbers steadily growing.
Neither side sought to engage; the Galman cavalry, as yet
unsupported by their foot soldiers, were content to watch. Duke
Ragener would not risk his single remaining squadron of horse
to push them back; there might be far greater forces just over
the horizon.

It was noon before the vanguard of the Vriesian army
reached the tower and village of Gedhabrú, where the long, low
hill of Nautshrygg, the bull's spine, pushed the River Gedha
into a great serpentine loop to the north. The army's line of
march led onto the mound, but at the far end, near the tower,
men were spreading out over the grass. The trebuchet carts had
been pulled off the road and lay like discarded toys. Men lined
the far crest, staring down towards the bridge, and none were
moving forwards. Fearing to learn what she might see, but
needing to know, Adelais nudged Allier to join them.

As she approached the castle she saw nothing to alarm her.
A squadron of Theignaulter cavalry was lined up beyond the
river, facing them. For a moment she was relieved, but curious
to know why they weren't riding north. Then she neared the
crest and an icy fear knotted her gut; about thirty tarrazim
archers lined the far bank. And the bridge lay in ruins with its
stone pillars poking through the water like an old man's teeth.
Adelais joined a knot of nobles standing near Ragener's
banner.

'*Skit!*' Hjálmar breathed out.

'Well, at least we know who set up the ambush.' Adelais
nodded towards the tarrazim. 'I'd like to have words with the
Count of Theignault.'

'I'll cut off his fucking balls.' Ragener looked on, slack-jawed
with disbelief. In the working of his mouth Adelais saw him
scrambling to think of an alternative.

'Where's the next bridge?' The full extent of their predicament was dawning on her. No bridge. No ford. And the Galman army on their heels.

'Half a day's ride, either way,' de Warelt answered. 'I think we can assume that he is ahead of us there, as well.'

Down by the bridge, a minor lord began shouting across the river, the words indistinct but the tone hurt, angry, pleading. A tarrazim loosed a single arrow and the lord crouched to take it on his shield.

'They're going to hold us here and let the Galmans finish us.' Jarl Magnus turned to look back along Nautshrygg. The river gleamed either side, almost turning the hill into an island. 'If you or *Frú* Revna are able to work any magic, now would be a good time. We have an unfordable river on three sides, and the Galman army up our arses. *Vidherum fjakkhenn.*'

We are fucked.

10.2 TAILLEFER

Taillefer found the Duke of Delmas's morning councils deeply uncomfortable. He could add nothing when it came to matters of war, though Delmas himself was warm with him; Taillefer had been useful in bringing the Hand and arranging its validation. A day north from Baudry, the day was still young but a dozen or more nobles and captains were all perspiring under padded gambesons, chain mail, and heraldic surcoats. The tent flaps were open to catch a dry summer breeze, but a miasma of sweat, leather, and oiled metal hung about the group, slick as sin.

And foremost among these nobles stood the cause of Taillefer's discomfort. He and Leandre de Fontenay avoided looking at each other. Taillefer suspected that de Fontenay had accepted that the three of them were so tightly linked to the story of the Hand that Leandre would not want to sully that mystique. Yet waiting for him to declare his intentions was like waiting for an axe to fall. So far, there was only a frozen silence. Taillefer saw Episkopos Juibert watching him and looked away in shame; here, close to the presence of the Hand itself,

Taillefer had been toying with impossible dreams of denying his faith and living quietly with Agnès at Molinot.

Other than Taillefer and Episkopos Juibert, one other man at the council was not armed; Othon de Remy wore his gold chancellor's chain over a rich cote-hardie. He stood by Prince Lancelin's elbow, close enough to murmur advice. Both had been rescued, humiliatingly, from the debacle of Baudry. Neither of them could be denied their right to attend the council. Taillefer almost felt sorry for his brother; the once all-powerful chancellor was being pointedly ignored by the entire Delmas faction.

Taillefer and Othon had spoken, briefly. Othon had expressed surprise, and perhaps a little admiration, at Taillefer's new standing with Delmas. 'Never thought you had it in you,' he'd said, assuming that Taillefer had been party to Delmas's plot to let Lancelin fail. He'd reminded Taillefer of the old dictum: 'Remember, brother, the pinnacle of power is slick with blood and shit.'

And with the enemy trapped south of the Gedha, Prince Lancelin seemed in a rush to prove himself, crying, 'we should harry them!' when the Vriesian entrapment was confirmed. Lancelin had little respect among the warrior lords. His bearing was all bluster, and his armour was too well fitted, as if shaped to show his figure rather than allow the movement a warrior needed in combat. He was sweating profusely. 'I will take a squadron of my nobles and wreak havoc on their line of march!' Lancelin dabbed at his forehead with a linen cloth.

'You will not.' Delmas spoke with unquestionable authority.

'Perhaps, Uncle, you would condescend to explain.' Lancelin had the high, strained voice of a princeling trying to assert his authority, yet who knows his own failure before he opens his mouth.

'We already have them precisely where we want them, marching onto the bull's spine.' Delmas's finger tapped the map where the Gedha made its long curve around the hill. 'We will let them pour themselves into the bottle before we ram home the cork.'

'But we will be well-armed knights against peasants on foot!'

Delmas turned to de Fontenay. 'How many horse do we have, my lord?'

'Fifteen hundred, Highness, and growing.' De Fontenay obviously knew the question was rhetorical. This was for Lancelin's education. Or humiliation.

'And how many foot soldiers does Ragener still have under his command?'

'We estimate around five thousand, Highness.'

Delmas nodded as if he'd needed this confirmation. 'Including all the berserkers who wiped this puppy's arse at Baudry.'

There was a collective intake of breath at Delmas's blatant insult to the man who claimed the throne. Lancelin flushed as red as de Fontenay's surcoat but seemed unable to find a response.

A lesser lord broke the awkward silence. 'And how are the Vriesians to be contained south of the river?'

'If they try to break out east or west, our cavalry will have them. We hold the bridges on either side and there are no fords. The Count of Theignault's tarrazim archers will prevent any attempts to repair the bridge and will kill any who throw away their armour and try to swim.'

'And what is the price of the Count of Theignault's... assistance?' Taillefer had not meant to speak. The question came from a pain within his heart; a hundred paces away the Hand itself lay protected by a ring of Guardians, and here they spoke of treachery and killing. It struck at the core of his imperfect soul.

'Vriesland,' Delmas answered. 'He will have the duchy, as my vassal.'

'But Vriesland should be a vassal of the king,' Lancelin squealed.

Delmas merely smiled until Lancelin turned away. Taillefer thought the boy might weep. Soon, perhaps, Delmas would have the whole army behind him. At that point, Delmas would invite Lancelin to renounce his claim to the crown. This much was now obvious even to Lancelin.

'Within one day we will have ten thousand foot soldiers with us. That is enough. Before the battle, the episkopos will bless the army from beneath the Hand, within sight of the enemy. I doubt any Ischyrians remaining with Ragener will fight after that.'

Taillefer shook his head. 'No, no—'

But Delmas talked over him. 'They will fight behind a shield wall, for that is the only way they know. We will smash that with a war-hammer charge, the broadest we can field on that hill, and push them into the river.'

Taillefer swallowed his fear and spoke loudly enough for all to hear. 'This is wrong, Your Highness! The Guardians never fielded the Hand in war. It is too holy to be used for base purposes.'

'They are all heathens now,' de Fontenay growled. 'Or those that are left to fight will be.'

'But this is not a war for the God, it is a war for land.'

The episkopos turned to glare at Taillefer. 'In wiping the heathens from the earth, we do the God's work.'

Could he really believe that?

'There.' De Fontenay waved his hand dismissively. 'Your superior in the faith has spoken.'

Their eyes met, and in that icy gaze Taillefer saw only contempt for a priest without moral honour.

'Yet I must caution you, my lord.' Taillefer knew his words, in front of Delmas, who would almost certainly be his king, would end all hope of preferment in Galmandie. 'The Hand is the holiest relic on earth. It will punish anyone who uses it for base purposes.'

'Yet you have borne it here from Fontenay.' Delmas looked surprised. 'Will you not bear it into battle?'

'If it were a battle for the faith, willingly. In a fight for lands, no.' Taillefer could feel his precious involvement with the Hand slipping through his fingers.

Delmas snorted. 'Well now is the time for all Ischyrians to unite and throw the heathens back to the northern wasteland they came from. Do you agree, Eminence?' He looked at the episkopos.

'Assuredly. We can restore the light of Ischyros to Vriesland.'

'Then strap that golden hand to a spear shaft, Eminence, and lead the army of Galmandie. Perhaps when we have defeated the Vriesians you can persuade de Fontenay to let you keep it.'

Across the pavilion, Othon's expression was quizzical, even bemused, as he watched Taillefer's fall from power and grace.

10.3 ADELAIS

There was only one place for the Vriesian line. In making its great
loop around the bull's back, the River Gedha had cut a waist,
narrowing the hill until it was only five hundred paces wide
between the low river cliffs to east and west. The river margins were
lush and green, but the spine of the bull's back was a coarse mat of
browning weeds and dry grass; the spring's trampled crops had not
been resown. To the north of this pinch-point, the ground rose to the
little castle above the village before falling to the wrecked bridge. To
the south, the land fanned out, stretching for half a league of fields
and grassland before reaching forest. A little after noon, the
Vriesian rearguard, de Warelt's squadron of cavalry, crossed this
plain, ushering in the last of the foot soldiers the way a farmer's dogs
bring home sheep. They all marched through a low fog of dust.

Adelais walked the 'waist' behind Ragener and a group of
Vriesian captains; Magnus and Hjálmar, three more jarls,
Sjóland, Armourer Knud, and a steward with a slate tally of
supplies. Either side of them, men were digging pits against
cavalry; narrow, steep-sided traps deep enough to break a
charging horse's leg. The terrain was baked hard and progress

slow, even though the men worked in relays with the few pick-axes available, or used spears to break the earth. On the softer soil near the river, other men were hammering in stakes, angled towards the enemy. The ground was too hard in the centre, and there were too few stakes; most had been left outside Baudry. The strategy was simple, it seemed; dig pits. Form shield wall. Wait.

Too simple. Adelais unbuckled one side of her armour and reached inside to scratch at the wound on her breast. It still itched, sometimes, though it was now just pale lines in her skin in the clear stave of *ansuz*, the god-rune.

Skuld had touched her there and told her that *ansuz* was the rune of enlightenment, of wisdom, and of magic. She'd said '*tiwaz* may win you a battle, at a cost, but only *ansuz* will win you the war.'

And if they didn't win this battle, they would have lost the war.

But how could they possibly win?

Ten paces away, two men were taking turns to swing sledge-hammers at the end of a stake, making a rhythmic pounding. The end of the stake was flattened and splintering but axes would sharpen it if they ever succeeded in rooting it firmly enough in the hard ground.

Óss er algingautr...

She scratched absent-mindedly, wondering why she was thinking of Humbert Blanc, the Guardian knight who'd been her protector and mentor during her escape through Galmandie. Humbert would have been appalled that the Hand was being used to lend divine blessing to a secular war.

'Princess?' Hjálmar turned to her. Someone had asked a question.

Her mind still wandered. Humbert had shown her a trick about bringing down charging cavalry...

Ok ásgardhs jöfurr...

'Leave her.' Ragener sounded contemptuous. 'She's working out how to throw thunderbolts at the enemy.'

His sarcasm did not sting. It planted a seed. A glorious seed. Thunderbolts, or firebirds? Adelais let her fingertip trace the scar.

Ok valhallar vísi...

The seed grew. And flowered.

'Master Armourer!' Adelais called after him. Knud turned, his eyes narrowing as he saw her reaching inside her armour. 'Do you still have those rope-bound stones? And oil?'

'Aye, mistress.' Knud licked his lips.

Fjakk him. But I need him. She scratched the itching *ansuz* scar anyway. *Óss er algingautr...*

'And how long are the chains that you use to haul your machines?'

'Forty paces each, mistress.'

She stood still, letting Ragener's party walk ahead. 'Then what if we...' At first she struggled to put her idea into words, but by the time Ragener and Magnus had reached the western-most river cliff, turned, and come back to them, the armourer was grinning. Grinning into her eyes, now, not her leather breasts. He interrupted the passing duke.

'Your Grace, we have a suggestion...'

The crews slaved through the afternoon and evening to assemble their trebuchets and fill their counterweights with bags of soil. In the late twilight of the longest days they each fired a single ranging shot; a soaked but unlit incendiary whose lighter weight would carry furthest. Adelais, waiting beyond the lines with Hjálmar and a guard of his berserkers, watched them soar over her head, black against a darkening sky. They rushed forwards to mark the points of impact by tying rags to nearby bushes.

But the plan was not without problems. She'd have to give a signal, and there was only one place where she would be seen all along the line, and that was on the road, in front of the shield wall. Even the tower was hidden from one end of the line by a fold of land.

Tomorrow, she'd have to face down the Galman charge. She was dry-mouthed at the thought. It was madness.

Unless this worked.

Afterwards, she stood on the road, staring towards the Galman camp nearly half a league to the south. All afternoon they had been arriving, setting up brightly coloured pavilions for their nobles, their banners pinpricks of colour like distant flowers. Now all she could see was their campfires; so many, it was like a city. Would Agnès be there? She looked up. No stars; a sheet of thin, grey cloud had slid over the sky in the late afternoon, turning the sun weak and watery. *Sætur Sif*, let it not rain.

'Do you still want to do this?' Hjálmar loomed beside her.

'Got any better ideas?' Adelais wished he didn't sound so uncertain. She needed to believe they could win.

'Let's go back.' He touched her arm, turning her towards their lines. He was right, of course; they should return. Already their escorts were edging up the slope, swords drawn, some stepping backwards up the road as they watched for any Galman patrols probing their defences in the twilight. Yet she wanted to stay out here, with him. Perhaps hold him, be held, because she wasn't sure either. For the second time that day she reached inside her armour to trace a finger, a fingernail, over her own itching breast.

Ansuz. To win a war.

CHAPTER ELEVEN

11.1 TAILLEFER

In the first ghost-light of day, the air was so still that the world seemed to hold its breath. Even the first birdsong seemed uncertain. As Taillefer and Malory walked through the Galman army, the smoke of the campfires rose spear-straight into the sky. Taillefer had let it be known that he would conduct the dawn office in the open, in front of the lines; already, men were leaving tents and makeshift shelters, throwing off their cloaks, stretching, and tramping through the lines to join him. The certainty of battle turned many men's minds to the God and the need for blessing. Others blew embers into flames. It was still dark enough for the sparks to flash like fireflies against ruddy, shadowed faces.

Malory carried a brazier and a small bundle of aromatic wood so that their prayers might rise sweetly to Ischyros. He was frowning as he sanctified the fire, making it holy even in this unholiest of settings. Their eyes should have been eastwards towards Alympos, but when the newly consecrated flame was burning well and they were waiting for their congregation to gather, they both looked north across the gently rising ground of the hill known as 'the bull's back'. Beyond that half-league of

open ground was the woman Malory thought was a Blessèd
One of the God, the woman who'd granted him pardon and
transformed his life. Soon the Galman army would advance on
her under the Hand she'd once touched. When she was taken
she'd be burned alive, and there was nothing either of them
could do about it.

The Vriesian camp was spread like a distant ants' nest
across the hill, below the tower of a small castle. In the half-
light, two wagons were rolling across the plain a few hundred
paces in front of the Vriesian line; a returning patrol said they
were sprinkling the ground, presumably as part of some foul,
heathen rite before battle. Taillefer and Malory made the sign
of the God together and turned to their congregation.

There was no sunrise, merely a lifting of darkness and a
sharpening of the horizon. The faintest of breezes now kissed
the day, bending the smoke of the campfires towards the north.
Taillefer and Malory stayed in front of the lines after the dawn
office, hearing those who wished to unburden before battle.
When the Duke of Delmas summoned him for a last council,
Taillefer left a long queue behind him. He resented that call; he
could give comfort among the penitents, but had nothing more
to say in council. Nothing that would dissuade them from
parading the Hand and claiming divine approval for a secular
war.

The strategy that Delmas outlined was clear; smash the
Vriesian line with a war-hammer charge. One thousand knights,
two hundred in each line, charging side by side, so close
together that their knees overlapped and the horses could not
evade. The first line to smash the shield wall, even at the cost of
their own lives. Second line to break through. Third line to
charge the Vriesian reserves before they could seal the gap.
Fourth line to take the shield walls in their unprotected rears.

Fifth line to mop up. Kill any who still stood. Seven thousand
foot soldiers to follow. No quarter unless ransoms were offered.
It would be a glorious day. Two hundred knights and three
thousand foot to remain in reserve.

'I shall lead the front rank.' Leandre de Fontenay's quiet
words silenced the pavilion, save for a few sharp intakes of
breath; to be the face of the hammer invited death. Even though
the outcome of the day was not in doubt, the veterans of many
campaigns said a third of the front rank would die as they
hurled themselves upon the shield wall. In the days of the
Knights Guardian, their warriors had competed to be allowed
the honour of this most valiant of roles, for if a knight were to
die thus, in a holy war, surely he would fly straight into the arms
of Ischyros? But in these more secular times, only volunteers
were accepted into the front rank.

And they already had enough; two hundred brave men.
Some were inspired by the Hand and had the light of the God
shining in their eyes. Others had something to prove besides
their faith; their honour; their courage. Others sought fame, so
that they could tell their children and children's children, '*I was
the face of the hammer on the field of Nautshrygg.*' Some simply
wanted to prove their masculinity.

And Leandre de Fontenay? What did he have to prove?
There was a heaviness, a weight about the man that perhaps
only Taillefer and Agnès understood.

'I shall lay my life and my honour before the God,' Leandre
added.

Delmas bowed his head in what could have been either
respect or sadness or both. It might have been to hide the dew
that sprang into that royal warrior's eyes; Taillefer had seen
genuine friendship grow between them. 'Then the God go with
you, de Fontenay. Would that I could ride beside you.'

'There must be one who commands, Highness.'

Delmas glared angrily at Prince Lancelin and gestured

towards de Fontenay. 'There, puppy! If you want brave lords to follow you, this is the price. It is called valour. It is leadership.'

'Then I too shall ride in the front rank!' Lancelin's voice was too high. He stood unnaturally tall with his nose lifted defiantly, as if he was straining for an extra finger of height. A young squire laughed nervously.

'No, you won't.' Delmas sounded tired. 'I'll have no man say I sent you to your death.'

'But I demand the right!' As Lancelin swallowed, his throat-apple bobbed comically above the level of his chain-mail coif and disappeared again.

'By Salazar, I am tempted.' Delmas breathed deeply before he waved in dismissal. 'Put him in the second rank, then. And place good men around him.'

After the lords had gone, only Taillefer, Delmas's squire, and the episkopos remained with Delmas in the pavilion.

'I know, I know. I should let him be killed,' Delmas answered his squire's unspoken question. 'But I shall have this crown by honourable means; he will yield it to me, and the lords who follow him will have nothing to resent. Besides, Ragener must sue for peace. Either that or they will all die, so the war-hammer probably won't happen, and I don't want that boy crowing a courage that was never tested.' He turned to the episkopos. 'Now, Eminence, go and do what you do best. Wave the Hand in front of the army. Tell them Ischyros is with them. I shall wait for Ragener to sue for terms.'

Even by the time the morning was halfway to noon, no emissary had come from the Vriesian lines. Two lines, as Delmas had predicted: a shield wall and a reserve, though they were still scattered, sitting on the grass over a thousand paces away, only loosely in position. Much closer to Taillefer, five lines of Galman knights waited in open order; they would close into the compact hammerhead formation on the neck of the bull's back as they neared the enemy lines. Some of the horses were becoming restive with inactivity.

Taillefer sat on his mare near Delmas, behind the Galman cavalry, in front of the foot soldiers; these would advance behind the war-hammer.

'He *must* come.' Delmas seemed insulted that Ragener was not suing for peace. 'I'll wipe them from the earth!'

Yet only a single rider moved into the front of the Vriesian lines; a tiny figure in golden armour, or a golden surcoat, on a black horse. It was too far to see details, but Taillefer knew instinctively that it was her. She cut a lonely figure, out there on her own. Was she waiting for something? It was a strange place to wait, in front of the shield wall where she'd be crushed by the charge.

'If Ragener's sending the witch to me, I'll not talk to her.' Delmas's horse had begun to fidget, bored with waiting. 'He can crawl here himself and beg.'

'She won't come.' Taillefer turned at the sound of Agnès's voice, his heart lifting. How did she do that to him? They'd hardly spoken since the temple outside Bellay, and even with the army looking on he was reacting to her presence like a boy with his first love. She rode her palfrey between Taillefer and Delmas; straight-backed, poised, immaculate. 'Shall I try and talk them out of this madness, Highness? Woman to woman?'

'My lady.' Delmas dipped his head. 'But you do not know the terms.'

'Oh, I understand the terms.' She rode on, not waiting for permission. 'Surrender or die,' she called over her shoulder. 'Nothing less.'

11.2 ADELAIS

Adelais nudged Allier into a trot, then a canter, towards Agnès. If Agnès thought she was excited to see her, she'd be right. Partially right. *Where* they met was important, and Adelais paced Allier so that she could slow to a walk before the marker-rags, and wait a hundred paces beyond.

Agnès's smile was strained as she approached. 'I still love those leather tits.' And her jollity was forced.

Adelais rapped one breast with her knuckles. It knocked like wood even through the cloth-of-gold tabard. 'No fun to play with, though.' They were flirting. Two women who had once almost been lovers, now at the head of two hostile armies. Six hundred paces behind Adelais were the two ranks of the Vriesian shield wall, wedged between the river banks. A similar distance behind Agnès the horizon was a forest of lances. *So many.*

'New toy?' Agnès pointed towards the tarrazim bow in its leather holder, hanging behind her saddle.

'I find it easier than a crossbow.' Adelais smiled ruefully, thinking of the time she'd used Agnès's hunting crossbow to defend a bridge. She dropped her hand to the quiver behind her saddle and touched the fletchings of her arrows. 'The man who owned it tried to kill me.'

Agnès's eyes widened, her shock plain. *That's something she didn't know. Good.* Adelais could not believe that Agnès would have had anything to do with the tarrazim.

'Oh, *kjúkling*, I wish we could find somewhere quiet.' Agnès's shock faded into sadness. 'Just us. Drink some wine.'

'Laugh a little.'

'While you brushed my hair again.'

'You could do mine now.' Adelais pushed her fingers into the plaited crown on her head. Her hair still wasn't long enough for maiden's braids. Another year, perhaps. If she lived. A strand fell loose and flopped in front of her eye, a corn-gold wisp against a flat, grey sky. 'It's grown a bit.'

'One day.'

'One day.'

They looked at each other. Their horses touched nostrils; they too were old friends. Agnès looked radiant, despite her sorrow. Her figure might have been a little more rounded...

'You're with child!' Adelais almost whooped in delight. Suddenly this was a happy time. 'So Leandre finally did his duty!'

Agnès looked down, a slight blush on that glowing skin. 'No. Not him.'

'Oh, you bad girl!' Adelais's laugh was high and giggling, even in her own ears. 'Does Leandre know?'

'He does. Things are somewhat... tense at the moment.'

They both looked over their shoulders at the watching armies, and erupted together into snorting, preposterous laughter. Agnès's eyes were now sparkling and a little moist.

'Oh, my friend, I miss you.' Adelais had never known a bond like this. 'I wish we could have that wine.' So many questions she wanted to ask.

'Miss you too. You know what's going to happen, *kjúkling*, don't you?'

'I know what might happen.'

'Twelve hundred horse. Ten thousand foot. They'll smash you.'

'They'll try.'

'Can't you persuade Ragener? Delmas is waiting for him to come crawling.'

'He won't.'

'But everyone could live. All for a little humbling...'

'Even me?'

'Well...'

'I wouldn't even ask. Even if I thought Delmas would let me live.'

'I was afraid you'd say that.' Agnès nudged her horse alongside, close enough for their legs to touch. 'I have a gift for you. From Elyse. And me. With love.' She reached into the scrip hanging from her belt and pulled out a small glass vial.

'The same potion?' Adelais turned the little bottle over in her hand. Elyse had given her one of these before, just in case it was the only way to escape death by torture at the hands of the anakritim. *One drop for pain, five and you'll never wake.* This time no rune had been cut into the wax seal.

'The same. Don't let them take you alive, *kjúkling*. They'll burn you.'

Adelais smiled rueful thanks as she slipped the poison into her own scrip, and sighed. They were silent for several heartbeats, looking at each other, until Adelais touched Agnès on the arm. 'I suppose we ought to let the men get on with their work.'

They clasped hands, forearm twined around forearm. Agnès was truly crying now. 'I hope, wherever it is we go to, after...' After death, she must mean. 'I hope it's the same place.'

'I'm not dead yet. One day I might even bounce your baby on my knee.'

They both smiled at the impossibility. Agnès tugged at Adelais's hand and they both leaned out of their saddles. They kissed briefly, fiercely, on the lips, and let their fingers trail their farewell.

11.3 FYLGJA

The wolf within her has no understanding of 'death'. There are simply endings and beginnings in the endless cycle of renewal. Prey that is warm with blood becomes meat, that the pack may live and thrive. Wolf-kind that grows old, falls sick, goes lame, also becomes meat, but for flying-kind or crawling-kind. Without endings there can be no beginnings. Without winter there is no spring.

Yet wolf-kind does not go willingly to its ending. When menace is near and cannot be overcome, it runs. If it cannot run, it fights while it has strength and claws and fangs; it does not submit. But wolf-kind does not walk into the midst of man-kind. It does not choose the path of greatest peril.

Many men are close, but the she-wolf is still safely hidden in the bushes where the land falls to a river. In front of her, battle lines have formed. The air is heavy with their tension, the way it is heavy before thunder; there will be many endings this day. The lines of men stretch away, up over a rise where the earth is brown and dry and empty. Round shields rest on the ground with their upper rims leaning against mail-clad stomachs or hips, forming a loose wall that will be lifted and tightened before battle is joined. Beyond the crest, the ranks of men sink as the ground falls, until the wolf can see only above their knees, their waists, their necks, but even beyond that they are there, she knows, all the way to where the land meets the same river on the far side of this great loop. The men have spears, axes, knives, swords; weapons that spell an ending for wolf-kind. Nearest to the bushes, on the wings of the army, are the most dangerous men of all; those with the bows that hurl fangs through the air.

Yet along that crest comes the girl, riding her warhorse slowly towards the men with shields, and the *fylgja*, that which is not wolf, swells with pride, for the girl is strong and proud. The *fylgja* knows the girl, she reads the warp and weft that flows around her; the uncertainty, the doubt, the weight of these men's lives upon her shoulders. She must be seen to be sure, because only then will they believe and obey. Stand. Fight.

There is another destiny that flows this morning. It is clearer with every stride that the warhorse takes. A shared destiny. An ending that is perhaps a beginning. The *fylgja* remembers a pact, made moons before in a sacred place.

What will you give to save her?

My life.

So be it.

The wolf within does not choose this path. It resists. Wants to run, but the *fylgja* commands, in the way that a pack elder might nip at a wayward cub; the girl is of the blood of the wolf. She is wolf-kind. Whelp of our whelp. And if we stand with her, men will believe in her. We *will* go to this ending.

Slowly, the she-wolf steps out into the open, in front of the wall of men. She holds her head low, sunk below her shoulders, and a wondering silence spreads along the line as the heads of men turn to stare, nudge one another, point at her. She senses their awe, for she knows she is massive in their eyes, and she snarls her defiance; without their weapons she could rip any of them into meat. Those nearest to her lift their shields and heft their weapons, but not to fight. Not yet.

Hesitantly at first, but with ever-growing power, weapons are slammed into shields; a steady rhythmic beating that honours the girl, the gods, the wolf. Two horse-lengths in front of the line, the girl turns her horse to face the enemy, and the beating becomes the chant of five thousand men, as one; deep, hoarse, mighty, so the very earth hums with their noise.

Hún úlfur! Hún úlfur! Hún úlfur!
She-wolf! She-wolf! She-wolf!

11.4 ADELAIS

Adelais had hoped that the wolf would come. As she rode back from her parley with Agnès, men were turning and pointing, all along one side of the shield wall, from the river to the crest. Adelais found her eyes dewing. This, she knew, was no warning, no insistence that she take another path. This was like a parent choosing to stand alongside their child at a time of trial, and for that she felt her chest swell.

While the wolf was a still hundred paces away, Adelais reached a gap in the shield wall where Ragener sat waiting on his horse, bulked out by gambeson and hauberk so that he seemed to overflow his saddle. A cluster of nobles waited behind him under the red eagle banner of Vriesland. Soon he would go to the highest point of the hill, beneath the tower, where he could watch and command.

'Terms?' Ragener called. He'd pushed his mail coif back onto his shoulders, and yellow hair tufted from beneath a leather under-cap. Lines of sweat shone on his cheeks.

Adelais halted in front of the line. She shrugged. 'Surrender or die. Delmas wants you to crawl.'

A flicker of uncertainty crossed Ragener's face, and Adelais groaned inwardly. *Don't waver now, you fat gyke.*

'Are you sure about this, girl?' Ragener waved his hand in a way that encompassed half his army. No swearing, for once. Five thousand men watched them; shield men with axes and war hammers to the fore, spear men behind. A reserve row. Trebuchets ready to fire, bowed and straining, their counterweights filled to capacity for maximum range. Brazier fires burning beside each. *Good.* Archers on the wings. Revna, sitting on a wooden platform with her *seidhkona* staff. Soon she would begin rune song.

And every forty paces along the shield wall, narrow gaps that could be filled, *would* be filled with a single step after her signal was given. Gaps where ropes lay in the grass, trailing out towards the enemy. Short lines of men stood by each rope, ready to lift and haul.

Was she sure? Of course she wasn't sure. They'd practised before dawn, by the flare of torches. Everyone knew their tasks. Would it work with a thousand knights charging at them? When men might fumble and fail in their fear? How the *fjakk* could she know?

She glanced towards the wolf as a pounding of weapons on shields began and swelled, as if the wolf cast a bow-wave of sound. It was spreading as others saw it, and she had to shout to be sure she was heard. She stood in her stirrups and bellowed at her duke, at everyone.

'Of course it will *fjakkinn* work! We're going to teach those Galmans they can't crush Vriesland!' As rousing speeches go, it was pathetic, but it was all she could think of at that moment. It should be Ragener inspiring his men, not her. She turned Allier and nudged him forwards, in front of the line, knowing the shield wall would close behind her. She looked right and left to be sure she was in the right place, where she could be seen even at both ends of the line where it dipped towards the river. *Here.*

The thump of weapons against shields was sounding all along the line now, and a chant began, in time with the blows.

Hún úlfur! Hún úlfur!

They should be calling for Vriesland, not for her. Or were they shouting for the wolf that had turned with her to face the enemy?

'Hello, Amma.' Adelais did not need to speak, but did. 'Thank you.' She could not be heard, anyway, and the wolf made no reaction. It was quivering slightly, as if it might turn and run at any moment. *Amma, please don't do that!* Three of them, together, in front of the lines: horse, wolf, woman, and each of them *skitting* themselves. Adelais envied Allier his freedom to lift his tail. Ahead of her, the Galman army had begun to move, a single, terrible mass still far enough away to flow slowly over the ground like spilt oil.

Oil. At dawn they had soaked the land. Every barrel they had, bar one; enough for the armourer to burn several towns, now poured away onto that dead, brown grass by the markers. She'd caught the stink of it as she rode back from talking to Agnès, but how much would have soaked away? Was this all for naught?

Adelais twisted to look up at the tower behind, where her own banner of the black wolf on a golden field hung straight out, flat to the ground. Her young standard bearer had a crucial task that day. Armourer Knud was up there with him, watching the approaching cavalry from the only place that gave him the height to see clearly. On the ground, the front ranks of the enemy would hide the rearmost. Knud would raise the wolf banner when the crews must put fire to the shot, and drop it when the moment came to let fly. After that, reload and fire again. Keep firing until that one remaining barrel was empty and every shot had gone.

Hún úlfur! Hún úlfur!

The men should save their breath and energy.

One thousand paces now. Adelais ran her fingers through her hair, mentally going over the advice of the veterans of other wars. Her braids were unravelling. *Concentrate!* Each line of knights will walk until they are within one hundred and fifty paces, then trot. They will not charge until they are less than one hundred paces from the shield wall, possibly as close as seventy, so that they can keep their formation and strike with fresh horses. There will be fifty paces between each line.

So much depended on how many lines of cavalry came at them. The ranging shots from the trebuchets had flown three hundred and fifty paces with the light, rope-wrapped, oil-soaked shot. They would aim to land the first shot into the midst of the rearmost line, or when the front line was at two hundred paces, whichever came first.

Eight hundred paces. *How many lines?* The Galman cavalry were a solid mass of armoured grey and bright heraldic surcoats. She could make out another line beyond, but it was impossible to tell how many more were coming. The whole nobility of Galmandie must be there.

Hún úlfur! Hún úlfur!

She didn't see Hjálmar approach. She was still peering into the distance when he touched her knee. He looked even broader in his gambeson and chain mail. His shield was still slung over his back, and his sword and war hammer hung on either hip. He cradled his grey-plumed helmet under one arm and his face was tight with strain.

'Come back, princess. You will be crushed between their charge and the shield wall.'

'Not if this works.'

'It's too risky.'

'And this is the only place where I can be seen by the whole army. We tried it. They all have to pull at the same time so I have to give the signal from here. You know this.'

'Let me send one of my berserkers to give the signal instead. They know this a death worthy of Valhalla.'

'My idea. I'll not send another to take my risk.'

'Princess, you are infuriating!'

'I love you too, troll-man.' Adelais spoke lightly, before she thought of the consequences. Would he die for those words? His eyes were shining now, but with such sadness. She pulled off a gauntlet, leaned forwards, and touched his cheek. It was the only bare skin showing. 'Go, my friend. Stay safe. I must do this.'

She watched him squeeze through one of the rope gaps in the line, pulling his helmet angrily over his head. She marked the point where his plume melded into the front rank.

Six hundred paces. She could hear them now; a sighing movement like waves on a distant shore.

The chant of *hún úlfur* faded. A louder, rattling hum behind her as men moved into their final positions, overlapped shields, planted their boots. Groped for hammer pendants or touched the man alongside. Gripped their weapons. Muttered invocations to the gods. Here they would fight and probably die.

Four hundred paces. A bright red surcoat rode the road towards her in centre of the front rank; the golden flowers of de Fontenay. *Oh, no.*

A strand of Adelais's hair fell loose and flopped over her face. Thoughts chased wildly round her head like a bird trapped in a barn. Why hadn't she worn a helmet? So she could be seen, of course. In a mad moment, she finger-combed the plaits from her head to let her hair fall freely as if she were a bride. It had not been cut for over a year and it came below her shoulders now. Definitely a woman. Yellow tresses, leather tits, and cloth of gold. In an inspired moment she pirouetted Allier, swinging her head to fling her locks wide, and bellowed for an army to hear.

'Today I am wed to Vriesland!' Yet it was all for show, just

making use of what was happening anyway. She did not deserve
the great roar that spread through the ranks. High on the tower,
the armourer spread his hand. Five. Five ranks of cavalry. *Fjakk.*
Too many.

The front rank was passing the markers. The ground trem-
bled to the ponderous tramp of a thousand horses, though still
they walked, a solid line stretching from side to side across the
bull's spine. They looked unstoppable. Now she could hear the
jingle of harness.

A horse slipped, skidded and recovered. Another crashed
into its neighbour, scrambled and fell. The oil was still soaking
the surface. *Takk til gudhanna.* Thanks be to the gods.

A sharper booming began behind her as Revna struck her
platform with her staff.

'*Týr er einhendr áss...*'

Tiwaz, the rune of Tyr, the one-handed god.

Allier began to dance beneath her, waiting for permission to
charge. Adelais clamped her calves against his sides, holding
him, calming him. His former master had trained him to leap
fearlessly at an oncoming enemy. Now she wanted him to
stand, unmoving, and face down a charge. And soon the
oncoming hordes would see what that same master had trained
her to do. *Dear Humbert.* Would he smile at her from his
Ischyrian paradise? She who muttered rune song? She who was
about to bring down the might of Galmandie?

If this worked...

'*Ok ulfs leifar...*'

Tyr, who sacrificed his hand that the gods might bind
Fenrir, the monstrous wolf.

'*Ok hofa hilmir...*'

A rune of victory.

Sacrificial victory.

Two hundred paces, close enough to hear the shouts of squadron commanders – 'hold, hold' – as the line kept perfect formation. Two hundred knights, riding so close their knees touched, filling the width of the bull's back. Here and there a destrier trotted, even cantered on the spot, and was quickly curbed.

She risked a glance behind. Wolf banner up. A ball of fire raged in the sling of each trebuchet. Steady, steady, not too soon.

'*Týr er einhendr áss...*'

Her mouth was dry. She could not even manage the spit to sing rune song.

One hundred and fifty paces. Cries from their squadron commanders, and the line began to trot, still knee to knee. The only thing between them and the Vriesian shield wall was now the line of stakes, each about forty paces apart, and a few shallow pits. They looked insignificant defences against cavalry.

Two mighty crashes behind her sent Allier rearing, fore-hooves flailing. She glimpsed the wolf beside her, cowering to the ground, but, as Allier's hooves came down, her eyes were on the fireballs arcing over her head, trailing filthy smoke.

Several horses in the Galman front rank also shied badly. Two threw their riders. The line closed back into almost perfect formation; some knights were looking over their shoulders, watching fires that seemed to hang in the air, slowly shrinking, before plummeting towards the earth.

And disappeared behind the wall of cavalry. Nothing. Perhaps a few screams, barely audible beyond the thunder of hooves. Adelais felt her shoulders slump, but brought Allier back under control and drew her sword. She'd play this game to the end.

One hundred paces. Coming quickly now, the line getting

more ragged. Still trotting. A few more heartbeats and they would charge. She must wait until they committed. Adelais raised her sword, and, as if at her command, a great gout of flame erupted into the air behind the cavalry as the oil-soaked ground ignited. Now there were definitely screams, of horses and of men.

'*Ok ulfs leifar...*'

Eighty paces, and Leandre de Fontenay's lance toppled forwards from upright into the couched position of the charge, the signal for two hundred more lances to come down, and for two hundred destriers to leap forwards into the mad gallop of the charge. They were silhouetted now against a wall of flame, twice the height of a mounted knight and more, that was spreading across the hill, and the earth shook with their coming.

Allier was spinning, unable to stay on the spot, bucking, demanding to be unleashed. She could not hold him for much longer. She reached out to the horse with her mind – *please, my friend* – and felt the bond as they melded into the dance of rune song; a hand-clasp, a union. They were one, tuned to the finest pitch, quivering.

'*Ok hofa hilmir...*'

All along the Vriesian line, men had picked up their ropes and were watching her, waiting, panting in their fear. Not yet. Too soon and they'd see the traps in time to stop. Too late and they'd be into the shield wall that bristled with spears behind her.

And she was between them.

So was the wolf, still here, hackles raised, snarling, backing towards the shield wall.

Seventy paces. Adelais lifted her sword as high as she could, holding Allier balanced between her fingertips and her legs so that she rocked with his dancing. Leandre de Fontenay was now a little to her right; he would strike near Hjálmar's place in the line. And behind him, in the second rank, another red surcoat with the retainer's badge of de Fontenay. Open-faced bascinet. Guy Carelet was riding into battle as a man-at-arms.

Allies. Friends. Hurling towards the man she loved. And horses, so willing to serve, so soon to die. It was all so *fjakkinn* senseless. And directly in front of her an unknown knight's lance was aimed at her chest in a way that made this madness seem very personal. The world narrowed to a single, shining point, with the bright colours of heraldry blurring behind it.

Adelais hardened her heart and brought down her sword, cutting air. The Vriesian rope men heaved, running away with their ropes, hauling the traps out of the grass.

For the stakes were not simply stakes, they were levers, and the ropes pulled them backwards so that they lifted other, heavier stakes from the ground, each heeled into a pit and guyed with cables hammered into the earth. Between the stakes hung the iron chains that had drawn the trebuchets; head-high at the posts, sagging to thigh-high in the dips, always too high for a charging destrier to jump with an armoured knight on its back.

A few lances lifted as men saw the trap and sat back, trying to rein in, but they were too close, too committed, and the chivalry of Galmandie crashed like a breaking wave at her feet. Dust burst from the earth like grey sea-spray under the impact of their bodies, and the mighty thunder of the charge erupted into a noise as overwhelming as the avalanche. The knight who thought he would kill her was pitched forwards onto his face, his lance slithering onwards down the track on its own. All along the line, the wave still tumbled, not yet spent, as men and fallen horses bounced forwards, some pulling lengths of chain with them, their bodies compacting into a new defensive wall.

For a moment Adelais could not move. She stared at the twisted, screaming wall of horse flesh and broken men, appalled at what she had done. 'I'm so sorry,' she muttered. *Sætur Sif, the poor horses!* Now that the avalanche was spent, it seemed almost quiet in comparison, though the air was full of the drum roll of hooves as the next line was driven into the chaos of the first; a line bright with heraldry but with little formation; lances at all angles, a line already breaking, for this was less a charge than a stampede away from the flames.

Beyond them, a third line was disintegrating, its horses galloping uncontrollably away from the burning madness of men and beasts across the middle of the hill, pushing the second line forwards, even breaking through it, so the heaps of fallen horses and men shook as more horses crashed into it, stumbled and fell. In front of Adelais, a horse tried to climb over, its eyes rolling white in its terror, rider swaying unbalanced in the saddle. One iron-shod hoof thumped into the shoulder of a screaming, grounded destrier and another into a fallen man's back before it fell, pitching the knight onto his side in front of the Vriesian line.

'I yield!' he cried, spreading his arms wide.

One shield lifted and slammed edge-downwards with a sickening, shovel-in-gravel sound, and for the first time in the battle Ragener's voice rang out, high and clear over the din.

'Ransoms! I want ransoms!'

He was still going to have to fight for them. Adelais shook herself out of a daze that could only have lasted a few heart-beats, and spun Allier, trying to make sense of the madness.

She was trapped in a narrow strip between the shield wall and a line of groaning, writhing bodies. To her left, the chains had worked; Vriesian spears faced twenty paces of open grass. In front of her, a wall of flame silhouetted a packed melee of cavalry where knights fought to control panicked mounts, unable either to continue their charge over the tangled, screaming mess to their front or to retreat through the wall of flame behind.

But to her right, the band of grass narrowed to a point where it merged with the Vriesian line; the first line of the war-hammer had been brought down by the chains but had broken the shield wall apart, leaving a gap for a few of the second line to punch through. Already the line was bowed, bulging backwards as Galman knights pressed into the breach.

Behind Adelais, a two-man width of the shield wall opened. Jarl Magnus stood in the gap, beckoning.

'Come, girl. You've done your job. Quickly, now.'

But her eyes were drawn to the right, where that handful of brave Galman knights were wheeling their mounts behind the Vriesian line, casting aside broken lances and reaching for axes or swords. Others were bunching into the gap, scattering bodies; a flow had begun towards the breach the way water will drain from a trough. Men were running from the Vriesian reserve line to support, but the cohesion of spear men and shield men was broken; now all was individual fights. And in the thick of the fight Hjálmar's grey-plumed helmet stood taller than all the others where he rallied his men.

Yet he turned towards her, looking for her across the chaos. And he did not see the Galman knight behind him until it was too late. Adelais screamed a warning but her voice was lost in the din of battle and Hjálmar was still turning, lifting his shield, when the mace fell.

11.5 TAILLEFER

Agnès had positioned her horse to stand alongside Taillefer. He tried and failed to imagine what it would be like to watch your husband lead the charge against your dearest friend; her face was taught with emotion. If they had been alone, he would have held her. But ten paces away from them Delmas and the remaining nobles also watched, and the entire reserves were spread across the fields behind them.

The advance had seemed so ordered, so mechanical. Five lines of cavalry in bright surcoats, walking forwards a little faster than the drab foot soldiers behind them. The massed ranks of infantry tramped forwards in their companies, banding the bull's back with broad lines of armour-grey. From Taillefer's vantage point on a slight rise, the companies looked like a single, vast insect; a woodlouse, perhaps, armoured and lined, crawling onwards on countless legs. The air thrummed with the noise of their advance.

Taillefer had never seen a trebuchet in action, and did not understand the shooting stars that soared upwards over the war-hammer, hung in the air, and plummeted towards the earth. He had time to think that those lines of light were almost pretty, until they burst in the middle of the last line of cavalry. One knight was struck directly; he and his horse folding inwards like a scrap of paper crumpled in a fist. His fall brought down two others. The other landed a little short, and bounced upwards with such violence that another knight and his destrier were bowled over backwards on top of each other. Both shots seemed to explode as they hit, scattering flaming fragments. They came down again in front of the lines of infantry and carved bloody, burning gaps through two ranks. Among the horses, the heraldic caparisons decorating one destrier had caught light and the beast was bucking and kicking, beyond all control, inflicting damage all around as it tried to escape the fire burning on its rump.

'Clever.' Delmas sounded impressed, though unconcerned. 'But too late. They should have shot at the first rank. They'd have taken out more in the next, and broken the line.'

'I think they intended to shoot into the rear.' Agnès's eyes narrowed, peering towards the points where the shots had landed, and where lines of flame were now spreading along the ground. Already that rear rank was disintegrating as horses that would willingly have hurled themselves at a shield wall panicked at the fires. Knights were surging forwards, lances upright, trying to curb their mounts, and the disorder was spreading from the fifth into the fourth rank. Somewhere beyond, the war-hammer must have met the shield wall; even above the din of the advance Taillefer heard a long, low rumble like distant thunder.

The fires met and blossomed in the middle of the hill, and Taillefer's view of the battle wavered in the heat, then disappeared in the centre behind a curtain of flame. On the wings of the advance, the war-hammer blended into a single mass, their colours muted by smoke. And the flames were spreading, flowing outwards from the bull's spine.

'Oil,' Taillefer murmured. 'They spread oil. I saw them. Thought it was a heathen libation.'

'I smelt it,' Agnès answered. 'And I didn't understand. Too busy saying goodbye.'

Two more fireballs dropped from the sky and burst within the furnace. One struck the hard surface of the road and bounced high. There was a terrible inevitability about watching its fall – six, seven, ten heartbeats later – into the middle of a company of infantry. Taillefer watched a wave of movement spread outwards through the army; a ripple of shock. The advance faltered. It would be madness to march into that wall of flame.

Delmas beckoned to an equerry. 'Tell them to go round the fucking sides!' He waved him forwards, through the lines.

Yet the flames now stretched from river cliff to river cliff and were edging towards them as dry grasses and undergrowth ignited. Men in the front rank backed away, arms raised in front of their faces.

'It is the God's punishment,' Taillefer whispered. 'We should never have brought the Hand to war.'

The first foot soldiers began edging their way along the river cliff, cowering as they went with their shields raised towards the flames above them. One of them seemed to stumble, and rolled down the slope towards the river. And another. Two more slumped as if suddenly too tired to continue.

'They have archers on the wings, Highness,' a noble remarked. 'The cliffs are too steep for an ordered advance.'

'I can fucking see that.' Delmas sounded exasperated.

More men dropped.

It was impossible to tell what was happening beyond the smoke. The noise of the battle assaulted their ears, even across a thousand paces of hillside; a ringing, a screaming, a grinding in which a thousand blows became one, as if some vast mill wheel was grinding metal and flesh against rock.

'Leandre...' Agnès spoke her husband's name so quietly that perhaps only Taillefer heard.

Taillefer closed his eyes as an unworthy thought crept into his mind; if de Fontenay were to die, so many issues would go away.

He made the sign of the God, silently begging forgiveness.

11.6 ADELAIS

Adelais bellowed a great, visceral scream towards the place where Hjálmar had fallen, both denial and protest, a scream that cut through even the din of battle and the constant drum roll of hooves. She knew she could not ride to him; she was in that strip between shield wall and chaos, which narrowed until the shield wall buckled in the face of the flailing hooves of fallen horses. And beyond that bloody merging, a block of Vriesian berserkers was trying to re-form the line. She did not even know if Hjálmar was beneath his own men's feet or the hooves of the Galman cavalry. An ever-growing number of knights was there, thrusting downwards with their lances at the warriors trying to reform the line. A small forest of Vriesian spears bristled back, trying to keep them at bay.

Adelais did not think that what she was doing was courageous. It was blind instinct to throw herself from Allier's back, grabbing the tarrazim bow and her quiver as she jumped. She called to Magnus to take Allier, but he too had seen and was turning back into the line, his shoulders lifting to shout. Adelais could not ride to Hjálmar, but she could scramble over the downed horses; the twisted ridge of their bodies was a pathway between the armies. She would not accept another death of one she loved. *Not again!* She would not let this fate be woven. Anger rose within her the way it had beneath the yew at Heilagtré, implacable, capable of hurling thunderbolts.

She reached for rune song the way she might reach for weapons, selecting them for their task. Not *sowilo* or *tiwaz*, not yet; she wanted defence before victory.

The leg of an injured horse thrashed wildly upwards at her from where it was trapped on its back. She dodged and sprung onwards from the beast's chest, slinging the quiver across her back as she ran, and reaching over her shoulder for an arrow.

Which rune would save him? She would not unleash the wild force of *thurs*. Not with Hjálmar down.

A man still lived between the animals; a mail-gauntleted hand groped upwards. She leapt the gap, leaving his groans behind her.

Algiz.

The stag-rune. The rune of protection.

Hjortin er konugur skógarins...

The stag is the king of the forest...

She'd almost reached the breach; here the horses lay piled on top of one another, two or three deep, making a vantage point of sorts, though its top still moved; they were not all dead. She scrambled up this hill of flesh and stood on the highest shoulder, above the level of the mounted knights. The nearest were barely three paces away, funnelling into the gap. Even she could not miss. They were too packed to charge, but those within reach of the Vriesian line had shifted their lances into an overhand grip and were stabbing into the shield wall. And she was on their unshielded side. Adelais nocked her arrow and drew until the strain across her shoulders demanded release—

... Ok dádýrsherra...

The hind's lord...

—and put it into the nearest knight's elbow. She'd been aiming at his body, but at this range the narrow, armour-piercing bodkin head went clear through his chain-mail sleeve, knocking him sideways in the saddle; he hunched to his right and dropped his lance with his arm now dangling useless.

A glance into the Vriesian lines. Where was Hjálmar? No sign of his plume. Must still be on the ground.

Ok elskadhur gudhanna...

Beloved of the gods.

Nock, draw. Again the unbearable tension across her back before she released it into a knight's chest as he jostled for space to fight. He too dropped his lance and rocked in the saddle. By the time he hit the ground she had another arrow ready.

She'd been seen. *Of course you've been seen,* some wild part of her mind told her. *You're standing on dead horses in leather tits and cloth of gold, shooting arrows at them.* She had to swing her aim away from the breach to put that arrow into the belly of a knight who cantered towards her, levelling his lance.

A twitch and lurch beneath her almost toppled her and she dropped to one knee. She turned, unsteady on the soft, moving hide of a horse, and loosed an arrow into the back of a man-at-arms near the fighting. Those already battling at the shield wall started to look over their shoulders, distracted as they realised men were dying *behind* them, and the shield wall was closing. Two berserkers were pulling a body from the crush by his armour-straps. A grey-plumed helmet hung low between the shoulders. Hjálmar! *Please gods, let him be alive.*

Elskadhur gudhanna ok elskadhur mynn.

Beloved of the gods, and my beloved.

Elskadhur mynn, elskadhur mynn. She knew it now.

Another knight came at her, merely trotting to let his horse pick its way through the debris. He wore an open-faced bascinet, and she could see into his eyes. She had a strange sense of communion with this man who was trying to kill her, almost as if they knew each other; a frowning face, age-lines fanning from the eyes, moustache overflowing the chain mail that framed his face, and a coat of arms of white diamond lozenges on a black field. She fired into that face, but he lifted his shield as she loosed and she had to jump sideways off the mound to avoid his strike. His momentum carried him past before he could correct his aim.

'Bitch!' he called, but not as if he meant it.

'Bastard,' she answered, almost amiably. It was a ritual response; her mind was full of the sight of Hjálmar's body being dragged clear. She nocked another arrow and scrambled back up the pile of horses until she could stand on their summit and strain to see if Hjálmar lived. It didn't occur to her to shoot white-diamonds in the back. All her attention was on Hjálmar. She even forgot to sing rune song. *Move, Troll-man!*

Adelais loosed her arrow into another knight's shoulder and was reaching for her quiver again when a mighty blow hit her in the back, punching her onto her hands and knees. For a moment Adelais stared stupidly at the blood-smeared point that had sprung out of her armour on her left side, angling out below her breast, but it was ripped out almost as soon as it appeared and she screamed as its edge sliced across her ribs, wrenching her around to face outwards, away from Hjálmar. The tumult beyond the battle lines filled her vision, outlined against flames, before she fell towards it, limbs flailing.

Adelais did not know how long she lay at the base of the mound. A few heartbeats only, perhaps, but for those heartbeats she knew a strange calm; the horse's body behind her was warm and soft against her neck. The sky above was flat grey, streaked with filthy smoke. She didn't have to worry. No one could expect any more of her. She took one deep, sighing breath and the pain across her side dragged her back whimpering into the moment.

She looked down, panting as shallowly as she could. The left side of her armour had been ripped open. If she reached round to the back with her right hand – *fjakk, that hurt* – she could feel the lips of the gash all the way to where a lance had gone in. She guessed it had slid across her ribs. Probably broken some of them. It hurt to breathe but she was not coughing blood.

Blood. She could feel it soaking her back and side, and pooling between her skirts and her *rass*. Must stop the bleeding. She blinked at the world, trying to make sense of it. More arrows were flying. *Good.* Must be coming in from the wings. Still long range; the arrows were punching at chain mail, not penetrating, though another horse went down, screaming. And in the distance, the sound of a shield wall moving in unison, the way she'd seen outside Baudry; the *hoo!* and stamp of an unbroken line. That too was part of the plan; trap them with chains in front and fire behind, then encircle them from the wings with the rearguard.

But Hjálmar dying, that wasn't part of the plan. Nor was a lance through her ribs.

She looked for her assailant. It could not have been messire of the white lozenges; he'd still been wheeling away after his failed charge and she couldn't see him anywhere. But a knight with a green, muzzled hound as his blazon was circling with a lance upright in his hand. He too wore an open-faced bascinet and his eyes were locked on her as he turned his horse, and there was not a glimmer of mercy in that stare. He was coming back for the kill.

Adelais groaned and rolled onto her knees. She just wanted it to stop. She managed to stand as the knight began his charge, and a new rush of blood flowed down her leg. She'd fight.

Wouldn't just stand and take it. Bow gone. Couldn't have drawn it anyway, but she could draw her sword, just, almost howling at the pain of that simple movement. Too late now for *algiz*. She needed power. Raw, conquering power.

Tiwaz. The rune of Tyr, the most honourable, the bravest of the gods. The rune of sacrificial victory.

Twenty paces. The knight launched his horse into a canter. *Týr er einhendr áss...*

Ten paces. The lance point began to drop. And, hemmed in by fallen horses, she could not move fast enough to avoid it.

Ok ulfs leifar...

And the leavings of the wolf.

Five paces. The point now level with her chest. She could even see her own blood on the blade. What had her grand-mother Yrsa taught her? '*You cannot change your dying-day. All that matters is how you face it*.' Adelais straightened, pushing through the pain, gripped her sword two-handed, and snarled her defiance.

Ok hofa hilmir...

She did not see the wolf bound down the hill of corpses behind her. She only knew that the knight's destrier leapt side-ways so that the lance's point went past her shoulder. She did not even have the energy to strike but turned, swaying, as the knight charged by. Adelais could not understand the writhing bundle of fur now hanging from the horse's neck, not until she recognised tail and claws and snout, and knew that the wolf was hanging by its jaws from the horse's throat. Within two paces the destrier's charge had become a bucking, screaming panic as it tried to shake the predator free. It backed away, rearing, flailing with its hooves, and went down on its haunches, throwing the knight backwards in the saddle.

The wolf was relentless, snarling bloody-jawed, raking with its claws until the suffering beast fell sideways, trapping the knight's leg beneath its body, and the wolf switched its attack to the knight, bounding over the horse so it could rip out the knight's throat. He screamed and tried to push the wolf away, then to throttle it with his hands around its neck. As Adelais tottered towards them, they were trying to choke each other, with the knight's chain mail stopping the wolf's teeth from closing. Adelais was still two paces away when the knight dropped one hand, drew his poniard, and plunged it into the wolf's side.

Adelais could scarcely lift her sword, not even to save the wolf. She was dizzy, almost fainting, both thinking and moving too slowly, but she staggered on. *Ísa*, the ice-rune, would bind a foe. It had worked with the Nornir on Heilagtré. *Íss er árbörkr!* But though her lips moved, no sound came, even when the poniard was pulled out, bloody, and slammed back. She did not have enough strength left to swing her sword; she could only reverse it into a two-handed, downwards grip over the man's face, and fall with it.

The screaming and the squirming stopped as suddenly as a cut thread, and Adelais slumped sideways, onto her wound. Her vision blazed with the pain of that impact, but she did not pass out. She found herself staring at the wolf's head across the knight's body. She lifted her arm, touched it gently on its crown, her bare fingers stroking warm fur.

'Amma,' she whispered, as the eyes turned from blue to sightless amber.

Her own sight was dimming; the colours of heraldry had softened to ash, and the sounds of combat were being beaten down by the relentless *hoo! hoo! hoo!* of an advancing shield wall, slow as the pulse in her head. Yet as the world faded, the voice of Skuld, the youngest Norn, she who weaves that which might become, rang clear and sad in her mind. *So be it.*

Adelais was jolted into awareness by some spasm behind her; she had slumped against the body of a horse, and the beast's final twitch thumped her between the shoulders. Her sight blazed open with the pain and she lay gasping, staring upwards at roiling thunderheads of smoke. Around her there was still the hiss and zip of arrows, and the stamping *hoo!* of an advancing shield wall, but it seemed quieter, as if the battle itself were falling asleep. She lifted her head.

Coming towards her through the drifting smoke was a scarlet surcoat. On foot. Gripping a sword. *Leandre de Fontenay lived?* But her vision sharpened. Guy Carelet. *Guy is going to kill me? We were friends, once...* A cluster of knights followed him, like a miniature procession, among them the knight with the white diamonds on his surcoat. All of them were dismounted and leading their destriers. All gripped drawn swords.

Adelais groaned. *Fjakk. Can't fight. Can't do any more.* She managed to roll onto her knees, and grasped at the handle of her sword, still pointing skywards from green-hound's face. Broken ribs grated with the effort, slicing agony from her spine to under her arm. She knelt there, supporting herself against the pommel, unable either to pull out the sword or to stand. She glared upwards at Guy. *What a skit way to go. At least I've got a sword in my hand.* She couldn't even speak, but she managed an animal snarl as Guy reversed his sword in the way she had done when she killed the green-hound knight. *And at least it will be quick.*

Yet Guy knelt in front of her, his chain mail rippling, and offered her the hilt. Adelais blinked, not understanding.

'Adelais, we yield to you.' His cheeks coloured, the words

awkward on his tongue. Behind him, white-diamonds also knelt. His mail-framed face smiled, wryly.

'I am Matheu, Count of Erinor, and I too yield, mistress. I have seen many deeds of valour this day, but I deem you the most worthy of my sword.'

Adelais blinked at him, not understanding. She put one hand to the hilt of Guy's sword, not in acceptance, but to steady herself.

'See, mistress.' Erinor twisted to wave at the field of battle behind him. 'The day is yours, at least on this side of the flames.'

Adelais tried to push herself more upright to see beyond his shoulder. Her skirts tugged at her backside and hip where the blood was plastering them to the skin. *Sætur Sif, the pain!* The surviving knights had been penned between two shield walls, perhaps two hundred paces apart, too tightly packed to form units and charge. Archers menaced them from behind the shield walls, armour-piercing bodkin arrows nocked and ready. A horseman wearing the royal sunburst on blue – *that must be Prince Lancelin* – was still mounted, his helmet jerking from side to side, his shouts angry and incoherent as all around him knights stepped down from their saddles, heavy with defeat.

Adelais allowed her head to fall forwards, her senses reeling. *So tired. Water. Need water.* She was only vaguely aware of Guy's hands reaching out to catch her as she fell.

11.7 TAILLEFER

'What the *fuck* is happening?' The Duke of Delmas peered along the bull's back towards the flames. Even at a thousand paces, the sounds of battle were a mighty din, like a host of blacksmiths. There were deeper noises, less sharp, that blended into one, continuous groan that might be the distant lowing of a great herd of cattle. Slowly, the sounds faded and were replaced by a distant chant – *hoo! hoo!* – that told every veteran that the Vriesians still fought. That too ceased, and an eerie, palpable unease spread through the Galman army. Ten thousand foot soldiers and the few hundred remaining knights stared at the wall of belching smoke. A thousand knights had disappeared beyond the flames. None had returned. No others could advance. Near Taillefer, men were muttering to each other; hardened veterans of many wars who had seen nothing like this. Several made the sign of the God, and looked over to where the Hand was raised in blessing within its golden case.

No one answered Delmas. Bushes were burning fiercely across the centre of the hill; yellow flame and grey smoke against the red and black of the oil fires. Another fireball soared through the smoke, burst in a spray of embers, and bounced towards them. It did no new damage; the army had retreated out of range, and anything that could burn was already alight, but it proved that the Vriesians were still fighting.

'Shall we send forward the reserves, Highness?' a noble asked. 'Along the wings?'

The centre of the hill burned like the pit of Kakos but the fires were not so intense near the river cliffs; green growth had not ignited and there was more smoke there than flame. It might be possible for brave men to break through on foot. No horse would ride into that.

'Not until I know what we're sending them against. Send scouts. A purse of gold to the first man who can bring me news, even if it is bad news.'

'They have archers on the wings, Highness. An advance in strength might succeed, at a cost. Isolated men would die.' Delmas's equerry was the only noble brave enough to oppose him.

'Then find a fucking boat! Go around them and tell me what's happening.'

'At once, Your Highness.' The equerry turned his horse away. He seemed relieved to have a task to fulfil. The rest of them had to wait. Agnès sat straight-backed and still on her palfrey; only the fretful movement of her fingers around her reins showed her nervousness. Taillefer wished he could reach out and hold her hand, in comfort and support. Around them, the troops began to take advantage of the pause to rest and sit on their shields. One captain, more considerate than most, sent a servant staggering along the line under the weight of a great water skin.

A brief, light breeze began to push the filthy air to the north-east, enough to glimpse the end of the Vriesian line; at this distance it was a solid block of darkness painted onto the hill-side. And it was intact. Unbroken. A new, disorganised line had been smeared across the bull's back in front of it, as indistinct as a pile of brushwood. There was movement, and possibly fight-ing, but the wind dropped almost as soon as it arrived, and the oily fog closed again over the hill.

But the fires were losing their intensity as the oil was exhausted. Soon it was only scrub that burned, though the whole hill smouldered. A half-company was formed behind a tightly packed wall of overlapping shields, and sent forwards on the western wing.

Before they reached the smoke, a trio of men came towards them, ghost-grey in the haze, their progress erratic as they stepped around isolated fires, but they carried the white flag of truce. The Galman half-company halted, waiting, as the trio's outlines hardened; a northern jarl and an escort of two, all with round shields, belted mail hauberks, and open-faced, nose-guarded helmets. Their weapons were sheathed. The jarl was arrayed in his war glory: a helmet that seemed to be formed in the shape of a stooping, golden bird with its wings stretched, and arm-rings of silver and gold that gleamed as he walked.

They paused in front of the Galman company until their flag of truce was acknowledged. When they trudged forwards their boots raised new smoke-trails of powdered ash from the hillside. All three of them held cloths to their faces. Two were coughing.

Taillefer thought it discourteous that Delmas let them come to him rather than meet them halfway. Perhaps he would have moved for Ragener, duke to duke. At least it meant that Taillefer could hear what was said when the trio stopped in front of Delmas. They were all filthy, despite the jarl's gold, and not only from the soot of the fires; their shields showed the bright scars of recent blows, and one berserker had a darkening spray of blood on his shoulder, though Taillefer could see no wound.

'You are Delmas?'

The duke nodded. He did not dismount.

'I am Magnus Finehair.' The jarl spoke with the lilting inflection of the north. 'Do you concede the field?'

Delmas spluttered. 'Concede?' He looked left and right across his army. Ten thousand faces looked back. 'What deludes Ragener into thinking I might admit defeat?'

Magnus Finehair seemed to have expected that reply. 'Because you have just lost your cavalry. All who attacked are now dead or prisoners.' He spoke loudly enough for his words to be heard by the troops nearby and murmurs of consternation spread outwards through the ranks. Soldiers leaned towards each other, swaying as the word was passed from man to man.

Agnès tensed, but did not interrupt.

Delmas breathed deeply. 'How?'

The jarl shrugged. 'They fell over. The gods were on our side.' He smiled without humour; he was not about to give away information freely.

'I have ten thousand men who have yet to fight.'

'And we have your Prince Lancelin.'

Delmas snorted as if to say *'and you can keep him'*.

'Together with about four hundred knights who had the sense to yield.'

A second wave of whispering spread outwards through the army.

'I still have twice your strength.'

Magnus Finehair shrugged again. 'Our shield wall did not break under your war-hammer. It will certainly hold against foot soldiers.'

'So what is Ragener proposing?'

'There are many of your knights that still live beneath their fallen horses. We will not break our ranks to help them while you are ranged against us. So we propose a truce to allow you to recover your dead and give them burial in the ways of your god. You may also take back any wounded who are likely to die. You

will need many carts. Those we think will survive will be held
for ransom. They will be cared for.'

Delmas looked around his nobles. All his council were
there, apart from de Fontenay. One by one, they nodded.
Delmas turned back to the jarl. 'Agreed. The truce to hold until
fair warning is given by heralds.'

'Never more than fifty men between the lines. No
weapons.' Magnus looked hard at the duke.

'On my honour.'

Magnus turned to leave.

'If you please, my lord...' Agnès called towards Magnus.
'My husband led the charge. Three golden flowers upon red?'

Magnus's face softened as he looked at her. 'Few survived
from the front rank, lady. I am sorry.'

'And what of Adelais, who stayed between the armies?'

'I saw her fall.' There was now real sadness in the jarl's
voice. 'She too fought bravely.'

Agnès slumped in her saddle as if under a physical blow.
Taillefer nudged his horse close, unable to touch her, but at
least able to look her in the face. Her eyes were shut and her
whole body clenched. He'd never seen her like that. As the
three northerners tramped back towards their lines, Taillefer
was only vaguely aware of conversations between Delmas and
his nobles.

'A truce, Your Highness? Now why would they suggest
that?'

'They probably think they can retake the far bank and
repair the bridge.' Delmas's voice. 'Then escape north with all
their valuable prisoners.'

'Yet we agreed.'

'They are going nowhere. Theignault's tarrazim will make
sure of that. Meanwhile, we will see what trickery they have in
mind and devise a strategy to beat it. And within a day our
valiant new ally will have crossed the next bridge upstream and

joined us with his forces. We'll have fresh cavalry.' Delmas snorted contemptuously. 'And I'll save that puppy Lancelin's arse a second time.'

Taillefer felt compelled to speak. 'Do you not think, Your Highness, that the God might be sending us a message? We have carried the Hand of Salazar into a secular war, and half the chivalry of Galmandie is dead or captive. Should we not at least listen, and pray?'

'You pray, Excellency. It's what you're good at. I'm going to win this fucking war.'

11.8 ADELAIS

Adelais was jolted awake by pain as she was lifted onto a stretcher. There were voices beside her. Guy Carelet arguing with berserkers as he was led away to captivity. She wished they'd shut up. *Breathing hurts. Everything hurts.* Being lifted off the stretcher in her tent was agony.

'More private here than in the dressing station.' Revna, her voice hoarse with rune song and exhaustion.

'Hjálmar? Where's Hjálmar?'

'He lives.' That sounded like one of his berserkers. Adelais tried to sit up, and yelped.

'Lie still, girl.' Revna again, lifting away Adelais's breast-plate. The two of them turned her on her side as gently as they could. Adelais could feel the blood pooled in the backplate, and a touch of cold air against her skin; the dress beneath must be ripped to pieces. 'Could you sit upright, on a stool? It will be easier to treat you that way.'

They lifted her under the arms, and as her head came up there was Hjálmar, coming through the tent flap, with his shield arm splinted and a lopsided smile on a swollen face. One eye was closing within a livid bruise, and blood matted his hair. She'd have laughed with joy if she could have drawn a breath.

'Hello, princess.'

'By the gods, you're ugly today.' Was that really all she could say? So much emotion filled her heart that she wanted to weep. Hug him. Tell him she'd thought he was dead. Instead she simply lifted a hand and touched his face as he knelt before her. 'You're hurt.'

'All bone, no brain. Shattered my shield and my helmet took the rest of it.' Hjálmar lifted his broken wrist in emphasis. His voice was slightly slurred. 'You've looked better yourself.'

'Did we win?' There were no sounds of battle.

'Not yet.' Hjálmar sounded hoarse as well. 'We are looking at ten thousand angry Galmans, but my father is negotiating a truce.

'Drink, girl.' Revna passed a leather flask to Hjálmar for her. 'This is going to hurt.'

Adelais swigged, and almost choked on the fiery spirit as Revna began to cut the dress from her back, exposing the wound. And her. Of all the ways Hjálmar could have seen her body, this had to be the worst.

'Revna's wanted me to get my clothes off for you for moons.'

Hjálmar did not laugh. Neither did she while Revna washed the wounds with wine; Adelais's fingers groped for Hjálmar's arm and clawed into the chain-mail half-sleeves hanging from his shoulder. Despite herself she let out a tight-lipped, nasal keening that did not quite become a scream. Hjálmar pulled her into him so that her face rested into the angle of his neck. He smelt of sweat and blood, old leather and oiled steel, but his beard was soft against her face. She wished he'd take his own armour off. She wanted to feel his warmth, not chain mail.

'Let it out, princess. There's no shame in crying.' His own tears ran wet below her ear.

'You need a bath, troll-man.'

'I'd say the backplate deflected the strike.' Revna's explo-
rations paused. 'Enough for the point to pass across the ribs, not
through them. I can see bone. Broken bone.'

'Probably wasn't charging at full speed,' Adelais panted.
She remembered how one assailant had trotted his horse
through the debris. 'Weak hit.'

'You'll live, if wound fever doesn't get you. I shall pack the
deepest cuts with dried bog moss and leave them open to drain.
It may prevent the wound fever. But you will scar.'

'Where's Allier?' Adelais mumbled into Hjálmar's
shoulder.

'Safe. One of my men has him.'

'The wolf died.' Memories were coming back. 'She
saved me.'

'I'd say your amma's job is done.' Revna's fingers pushed
gently into the wound and Adelais swigged again. This time she
did not choke, just grabbed at Hjálmar's back. It was several
heartbeats before she could breathe and speak.

'Why "done"?'

'You were already marked with *ansuz,* the god-rune.
Remember, Odhinn hung on the tree of Yggdrasil to gain the
wisdom of the runes, his side pierced by a spear. To those who
follow the old ways, you are now almost a goddess yourself,
twice marked by the All-Father.'

Adelais yelped as another tuft of moss was pushed into the
open wound. 'I think I'll settle for just being a *princess.*'

Hjálmar moved her away from his shoulder, enough to look
into her eyes. His were grey and full, gentle and questioning.
She had loaded her words on purpose, and she made a small
nod, enough to tell him she'd meant it. It was like a promise.
His 'princess'. Hjálmar pulled her into him again, a little too
hard.

'Easy, troll-man.'

She winced as Revna bound the rest of her wounds with bandages.

'Hjálmar Magnusson, go and fetch food for her.' Revna dismissed him as if he were a child.

'Not hungry.' Adelais wanted to sleep. On a feather bed. Face down.

'You've lost a lot of blood. You need food. While he's gone I'll help you into fresh clothes. And then there are others who need my care, even more than you.'

Yet she found it too uncomfortable to lie flat, so when she was dressed, Hjálmar's men put a chair outside her tent that they'd scavenged from the castle; a fine chair with arms such as a lord might use at a feast. She sat enthroned, with Hjálmar at her feet so that she might lean forwards against his back and ease the pressure on her chest. Even with his *rass* on the ground their heads were almost level. He'd shed his armour so her cheek rested against the warm skin of his neck. An impromptu court formed around them like an honour guard; berserkers and foot soldiers, wounded and whole, some standing, some sitting, all looking towards her with wonder in their eyes. *Please don't. I don't deserve adoration.* Many brought her offerings of food or mead or wine. Hjálmar insisted that food would help with the blood loss, so she nibbled at bread soaked in honey, and left sticky crumbs on his shoulder.

The wine was more welcome; it numbed the pain and allowed her exhaustion to surface. As the day faded they were both a little drunk. She yearned for somewhere comfortable to lie. Not on Hjálmar's back, companionable though that might be. Not on her thin bedroll, where stones and lumps below pushed at her wounds.

'Do you think,' she murmured into Hjálmar's ear, 'that somewhere in that castle or town there might be a bed?'

Hjálmar looked over his shoulder and made wide, lascivious eyes at her. 'Is that an invitation at last?'

Adelais was too tired even to punch him. 'I want to lie face down, on a soft bed.'

'Face down is possible. Quite fun, actually.'

'And I want to sleep.' And she was too tired even to flirt. He saw the look in her eyes and sent two of his men to find the biggest, softest mattress in castle or town, and bring it to her pavilion. While they waited, she slumped forwards and slept, rocked by his breathing.

Jarl Magnus came to them as the sun was sinking. Adelais stirred, a little embarrassed to be found in such intimacy with his son.

Magnus did not seem concerned. 'The truce holds, for now. They are clearing the dead from the field. And Duke Ragener requests your presence, mistress.' There may even have been a sparkle in his eye. 'Can you walk?'

Adelais tried. She was stronger after the food and could stand, just, with Hjálmar's support while the black spots in her vision faded into dizziness. But no, she couldn't *fjakkinn* walk. Her back had stiffened into a solid sheet of pain. She let them buckle her back into her wrecked armour and lower her into the chair.

'His Grace will have to come to me.' She didn't mean to be disrespectful. *Too much wine.*

Magnus shook his head, smiling, and waved forwards four berserkers. They tied spears to the legs of her chair and carried her through the tent lines to an open space behind their lines, low down between the castle and the river. Hjálmar marched at her side, shouting at them to be gentle. Perhaps a thousand men packed the space, forming a hollow box that had Duke Ragener at its centre. Most were still armed for battle, as if they were about to form a shield wall. At the sight of Adelais, they hefted their weapons and slammed them into their shields; Adelais was borne into the box on thunderous roars. They echoed from the castle walls behind her and rose to deafening punches that made her want to stop her ears. *Hún úlfur! Hún úlfur! Hún úlfur!*

They put her chair down in front of Ragener, and Magnus helped her to stand. He had to grip her under the arm to keep her upright. Ragener held up his hand for silence, and in this new quiet spoke for all to hear. Adelais supposed she ought to listen; it was in her honour, but, somewhere nearby, beyond the tent lines, a horse was screaming and she felt only the crushing guilt of its agony.

'Kneel.' Magnus spoke into her ear. A footstool had been placed in front of Ragener. 'I will help.' Between them, Magnus and Hjálmar lowered her onto her knees. She wondered if she was being asked to repeat her vow of fealty.

'For your deeds and valour this day,' Ragener's voice rang out, 'I dub you Lady of Nautshrygg,' he brought his sword down gently on each shoulder in turn, 'and award you the golden spurs of knighthood.' In the midst of a mighty roar of approval, Ragener himself knelt to buckle a pair onto her heels. He had to put his mouth close to her ear to be heard over the noise. 'And never forget your oath of fealty, girl. To *me*.' When he straightened, his smile did not reach his eyes.

Adelais was light-headed. She carried the terrible weight of many deaths, both men and horses, yet she began to laugh at the sight of Ragener staring at her armoured tits and wondering how to dub a woman a knight. It was all such a sham. But her laughter verged on hysteria, because the horse was still screaming and she wanted to run to it and say sorry and give it peace. The air reeked of fire, and blood, and the sickly smell of guts.

Adelais slumped back into her chair, gripping its arms as

she was hoisted back onto the berserkers' shoulders. As she was turned, a trebuchet came into view above her, its arm pointing straight into the sky, the crew lined up beneath, looking at her. They were laughing, smiling, pleased with themselves. She was carried up the hill towards them while all around men punched weapons into the air, slapped each other on the back, and bellowed their victory. *Hún úlfur! Hún úlfur!* Some had slung their shields over their shoulders and found drinking horns. She wanted to be somewhere quiet, with friends who would understand. Hjálmar. Agnès. Friends she could cry with. Be a woman, not an emblem carried around wrapped in gold like the Ischyrians' *fjakkinn* hand.

Her chair lurched as the berserkers forgot to be gentle and Adelais twisted, gripping the arms, until Hjálmar saw her pain and made them put her down.

When she could open her eyes and speak she found him kneeling beside her, looking into her face. A small circle of calm in the midst of uproar. One of his eyes was almost closed now. She took his uninjured hand in hers. It was so large it fully encased her own as she stroked the callouses on his palm.

'You're hurting too.' His splinted arm had knocked her chair as he knelt beside her. She'd seen him wince.

'It will heal. So will you.' He looked at her intently. His eyes were full of emotion. If they'd been alone, she'd have kissed him. But not here. Not in front of the army. Beyond Hjálmar's shoulder, a shining-faced berserker was pointing at a dried blood-splash on the sleeve of his hauberk, and bellowing the story of his kill to any who would listen.

'I thought Ragener would be happier.'

Hjálmar's fingers tangled gently with hers, saying more than could be spoken. 'It is your day, princess, not his. The army knows that, and so does he. Right now, they would do anything for you. They'd die for you. And they're ignoring him. Dukes don't like to be displaced.'

'By a woman.'

'By anyone.'

Adelais fretted at his hand.

'I'm frightened to love you, troll-man. Everyone I love dies.'

'Will you let me take that risk?'

'I think we're both already taking it.' She lifted his hand to her lips. It seemed even heavier than before; she had so little strength left. 'Do you think they've found me that bed yet?'

But one eye still gleamed in his battered face. It hinted at more than she wanted, at that moment. She thought she would probably spend her life with this man, whether that life was measured in days or decades, but she brought a hand up between them.

'One day, soon,' Adelais drew a cross on his chest, 'we will know the passion of *gebo*, the rune of love, the giving of ourselves.'

She lowered her hand and drew an arrowhead on his belly. 'It will also be the fire of *kaunaz*, the giving of bodies.'

⟨

'But tonight, will you just stay with me? Be with me? Perhaps hold my hand?'

Hjálmar rose to his feet, calling his men to carry her.

Adelais gasped as she was once more hoisted onto their shoulders and her bearers paused, thinking she was in pain, but she had just caught her first glimpse of the extent of the devastation. A line of carts raised a low fog of dust as they queued across the charred earth of Nautshrygg. At their head, a tangled hedgerow of bodies, of horses and of men, marked the line of the chains. Gangs of Galman soldiers laboured to clear it. Some of the destriers still lived, and kicked; here and there axes swung a brutal mercy.

More carts lumbered away, piled with dead. Well-armed Vriesians ensured that items of value stayed in the Vriesian lines – suits of mail, swords, gold spurs. The dead were being stripped of their armour and reclothed in their surcoats before their bodies were thrown onto the carts. Some destriers were being butchered on the spot; the army would feast on horseflesh this night. A great mound of dismembered carcasses was being built to one side for a later pyre. Staring horse-heads, hooves, gut-trailing torsos.

I did that. All those poor horses. To the Vriesian army, Nautshrygg meant victory against all odds, even if they might have to fight again on the morrow. To her, if she lived, it would always mean the suffering of destriers who had carried their masters so nobly and bravely.

'Take me there,' she begged, pointing towards the carnage. She needed to face her guilt, the way a dog needs to lick its own vomit.

'No closer.' Hjálmar made them stop thirty paces away. His berserkers formed an open line between her and the labouring Galman soldiers. The set of the Galmans' shoulders screamed anger, not defeat. She lifted her eyes to the horizon. A thousand paces away, their camp seemed no smaller.

'I thought they'd go home.' Adelais realised she sounded tired and a little lost.

'They will come again, I am sure,' Hjálmar sighed. 'They have ten thousand men who have yet to fight. We have under five, and some of us are wounded.' He lifted his wrist. 'Our best hope is to send boats across the river tonight, and try to clear the tarrazim from the far bank. If we can rebuild the bridge, we'd have the option of retreating.'

'Hasn't there been enough killing?' Adelais watched the cartloads of dead.

Hjálmar snorted. 'It goes on until either Ragener or Delmas gives in. And they are both too proud to concede.'

'For a while I thought we were safe. You were safe.'

'Well, we won't trick them with chains again. Do you have any more magic in mind, princess?'

Adelais didn't answer. Below them, a dead destrier had just been drawn clear of a knight's body, down where the fighting had been thickest. That destrier had probably been in the pile under her as she shot her bow. Pressed into the earth beneath, a dirty, bloody surcoat bore the three golden flowers on red of de Fontenay. The way the great helm lay at an impossible angle told Adelais that there was no hope, and her tired heart sank.

Oh, Agnès, will you ever forgive me?

'Hjálmar,' she so rarely used his given name that he turned to her, frowning. 'Will you please send someone to find a captured man-at-arms? Guy Carelet. Same surcoat as that knight. Retainer's badge.'

Agnès should hear this from a friend.

11.9 TAILLEFER

A man-at-arms in the de Fontenay livery brought Agnès the news just after sunset. He walked alongside the final cart of the day, a lone, swordless honour guard for his lord's body. Taillefer did not at first recognise Guy Carelet, the young man who'd escorted him and Agnès from Harbin to Fontenay; he walked round-shouldered, like one burdened by age.

Agnès had passed the afternoon on a chair near Delmas's pavilion, staring north over the battlefield, attended by Brother Thanchere and a small cluster of de Fontenay knights who had been held in reserve. Taillefer had not gone to her, though he yearned to offer her more than priestly comfort. It had been a time when all the priests with the army worked without ceasing. When the carts of dead began arriving back in the Galman lines, Taillefer had organised their reception; a clerk recorded their names, at least where they could be identified by friends or by their heraldry, and a relay of priests conducted a brief Office of the Dead for each. Taillefer consecrated a field where gangs of soldiers dug a great pit. Other teams carried the bodies to the pit, packing them close. Sometimes a friend would say a few words before the soil was thrown in. They all worked in a buzzing cloud of flies, with their nostrils assaulted by the smell of shit and guts.

Ragener had made a mistake in allowing bodies to be recovered before the battle was conceded. Taillefer sensed the mood change from despair to anger. When Delmas ordered the next assault, his army would be driven by a thirst for vengeance. The carts also brought news that Adelais lived, and had been awarded the golden spurs; there were celebrations in the Vriesian lines. Galman soldiers muttered that they'd wipe that laughter from their faces before long.

And the news brought by that man-at-arms was the greatest blow of all, for de Fontenay had been revered. This was a lord of high, untainted honour; the custodian of the Hand. The stricken look on Guy Carelet's face told his tidings without the need for words. Agnès rose to receive him, like a queen among her nobles, so stiff-backed in her grief that she seemed imperious. Taillefer left his work with the dead, and joined them as Guy looked down and shook his head.

'Did he suffer greatly, Guy Carelet?' Agnès made no other greeting.

'I think not, my lady. There are no wounds on his body. It may have been the fall...'

'And you are released?'

Guy shook his head again. 'I gave my parole, lady. Adelais asked that I bring the news to you myself.'

'That was kind. How does she fare?'

'She is sorely wounded. She asked me to bring her condolences, and hopes that you will forgive her. She prays this will not destroy your friendship.'

'My husband *chose* to lead the charge. There is nothing to forgive. Tell her I still hope that one day she will bounce Lord Leandre's heir upon her knee.'

There were gasps around her at that revelation.

'He knew?' The Duke of Delmas elbowed his way into the circle around Agnès.

'Aye, Your Highness.' Agnès dropped her eyes in a way that could be seen as coy embarrassment rather than guilt.

'And still he volunteered to be the face of the hammer! Fear not, my lady, we will avenge him.'

'I do not believe he would desire vengeance, Your Highness.'

'But he'll get it.' Delmas turned to Guy. 'Boy, honour your parole. Go back and whisper to your friends that they need not fear how to find their ransoms. The Count of Theignault's cavalry will be with us tomorrow, and no pagan trickery will stop us this time. We will slaughter them all.' Delmas made a courtly bow to Agnès and left them, emotion tightening his face.

Agnès signalled to Taillefer to remain. 'Brother Thanchere, Diakonos Taillefer, would you spare me a moment?' She was visibly, brittly in control of herself, staring fixedly after Guy's departing back. Taillefer thought that if he touched her, she'd crumble.

'My husband's lands and properties pass to me on his death, until his heir comes of age. That includes the Hand, if anyone can be said to "own" it. Perhaps we might discuss its future? And, in particular, its role in this war?'

CHAPTER TWELVE

12.1 GAUTHIER

'Wound fever. *Skit*, that's quick.' It was only dawn on the morning after the battle, and the apothecary-surgeon working his way down the line of injured men groaned as he gestured towards two orderlies. 'Get him out of here, before it spreads.'

Gauthier followed the man's stretcher as he was carried from the makeshift infirmary under the castle's walls. The wounded man was Ischyrian, even though he'd fought for Duke Ragener; Gauthier had seen the hand pendant on his chest. A Sjólander by his garb, and there had been no reason why his wound should be fatal; a lance under the shield into the foot. Painful. Possibly crippling. But not lethal.

Until the sweating began. Already the Sjólander was delirious, burning with fever, and raving about the punishment of the God. Gauthier, in his priest's robe, could work on that.

Gauthier had seen this before. Some battle wounds healed cleanly, while others turned hot and leaked bad humours. In a few hours, the fever took over the whole body, bringing sweats, delirium, and death, sometimes within a day. There were remedies; he'd heard about white willow bark and vervain, though the town's small stock of herbs was long exhausted, and once the fiery humours took hold there was little hope. The faithful would pray hard, and pay well to have a priest pray with them.

It never worked.

Gauthier had spent much of the night within the small castle's walls, where the courtyard was packed with captured knights, some wounded, all Ischyrians. They welcomed his prayers and blessings. So what if a few coins changed hands? He was bringing comfort. Outside the walls they were mostly heathens and they'd sent him away with an obscenity, but he'd been summoned to this Sjólander and the man looked as if he had coin about him.

Gauthier stretched away the night's aches, surprised that the day had come so early. Of course. It was the hay moon. Surprised also to see Duke Ragener wandering beneath the walls with bloodshot eyes and the pasty look of one who has drunk too much or slept too little, or possibly both. He was hatless and dishevelled.

'You have risen early, Your Grace.' Gauthier's robe was his passport to talk to anyone, and, after three moons on this campaign, Ragener knew him, at least by sight. Gauthier had even heard his unburdening, once. He didn't ask for coin with the duke. The knowledge he got was so much more valuable. Gauthier let the Sjólander go. The man would live a little longer, and the chance to talk to Ragener was too good to miss.

'Somebody stole my fucking mattress.' Ragener ran his fingers through his hair and lifted his chin towards the two orderlies tramping away with their burden. 'What are they doing with him? He's still alive.'

'He has wound fever, Your Grace. The apothecary-surgeon insists that those afflicted are set apart. He says it spreads swiftly between those with open wounds, if they lie close. There comes a time when not even prayer can save them.'

Ragener grunted. He paused near the gates from the castle onto the bull's back and scratched his belly, surveying the scene of battle. The smell of fire was still strong on the air. Tent lines stretched either side behind the partly cleared line of fallen Galman knights. Soon, more Galman carts would come to continue their grisly work. Gauthier made a diffident little cough to attract Ragener's attention.

'I saw two of Jarl Magnus's berserkers carrying a mattress at sunset last night, Your Grace.' Such a joy to be able to pass on that information. 'I believe they carried it to Lady Adelais's pavilion.'

'Fucking woman.'

'The northerners think highly of her. *Very* highly.' Gauthier emphasised the words, probing subtly for Ragener's reaction. 'It was a wise decision to honour her so publicly.'

'She's *my* vassal, not Magnus Finehair's. She'd do well to remember it.'

'The men talk of her as if she were a goddess. One might wonder who they think leads Vriesland.' *People are so easy to manipulate, once you know their weaknesses.*

'If she challenges my authority, I'll show her just how mortal she is.' Ragener stared towards the nobles' tents.

Gauthier looked around to make sure they could not be overheard. The only living things within fifty paces were four ravens sitting in the embrasures of the battlements. The filthy birds had probably gorged on the dead.

'Her wounds would prevent her playing any further part in the fight, Your Grace, if battle is rejoined.'

'What do you mean, Pateras?'

'I mean she can do no more.'

Ragener twisted to look Gauthier directly in the eye. 'What are you saying, priest?'

'I believe her value to Vriesland has all been spent. And if you will permit a humble priest to comment, Your Grace, the balance of power in Vriesland is changing. Theignault has already gone over to the Galmans, and a marriage between the son of Magnus Finehair and Adelais of Nautshrygg would create a powerful union. An *immensely* powerful union.' Gauthier thought he was better at weaving fates than any northern bitch would ever be.

'You think they will wed?' Ragener turned to stare at the woman's tent.

'They are clearly very close. I believe Hjálmar Magnusson stayed with her last night.'

Ragener snorted. 'Fucking woman should have died on the battlefield. Better a dead goddess than a live usurper.'

Gauthier breathed deeply before committing himself. Sometimes a strategy leapt at him. It seemed so wonderfully simple that he had to test it from all angles. Yes, this would work.

'It could still be arranged, Your Grace. She might die of wound fever. So unfortunate, after her victory.'

There was a long pause before Ragener answered.

'Now why would a priest say something like that?'

'I desire a strong, *Ischyrian* Vriesland, Your Grace.'

Another pause.

'How would you do it?'

It would be so easy. So innocent. 'Her bandages must be changed. If cloths that have been taken from one with this deadly fever were bound to her wounds, then she too will be infected.'

'Do they always die?'

'If the fiery humours spread to fill the body, very few survive. It is as the God wills. But I would need Your Grace's help to pass through her guards.' Two berserkers sat on their shields outside Adelais's tent and Gauthier knew there was another at the back.

Ragener too looked around them. He took several breaths while he made up his mind. 'I am minded to visit Lady Adelais this morning to ask how she fares. Come to me when you have the necessary materials?'

Gauthier inclined his head. 'I am Your Grace's humble servant.' And he could expect Ragener to be generous. Gauthier had never taken a fee from two masters for one killing before.

12.2 ADELAIS

Adelais's whole back was a layered sheet of pain; cut skin over
ripped muscle over broken bone. Revna returned once, briefly,
and said her small stocks of herbs were exhausted and alas there
were others who needed her help more. Adelais's wound was
leaking and needed new bandages, but those too were in short
supply. Hjálmar said Revna looked exhausted. Adelais, with her
face in a pillow and her fingers clawed in the mattress, had not
noticed.

Herbs. Adelais remembered Agnès's gift, the phial in her
scrip. *One drop in wine will dull any pain, two and you will
sleep for half a day.* She showed Hjálmar where to find it, and
they allowed two drops to fall into a goblet they then shared. He
too was suffering.

A warmth spread within her, gentler than any pillow. The
claws in her back released their grip, slowly dulling to the level
of a bad toothache. Her breathing eased as each suck of air came
without the price of grating bone. Laying half on her side, facing
Hjálmar, she was almost comfortable. Almost happy. He'd
spread a bedroll beside the mattress and lay on his side, good

arm uppermost, with his splinted forearm angled awkwardly between them.

'Wish we could hold each other.' In this dreamlike state Adelais could forget the interrupted battle and think of what might be. What she wanted to be.

'At least I can touch you.' Hjálmar looked into her face, seeking permission, while he slid his hand under the cover. It rested on her bare back, well below the bandages, with great gentleness. He had lovely grey eyes; tender and full. She smiled her encouragement and he began to stroke her. A lover's touch.

'I'll be ugly.' She was frightened at what he might see when those bandages were taken off.

'But you'll always have the cutest little *rass*.' His hand slipped lower. She liked that. *Soon, troll-man*.

Yet not even his fingers, teasing her into the moment, could prevent the drug from taking hold.

Duke Ragener came to see them when the day was still young. Adelais was still befuddled from the drug, and Ragener's presence was like having an oversized house-dog blundering around the confined space of the tent, wagging its tail, when all she wanted to do was sleep. He did not stay long, thank the gods.

'I brought someone to dress your wounds,' Ragener announced as he left. He made it sound as if dressing wounds was a jolly entertainment. Adelais, laying face down, could imagine him running his fingers through his hair.

'Where is *Frú* Revna?' Hjálmar's voice was slurred gravel, like a drunkard woken from his cups.

'I work with *Frú* Revna,' came a soothing, amiable voice from the tent flap. 'My name is Pateras Gauthier.'

'Priest!' Hjálmar growled at him. 'Bring us Revna.'

'She labours tirelessly in the infirmary, and our beliefs are set aside when so many are hurt. See, she has sent you fresh linen!'

Adelais managed to look over her shoulder. The sandy-bearded priest was vaguely familiar.

'Let him in,' Adelais mumbled into her pillow. Then perhaps she could sleep a little more. Maybe risk another drip of that potion. She was rather touched that a devout Ischyrian would minister to an avowed 'witch'.

She was surprised at his gentleness as he sponged away the caked bandages, though the cloth snagged like fishhooks in her skin. Hjálmar sat beside her, squeezing her hand and growling at Pateras Gauthier, as if the priest were the source of the pain rather than the means of its cure.

'I wish,' she gripped Hjálmar more tightly while a crusted scrap of bog moss was picked from her wounds, 'the faiths could work together all the time.'

'Devoutly to be desired,' Pateras Gauthier answered. 'Now, it would be easier to bind your wounds if you were kneeling.'

Hjálmar helped her onto her knees, holding a loose shirt across her body to preserve her modesty. Neither of them would have seen much, anyway, with her head resting into his chest, but it was awkward to have a stranger's hands reach around her. Pateras Gauthier was less gentle with the bandages than he had been with the cleaning; the tug as he tightened the final knot was harsh enough to make her gasp and claw at Hjálmar's shoulders.

'Easy, priest!' Hjálmar's snarl was as threatening as a fist.

'Looser, and they will slip. There, 'tis done.' Gauthier's voice had hardened too.

Adelais could not speak, not even to thank him. She did not see him leave, but stayed with her face in Hjálmar's chest, like a hurt child clinging to a parent's bulk.

'Will you lie down?' Hjálmar eased her away until he could look into her eyes.

Adelais liked the way he was looking at her. She could stay like this for a long time. 'I'll sit. It's easier, I think. Nothing pushing against my chest. Will you help me dress?'

Of all the ways he might see her body, why did it have to be when she was bandaged, vulnerable, and stripped of all allure? Revealing herself to him should be intense and seductive, not this brief, chaste exposure while she dressed. Yet he made the moment tender. Loving, in a way that promised a lifetime of caring. When she was decent, he cupped her face in his hands and kissed her gently – another promise of what would also be, soon, when she was ready.

In the mid-morning, Revna returned, looked at Adelais's bandages, nodded her approval, and lay down on the fine mattress. Within moments she slept in the way of one who has laboured a night and a day without rest. After another drip of potion in her wine, Adelais too found an awkward way of sleeping in the chair, so she was only vaguely aware of Hjálmar being called away to a council with Duke Ragener. When he returned, his face was furrowed with worry. The overnight attempts to retake the far bank of the river had failed; there were simply not enough boats in the town to land in sufficient force. Fifty good men had died, cut down by tarrazim arrows or drowned under the weight of their armour as the boats were upturned. There was now little hope of rebuilding the bridge during the truce.

Worse, they were running out of all food except horse flesh, and that would soon be putrid in the summer's heat; they were effectively besieged between the river and the enemy. The stores in the town would not have produced a single meal for the army, which had only what it had carried. They had enough for two days, on reduced rations. They'd fought the Galmans to a standstill only to be starved into submission.

Adelais felt strangely detached from the news. Her back was on fire.

She was woken by a hand on her brow. She looked up into Revna's face, all lights and shadows above a candle. Why was it dark so quickly? And why did she have this terrible headache? Her mouth was so dry that her mouth might have been cut from rough stone.

'Can you stand, girl?' Revna was frowning. Everyone was frowning today.

Stand? She could do better than that. If this headache would go, she could spread her wings and fly like an eagle. Adelais grinned through the pain, opened her arms to show Revna, and screamed.

'*Someone cut off my wings.*' Who would do such a thing?

Priest. She remembered a priest, cutting at her back. But Hjálmar had held her while he did it. So that couldn't be right.

Hands lifted her under her arms, enough to pull the skirts of her robe up from under her *rass*, exposing her back. As the cloth was thrown up, over her head, she leaned forwards to show Revna.

'Look what they've done to my wings.' She sobbed with frustration. She could hear Revna sniffing at the bandages. The candle moved so that the shadow of Adelais's skirts, piled up towards her neck, widened and filled the floor of the tent, fluttering. *Ah, there they are. They look huge against the light.* She sighed with relief.

'Wound fever. Help me get her down.'

Adelais was lifted onto the mattress, face down again. That hurt. Perhaps she wouldn't fly for a while. Especially as Hjálmar was there, holding her hand, love in his eyes and tears in his beard.

'I need willow bark and betony, wormwood and vervain, but all my herbs are finished.'

If Revna needed herbs for the wounded, then Adelais would fly away and fetch some. She moved her hands up level with her shoulders and took several gulping breaths before she pushed.

'Hush, princess.' Hjálmar's hand rested on her hair, stroking her head. She liked that. Somewhere nearby came the thump of a staff into the ground, and the high, keening call of rune song.

'*Úr er skýja grátr, ok skára thverrir, ok hirdhis hatr...*'

Úruz, the rune of healing. *Good.* She needed a little strength. Adelais drew on that power.

'Back soon,' she whispered, and screamed again with the pain of the first downbeat.

After that first agony it was easier, though she only made it as far as the battlements. Was it dawn already?

'Time has no meaning,' a raven answered her thought, croaking like an old woman. 'There is only that which has already come into being, and that which is happening, and that which may yet come to be.' Adelais knew that voice.

'*Frú* Urdhr?' In the way of dreams, it was entirely natural for one of the Nornir to sit beside her on the battlements in raven form. A very old, care-worn raven.

Urdhr made no answer, but flapped off over the head of Duke Ragener, who stood below them staring at the battlefield. He was talking to the priest who'd cut off her wings. *But he can't have. I've just flown here.* Ragener looked upset. Adelais wanted to tell him not to worry, she would fly away for herbs and bring them back for his wounded men, but her words rattled outwards as meaningless cawing, and Ragener continued his talk with Pateras Gauthier.

'Fucking woman should have died on the battlefield. Better a dead goddess than a live usurper.'

Who are they talking about?

The priest turned and looked up at her. 'It could still be arranged, Your Grace. She might die of wound fever. So unfortunate, after her victory.'

Me!

Adelais cawed her anger. '*Dhú svikulli ræfillinn!*' You treacherous bastard!

'How would you do it?'

And I won his fordæmdur battle for him!

'Her bandages must be changed. If cloths that have been taken from one with this fever were bound to her wounds, then she too will be infected.'

'Do they always die?'

'If the fiery humours spread to fill the body, very few survive. It is as the God wills. But I would need Your Grace's help to pass through her guards.'

Ragener also turned, looked up at the battlements, and stared her in the eye. 'I am minded to visit Lady Adelais this morning to ask how she fares. Come to me when you have the necessary materials…'

Adelais flapped over their heads, clawing at their hair until they ducked, folding over themselves; now she was becoming smoke on the wind, and the sun was high in the sky and the armies were ranged against each other. A younger raven called to her from the battlements in the voice of the Norn Verdhandi, telling her to watch the warp and weft of fate of the imminent *now* as it came into being.

Is this coming to pass today? Tomorrow? Is this already happening?

'Time has no meaning.' Verdhandi repeated Urdhr's words, waving a wing towards the ranks of Theignaulter cavalry advancing over the burned ground towards the Vriesian shield wall. The Count of Theignault himself rode at their head, disdaining a great helm so that his commands might be heard. His dark beard fell like a knife-blade over the chain mail around his neck. Below Adelais, on a *seidhr*-platform beneath the walls, Revna pounded her staff at half the pace of a slow heartbeat, and sang the rune song of *tiwaz*.

'*Týr er einhendr áss, ok ulfs leifar, ok hofa hilmir...*'

Tiwaz, the rune of victory. Yet what had Skuld told her in far-off Heilagtré? '*Tiwaz* will win you one victory, but only *ansuz* will win you the war. Remember the god-rune.'

And they had had their one victory. Should Revna be singing *ansuz*, not *tiwaz*? And Adelais ought to be singing with her, combining their power, but the pain in her back was spreading around her chest, squeezing the breath from her body. She was forced to watch silently as the count waved forwards riders on great draught horses; ten, twenty, or more, bunched in the centre. They wheeled in front of the lines of chains, all raised and newly staked now the element of surprise was spent, and tossed grappling irons over the chains. They rode back towards the mass of Theignault cavalry with little loss from the Vriesian archers on the wings. They trailed ropes, and they galloped until they were out of range and other draught horses joined them, adding their weight to the lines. The defensive chains were dragged out of the way with insulting ease.

Now the war-hammer formed. Only twenty abreast this time, the width of the cleared path, but they would strike the Vriesian shield wall like an axe into firewood. Adelais's chest tightened further as she saw Hjálmar among his men, sword in hand, with his injured arm strapped to his hauberk and his shield slung around his neck. Trebuchets fired, sending lumps of rough masonry now all the prepared shot was gone, and the ranging was poor. Two riders went down, and the charge came on, shaking the ground, until it hit the shield wall with the sound of a hundred anvils struck as one, a thousand drums, one thunderclap of the gods.

Adelais could not breathe, could not even scream as the shield wall shattered and the man she had dared to love died under the hooves. *I should never have let myself love him. Never allowed him to love me. I am truly the tree that calls the lightning.* She tried to fly to him but this time the agony across her back told her that her wings were truly wrecked, and she slumped back to the stone, condemned to watch the second line of the charge ride over his body. And the third.

Revna's rune song ended abruptly as a lance pierced her throat, scattering her bird-skull necklace over her *seidhr*-platform. By then the fight was dividing into two, as isolated ends of the shield wall formed doomed defensive circles and Ragener fled through the gate beneath her into the castle to take refuge with his house-guards and prisoners.

No tears came. Perhaps ravens can't cry. Yet there was one who landed beside her with a flutter of feathers and spoke words of comfort in the high, girl-woman tones of Skuld.

'I should have warned Revna.' Adelais could not speak, but Skuld was in her mind, and she in hers. 'Told her to sing *ansuz*.'

'What matters most is *who* sings *ansuz*. It is the god-rune. The All-Father has marked you with it.'

'I cannot sing. Can hardly breathe.'

'We are speaking. You can sing.'

'Has this already come to pass?' Adelais looked down at the lost field, where a horsehair plume trailed from a pile of tangled bodies. If that was real, the world had lost its meaning.

'There is that which is coming into being, and fates that are yet to be woven. If you believe you can weave fates, then weave another.'

'With *ansuz*?'

'*Ansuz* is the god-rune, the stave that is the doorway to all that Odhinn learned when he hung upon the tree of Yggdrasil, his side pierced by a spear. Pass through *ansuz* to know the wisdom of all that lies beyond. Only then will you unlock the breath of life.'

'Then all this has yet to come to pass?' Adelais still stared towards Hjálmar's corpse.

'This fate is being woven. But you are the *örlaga vefari*; if you can find the strength now, and then the wisdom, you might weave another.'

'Then help me to sing, my friend.' For Adelais had no breath. The pain in her back had sunk to a burning numbness, but a tightness had wrapped itself around her chest like a giant's arms, squeezing out her life. She, they, began. *Must sing!*

'*Óss er algingautr...*'

Adelais folded over with the effort. Below her, Revna's sightless eyes stared back.

'*Ok ásgardhs jöfurr...*'

She stretched out her arms one last time.

'*Ok valhallar vísi...*'

And flew. It was a feeble flapping that carried her only far enough for her to fall into the heap of mangled dead below. New dead. Old dead. Man-dead. Horse-dead. And a dead she-wolf who lifted her head and stared at her with blue, caring eyes.

'Come, *mynn litla Sif*, you are not in Valhalla yet.' The wolf nudged her with its nose.

'Am I dead too, Amma?' Adelais found she could talk to her amma's *fylgja* without speaking, just as she could with Skuld.

'Soon, child. Come, let me carry you.' And the wolf breathed into her face, enough air for Adelais to beat her wings and lift herself onto its back. She locked her claws into its pelt and rested against its neck, soaking in the warmth of childhood.

The wolf made a mighty bound that carried them soaring through the clouds to where an ancient tree stood on a hilltop, trailing just two branches in the shape of the scars on her breast, the god-rune, *ansuz*.

Two more ravens rested on its branches, and a single, huge wolf watched them approach from its base. The tree began to turn, its branches becoming the flapping cloak of an old man who leaned on a staff and stared at her over his shoulder. Only the power in his single eye told her that she looked upon the god, not upon a weary traveller.

'You have done well, young woman. But have you done enough?' Odhinn's voice had the rumble of mountains grinding together, and the softness of spring leaf.

'What more can be done, All-Father? Am I not dead?'

'You can accept death or find a reason for living.'

Adelais gestured towards Hjálmar's body, lying far away. 'I am tired of being the cause of men's deaths. If I have done well, then grant this man his life.'

'Before yours?'

'Mine is already taken. His fate is still being woven.'

'The *Valkyrjur* are flying. He will be chosen. You may feast together in my hall.'

Yet Adelais would sacrifice an eternity in Valhalla for the chance to touch his face and look into his laughing, living eyes. He deserved the chance to find that too, even with another woman.

'Grant him life, All-Father.'

Odhinn turned to stare into the distance, where the edge of the sun touched the horizon with dazzling fire. *Already? Time has no meaning indeed.* He pointed towards it with his staff and drew threads of fate in the air; sharp, angular strokes that formed the pattern of a rune.

'*Dagaz*,' he said, 'is awakening and dying. It is pleasure and pain, body and soul. It is the rune with no beginning and no end, for in *dagaz* death and life are one. You are now in *dagaz*. Walk on, young woman, and find the wisdom to know sunrise from sunset. If you find that knowledge, you may yet weave the fates of nations.'

Dagaz, that most enigmatic of runes, had been in Revna's runecast. Was this an ending, or a beginning, or both? Adelais slipped off the wolf's back onto her legs, for now she walked upright, as woman not raven. She put her arm around the beast's neck. She felt no pain in that movement; pain had been part of her physical body and she had left that behind, in a tent on Nautshrygg.

'Come with me, Amma. I can't do this alone.'

'Child, you can only do this alone.'

Adelais hugged the wolf, locking her fingers into its fur, putting a young lifetime of love into that fierce embrace, for she knew that this was truly farewell. The wolf nudged her again with its nose.

'Go, *mynn litla Sif*.'

Adelais turned and stepped forwards into the light.

12.3 TAILLEFER

It took half the day for all the Theignaulter cavalry to arrive in the camp. By then the flow of carts from the battlefield had slowed to a trickle, and the ostensible reason for the truce was over. They would attack on the morrow, Delmas announced, to give the horses chance to rest. It was pointless charging on spent horses.

In the afternoon, Episkopos Juibert himself conducted Leandre de Fontenay's burial. He would lie, at Agnès's request, in a solitary grave where his body could later be identified and exhumed so that he could rest with his ancestors at Fontenay. Fifty Guardians lined three sides of the grave, all in the distinctive, illicit, red lion on white surcoats, and all armed. The remaining de Fontenay knights closed the square. Beyond them, hundreds had come to honour the man who'd led the charge.

Only Agnès, Delmas, the episkopos, and Taillefer stood within the square, listening to the episkopos speak of duty and sacrifice in the name of the God. His eloquence was tainted by the need to swat flies away from his face. Agnès stood still, holding a square of lace to her face – not, Taillefer suspected, in grief but to mask the smells with the perfumed fabric; her scent

was rich, sophisticated, and alluring, even when no enticement
was intended.

No one expected her to speak, yet when the episkopos was
done she lowered the lace and called to the multitude in a high,
clear voice.

'Leandre de Fontenay was a man of high principles and
honour. A knight who knew his chivalric duty. A lord who was
loved by those he led.'

Murmurs of assent spread through the crowd.

'When he took the decision to reveal the existence of the
Hand of Salazar, he unleashed events that brought us all here
today, and to the condition we in are today. In future years holy
men will debate whether the God approved of his decision, or
showed his displeasure.'

'Lady Agnès...' Episkopos Juibert touched her sleeve but she
shook him off.

'Today the custody of the Hand falls to me. I too must
answer to Ischyros for the decisions I take.'

'My lady this is not agreed...'

Agnès turned to Juibert and Delmas with a regal smile upon
that lovely face. 'My lords, I need no man's agreement. I am my
husband's heir.'

Juibert and Delmas looked at each other, clearly wondering
how forceful they could be with a grieving widow, at her
husband's graveside, and in front of an army.

'However,' she called loudly enough to be heard far back in
the crowd, 'I know of three of my husband's wishes, that I now
dedicate myself to implementing. Firstly, that the Hand be
returned to the protection of the Knights Guardian. Their
numbers are still small, but until their order is once again rati-
fied and strong, I pledge the support of all men under arms
within the de Fontenay domain. Secondly, my husband wished
that Diakonos Taillefer of Harbin be the Hand's spiritual custo-

dian. And thirdly, I further pledge that no person will ever be charged to look upon this holiest of relics.'

'That's enough, woman!' Juibert reached for her, but Taillefer stepped in between them, and Brother Thanchere restrained Juibert from behind. Juibert shrugged him off but made no further move towards Agnès, struggling to recover his dignity.

'You'll never get your hands on it,' the episkopos hissed.

'Too late, Eminence.' With great reverence Taillefer knelt and picked up a plain, oak casket from the ground. 'You will find your gold reliquary is empty.' He offered the casket to Agnès on his knees.

Agnès opened the box as if displaying a book, held it high above her head, and turned so that all might see.

'And in witness to that pledge, behold the Hand of Salazar!'

The Guardians and her knights fell to their knees in unison, making the sign of the God. Beyond them, the army gasped in awe and followed suit until only Delmas and Juibert were on their feet. Then they too knelt, with visible reluctance.

'Very well, woman.' Delmas spoke quietly, between gritted teeth. 'What do you want?'

'Let's start with a seat on your council,' she whispered, closing the casket and placing it into the hands of Brother Thanchere.

Taillefer knew that his face was shining. He hoped this would be taken as adoration for the Hand, not for the petite woman who had just outfoxed an episkopos and a royal duke. With a little help. If the diakonos who brought the Hand from Fontenay could not be allowed a few moments of private prayer with the holy relic, who could?

Yet events had moved with such speed that they were yet to agree a strategy for what should follow this public declaration of custody. He, Agnès, and Thanchere must decide that immediately.

. . .

If Agnès felt any triumph at her coup, it was short-lived. As the crowd dissipated, Guy Carelet stood again on the road from the battleground, waiting for a chance to speak to Agnès.

'Another message, Master Guy?' She looked suddenly tired. It was easy to forget, amidst the machinations over the Hand, that her husband's grave was at her feet. 'Who from, this time?'

'Hjálmar Magnusson, my lady, the son of Jarl Magnus. He knows that you and Adelais were good friends.'

'Were?' There was more alarm in Agnès's voice now than there had ever been for her husband. 'She is dead?'

'She lives, my lady, or at least was alive when I left, but she has wound fever. I am told she raves, for much of the time, though she has moments of lucidity. Hjálmar says I am to offer you safe passage into the Vriesian lines. If you can bring healing herbs such as willow bark and vervain it *may* help, but now is the time for those who love her to gather at her bedside. He fears she will not live long.'

12.4 ADELAIS

Adelais walked in a hinterland towards a sun that never rose and never set, but cut the horizon in an eternal, dazzling curve. She reached towards it, shielding her eyes from the glare, and found that her fingertips trailed gossamer strands, fine as spiders' webs, the way the Nornir's hands had woven threads of fate in Heilagtré. She waved, experimenting, and drew the lightning flash of *sowilo*.

How very appropriate. The sun-rune, a rune of hope. She began to sing, and found her words formed a mist, as if the air was winter-chill. The words danced over each other, weaving into glowing ropes.

'*Sól er skýja skjöldr, ok skínandi rödhull, ok ísa aldrtregi...*'

The sun is the shield of the clouds, and shining ray, and destroyer of ice...

It had brought the avalanche in the mountains. Adelais paused in wonder, and the shimmering strands of *sowilo* faded. This would be fun, if only she could share it with Hjálmar.

Soon they would feast together in Valhalla. The All-Father himself had promised. Would they have warm skin in Valhalla? Would she be able to touch him, and feel his beating heart?

And would she have to share his company with all the *einharjar*, the legions of valorous dead? It was said that the *einharjar* feasted by night and fought by day, and so it would be until the final battle of Ragnarök. She'd rather have a meadow bank, in summer, where they could touch and laugh and be tender.

So what rune should she sing, if she was truly the fate-weaver? How could she prevent the fate that she had seen? Were she and Hjálmar, and all the northerners on Nautshrygg, doomed to enter Valhalla as victims of a heroic defeat? How could she stop the endless fighting between Vriesland and Galmandie, between Ischyros and the old gods? Adelais opened her arms towards the light, filled her chest, and sang.

'*Odhala er gjöf höfdhingjans, öruggur aflinn og löglegt frels, réttur allra kynslódha...*'

Odhala is the chieftain's gift, safe hearth and lawful liberty, the right of all generations...

Adelais shaped the mist of her song with her hands, threads binding threads into the *odhala* rune. *Odhala*, the rune of ancestral right, the hearth-rune, the rune of tribe and home and justice. Revna had said when it appeared in her runecast with *tiwaz* it meant victory for the old ways, at a cost. Was she the cost? It formed a shield wall of burnished brass around the sun itself...

... and turned to cloud, then mist, then vapour. Useless.

Adelais knew then that she must be alive to weave fates. Before *odhala* must come rebirth. Only then would her song be heard, for in this halfway hinterland, life and death had become one, time had no meaning so there was no future, no past, no fate, only the eternal 'now'.

It was a jest worthy of Loki that she should be promised Valhalla yet chose to live, while on the hill of Nautshrygg were four thousand berserkers who sought a valiant death that they might be chosen for Valhalla.

She faced the sun and sang again.

'*Bjarkan er laufgat lim...*'

Bjarkan, the rune of the earth mother. She'd sung it once for concealment and protection as she 'escaped' from Duke Ragener's castle, but it was also the rune of rebirth and becoming.

'*Ok lítit tré...*'

The rune of renewal.

'*Ok ungsamligr vidhr...*'

Yet this time her words formed no threads. She was within a tent, full of weeping people. Revna, sitting on a stool and pounding the ground with her *seidhkona* staff, singing rune song in her high, keening voice. Outside, the sun was rising, *really* rising, and Adelais sensed Revna's waning power; she would have been singing rune song for a whole night. Yet she caught glimpses of threads as *bjarkan* danced with *úruz* and the earth mother took strength from the bull's might.

'*Bjarkan er laufgat lim...*'

Jarl Magnus was there, lifting the limp wrist of a blonde-haired woman lying face down at their feet. He was looking at Hjálmar and shaking his head.

'*Ok lítit tré...*'

Hjálmar's tears gave her more strength than any rune song. She would spare him that pain. And other pains that would follow.

'*Ok ungsamligr vidhr...*'

And Agnès, *Agnès*, the fine noblewoman who sat weeping on the earth, stroking the woman's head. *Why can't I feel that?*

The woman's back was lacerated; great slicing cuts stretched round to the side, towards the breast, red with the hot humours of wound fever, purple-white with the onset of corruption. Adelais lay over that wrecked back, inhaled the strength of both *bjarkan* and *úruz*, and breathed.

'*Bjarkan er laufgat lim...*'

And coughed.

And felt pain.

When she opened her eyes she was looking at Agnès, now lying on the ground with her hair in the crushed grass of the tent, so close they might be lovers on a pillow. *Shouldn't be Agnès. Should be Hjálmar. But having Agnès here is good. In many ways.* Agnès's eyes were red and full, and she was half laughing, half crying as she stared into Adelais's face.

'Hello *kjúkling*,' she said.

Adelais took several breaths. Light, panting breaths. She hurt. Badly. But there was a memory, an inspiration, like a dream that has to be spoken at the moment of waking or will be forever forgotten. Important. So important it would weave the fate of nations. She had to make it real. Now.

'Agnès.' Another gasp. 'How do both sides win a war?'

At least, that was what she wanted to say, but the words were locked in her mouth. Agnès's concern was etched across her face. '*Shh, kjúkling.* You must rest,' she said as she moistened Adelais's lips with a sponge. Adelais sucked at it until she could swallow, then croak, then whisper.

And she shared with Agnès the wisdom of Odhinn.

CHAPTER THIRTEEN

13.1 ADELAIS

By the time the sun had fully risen, Adelais could talk. She felt as if she'd drunk a river of water, and she was still thirsty. She'd also eaten a little bread and honey, and though a weight of tiredness pushed her downwards she felt strong enough to sit, if someone held her arm. It was more comfortable that way, when her own weight did not press on her ribs.

Yet she floated in and out of a dream world, rambling. She could *feel* the tension in the air, for today they would fight. Again. Hjálmar and so many others would die.

'Battles don't win wars,' Adelais raved at Revna and Agnès as they helped her dress. 'Battles make more battles, the way dogs make puppies.' Her grandmother's staff lay against her chair and she grabbed it for support, trying to stand.

Yet Revna and Agnès only hushed her, easing her back into the seat, and she was too weak to resist. Why could they not see the wisdom of Odhinn? She foresaw a future of endless wars, between Galman and Vriesian, between Ischyros and Odhinn, the prophet Salazar and mighty Thor, between hard-faced Tanguy and the laughing, loving Freyja. For in this moment Adelais was *spakona*, prophetess, and though they would lose this battle, the next generation would fight another, and another, and the land would bleed forever.

Outside her tent, the air screamed with the insect whine of sharpening weapons. Above that came the sound of trumpets, brazen, challenging. Adelais frowned, not understanding, until Jarl Magnus pushed back into her tent, with Hjálmar at his heels. Both were fully armed for war.

'The heralds have announced the end of the truce,' Magnus told them. 'The battle lines are forming. Those *fordæmdur* Theignaulters have switched sides. They have a thousand more horse to throw at us. Lady Agnès, you must go now.'

Hjálmar stepped forwards to make his farewells, his broken, splinted wrist strapped to his chest, and Adelais almost wept as the memory of his death came surging back.

I will not let this fate be woven.

Adelais seized Yrsa's staff and brought its tip down into the earth, as forcefully as her broken body would allow. It was enough to shake the ground with all the power of Heilagtré, and the earth reverberated to a silent thunder. '*Óss er algingautr...*'

Agnès's eyes flew wide in shock. They'd all felt it. Adelais could see threads streaming from her staff, gossamer-fine. Could they see them too?

'*Ok ásgardhs jöfurr...*'

Ansuz, the god-rune.

'*Réttur allra kynslódha.*'

They were staring at her, waiting, wondering.

'Ragener must sue for terms.' Adelais gasped. She'd found a moment's clarity.

'There is no honour in that.' Magnus sounded cautious.

'You will die. He will die.' Adelais pointed at Hjálmar. 'We all will.'

'If this is our dying-day, then we will face it well.'

Adelais had no time for Magnus's stubbornness. 'And you will feast in Valhalla this night. I shall feast with you. This the

All-Father has promised. Yet there is another fate that can be woven.' She closed her eyes, summoning strength. *Sætur Sif, keep me lucid.*

'Lady Agnès has the ear of the Duke of Delmas. She, after all, lured Ragener into this war.' Adelais spoke without malice, but Agnès winced. 'She is now going to persuade Ragener of the terms that Delmas *might* agree.'

'Which are?' Hjálmar and Magnus spoke together.

Adelais closed her eyes, forming her words, while her hand touched her chest. *Ansuz*, to win a war.

Adelais heard that Ragener needed little persuasion; he knew the ruse with the chains would not work again. The armies dismounted or sat on their shields, staring at each other across a thousand paces of scorched ground, while heralds agreed how the negotiations were to proceed. Principals to be Ragener and Magnus, and Delmas and Theignault. Lady Agnès de Fontenay also to be permitted to attend and observe as the new custodian of the Hand. Likewise, Lady Adelais of Nautshrygg on the Vriesian side, if she was able. Five men-at-arms per side as escorts. Unarmed pages to hold the horses. Delmas insisted that a priest also be present to witness the swearing of any agreement. Diakonos Taillefer was mutually acceptable. The truce to hold for now.

Adelais was borne from her tent by four berserkers, her chair once again strapped to spears, with Hjálmar at her side. She'd wanted to attend on Allier, riding proud, but her legs would not support her. 'What if you fall,' Hjálmar asked, 'on those ribs?' So she swayed behind Ragener and Magnus like a piece of baggage, so light-headed she might still have been drawing runes in the clouds. Perhaps she should not have taken the last drop of Agnès's potion. *One in wine for pain.*

A pavilion had been erected between the armies, beyond

the burned swathe. The land still stank of fire, and their feet raised clouds of ashy dust.

Delmas did not keep them waiting long. A trestle table had been set up in the pavilion, set with goblets and jugs of wine. Adelais waved hers away. *Mustn't sleep now.* She watched the Galman procession approach, trying to read Agnès's eyes. *Has she succeeded?* The nobles rode, but Taillefer de Remy walked, carrying a box reverently across his arms, surrounded by five men-at-arms in the red lion on white surcoats of the former Guardians. That, she had not expected. Surely the Guardian order was proscribed?

Ragener and the Vriesian party stood when Delmas and the Galmans were announced, but Adelais stayed in her chair. She could not stand. Simply moving from her carrying-chair to the table had exhausted her, but her heart quickened in hope as Agnès gave her an almost-imperceptible nod.

Flowery compliments crossed the table, butterfly-light, from faces cold as iron. Taillefer laid his box gently in front of him, and all the Ischyrians made the sign of their god. Even Ragener made a token, fumbling movement. The five Guardians lined up behind the Galman nobles, their hands resting on their sword hilts.

'The Hand of Salazar,' Taillefer announced. 'Should we agree terms, an oath sworn on this holiest of relics will endure for all time.'

'And on what will you swear?' Delmas lifted both hands in a gesture that included Ragener, Magnus, and Adelais.

Magnus pulled an elaborately carved, gilded arm-ring from his forearm. 'This ring was forged when the gods were young. All oaths of my people have been sworn on it from time immemorial. Any who breaks such an oath is considered an outlaw and may be killed. On this will I swear.' He laid it beside the box.

'And I.' Adelais was struggling to think clearly.

Ragener looked relieved that no one had asked him on which artefact he would swear.

The nobles sat, carefully timing their movements to sit at the same moment. 'Trust is so important, is it not?' Magnus added, glaring across the table at the Count of Theignault.

'So, to terms.' Ragener sounded confident. Almost affable; a man who believes he can keep his duchy, or most of it. 'If the Galman army withdraws south of Baudry, Vriesland will cede the county of Theignault to Galmandie.'

'They already have Theignault, you fool,' the count sneered. 'Haven't you noticed where I sit?'

'Galmandie can have the county,' Ragener responded, 'but I want the count.' He pointed across the table. 'Treachery cannot be rewarded.'

Theignault laughed in his face. 'I think Duke Ragener has been drinking the mushroom tea his northern witches brew. It makes wonderful dreams, I'm told.'

'I agree to those terms.' Delmas looked over his shoulder and beckoned to the Guardians. Two stepped forwards and seized Theignault by the arms in what was clearly a prearranged move. He squirmed, he raged, and then he saw Delmas's face and knew. The betrayer was himself betrayed.

'But I was to have Vriesland!' Theignault bellowed, red with anger.

'I need vassals I can trust.' Delmas looked grim. 'What will you do with him?'

Before Ragener could answer, Magnus turned towards Adelais. 'Lady Adelais?'

Adelais gripped the arm of her chair until her fingers hurt, forcing herself to think. *Ansuz* had given her wisdom, had it not? The essential quality of rulers? And ruling meant taking hard but just decisions.

'Are the tarrazim still on the north bank?' she asked, looking at Hjálmar.

'They are.' He nodded.

'And what do the tarrazim do to anyone who hires them and cannot pay?' She held eye contact with Hjálmar, drawing on his strength.

'They kill them. There are no exceptions.'

'Then tie him to the bridge, without his armour. Let the tarrazim see that there is no chance of them being paid. I suggest you take off his surcoat and strap him to my chair to take him away, lest any of his men feel protective.'

'Excellent!' Ragener thumped the table, trying to re-assert his control, but Delmas was still looking at Adelais, a half-smile on his lips and, for the first time, respect in his eyes. Adelais looked beyond his shoulder, towards the Theignaulter troops waiting at their horses' heads, five hundred paces away. They would think it was her being carried back to the Vriesian lines, not the count.

'And?' Delmas prompted her.

Adelais breathed deeply. *Odhinn give me wisdom.* She whispered the rune song of *odhala* as she exhaled.

'*Odhala er gjöf höfdhingjans, öruggur aflinn og löglegt frels, réttur allra kynslódha...*'

'Duke Ragener said it himself. Treachery should never be rewarded.' Adelais nodded to the berserkers behind her. 'Bind him.'

'*What?*' Ragener started to rise from his chair but was grabbed by two of Magnus's men. 'I am your duke! You swore fealty!'

'You lost all rights to my loyalty the moment you ordered my death.'

'I did no such thing. Stop that, you vermin!' Ragener struggled as he was bound.

Adelais looked across the table at Delmas. 'He allowed a priest to infect my wounds,' she explained.

'And why would I do that, you stupid bitch?'

'Because I had fulfilled my purpose, and a union with Hjálmar Magnusson would make Jarl Magnus too powerful in your duchy.'

'You are mad!'

'No, I heard every word. And you are now a prisoner of Galmandie. You can take Duchess Severine with you, though I think she may prefer to live elsewhere.'

Both Theignault and Ragener raved, cursing, as they were taken away. Magnus and Delmas eyed each other across the table, warrior to warrior, each beginning a smile of amusement that broadened as the prisoners' shouts faded.

'What happened to the priest?' Delmas asked.

'My men were not gentle, I'm afraid.' Magnus did not sound apologetic. 'They flayed his back and packed his wounds with bandages that they'd taken from Lady Adelais. We'll turn him loose once he starts raving. Do you want him?'

'He's not one of mine. Probably belongs to Theignault.'

'Then his life is in your god's hands.'

Delmas shrugged. 'So be it.'

'No,' Adelais interrupted. 'Strip him of his priest's robe and tie him to the bridge beside Theignault. Justice must be seen to be done.' And it would be a quicker end than the ravings of wound fever.

'Remind me never to upset you, Lady Adelais,' Magnus chuckled. Across the table, Agnès's eyes widened before she inclined her head, smiling.

'The ransom for Prince Lancelin is set at five hundred thousand gold crowns,' Magnus said without blinking.

'An impossible sum.' Delmas lifted his hand dismissively.

'Precisely. A sum we never expect to be paid, though I am sure you will use it as pretext for taxes.' Magnus leaned forwards, his manner now conspiratorial rather than confrontational. 'Let us talk plainly, Highness. You do not want him back. We do not want Ragener back. Do we understand each other?'

A slow grin spread across Delmas's face.

'You take Theignault. You return home with honour and spoils. You withdraw your army south of Baudry. Vriesland is independent, with the River Dalsven as the boundary, as in former days. Other noble captives to be ransomed. We too go home with honour and the promise of riches.'

Delmas snorted. 'I could crush you against the walls of that little castle. I need pay no ransoms.'

Agnès cleared her throat and spoke for the first time. 'Perhaps Your Highness had already thought of helping the families of ransomed nobles by distributing the wealth of Theignault?'

'But I could keep Theignault and recover the captives.'

'At the cost of many more dead. And Your Highness will of course remember that I have custody of the Hand.'

Delmas tensed. 'Which means?'

'That if you do not accept these fair and honourable terms, Your Highness, I am minded to remove the Hand from your army, under the care of this growing band of Guardians and Diakonos Taillefer of Harbin. The battle might not be as easy as you think. The army that followed the Hand so eagerly to war will also follow it away, now that they have reason to doubt the rectitude of the cause.' Agnès smiled sweetly, and Adelais loved her for it.

So, it seemed, did Taillefer de Remy, who looked at her with the adoration of a hound for its mistress. *Did anyone else see that? Is he the father? A priest?*

Delmas began to laugh; a slow, shoulder-shaking rumble that erupted into a bark and a table-slap.

'I think, my lords, and ladies, that we are all agreed?' Taillefer de Remy stood. 'We can have clerks draw up a document, but on these principles, do we swear?'

They all stood, even Adelais, who had to be supported by Hjálmar. She did not mind that.

'On ring and Hand, my lords.' Taillefer touched the box.

Magnus and Delmas placed their hands on the sacred objects. They both looked at Adelais, inviting her to share the moment. Magnus slid his oath-ring within her reach.

'On ring and Hand.'

Afterwards, Agnès came to sit by Adelais. The principals of both sides were riding back to their lines, leaving the two women in possession of the field. Hjálmar loitered at a respectful distance, waiting for his men to return with her chair. Taillefer de Remy waited fifty paces on the opposite side, holding the reins of Agnès's palfrey. A Guardian beside him cradled the box with the Hand.

Adelais took deep breaths while her vision spotted and the world swirled. *It is finished.* Agnès held her hand. She might have toppled sideways, otherwise.

'You did well, *kjúkling*.'

'*We* did well. You were very brave with Delmas.'

'And you with Ragener.'

'I promised him once that I'd shrivel his balls. This is much better.' Adelais looked her friend in the eye. Seated, they were more of a height. 'Can you forgive me, Agnès?'

'For what?'

'For Leandre. All this.' Adelais waved across the plain towards the Galman grave pits.

'He brought it on himself. I think I shall miss him. He was a good man. Decent. Honourable.'

'I know.'

'Though in some ways this might even be convenient.'

'The diakonos?'

'How did you guess?' Agnès sounded alarmed.

'You've got to stop him making puppy eyes at you.'

'Oh.' Agnès lifted her chin towards Hjálmar. 'And you'll take the giant?'

'I think we'll take each other.'

'Is he built in proportion?' The old sparkle was back in Agnès's eyes.

They began to giggle. Adelais didn't know, but she'd enjoy finding out. When it didn't hurt to laugh.

'Bring him to Fontenay, one day. You and I can drink wine together, and brush each other's hair.'

'And I can bounce your baby on my knee.'

Agnès held both of Adelais's hands, squeezing them tightly in the moment of parting.

'You know you are ready to rule, don't you, *kjúkling?* With Ragener gone, Jarl Magnus will lead Vriesland. One day you will be a duchess.'

'I don't want to rule.'

'That's why you are ready.'

PART SIX

EPILOGUE

CHAPTER FOURTEEN

14.1 ADELAIS

Adelais and Hjálmar were wed in the harvest moon, two moons after the battle. She was not yet fully healed, but the pain of her wounds was fading and she could move without wincing. They married in a place and style of their choosing, not the Vriesian court. Adelais rejected the ducal castle in Siltehafn, where the nobility wanted to celebrate with lavish feasting, and chose instead Yrsa's sacred island of Freyjasoy. Those that came, and they were many, had to sleep in barns or in longships moored on the quayside. Neither would she allow the payment of a bride price, as her father wanted. She and Hjálmar exchanged swords and rings, in the customary way, but she gave herself freely and wholly; she was not some heifer to be sold at market. Besides, she had no need; her share of the ransoms would buy her a noble's domain of rich land, if she wanted.

At dawn on the morning of the ceremony, Adelais walked alone around Freyjasoy, thinking of her grandmother. Yrsa felt close in this place, almost as close as she had through the warm fur of a wolf. Adelais scanned the shadows beneath the fir trees, hoping for a glimpse of a grey coat and a snow-white bib, but the island was empty, smiling with her in early sunlight. The only sign of life was a seagull that tumbled playfully around her head. She laughed with it as it made the high, screeching calls so akin to the keening of *seidhr*. Its folding wings even formed the *jera* rune as it flew away.

She was being fanciful, but *jera* was a good rune for a wedding. The rune of plenty, 'the boon to men, and good summer, and thriving crops.' *Ár er gumna gódhi, ok gott sumar, ok algróinn akr.*

Frú Revna officiated, in the sacred grove that had seen untold generations of both betrothals and pyres. So many came that the feast afterwards overflowed her father's barn and spilt out into the fields. Adelais and Hjálmar pledged each other with the loving cup, weaving verses in each other's praise that delighted the crowd with raunchy innuendo.

'Mead I bring thee, thou root of oak...'

While the guests could still stand, Hjálmar and Adelais were led back to Freyjasoy amidst a chorus of ribald songs and suggestive comments. Yrsa's old cottage was to be their home for the five nights of feasting. From that night, their presence at the celebrations would be welcome, but not demanded; the cottage had been well stocked. Adelais pushed out the last, most intrusive of revellers, and stayed with her back against the door, looking at Hjálmar, listening to the noises fade across the causeway. She felt flirtatiously tipsy as she savoured the moment when appetite for each other became hunger. Hands slipped inside clothes, uncovering, exploring, and hunger grew into a desire so powerful that their very skin became both a blessing and a barrier.

Hjálmar did not understand when she murmured, '*Oh he is, Agnès, he is*'.

She'd tell him later. Much later.

14.2 ADELAIS

By the time the leaves were turning, Adelais was learning to read and write. Her first letter, in a simple, childlike script, was to Agnès. She had a reply in the frost moon, while the roads were still open, that spoke of the challenges of managing great estates while big with child. (*'One is enormous, kjúkling!'*) Agnès also wrote that Taillefer had been made an episkopos by the new high priest, and was charged with building a new temple at Fontenay to house the Hand. Even though he and his brother were estranged, he had been saddened by Othon's arrest and execution on trumped-up charges of treason. The letter ended *'I miss you. Come and see us!'*

Agnès repeated her invitation in the snow moon, when she sent news of baby Humbert's safe birth, but Adelais's hopes of visiting Fontenay that year were dashed when Magnus moved back to his ancestral hall in the north. There had been longship raids along the coast, and a jarl must defend his people. Hjálmar and Adelais became law speakers in Siltehafn, administering justice jointly. Adelais took particular pride in the new centre for healers, both Ischyrian and *seidhkonur*, that she established with ransom monies. She and Hjálmar made a good team, but it was a time to establish themselves rather than take prolonged absences.

In the worm moon of the following year, a letter came from Agnès that Adelais could not ignore. *'There are times when one needs a friend. Someone to whom I can tell anything, and whom I trust totally. Can you come?'*

She gave no other details.

Adelais set out before the end of the moon, as soon as she could transfer responsibilities, leaving Hjálmar to rule alone.

14.3 ADELAIS

As she travelled south, Adelais thought this might be Allier's last long journey. She did not know his age, but there was a slight stiffness to his walk on cold mornings. He had earned his time in pasture, with his mares. Adelais had high hopes for his latest colt.

She retraced her route out of Galmandie of two years before. It had never occurred to her to repair Ragener's ridiculous armour, now forgotten in a dusty storeroom, but it seemed natural to hang Humbert's sword from her hip, despite her escort. Eight warriors rode with her, each bearing a round shield with the leaping-wolf blazon of the Lady of Nautshrygg.

Their road south crossed the field of battle. It was newly ploughed, and combed of all traces of battle save the grave mounds, a charcoal darkening of the earth, and the statue of a destrier she'd had erected where so many horses fell. Their deaths were still her greatest regret. If Allier remembered any of their previous journey, it only showed once, when Adelais walked along the riverbank at Bellay to throw flowers into the river at the place where Humbert Blanc had died. Allier broke free of his groom and surged ahead of her in that high-stepping, powerful trot that shouted '*warhorse*' to all who saw. He paced the bank with his head held high, whinnying, until Adelais gathered his trailing reins and stroked his neck. She wept with him until he consented to be led away.

They reached Fontenay as dusk was falling, when the lamb moon was nearly full. Adelais had last seen the château as a fugitive, clad in ragged men's clothes and facing a winter with nothing but stolen sandals on her feet. She'd looked at the line of bone-white, pinnacled towers shining above the valley's mist and thought it a cloud castle, far beyond her reach. Now she rode up the hill to its gates on a destrier, surrounded by her entourage. Their party, and its blazon, had been sighted from afar and Agnès came bouncing down the steps from her hall to greet them; the chatelaine of half of Jourdaine reduced to girlish breathlessness in the excitement of Adelais's arrival.

After their initial embrace they linked arms and Agnès steered Adelais towards her private apartments, gushing a non-stop stream of welcome. 'We will feast on the morrow. Taillefer will come. Tonight we talk, just you and me. I have ordered a bath prepared, and food in my chambers. But first you must meet little Humbert. Oh, it is so good to see you...'

That night, they groomed each other's hair, in their ritual of friendship, as they once had in the hunting lodge. Agnès had a mirror in her chamber; they could look at each other as they brushed and see the nuances of shared stories in the sparkle of an eye. Their tales were not of statecraft and the management of great domains, but of the escapades of little Humbert, so adorable to Agnès and so challenging for his nurse, or Adelais's hair, now three years long and Hjálmar's great delight. Adelais let Agnès choose the time and manner for telling her the reason for her letter.

'No children, yet?' Agnès brushed Adelais's tresses into a golden river, but her eyes were on Adelais's reflection. It was a question only the best of friends could ask sensitively.

Adelais shook her head. 'Sometimes I miss one moon, occasionally two, once three. I fear that crossbow bolt damaged me forever.'

'Oh, you poor girl.' The compassion on Agnès's face prompted Adelais to stand and accept her hug.

'It is a sadness for both of us.' Adelais spoke into Agnès's hair, lying like silk against her cheek. 'It's fun trying, though.'

'He gives you joy?' Agnès pulled back, an impish smile on her face.

'Oh, yes.' Perhaps later, after more wine, Adelais would tell her just how much joy. But for now they simply grinned at each other in unspoken understanding. 'And you have written much about Taillefer?' She made that a question.

'Let's just say I turn away all suitors. We meet at the hunting lodge when we can. "Time out of time", we call it. I'd rather a few snatched days with the man I love than a lifetime with someone else.' Agnès's green eyes shone in a clear-skinned, radiant face. She stood on tiptoes to whisper in Adelais's ear, though there was no one else that could hear. 'Your belt works beautifully, by the way.'

Adelais laughed, but she knew there was more that Agnès wanted to say; a sadness or a worry that was waiting for the right moment to be teased out. They were coming to the issue.

'You have not been discovered?'

Agnès shook her head. 'Elyse is totally loyal. And I am sure our meetings are still private. We arrive at the lodge and leave separately, and I only take people I trust. Elyse's son Eloi. Rossignol. My maid, Mathilde. You remember Mathilde?'

'Of course. Guy?'

Agnès shook her head slightly. 'Perhaps when he is a little older.'

Adelais searched her friend's face. They still held each other, close enough for Adelais to feel Agnès's warmth through the linen shifts that they both wore. Agnès had grown a little fuller in her figure with motherhood and the passage of nearly two years, more matron than maiden.

'Agnès, are you with child?'

Agnès blushed and looked down. 'We tried so hard to be careful. Only met at certain times of the moon. But it's so hard to pull apart when...'

'I know.' Adelais smoothed her hand across Agnès's back. 'Oops.'

'Yes, oops. One can't pass this one off as Leandre's.'

'How many moons?'

'Three. It will come sometime around the hunter's moon or the blood moon.'

Adelais dropped her hands and sat down, facing the mirror. It was the jest of the gods that she and Hjálmar should want children but she could not carry them, while Agnès had conceived too easily. Twice. And if she gave birth to an illegitimate child in Ischyrian Galmandie, her nobility would be no protection; she would be dishonoured and labelled a harlot.

'You and Taillefer could run away together. He could renounce his priesthood.'

'His faith is important to him.' Agnès picked up the brush and started again on Adelais's hair. They were both quiet for a while. This news would take time to digest.

Adelais scratched absent-mindedly at the scars on her chest, thinking. *Ansuz.* Wisdom. She began talking tentatively as an idea formed.

'Do you have a good steward? One you can trust to run your affairs in your absence?'

'Yes, I suppose.' Agnès watched Adelais intently.

'Then come back to Vriesland with me, with little Humbert and those you trust. You'll leave here as Lady de Fontenay, and you'll arrive in Vriesland with a name and a story we can agree, perhaps as a 'newly widowed' friend.'

'But courts talk. Siltehafn will be no different to Villebénie or Fontenay. There would be gossip.'

'I have a place in mind. A small manor called Aldingardhur. It was Duke Ragener's gift to me when he thought he could bed me. A pretty place, about ten leagues from Siltehafn. A day's ride when the roads are good. Just a hall, orchards, fields, and about sixty people to work them. It's yours for as long as you want. And I would so love the chance to look after you as you have looked after me.'

'But I'd need to be away for eight, nine moons...'

'You could tell everyone here it's for a short visit, and then you could have an "accident" that stops you travelling back to Fontenay before the winter. Say you've broken a leg, or something. And remember, lords go away to war for much longer. It's what stewards are for.'

Agnès stared at her in the mirror, her eyes wide with hope. 'But I'd have to leave the baby behind in Vriesland.'

Adelais reached over her shoulder and clasped Agnès's hand. 'I can't take that pain away from you, but there is a long tradition in the north of fostering or adopting children. I will talk to Hjálmar, but I think he would be honoured to raise your child as our own. I can promise you now that she will be loved, that you and Taillefer will always be welcome to visit, and that when she is old enough to travel she can come and stay in Fontenay.'

Agnès's mouth worked as if she was trying to say something, but could not find the words. Eventually she took a deep breath and spoke. 'She?'

Adelais did not know why she had said that. She turned on the seat and put her face against Agnès's shift, over her tummy.

She looked up for permission before she slid her hand under the hem and upwards until she could rest her fingertips on that slight matron's hill below the navel. It was still too early for discernible heartbeat or kicking; the heat, the life, were all Agnès's. But if she closed her eyes she could sense a faint humming in the web of fate, as subtle as a leaf fluttering on a distant tree. A birch tree. And the humming whispered a rune. *Bjarkan.* That most female of runes.

'She,' Adelais confirmed, and bent to kiss the place. 'Hello, *kjúkling,*' she whispered.

A LETTER FROM G.N. GUDGION

Thank you so much for choosing *Blood of Wolves*. I hope you've had as much fun reading Adelais's adventures as I have writing them. She's a character that took such a hold on my imagination that I feel we have written this together.

Blood of Wolves completes the Rune Song trilogy, but I am planning other works. If you'd like to keep up to date with all my latest releases, just sign up at the following link. Your email address will never be shared and you can unsubscribe at any time.

www.secondskybooks.com/gn-gudgion

If you liked *Blood of Wolves*, could you do me a huge favour? I so appreciate feedback, and reviews really help new readers discover the books. Reviews don't have to be long; it just takes a few words and a star rating on the website of your retailer, or even a simple star rating. Thank you.

Would you like to know the story behind the story? My sources of inspiration? There is a real-life Allier, for example. Or would you like me to talk to your book club? You'll find more Adelais-related material and a 'contact' page on my website. While you are there, do please subscribe to my own email list. When you do, there are free stories to download.

I shall be excited to hear from you.

www.geoffreygudgion.com

facebook.com/geoffrey.gudgion.author
x.com/GeoffreyGudgion
instagram.com/GeoffreyGudgion

ACKNOWLEDGEMENTS

As with *Hammer of Fate* and *Runes of Battle*, particular thanks go to my family for their love and encouragement, and to my agent Ian Drury for his support.

Huge thanks also to my editor Jack Renninson and his team at Bookouture/Second Sky: Angela Snowden for forensically detailed copy editing (and creative input), Alex Holmes, Mandy Kullar, Natalie Edwards, and Lizzie Brien for editorial, Faith Marsland for proofreading, Lance Buckley for cover design, Melanie Price and Ciara Rosney for marketing, and Noelle Holten for publicity.

Preparations for publishing *Hammer of Fate* and *Runes of Battle* were already well advanced before I heard Matt Addis's outstanding audiobook recordings, so this is my first opportunity to thank him for the series publicly. Matt has brought the characters to life, making them unique and individual, and has woven such drama and emotion into his narration that they are a joy to hear. You will find his website here: www.mattaddis.com

While building Adelais's world I read many sources about medieval life and beliefs, in particular:

- *Whispers of Yggdrasil*, a blog by Arith Härger.
  There is a wealth of published material on runes and *seidhr*, the practice of sorcery in pre-Christian Nordic cultures. Among the frequently contradictory sources, I have found Arith to be a

rich and credible mine of information at both the academic and esoteric levels. A novelist weaves facts into imaginary worlds, and while acknowledging Arith's considerable input, I make no claim that he endorses the warp and weft of my story. www.arithharger.wordpress.com

- Wikipedia provided the public domain, Icelandic versions of rune poems and their translations. Those familiar with rune lore will know that there are no surviving Icelandic rune poems for either *ansuz* or *odhala*; the lines used for these runes in *Blood of Wolves* are my own.

Printed in Great Britain
by Amazon

39451918R00243